Dear Reader:

You are about to meet Maeve Tremayne, an extraordinary vampire heroine whose unusual powers transcend the familiar boundaries of time and place. She literally moves between centuries and across continents whenever her strength and compassion are needed. Her sense of justice and capacity to love make her more passionate than any mortal woman you've ever known.

Maeve becomes a catalyst for change in the vampire world she has inhabited for several centuries. She will be called upon to attempt to rid the world of a powerful, self-centered immortal named Lisette, a dangerous rival whose whims threaten the survival of all vampires, angels, and warlocks—as well as all ordinary humans.

My new novel is about empowerment, about a brave young woman and a heroic man who heal in their own special ways. Together they become incredibly stronger and unforgettable. I invite you to join them in their exciting quest for peace and eternal love.

All best,

Linda Lael Miller

❊ ❊

Turn the page for rave reviews
of Linda Lael Miller's bestselling vampire romance,
Forever and the Night . . .

Berkley Books by Linda Lael Miller

FOREVER AND THE NIGHT
FOR ALL ETERNITY

For All Eternity

LINDA LAEL MILLER

B
BERKLEY BOOKS, NEW YORK

FOR ALL ETERNITY

A Berkley Book / published by arrangement with
the author

PRINTING HISTORY
Berkley edition / November 1994

ISBN: 0-425-14456-9

BERKLEY®
Berkley Books are published by The Berkley Publishing Group,
200 Madison Avenue, New York, New York 10016.
BERKLEY and the "B" design
are trademarks belonging to Berkley Publishing Corporation.

PRINTED IN THE UNITED STATES OF AMERICA

10 9 8 7 6 5 4 3 2

*For Wendy—again, always, just because.
You're still the best thing that ever
happened to me.
I love you, Sweetheart.*

"We are shaped and fashioned by what we love."
—*Von Goethe*

CHAPTER
❧1❧

Bright River, Connecticut
The present

Vampires are not supposed to cry.

So Maeve Tremayne told herself, in any case, that day in midsummer, as she stood in the echoing entry hall of her brother's house, gazing through a sheen of tears at the bouquet of dead roses he'd left for her.

The pale, shriveled petals lay scattered across the dusty marble tabletop, their curled edges the color of tea. Clearly Aidan had been away for some time.

Maeve took a certain bittersweet solace in this confirmation that her twin had not forgotten his promise to let her know whether his grand and foolhardy experiment had met with defeat or triumph.

1

The message of the roses was unmistakable: Aidan had surrendered his immortality to become a man again.

Maeve reached for a papery white petal, turning it slowly in her long, pale fingers. Aidan had never known a moment's happiness as a vampire, she reflected, in an effort to console herself. He had, after all, been changed against his will by a vindictive lover, the legendary Lisette.

For more than two centuries Aidan had despaired of his wondrous powers, instead of glorying in them, as Maeve had in her own. Even now it amazed her that her brother hadn't appreciated the extent of his gifts; vampires could travel through time and space at will, manipulate objects and human beings by mental tricks, disguise their presence from any lesser creature and most equals, and think with the entire brain, rather than just a small portion, as mortals did.

Oh, yes, vampires were far superior to those pitiful creatures, with their fragile organs and brittle bones. Immortals were able to see and hear as well or better than the average alleycat, and except under very bizarre circumstances, they need not fear the specter of death that awaited all humans.

Maeve shuddered, remembering the nightmare scene that had taken place only a few months before in an isolated graveyard on a hilltop behind an ancient abbey. Aidan had nearly died the most horrible of vampire deaths, a hellish, fiery ordeal triggered by the light of the sun.

Damn Aidan and his fatuous nobility, she thought. He'd gone willingly into Lisette's trap in an effort to rescue another nightwalker, his friend Valerian. If it hadn't been for Maeve herself, and for Tobias, one of the oldest vampires on earth, Aidan would have perished, screaming and writhing in the snow.

Maeve gathered petals in both hands and pressed them to her face. She caught their faint scent and tucked it away among her memories to recall at another time.

"Aidan," she whispered brokenly. "Oh, Aidan."

She was alone in the vastness of creation now, Maeve told herself, parting her hands and letting the rose petals rain gracefully down upon the tabletop. She had only enemies and acquaintances, but no friends.

Vampires were not particularly social creatures, since they feared certain angels and warlocks, as well as seemingly blundering humans who were in truth ruthless hunters, out to destroy them. Moreover, blood-drinkers mistrusted each other, and with good reason, for they tended to be greedy and unprincipled, unabashedly devoted to their own best interests.

Maeve sighed and wandered into Aidan's study, where he had worked so many nights on those damnable journals and sketches of his. He had always fed early, if possible, and then returned to this great, ponderous, lonely house to pretend he was a mortal, with a piddly life span of seventy-six years or so. It still mystified her that he'd admired them so, these awkward beings who were almost completely oblivious to the marvelous powers evolving in the secret depths of their own spirits.

She took the first volume of Aidan's many bound journals down from the shelf and felt a stab of grief when she saw the sketch of herself and her brother on the initial page. She recalled their human beginnings, in eighteenth-century Ireland, when they'd been born to a bawdy but very beautiful tavern wench, with a rich English merchant for a sire.

Alexander Tremayne had taken good care of his

by-blows, Maeve had to confess, considering that he had another family, a legitimate one, back in Liverpool. His great sin, the one Maeve would always despise him for, had been in separating the twins when they were just seven years old.

Just prior to that fateful parting, Aidan and Maeve's flighty, superstitious mother had taken them to an old gypsy fortune-teller. The crone had studied their small palms and then rasped, "Cursed! Cursed for all eternity, and beyond!"

At that, the ancient creature had risen from the steps of her colorful wagon and tottered inside. Moments later she had returned with duplicate medals, rosebuds shaped of gold and suspended from sturdy chains. With great ceremony she had hung a pendant around each child's neck.

"These cannot save your souls," she'd said, "but they will remind you to uphold the qualities of mercy and faith, no matter what befalls you. From those will come your strength and your power."

Maeve had kept the gypsy's gift ever since, taken comfort from it after she was sent away from her mother and brother.

From an upstairs room in an Irish tavern, Maeve had gone to a nunnery, where she'd been taught to sew, weave, and embroider, as well as to read and write. Aidan had been sent to an expensive school for boys, far away in England, and he, too, had kept his pendant close.

The two children had soon discovered an eerie ability to communicate via images held in their minds, and that contact had been Maeve's consolation during dark, lonely hours.

Then, when Aidan had reached young manhood, he'd met Lisette, the most powerful of all female vampires, and had mistaken her for a mortal woman. In the end Lisette had murdered Aidan, and then restored him as a nightwalker by giving him back his own blood, altered.

When Maeve had discovered the truth, through the offices of an exasperating, impudent, and unbelievably handsome immortal called Valerian, she was shattered. From then on, she knew, all eternity would lie between herself and Aidan, for he would live forever, while she was destined to grow old and die.

Valerian had graciously explained the benefits of becoming a vampire, as well as the obvious drawbacks.

On the one hand, an immortal could do virtually anything he or she wished, on the strength of a single clearly focused thought. The world, even the universe, was their playground. But on the other, Valerian had said with a shiver, there was no doubt that if the fundamentals of religion were true, all vampires would surely be damned. There would be no help for them, and certainly no mercy; if they were judged before the courts of heaven, they'd be cast into the Great Pit as well.

Raised in a convent, Maeve had heard plenty about hell and been taught to fear it with her whole soul, but she was also irrepressibly adventurous. Moreover, she could not bear for Aidan to leave her behind, and, in the last analysis, the consumption of blood seemed a small price to pay for the privileges vampires knew.

After all, she wouldn't have to kill her victims if she didn't choose to, and even in her innocence she knew there were plenty of scoundrels in the world to take nourishment from. She needn't pick on anyone with an honest heart.

When all these matters had been carefully reviewed, Maeve made her decision and asked Valerian to make her a vampire, since she knew Aidan would never consent to do it himself. At first, Valerian had refused, but he'd been attracted to Maeve, too, and she'd used the fact to her advantage.

Eventually Valerian had changed her, and it was not at all the unpleasant experience Aidan had described. In fact, Maeve had known unbounded ecstasy that night.

Aidan had been enraged when he discovered that his sister had followed in his footsteps; he'd called her all sorts of a fool and cursed Valerian to rot under a desert sun, and then he'd simply vanished.

For a time Maeve had been Valerian's lover, as well as his apprentice. He had introduced her to the pleasures of vampire sex, a mostly mental pursuit vastly superior to the comical wrestling humans seemed to enjoy with such abandon. Since Maeve had been a virgin when Valerian transformed her, she'd been spared the indignity of sweating and straining and thrashing under some man's thrusting hips the way mortal women did.

Valerian had introduced her to many other things besides the intense delights of mating, of course. She'd learned all the nightstalker's tricks and learned them well. One night, when she caught Valerian playing vampire games with a beautiful fledgling named Pamela, Maeve had decided to strike out on her own.

She'd done well, too, eventually reconciling with a still-vexed Aidan and hurling herself into one wonderful adventure after another.

Now, as Maeve stood in the deserted room that had once been her brother's favorite retreat, holding the golden rose pendant between two fingers, she struggled to accept another reality, another turning in the road.

She must leave Aidan to his humanity, though the temptation to seek him out was almost irresistible. It was to be hoped that he'd made a happy life for himself.

Maeve figured she would never know; Aidan was dead to her, and she to him, and there could be no returning to their old bonds.

There was nothing to do now but feed and retire to the attic studio of her home in London, where she liked to go when she was sad or injured. There she would sit at her loom, letting her thoughts drift while she worked the shuttle, allowing her deeper mind to dictate the image that would appear, as if by magic, on the resultant tapestry.

Gettysburg, Pennsylvania
July 14, 1863

When Calder Holbrook slept—a rare event in itself— his dreams were haunted by the bone-jarring thunder of cannon fire and the screams of schoolboys-turned-soldier. Not a moment passed, sleeping or waking, when he didn't want to lay down his surgical instruments and go home to Philadelphia, but he couldn't leave the wounded. The color of their tattered uniforms meant nothing to him, though some of the other doctors refused to treat "the enemy."

That particular summer night was hot, weighted with the metallic scent of blood and the more pungent stenches of urine and vomit. After operating for twenty hours straight, Calder had stretched out gratefully on the soft, cool grass covering an old grave, there in the sideyard of the small clapboard church, and plunged headlong into a fitful slumber. In the early hours, well before dawn, something awakened him, something far more subtle than the cries and moans of the injured boys inside, sprawled end to end on the pews.

Aching with despair and fatigue, Calder lifted himself

onto an elbow and scanned the churchyard. There were so many wounded, such an impossible number, that they spilled out on the crude sanctuary to lie in neat rows on the grass. Even so, this was only one of many improvised hospitals, all overburdened, overwhelmed.

Some of the patients shivered or sobbed in their inadequate bedrolls—if they were lucky enough to have a blanket in the first place. Some moaned, and some had suffered only minor injuries and were just marking time, waiting to be sent home or to rejoin the Union troops at the front. The Confederates, of course, would be marched to some prison camp, or hauled there in whatever rickety wagon could be spared.

Calder came back from his musings and squinted. Something was different; he had an eerie, fluttery feeling in the pit of his stomach, made up partly of excitement and partly of fear. He dragged himself upright, his back against the cool marble headstone, ran blood-stained fingers through his dark hair, and strained his tired eyes.

And then he saw her.

She was a creature made of moonlight, moving so gracefully between the rows of fallen soldiers that she seemed to float. Her gown was pale, sewn of some shimmering, gauzy fabric, and her ebony hair tumbled down her back in a lush cascade.

Calder rubbed his eyes, then the back of his neck, mystified, certain that he must be hallucinating, or at least dreaming. This was not one of the good women of the town, who had been assisting so tirelessly with the injured of both sides since the terrible battle earlier in the month; none of them would have worn something so impractical as a white frock into the midst of such filth and overwhelming gore.

An angel, then? Calder wondered. Some of the

stricken boys had spoken of a beautiful guardian spirit who came in the night and gave nurture and comfort to those who were the nearest to death. Of course, they'd been seeing what they wanted to see, being so far from their mothers, wives, and sweethearts.

Calder narrowed his eyes again, trusting neither his vision nor his reason. The woman did not vanish, as he had expected, but instead knelt beside a sorely wounded lad and drew him against her bosom with such tenderness that Calder's throat tightened over a wrenching cry.

Her glorious hair, seemingly spun from the night itself, was like a veil, hiding the lad's head and shoulders from view.

Calder finally gathered enough of his senses to scramble awkwardly to his feet. "You, there," he said in a low but forceful voice. "What are you doing?"

The creature raised her head, her exquisite face pale and glowing like an alabaster statue in the silvery wash of the moon. The boy lay in her arms, his head back in utter abandon, an expression of sublime jubilation plain in his features. Even from that distance, Calder knew the soldier was dead.

The doctor scrambled to his feet, swayed slightly from weariness and hunger, and started toward the woman. She laid the boy on the ground with infinite gentleness, bent to kiss his forehead, and then rose gracefully to her full height. Just as Calder drew near enough to see her clearly, she raised her arms and clasped her hands together, high above her head. She favored the physician with one brief, pitying smile, and vanished like so much vapor.

Calder gasped, shaken, terrified that he was at last and indeed losing his mind, and oddly joyous, all of a piece. After a moment or so he composed himself and crouched beside the boy the woman had held so lovingly, searching with practiced fingers for a pulse.

There was none, as he had expected, but Calder felt the familiar mixture of rage and grief all the same. The soldier had obviously been trying to grow a beard, and he'd produced peach fuzz instead. His features were more those of a child than a man.

Damn this war, Calder thought bitterly, and damn the politicians on both sides for sending mere children into the fray. He was about to straighten the boy's head, and cover him so that the overworked orderlies would know to carry him away in the morning, when he noticed the odd marks at the base of the lad's throat—two neat puncture wounds, just over two inches apart.

"What the hell?" Calder whispered.

Tom Sugarheel, an earnest but largely incompetent fellow who had been dragged out of some second-rate medical college and pressed into government service, suddenly appeared, squatting at Calder's side. "That'll be one less to bawl and snuffle for his mama," the other man said.

Calder reminded himself that he was here to attend the sick and injured, not to kill, then glared at Sugarheel. It galled him to ask an opinion of this oaf, but sometimes even idiots possessed insights that escaped other minds. "Look at these marks," he said, pointing to the boy's throat. "Have you seen anything like this before?"

Sugarheel shrugged, reaching into the torn, blood-stained pocket of the dead lad's dark blue tunic. "Not as I recollect." He found a small tintype, probably intended for the soldier's mother or young bride, and ran a dirty thumb over the cracked glass while he pondered the already fading throat wounds. "Looks almost like something a snake would do."

"You're the only snake in the immediate vicinity," Calder pointed out impatiently, snatching the photograph in its blood-speckled leather case from Sugarheel's grubby grasp. "Rustle up a couple of orderlies, and don't touch this boy's personal belongings again."

Sugarheel's expression was wry and defiant. "Most of these lads carry a paper with the name of their folks and such. I just wanted to make sure his kin got any valuables he might have."

Calder felt a crushing weariness, deeper than physical exhaustion, something that lamed the spirit. "That's the chaplain's duty, not yours. Make no mistake, *Doctor*—if I catch you stealing, be it from the quick or from the dead, I'll cut you open like a bloated cow and fill your guts with kerosene. Is that clear enough, or were there too many syllables for you?"

Hatred replaced the amusement in Sugarheel's narrow, pockmarked face, but he didn't respond. Instead he got to his feet and ambled off to fetch the requested orderly.

Calder rose a moment later, after silently bidding the fallen soldier Godspeed, and stumbled back to the soft mound, hoping to sleep again, knowing with despairing certainty that he would not.

Maeve reached her new lair, a long-abandoned wine cellar in an old villa in nineteenth-century Italy, just moments before the light of the morning sun came flooding over the low hills to blaze in the olive groves and vineyards and dance, sparkling, on the sea. The inevitable sleep overtook her, and she sank into utter unconsciousness. All levels of her mind were blank, as usual, empty of the random images and fragmentary dreams some vampires experienced.

When she awakened, however, hours later, at the

precise moment of sunset, a man had taken up residence in her thoughts—a *mortal* man, no less. He was very handsome, in a patrician sort of way, with dark hair, good teeth, and broad shoulders, but Maeve still resented the intrusion. Why, she wondered pettishly, should she find herself pondering the likes of a beleaguered army surgeon like Calder Holbrook?

Maeve rose from her improvised bed of dusty crates and smoothed her hair, feeling even more irritated at the realization that she'd taken the trouble to ferret out his name before leaving the Civil War field hospital for more pleasant surroundings. She had no particular fascination with human beings—beyond feeding on them when the need arose, that is.

In a flash, much of the doctor's history flooded, unbidden, into Maeve's mind. Calder Holbrook was the second son of a wealthy Philadelphia banker. He'd graduated from Harvard Medical School with honors and taken further training in Europe. He'd been married once, to a selfish socialite who had deserted her husband and their small daughter to run away with a lover. Holbrook had endured this betrayal with admirable equanimity, but when his beloved child had perished of spinal meningitis a year later, he'd turned bitter and cold, devoting himself to his work. His father had begged him to spend the war years in Europe, advancing his studies, but Holbrook had accepted a commission and left his comfortable life in Philadelphia without so much as a backward glance. . . .

Maeve put her palms to her temples and closed her eyes, trying to stop the onslaught of images and emotions, wanting to know nothing more about Dr. Calder Holbrook. All the same, she was well aware that she would see him again, whether she wished it so or not.

Exasperated, Maeve formed a picture of her grand house in London, with myriad comforts of the twentieth century, and centered all her inner forces on the desire to be there. In an instant she found herself standing in her own lush suite of rooms.

Moving rapidly, as if to shake persistent images of a doctor from her mind, thoughts of a man as sorely wounded as any of his patients, Maeve exchanged her white dress for a comfortable gown of red velvet. It was a simple creation, really, loosely fitted at the waist, with wide sleeves tapering into cuffs that buttoned with jet. After brushing her hair, she left her private apartments, walked along the wide hallway, and climbed the attic stairs to her studio.

She must feed soon. Maeve was not one for starving herself, knowing as she did that her powers, rare even among vampires, as well as her unflagging strength, came from the blood she took each night. Besides, she looked forward to the sweeping, thunderous joy that always overtook her during that intimate communion.

When she opened the door to the studio, however, and saw her loom awaiting her there, Maeve was drawn to it. During those early, wildly painful nights when she'd first known that her brother had either ceased to exist or somehow been restored to all the faults and frailties of humanity, weaving had been her only solace. She had not seen Valerian during that time—for all she knew or cared, her former lover and mentor was rotting in some crypt with a stake through his heart—nor had she encountered her acquaintances, the Havermails, or any of the members of the Brotherhood. Indeed, Maeve had taken care to avoid all other vampires, fearing they would sense her unusual vulnerability and close in on her like so many frenzied sharks.

Maeve had no illusions about blood-drinkers; except for Valerian's odd fascination with Aidan, and the deep bond that had once existed between her brother and herself, she had never known one to harbor true affection for another.

The pull of the loom was strong, stronger even than the unholy thirst.

She found the long box that contained her many spools of colored floss, then seated herself on the stool facing the primitive mechanism. Soon the shuttle was making its comfortingly familiar, rhythmic sound, and Maeve lost track of time, sublimating even the ravenous hunger she felt.

When a form suddenly towered opposite her, she cried out, startled. In the next instant, she was furious, for Maeve had not been caught off guard in such a fashion in nearly two centuries.

Valerian was examining the growing tapestry, a frown creasing his handsome brow. The scars from his grave-yard encounter with Lisette, the one from which Aidan had so nobly attempted to save him, were now almost fully healed. His lush mane of chestnut hair had grown back, thicker than ever. The old mischief flashed in his blue eyes, though this was tempered by a certain quiet sorrow.

"You really ought to be more vigilant, my dear," the seasoned vampire said, leaving off his former thoughtful inspection of the half-finished tapestry to round the loom and stand at Maeve's side. "Suppose I had been Lisette, or some wandering warlock?"

Maeve was embarrassed, and that made her angry, for her besetting sin had always been pride. "Had you been Lisette," she said, seething, "or 'some wandering war-lock,' instead of your pompous and arrogant self, you probably would have had the decency to knock at the door."

Valerian arched one eyebrow and studied her with a wry expression, though the sadness in his gaze did not lessen. He had suffered, and in spite of herself, Maeve felt a twinge of pity for him.

"I see no reason to continue this nonsensical debate," he said. "The point is, I am here."

"You'll pardon me if I don't touch my forehead to the floor three times or kill the fatted calf," Maeve retorted with slightly more charity in her tone.

Valerian laughed, but despair rang in the sound, as well as mirth. "What a relief to find that you haven't changed—you're still the same saucy, peevish chit I transformed these many years ago."

Maeve narrowed her dark blue eyes. When Valerian reminded her of her making, it was usually an indication that he wanted something. "Next you'll be pointing out that you taught me everything I know," she accused.

"Didn't I?" he asked lightly.

"No!" Maeve cried. "I can't count the number of times you nearly got me burned, beheaded, or staked through the heart in my sleep." She paused, calming herself slightly. "Come, Valerian—no more hedging. What do you want?"

He sighed dramatically—pure affectation, since vampires do not breathe. "I'm surprised you haven't asked about Aidan," he said softly.

Maeve felt dizzy, as if she'd taken a blow. "I know he gave up his immortality," she replied. "Nothing matters beyond that."

"Oh, no?"

Maeve lifted her eyes, met Valerian's penetrating and somewhat hypnotic gaze. "He is well?" she asked, quickly and in a low voice. At the other vampire's slight hesitation, she whispered in a furious rush, "*Damn* you, Valerian, *is he well*?"

Valerian engaged in a slow scowl. "He and that Neely creature are married now, and they're expecting a child." He stopped for a moment, bristling with distaste. "They're actually living in a *motorhome*," he went on, "like a pair of latter-day gypsies!"

Maeve laughed, amused at Valerian's snobbery, but the sound was a bitter one because she had realized the danger. Her expression turned deadly serious. "You've been following Aidan about, haven't you? You idiot— you've probably set half the ghouls in creation on his trail!"

The accusation made Valerian draw himself up in an imperial swell of annoyance. As usual, he wore tailored evening clothes and a cape, and in one hand he held a very expensive top hat. The attire served to accentuate his natural majesty of countenance.

"I veiled myself," Valerian said scathingly, glowering down his nose at a thoroughly undaunted Maeve. "No other vampire, not you or even Lisette herself, would have sensed my presence." He seemed to deflate a little then, though the change was nearly imperceptible, and Maeve could not be certain whether she'd seen or just imagined it. He examined his perfectly manicured and buffed fingernails. "The truth is, I was bored to distraction within a week," he finally allowed in a moderate tone of voice. "I'd forgotten what mundane lives humans lead."

Maeve was frowning and, being unusually adept at such things, even for a vampire, Valerian read her thoughts. He smiled gently and reached out to raise her chin with an index finger.

"There, now," he said. "Don't be worrying about your foolish brother, my sweet. Only Lisette has reason to quarrel with our Aidan, and I've stolen all memory of him from her mind."

"However did you manage?" Maeve asked, surprised. "Don't tell me you actually approached her again, after she staked you out in that graveyard to be destroyed by the sun!"

"It was easy," Valerian scoffed. "When her plan backfired and she herself was nearly caught by the light of day, she was badly disfigured. Being a vain creature, Lisette has secreted herself away. Most nights she does not even rise to feed."

Maeve left the stool and went to the tall leaded windows that looked out over London. "Lisette is dormant?" she asked casually, knowing all the while that she wasn't deceiving Valerian; that was virtually impossible.

"For the most part," Valerian replied, moving silently and swiftly to her side and pretending an interest in the lights of the city.

"So that's why you've come," Maeve said. "You hope to destroy her, and you want my help."

Valerian didn't reply immediately. When he did speak some moments later, his voice was oddly hoarse and grim with determination. "Lisette is a scourge on mortals and immortals alike," he said. "When she rallies—and believe me, Maeve, she *will* find her old strength—she will be more dangerous, more unreasoningly greedy, than ever before. I have seen her return from one of her monumental sulks innumerable times. She goes on rampages, feeding on innocents, changing most of her victims into vampires, and killing those who are too weak to make the transition. It must not be permitted to happen again."

"Why do you want me to help? There are others who are older and more powerful."

"You know very well why I want you," Valerian replied tersely. "Lisette is the undisputed queen of all vampires, and you, my difficult darling, are her logical successor."

CHAPTER

🙢2🙠

Maeve was particularly hungry and rather weak, having missed her feeding that night, and she was impatient with Valerian and his penchant for high drama. She turned to look up at him, there by the towering windows in the studio of her London house, and folded her arms. "Suppose I tell you I have no desire to be the vampire queen? What if I simply want to go on living strictly for myself, the way I always have?"

Valerian's smile was almost—but not quite—a smirk. Even he would not have dared that, for he knew better than anyone that she was his equal, in power and in skill. "I would not believe a word of it—there is something of your heroic brother in you. Besides, you have no choice in the matter, darling. It seems to be fated."

"*Fated*," Maeve scoffed quietly, but she felt troubled on some deep level of her being. "Nothing is fated for vampires—we are not a natural creation, remember. We have no place in the grand scheme of things."

"Alas," Valerian said, with another of his theatrical sighs, "you are right, my darling, but you are wrong, as well. Some thousand years after the first vampires came into being on Atlantis, other supernatural creatures waged war against our kind. Blood-drinkers were forced into hiding, and still we were nearly destroyed. Then, in meditation, one of the elders saw a vision—a battle between Lisette and a new queen, blessed—if that's the proper word—with powers more formidable than any vampire has ever possessed."

"What does that have to do with me?" Maeve snapped, fearing sorely that greatness would be thrust upon her, whether she desired it or not. She liked her existence just the way it was, though she would have preferred to be spared the grief Aidan had caused her, of course. "There are other strong female vampires, you know. Your friend Pamela, for instance. And then there is Dimity—"

"Do not waste my time," Valerian snapped, interrupting Maeve with an imperious wave of one hand. "Pamela loves her own pleasure too much, and it is rumored that Dimity consorts with angels. There is no one but you, Maeve. You must help me destroy Lisette before she regains her former strength and wreaks havoc on the natural and supernatural worlds alike."

Maeve was honestly baffled. "Why do you care?" she asked. "Pardon my saying so, Valerian, but you aren't known for your generosity and self-sacrifice—especially on behalf of human beings."

Valerian turned his head for a moment, but Maeve saw nearly fathomless grief in his magnificent profile all the same. *Saints in heaven,* she thought, *he misses Aidan even more than I do.*

"I've changed," he said finally. He looked at her again then, with a mischievous, slanted, and slightly haunted grin. "Somewhat."

Maeve felt a small rush of affection for her old friend and erstwhile adversary but offered no response to his statement. Instead, after a few poignant moments had passed, she sighed and said, "I must feed—the sun will be up soon."

"You'll think about what I've said?" Valerian asked.

Maeve gave a reluctant nod and watched with grudging admiration as the other vampire drew back, swirled his expensive cape, and vanished into a shifting vapor. She'd never known another nightwalker with Valerian's flair for showmanship.

Maeve's temptation to return to the American Civil War, and thus to Dr. Calder Holbrook, was monumental. As an exercise in self-discipline, and because she would be damned and double-damned before stooping to consort with a mortal the way Aidan had, Maeve turned her thoughts in another direction.

She blinked and found herself in her suite, on the floor below. The housekeeper, Mrs. Fullywub, a chronic insomniac, was there, neatly folding the jumble of silky lingerie in one of the bureau drawers.

The pleasant woman started at Maeve's appearance. "Dear me," she fussed, "I wish you wouldn't do that. I don't believe I'll ever get used to it."

Maeve smiled, went into her walk-in closet, which had been a dressing room in earlier times, and selected a pair of tight blue jeans, a black leather jacket with studs, and a tank top that resembled a man's undershirt. Scuffed boots completed the ensemble.

Mrs. Fullywub shook her gray head. "Don't tell me you're going about with one of those American motorcycle gangs now," she said. "They're mostly bad company, those people."

Maeve changed hastily. "For my purposes," she answered, "bad company suits best."

"I suppose you're right." The housekeeper sighed with motherly regret. "Still, I hope you'll pay close attention to whatever is going on around you. You remember what happened to your brother, when he mistook a warlock for one of us poor, hapless mortals."

Maeve applied mousse to her hair and combed it through with splayed fingers, giving the formerly smooth tresses a wild, spiky look. She ignored the mirror above the dressing table, since it would not reflect her image anyway. "I'm nothing like Aidan," she said, somewhat testily. "And you needn't worry about me."

"You're more like him than you think," Mrs. Fullywub insisted, "and not a moment goes by that I don't fret for your safety. You have powerful enemies, don't forget."

Maeve raised her hands over her head, palms touching, fingers interlocked. "Good night," she said, and disappeared.

Moments later Maeve reassembled in a place Valerian had introduced her to long before, a bar called the Last Ditch. The term suited the filthy dive; "hell" would have been a more apt name, but that one was taken.

Smoke filled the crowded bar, tinting the air a greasy blue, and the singular smells of unwashed humanity were more pungent than ever. Maeve twitched her nose, revolted, engaging in a brief and wholly idle wish that vampire senses were not quite so keen.

She noted a warlock near the jukebox and nodded to

let him know she was aware of his presence. He returned the courtesy and added a smile and a jaunty salute.

Go to hell, Maeve told him. It was easier, with all the noise of the bar, to speak mentally.

The warlock's smile enlarged a little. *If I get there before you,* he replied, *I'll save you a seat.*

Maeve shuddered slightly in spite of herself. Long ago, in the eighteenth-century nunnery where she'd spent most of her childhood, the good sisters had taught her to fear the devil's hearth to the very center of her being. It was a fixation that she, like Valerian, who had been human in medieval times, had never quite been able to shake.

She said nothing more to the warlock, but instead scanned the crowd for a deserving victim.

She passed over the ones who were merely misguided, and those who suffered from some hidden wound of the mind or spirit, looking for someone who relished evil and practiced it willingly.

She was in luck, for there was a noted politician present, though he'd taken care to keep a low profile. He sat at a corner table, pawing a vacuous young girl who wore too much makeup and too few clothes.

Maeve made a low, purring sound in her throat and sashayed toward the senator's table, slim, rounded hips swaying, thumbs hooked saucily in the pockets of her leather jacket. "Dance?" she said.

The girl stuck out her lower lip, and tears brimmed in her eyes as the politician clambered to his feet, upsetting his chair in his eagerness to accept Maeve's invitation. Seconds later he was in her arms, and they were moving slowly to the music, swirls of smoke eddying around them, drifting even closer to the deep shadows next to the bandstand.

The senator never stood a chance.

"Don't you think you're cutting it a bit close?" Tobias demanded when Maeve popped into her special chamber underneath the London house, soon after her feeding. "The sun will be up in five minutes."

"What are you doing here?" Maeve countered, pulling off her jacket and tossing it aside. "Don't you have a satin-lined coffin waiting for you someplace?"

Tobias shook his head. He looked young, with his slender frame and eternally boyish features, but in fact he was a founding member of the Brotherhood of the Vampyre. He had been among the first blood-drinkers created, long ago on the lost continent, during a series of medical experiments.

"Such a bold creature," he said. "You remind me of your brother, Maeve—you seem to have no sense of what is appropriate, and that fact may well be your undoing."

Maeve tossed her hair, wishing she could brush out the sticky mousse, but there was no time. Soon the consuming need to sleep would drag her down into the darkest depths of her own mind. "It's beginning to get on my nerves," she confided, sitting down on the row of crates to kick off her motorcycle boots, "the way everybody keeps comparing me to Aidan."

Tobias, apparently in no hurry to return to his own lair, wherever it was, leaned against the dank brick walls and folded his arms. He was clad in a plain tunic, colorless leggings, and soft leather shoes. "It's natural, I think—you are his twin, after all."

Maeve tried to be polite to her uninvited guest, though she could not quite bring herself to smile. She'd just dumped a state senator in a crumpled heap behind the

Last Ditch, seriously anemic but alive, and his blood had left her feeling a little ill.

"I *was* his twin," she corrected her elder. After that she paused and then made an effort to be polite. "Please forgive my tart manner, Tobias—it must be the costume."

Tobias took in her tough-chick getup with quiet amusement. "Indeed," he agreed. His expression turned serious in the next instant, however, and he went on. "Word has reached the Brotherhood that Valerian has been attempting to incite some kind of rebellion against Lisette. Is this true?"

Maeve felt uncomfortable; for all her quarrels with Valerian, she was no snitch. Besides, she owed the other vampire a debt, since he'd given her immortality in the first place. "What if it is?" she asked moderately. Even respectfully.

Tobias might have sighed then, had he been human, or even a little inclined toward feigning their singular traits. Instead, he just looked resigned and weary. "Valerian has been a nuisance since his making," he said. "Still, I personally find him entertaining, and therefore I tend to overlook his . . . foibles." The elder paused, regarding Maeve with a searching stare for a long moment before continuing. "Did he ask you to lead some kind of campaign against Lisette, as we suspect?"

Maeve hesitated, then remembered that it would be absolutely useless to lie to an elder. Her thoughts were probably as clear to him as if they were goods on display in a shop window. "Yes. For some reason I cannot quite grasp, Valerian sees me as the next queen. But don't worry—I'm not interested in a political career." Exhaustion swamped her, tugged at her consciousness, and she marveled because Tobias seemed unaffected by the

vampire's need to lie dormant during the daylight hours.
"I hope you're—not planning to—sleep here," she
struggled to say. "I have a—reputation to consider—
you know."

He bent over her. "You must not confront Lisette," he
said clearly. "She is more powerful than you can ever
imagine, and we will all suffer if she is angered. Besides,
it is not ours to protect humans—that is the task of
angels."

"Angels," Maeve repeated softly. And then she drifted
into the dreamless place where vampires slumber.

Gettysburg, 1863

The battle had ended days before, Calder reflected as he
moved among the wounded. The little church on the
outskirts of town still brimmed with them, as did the
whole of Gettysburg, and the graveyard had long since
been filled. In many ways the aftermath was worse than
the fighting itself, for there were no surges of adrenaline
now, no stirring drumbeats and certainly no talk of glory.
This carnage around him, the crushed or sundered limbs,
the blinded eyes and deafened ears, the putrid infections
and the dysentery, *this* was the true nature of war.

A boy dying of gangrene clutched at Calder's wrinkled
shirt as he passed, grinding out a single word.
"Doctor—"

Calder braced himself, knowing the child-soldier was
about to plead for something to kill the pain, and there
was nothing. The supply of morphine, inadequate in the
first place, had been exhausted long before. "Yes, son,"
he said gruffly. "What is it?"

"I reckon the Lady will come for me tonight, as she
came for those others I heard about," the lad said. Instead

of desperation, Calder saw hope in the youthful face, along with agony. "She'll take me home to heaven."

Several moments passed before Calder's suddenly constricted throat opened up again so he could speak. A week had passed since he'd seen the beautiful specter, and every moment of that time he'd been telling himself she'd been a figment of his imagination. "The Lady," he said, somewhat stupidly.

The boy released his hold on Calder's shirt. "You ever see her?"

Calder sighed. He was on the verge of collapse as it was, and he didn't have the strength to lie. "I thought I did," he admitted. "What's your name, lad?"

"Phillips, sir. Private Michael Phillips, Twentieth Maine. I fell when the Rebs tried to take Little Round Top." Again the boy grasped at Calder, this time closing grubby fingers around his wrist. "You get them to take me outside and lay me in the sweet grass," he rasped. "They say she won't come inside the church—that's mighty strange, for an angel, don't you figure?—and I want her to take me."

Tears stung Calder's eyes, and he looked away for a moment. Damn, but it still galled him that he couldn't save them all, every last one, instead of just a few lucky ones here and there. After all this time in medicine, first as a civilian and then as an Army surgeon, he continued to find the reality nearly unbearable. "You seem to know a lot about this Lady," he said.

"She's about all anybody talks about," Phillips replied weakly. It was plain that he was barely holding on, and the stench of his infection came near to choking Calder. "Will you get me outside, Doctor, so's she can find me?"

Calder raised a hand and signaled for a pair of orderlies. They were actually ambulatory patients, these ready helpers, one of them hailing from Richmond, Virginia, the other from somewhere in the New Hampshire countryside. For them, the fighting was over; one would be sent home, with a permanently lame leg to remind him continually of his brush with glory, and one to a prison camp.

"This is Private Michael Phillips." Calder performed the introductions with proper dignity, once the orderlies had reached him. "He wants to see the blue sky when he looks up. Get a stretcher and find a place for him outside."

"Yes, sir," said the boy from Richmond.

As gently as they could, the Yankee and the Confederate shifted Phillips onto a canvas stretcher stiff with dried blood and hauled him through the open doorway and down the steps. Calder followed as far as the church porch and stood watching them, gripping the rail.

He should have been thinking about home, he supposed, or about those peaceful, idyllic days before war had torn the nation into two bleeding parts. Instead his mind was full of the mysterious woman he'd seen moving among the fallen soldiers that night a week before. Had she been real? he wondered yet again. After all, he hadn't been the only one to see her—she was the hope and comfort of many of the wounded, and their description of her matched the vision Calder himself had glimpsed.

His hands tightened over the railing until the knuckles ached. The reasoning, scientific part of him said she could not be an angel or a ghost as the others believed. No, as beautiful and real as the Lady was, she was merely a projection of all their tormented brains—his, those of the other doctors and orderlies, and, most of all, those of the patients themselves. The power generated by such grief and suffering had to be formidable.

Calder watched as Phillips was carefully laid out on the grass, in a space left by a boy who'd passed on that morning, and found himself wishing with his whole heart that the Lady was real. Just then, he very much needed to believe in some benevolent force, however strange and inexplicable.

He got through the rest of that day by rote, and at sunset a messenger rode in, painted with dust and so weary he could barely sit his horse, bringing word that four doctors would arrive within the week to relieve Calder and the others.

The news filled him with both relief and despair. He was mentally and physically exhausted; soon he would be of little or no use to the fallen soldiers around him. Still, he hated to leave them, and, even more, he feared that he would never see the Lady again.

That night, while Calder sat waiting, his back to a birch tree, she returned. It was about two in the morning, he reckoned, though he did not take out his pocket watch, and she went straight to Phillips.

Calder was fascinated, stricken by her beauty and her magic, unable to move from his post by the tree and approach her as he'd hoped to do. Instead, he simply watched, powerless and silent, while she smoothed back the dying child's rumpled, dirty hair and spoke softly to him.

As Calder looked on, the lad raised his arms to her, like a babe reaching for its mother. She drew him close and held him tenderly, and for a moment Calder believed she truly was an angel.

She rocked the boy against her bosom for a sweet, seemingly endless interval, then bared his fragile neck and buried her face there. Phillips shuddered in her arms and then went still, with that same trusting abandon in his bearing that Calder had seen in the other soldier, the one she'd taken on her last visit. The Lady seemed to nuzzle him, and when she lifted her head, her gaze met Calder's.

He felt some kind of quaking, deep in his being, but even then he knew it stemmed from excitement, not fear. He willed her to come to him, and she did, drifting along with steps so smooth that she appeared to be floating.

When she stood only a few feet from him, her dark tresses tossing in the slow summer breeze, her pale skin bathed in moonlight, he believed in whatever she was, believed with the whole of his spirit.

"Who are you?" he managed to whisper after a long time. His voice was a raspy sound, scraping painfully at his throat.

She drew nearer, knelt beside him, and touched his hair. At first he thought she wasn't going to speak, because she was just a vision, after all, and therefore without a voice. Then she smiled, and Calder felt a pinch in his defeated heart as she said, "What does it matter who—or what—I am?"

"It matters," he confirmed.

"Perhaps it does," she said. She removed the pendant she was wearing, an exquisitely wrought golden rose on a long chain, and put it around Calder's neck. "Very well, then. I am quite real, and this shall be your proof."

"You truly are an angel," Calder marveled hoarsely.

She laughed softly. "No," she said. "My name is Maeve, and I am quite another kind of specter." She searched his eyes for a long moment, an expression of infinite sadness in her face, and then lightly kissed his mouth.

He felt a surge of sensation, both physical and emotional, and was completely lost to her in the space of a single heartbeat. He groaned and closed his eyes, and when he opened them again, she was gone.

Calder was paralyzed for a time, full of confusion and wonder and a peculiar, spiraling joy, but when he could move, he groped for the pendant. It was there around his neck, real and solid to the touch.

"Maeve," he repeated, in a whisper, as though the name itself had the power to work magic in a world sorely in need of just that. "Maeve."

Maeve was distracted as she worked at her loom that same night, her mind full of Calder Holbrook. She had been foolish to approach him and worse, to speak to him and leave her precious pendant, like some smitten maiden in a troubador's song.

She felt a surge of emotion that would have caused her to blush, had she been human. For all practical intents and purposes, she thought, she *was* a virgin. While she and Valerian had often engaged in torrid bouts of mental sex after her making, no man had ever touched her before that. Now, no man ever would.

The idea was oddly painful, and that made Maeve furious with herself. She had, after all, vowed never to become involved with a mortal, and she wasn't the least bit like the legendary Lisette, who enjoyed bedding human lads at the height of their physical prowess.

Maeve murmured a curse, trying to shake the images that suddenly filled her mind, images of herself, coupling with Calder Holbrook. The effort was futile.

"It would be dangerous," she said aloud, at once irritated and dizzy with desire, working her shuttle so forcefully that it was in danger of snapping. "Such a thing must never be allowed to happen!"

But Maeve still felt the hot, powerful yearning, stronger even than the need for blood. Knowing that at the height of her savage passion she might well lose control and actually kill her lover did nothing to ease the wanting.

She had always been so pragmatic, oblivious to the charms of humans—beyond drawing sustenance from them, of course. What was happening to her?

"Whatever it is," a voice intruded, "you'd better put a stop to it before you end up mortal, living in a motorhome and making babies."

Valerian. For once Maeve was glad to see him.

"Thank you for announcing yourself," she said coldly. "And for rifling through my thoughts like a pile of rummage in a market stall!"

Her visitor was dressed in unusually ordinary clothes, for him. He wore blue jeans and a sweatshirt with a picture of a wolf on the front.

"Tsk-tsk," he scolded. "You have much greater problems than my abrupt entrances. Lisette is prowling, Maeve. It is happening."

The news wrenched Maeve out of her self-absorption without delay. "What do you mean, she's 'prowling'?"

"Just that. Lisette is not merely taking blood, as the rest of us do, she's creating new vampires. Indiscriminately. And they are ugly, mindless creatures, with no more discretion than army ants."

Maeve abandoned all pretense of working at her weaving, and slipped off her stool to approach Valerian. "Does the Brotherhood know of this?"

Valerian's expression conveyed both amusement and well-controlled fury. "They choose to ignore it."

Maeve recalled her visit from Tobias. "Then perhaps

you should follow their lead, Valerian. I've already been instructed not to interfere with Lisette."

For a moment it seemed that Valerian would explode with frustration. "Don't you see what will happen if she isn't stopped?" he demanded when he'd composed himself again. "The world will be overrun with these monsters, and if that's allowed to continue, there will soon be no humans to sustain us." He gripped Maeve's shoulders in strong hands and looked deep into her eyes. "But it will never come to that, Maeve," he went on, "because Nemesis will be forced to step in. He will mobilize armies of angels and destroy not just Lisette, but every vampire on earth. He's been itching to do just that for centuries, and this may be all the excuse he needs. Remember—as a warrior, it is his charge to protect the mortals his Master so cherishes!"

Maeve felt cold. "Surely the Brotherhood has considered—"

"Please!" Valerian scoffed furiously. "What has happened to your brain, Maeve—are you thinking with only a tiny portion as mortals do? The Brotherhood is a group of doddering old fools who have long since lost touch with the true state of affairs."

Maeve raised the fingertips of her right hand to her mouth, taken aback. Valerian's words had been bold, even for him. "Be careful," she warned after a moment of recovery. "It may not be Lisette our Brothers rise against, but you. As it is, they think you're rash and hot-headed, and they've warned me not to listen to your wild ideas."

Valerian's brow furrowed as he frowned. "Since when does anyone—the Brotherhood included—tell the illustrious Maeve Tremayne what to think and whose words to heed?"

She did not reply, for Valerian's question had struck its

mark. Maeve valued her right to choose her own path and make decisions for herself above everything but her singular vampire powers.

The older blood-drinker smiled now and cupped his hands on either side of her face. "All I ask," he said quietly, "is that you look at what Lisette is doing. Once you've seen, you can make your own judgment."

Maeve started to argue, but the words stopped in her throat. Instead she simply nodded.

Valerian wrapped his arms around her, and the embrace became a nebula, spinning faster and faster. Maeve clung to the front of his shirt with both hands and devoutly hoped he knew what he was doing.

When the whirling stopped and they were still, Maeve was ruffled, and she pushed herself out of Valerian's arms with slightly more force than necessary.

"Why do you always have to be such a show-off?" she demanded. "Why can't you just will yourself from one place to another, the way the rest of us do?"

Valerian's eyes laughed, though his mouth was solemn. He raised a long finger to his lips. "Shhh," he whispered.

Maeve looked about and realized they were in a hospital, and judging by the high-tech equipment, she determined the time was the late twentieth century.

A nurse rounded the corner and stopped cold in the dimly lit corridor, clutching a medical chart to her chest. She was staring at Valerian and Maeve with her mouth open.

"You don't see us," Valerian said cordially, approaching the poor startled creature, who was now as immobile as a small animal blinded by a bright light. He rested the back of one hand against her forehead and repeated his words, this time gently, like a parent comforting a distraught child.

The young nurse stiffened for a moment, as if a charge had gone through her slender form, then proceeded down the hall, her conscious mind clear of impossible creatures knitted of shadows.

Valerian watched her go, a sort of affectionate concentration evident in his handsome face, and then gestured for Maeve to follow him. She did and found herself in a cold, sterile room with metal cabinets lining the walls. There was a human in attendance, but Valerian rendered him unconscious with a touch to the nape of the neck.

Barely a moment later a metal drawer slid open, seemingly of its own power. Maeve watched in disbelief as a bluish-gray corpse sat up and swung down from its storage place as nimbly as an athlete, though the body was that of a very old man.

The sight made Maeve shudder, though she'd seen many macabre things in her time; the thing was a vampire, and yet it seemed unaware of itself, unaware that two other blood-drinkers were nearby. It crept slowly toward the sleeping mortal, fangs glinting horribly in the fluorescent night.

"Do something," Maeve whispered, for the moment too repulsed to move.

Valerian stood still, his arms folded, his manner thoughtful and unhurried. "There—a specimen of Lisette's work," he said. "And this is only the beginning of the nightmare."

CHAPTER
❖3❖

The hospital morgue was utterly still.

Maeve started as the living corpse reached the mortal attendant, who had awoken and was now catatonic with terror, and closed waxen fingers over his shoulders.

After casting a contemptuous glance at Valerian, who was watching the process with a mixture of clinical interest and smugness, Maeve finally shook off her own morbid fascination and stepped forward.

She had never, since the night of her making, consumed the blood of an innocent, and she would not stand by and watch while another vampire did so.

"Stop," she said clearly, her voice charged with warning.

The freak looked at her stupidly, clearly confounded,

but its hold on the mortal did not slacken. Its face was all
the more hideous, it seemed to Maeve, for the ragged
vestiges of humanity that still showed in its features.

Maeve knew that reasoning would not reach the
creature, nor would the threat of greater powers, for it
was conscious of nothing but its own mindless, unceasing hunger. Feeling a strange, disconsolate pity even as
she moved to destroy, she reached out and closed her
fingers over the creature's clammy throat.

"Be careful," Valerian coached dispassionately, sounding a little like a university professor overseeing a flock
of mediocre students. "Its bite may be venomous. We
don't know much about these aberrations, you know."

"Thank you so much for your input," Maeve replied,
her gaze never shifting from her prey. She gave the ghoul
a hard shake, and its grasp on the human, now blathering,
was broken. The mortal scrambled to safety, making a
low and wholly pitiful whimpering sound as he went.

Maeve did not pause to watch the attendant's flight,
but instead concentrated on forcing the lesser vampire
onto a shining steel autopsy table. She hissed an order,
and Valerian finally troubled himself to stir, handing her
a pair of scissors.

Maeve subdued the demon when it struggled, dared to
murmur a prayer for its true soul, and drove the long,
narrow blades of the scissors through the beast's chest
wall and straight into a heart that had long since stopped
beating.

The monster would not rise again.

A clamor stirred in the outer hallway; clearly the
terrified attendant had been carrying tales about the
strange and fearful goings-on in that eerie way station for
the dead.

Valerian sighed. "We'd best get out of here," he said.

"In a few seconds a horde of panicky mortals will come bursting through the doorway, and I would rather not deal with the poor wretches at the moment."

Maeve glared at him, even as she raised her hands over her head for a swift departure.

To Maeve's frustration, when she reassembled herself in the center of an ancient stone formation in the English countryside, the place where rumor had it that Aidan had been found, months before, Valerian was already there.

"Well," he began, in that imperious tone that came so naturally to him, "do you believe me now?"

Maeve was still shaken and not a little disgruntled, for she had felt a potential strength stirring in the being she had destroyed, a primitive agility that would be terrible if it were ever properly channeled.

Still, she did not want Valerian to be right.

About anything.

"Any vampire could have made that—that thing," she said. "We have no proof that Lisette was responsible."

Valerian gave a raspy, tormented cry, full of profound exasperation. "Very well," he snapped. "Let us suppose, for a moment, that Lisette is not the culprit. The fact would remain that we are dealing with a renegade of some sort—one that must be stopped."

Maeve felt a chill, even though the night was warm, and a painful sense of desolation settled behind her heart, leeching her strength. She missed Aidan more sorely in those moments than she ever had, and yearned for his counsel.

She spoke patiently. "It could have been a random episode, an act of passion or revenge. We have no reason to believe it will be repeated."

Valerian gazed deeply into her eyes. "You are fooling yourself," he told her, touching a deep, well-hidden nerve with his words. He knew her so well and often taught her things about herself that she would rather have ignored. "This is no time to bury your head in the sand, Maeve— the existence of all vampires may depend on the choices you make."

She turned from him, let her forehead rest against one of the cool, towering stones that had witnessed her brother's transformation from blood-drinker to mortal. Weariness swept over her, and for the first time in over two hundred years she wanted to retreat, as Valerian and others had done through the centuries, to lie dormant in some hidden tomb until the challenges facing her now had passed.

"Perhaps," she finally said after a long while, still not looking at Valerian, "vampires should not be saved. It could be that our time has ended—"

Valerian gripped her shoulders and wrenched her around to face him. "You cannot stand back and allow this to happen," he growled, showing his fine white teeth, including the sharp incisors that were only slightly longer than their counterparts. "The rest of us have sacrificed much—indeed, our very souls—for our immortality and our singular powers. Do you think that would be the end, if we all perished, that we would lie peacefully in our graves, oblivious to the universe around us? You must know that we would be sent into the pit, multitudes of us, to suffer agony for all eternity. Will you condemn us to such a fate, Maeve? We who have been your friends—your lovers?"

Maeve felt a stab of conscience, a certain annoyance, and no small amount of fear. "I have had only one lover," she was compelled to point out, even though the fact had no relevancy to the dilemma she faced.

Valerian narrowed his magnificent, mesmerizing eyes.

"Vampires are not creatures of conscience or charity," he admitted softly, "but we are living beings who feel sadness and pain, as well as pleasure—and far more keenly than mortals do. Will you not fight for us? Will you not defend us, your sisters and brothers?"

"Why me?" Maeve cried in an agony almost as great as the one she'd endured when Aidan abandoned her. "Why not you? Or Tobias?"

The vampire laid his hands on either side of her face. "Deep inside, in the center of your mind and heart, you know the answer, Maeve," he said, his voice soft and grave. "Some unconscious consensus of the species has appointed you to take up the sword in our behalf."

Maeve was silent for a time, considering. She hesitated so long, in fact, that the first pinkish-gold light of dawn was tracing the horizon before she replied. "I will find out what is happening, but that is all I am willing to promise."

Valerian, to her weary annoyance, was smiling as she locked her hands together high over her head and vanished.

Calder Holbrook sat glumly in his father's august study, an overfull snifter of brandy close at hand, gazing out one of the windows overlooking the formal rose garden that had been his mother's pride. In one hand he fingered the necklace the Lady had given him, as though it were a rosary instead of a simple pendant on a chain.

Only a few feet away, in the carefully cultivated soil of the garden, the roses conducted a silent riot of color, their reds and pinks and yellows gaudy and rich in the afternoon sunlight. It seemed ironic to Calder that such shameless beauty could exist in a world where young boys played soldier, blowing each other to shreds at the behest of politicians and merchants and bankers.

"You needn't go back, you know." The voice came from the broad archway behind Calder, the doorway leading into the main part of the house, and, though it was unexpected, it did not startle him.

He did not turn to face his father, but instead closed his fingers tightly around the strange, simple pendant. His inner organs seemed to stiffen as he bolstered himself against this quiet, ruthless man who had sired him.

"Do not suggest buying my way out of the Army again," he warned. "I volunteered and I will serve my time."

Calder could imagine Bernard Holbrook's rage, as fathomless and cold as a well lined in slippery stones. "When will I understand you?" Bernard asked, and the clink of crystal meeting crystal echoed in the muggy, ponderous room as he poured a drink of his own.

Calder sighed but did not turn his attention from the lush roses, which seemed to frolic even in the still air, like trollops in gaudy dresses. "Perhaps never," he replied. "We are too different from each other."

"Nonsense," blustered Bernard, who preferred not to entertain realities that weren't to his liking. William, Bernard's elder son and Calder's half brother, looked and thought like their father and was a fawning sycophant in the bargain, but that apparently did not satisfy the old man. "Nonsense," Bernard said again. "You are flesh of my flesh, bone of my bone. We are more alike than you want to believe."

Suppressing a shudder at such a prospect, Calder dropped the pendant into the pocket of his starched linen shirt—he had long since tossed aside his suit coat—and summoned up a somewhat brittle smile. "Think what you wish, Father—as you always do."

Bernard was a portly man, with a wealth of white hair, a ruddy complexion, and shrewd blue eyes that were often narrowed to slits in concentration. Whatever his other faults, and they were many, his mental powers were formidable, and he could discern much that would escape a lesser mind.

"Surely you won't try to convince me that you—even you, with your curious ideas of mercy—actually *want* to go back to another of those damnable field hospitals. Good God, Calder, the places have got to be horrible beyond comprehension."

Calder's broad shoulders sagged slightly. "They are," he confessed in a tone that betrayed more than he would have revealed by choice. He rubbed his temples with a thumb and forefinger, remembering the incessant screaming, the sound of saws gnawing at bone, the vile, smothering stenches.

Bernard took a pensive sip of his brandy, looking out at his late wife's roses as though in fascination. Calder knew the expression was deceptive; he would have wagered the last decade of his life that the older man didn't even see the blossoms. Finally, when he was damn good and ready, he spoke again.

"Why, then, do you insist on going back?" he asked, and for a moment the question seemed reasonable to Calder, and he did not know how to answer. "Well?" Bernard prompted when an interval had passed. "Is it because you want so badly to spite me?"

Calder sprang from his chair, invigorated by a sudden rush of fury, and turned his back on the man who had sired him to gaze up at the woman in the portrait displayed above the mantelpiece. "Damn it, Father," he bit out after several seconds when he did not trust himself to speak, "when are you going to realize that the sun and the planets do not revolve around you?"

"When," Bernard countered quietly, "are you going to realize that in throwing your life away like this you injure yourself far more grievously than you could ever hurt me?"

Slowly Calder turned to face the other man. "I am not 'throwing my life away,'" he said coldly in measured tones. "I am a *doctor*, Father. Is there a more logical place for me to be than in the midst of suffering and pain?"

"Yes," Bernard said with a patient sigh. "You could be a society doctor, like many of your schoolmates, and treat rich ladies with the vapors."

Again Calder felt such contempt that he dared not speak. Instead he moved close enough to the place where he'd been sitting to retrieve his half-finished brandy. He tossed back the contents of his snifter and felt the fire spread through his veins, the sudden, almost painful slackening of the muscles in his neck and shoulders.

"Calder," Bernard went ruthlessly on, his voice level and sensible like that of a snake charmer. "Listen to reason. I have friends who can arrange an honorable discharge. You can spend the rest of the war in Europe if that's what you want, learning those new surgical techniques you're forever yammering about."

Calder closed his eyes, shaken and ashamed. A part of him wanted to do as his father urged, to flee the carnage plaguing his own continent and lose himself in the knowledge he craved, to pretend there was no unnecessary pain in the world, no savagery.

"No one would blame you," Bernard pressed, probably sensing his advantage.

Calder came back to himself in a flash of conviction and hurled his empty snifter against the polished black marble of the fireplace. The crystal shattered into thousands of glittering shards, and he wondered if that was not how God must see His creation: as broken, shining bits of something originally meant to be beautiful. "*I* would blame me," he said softly.

Bernard sighed again. "Would that your sainted mother, God rest her soul, had taken her stubbornness to the grave with her," he said, "rather than leaving it in your keeping."

Calder said nothing. He was, in fact, already looking toward the doorway, yearning to be away.

As had ever been, Bernard did not seem to know when to quit. "If you will not put the war behind you for your own sake," he said, "then do so for mine. I need you here, under this roof."

"You have William," Calder replied, unmoved.

Bernard offered no comment on that statement; he could not fault his elder son without faulting himself, for they shared the same thoughts and feelings and opinions. "Why in the name of heaven do you hate me so much?" he asked. "You have never been abused, and you have lacked for nothing. I saw that you had the finest possible education, even when you insisted on wasting that marvelous mind of yours on ordinary medicine. Tell me—I think I deserve to know—why is it that you have chafed and strained against me from the time you learned to grip the rail of your baby bed and hold yourself upright?"

Calder raised his eyes to the lovely, guileless face in the portrait over the mantel, the face of his mother. Somewhere deep in his mind her sweet voice echoed, shaping the words of some silly lullaby.

Finally he turned to Bernard. "I don't hate you," he said. "I cannot spare the energy hatred demands."

"But you do not love me, either. You never have."

"Wrong," Calder said in a low, insolent voice. "She loved you once"—he gestured toward the painting that dominated the room—"and so did I. Until I saw that you were destroying her with your polite cruelties and gentle betrayals."

Bernard threw up his hands, then let them slap to his sides in frustration. His face was redder than usual, and the white line edging his mouth gave evidence that he was shocked as well as infuriated.

"Great Scot," he whispered. "After all this time, are you telling me that you have scorned my every effort to be a father to you because of a few fancy women?"

"She thought you loved her," Calder said, looking up at his mother's face, feeling again the terrible helplessness and despair he'd known as a small child. She'd wept over her errant husband, the beautiful, naive Marie Calder Holbrook, until Calder had thought his own heart would break. And in the end her abiding grief had caused her death.

"Marie was weak," came a third voice from the inner doorway.

Calder's gaze shot to his half brother, who was fifteen years his senior. William might have been a comfort to Marie, even a friend, for he'd been quite near her own age; instead, he had tormented her for taking his dead mother's place in that yawning tomb of a house.

A charge moved in the room, a silent crackling, nearly visible for its sheer strength.

"Do not tempt me to do you harm, brother," Calder said to William. "The pleasure of the prospect is very nearly more than I can resist."

William, who would look exactly like Bernard in another thirty years, started to speak and then wisely restrained himself.

Calder pushed past him to enter the wide hallway just beyond.

Bernard shouted his name, but Calder did not turn back. Instead he kept walking, his strides long, until he was far from the great house and the others who lived beneath its heavy slate roof.

Benecia and Canaan Havermail were having one of their ludicrous tea parties when Maeve appeared in the ancient graveyard behind their family castle.

Benecia, a gold-haired wisp of a girl, and Canaan, her younger sister, who was dark of coloring, appeared at first glance to be children. They were in fact vampires, with some four centuries of grisly escapades behind them, and all the more terrible for their doll-like beauty.

Seeing Maeve, Canaan clapped her tiny, porcelain-white hands. Her nails were delicate pink ovals, microscopic in size and smooth as the interior of a sea shell.

"You've come to have tea with us!" she cried in childish delight.

Maeve felt a pang, looking upon this exquisite monstrosity, and wondered again if she hadn't been right, during her last encounter with Valerian, when she'd suggested that it might be better to let all vampires perish.

"Sit down," Benecia trilled, drawing back a dusty chair. Her golden sausage curls bounced in her eagerness to welcome the unexpected guest.

Maeve took in the scene without speaking or moving. The tea table was a dusty monument, smudged with moss and draped with the weavings of spiders, but it was the other guests that gave her pause.

The sisters had disinterred two corpses and a skeleton, no doubt from graves in other parts of the cemetery, and arranged them around the tombstone-table in a hideous parody of a favorite human tradition. One body, mummified by some strange subterranean process to a hard brown thing, mouth open wide as if to scream, had been neatly broken at the waist so that it would sit like a proper guest. The other was a gray, dirty thing, with rags hanging from its frame, its bony, long-dead fingers curled around a pretty china cup. The skeleton was perhaps the least ludicrous of the party, for it was clean of grave-dust, and no atrophied muscles clung to its ivory smoothness.

Maeve shook her head, marveling, not bothering to decline the invitation to join in the festivities. Before she could speak, a fourth creature lumbered into view, and she gave a little cry of amazement when she recognized what it was.

The grayish corpse, only recently dead, had been changed, like the poor creature Maeve had destroyed in the hospital morgue, into a low-grade vampire.

"Where did you find this beast?" Maeve demanded of the ancient children as the blood-drinker went from one horrible guest to another. It bared its long fangs as it wrenched one after the other to its mouth, then tossed each aside in blind frustration when there was no blood to drink.

Benecia, the elder of the two most terrifying fiends in the lot, batted her enormous china blue eyes in feigned innocence. "We stumbled across him when we were out feeding," she said in a sweet voice underlaid with vicious determination. "He's perfectly dreadful, isn't he?"

Canaan had plagued the wretched thing into chasing her, and she giggled with all the merriment of a human child frolicking with a kitten. In that moment Maeve understood her brother Aidan's revulsion for the ways of vampires as she never had before.

"We've named him Charlie," Benecia said cheerfully.

Maeve tried again. "Where did you find him?" A suspicion dawned in her mind, ugly and totally feasible. "Or did you make this abomination yourselves?"

Canaan stopped her happy dance to stare at Maeve, and Benecia was still as well.

"Tell me," Maeve ordered.

Hatred flashed in Benecia's cornflower-blue eyes, with their thick, fringelike lashes. She answered in a respectful tone, though her words were flip.

"Of course we didn't make him ourselves, Auntie Maeve," she said with acid goodwill. "We only *drink* from mortals, we don't change them."

The corpse had stopped scrambling after Canaan to stare at Maeve, round-eyed and slavering. She suppressed a shudder.

"Then where did he come from?" she insisted.

"We told you," wailed Canaan, stamping one impossibly small, velvet-slippered foot. "We *found* him. He was wandering outside All Souls' Cathedral in London."

"Were there others like him?" Maeve asked distractedly. With the formidable power of her mind, she reached into the skull of the pitiful creature before her and found no consciousness there, no vestige of a mortal soul.

Benecia shrugged, then bustled to put the tattered fragments of humanity Charlie had disturbed back into their chairs. "*If* there are more, we didn't see them."

Canaan was glaring at Maeve, her small arms folded

across the ruffled bodice of her pink taffeta dress. "Mummy's still hunting, if you wished to see her."

"Get me a sharp stick," Maeve ordered, drawing the hapless, unresisting creature toward her by the strength of her thoughts.

"You're going to stake him?" Benecia and Canaan cried in eerie unison, their voices ringing with mingled horror and eager anticipation.

"Just do as I tell you," Maeve snapped, mentally pressing poor Charlie to the rocky ground.

Canaan brought a piece of half-rotted wood that had probably served as a marker for one of the graves, in some long-ago time.

Maeve centered the stake over the beast's cold chest with one hand and took up a rock with the other. Destroying the other creature had been relatively easy, if horrible, but this instance proved more difficult. When she pounded the wooden point past skin and tissue and bone, however atrophied, the thing shrieked in rage and pain. Maeve felt sick as she struck wood and stone together, over and over, until the screaming ceased and the monster was truly dead.

When she looked up from her task, Benecia and Canaan were looking on, faces white as moonglow, eyes gleaming with pleasure. They reminded Maeve of wolves held at bay by firelight, yearning to spring, to tear and plunder with sharp teeth.

"Be gone!" Maeve cried in disgust, trembling slightly as she rose to her feet. She did not wish to be other than what she was, a practicing vampire, even after what she had just experienced, but she did long for a confidante, a mate, a kindred spirit who would lessen the horror.

Yet again, her thoughts strayed to Calder Holbrook, the American doctor. There was something in him, some combination of talents and foibles, that grasped at her heart and would not let go.

Instead of seeking him, however, Maeve focused her attention on Valerian, leaving Charlie's still body to the ravenous hunger of the dawn.

She found her erstwhile mentor in a harem, clad only in a loincloth and a blue silk turban trimmed in pearls and sporting a magnificent emerald for a clasp. The scantily clad dancing girls surrounding Valerian scattered with little cries when Maeve took shape in their midst.

"I might have known you'd be someplace like this," Maeve huffed, looking around her in contempt while Valerian raised himself gracefully to his feet and dismissed the dancers with a clap of his hands and a few indulgent, smoky words.

Valerian chuckled, folding his beautifully sculpted arms over an equally well-shaped chest, and arched one eyebrow. "Are you jealous?" he drawled.

The very suggestion made Maeve dizzy with fury. "Most certainly not," she snapped.

Valerian removed his turban and set it carefully aside, then, with a sweeping gesture of his hands, magically clothed himself in his usual formal garb, cape included. He'd been on a Dracula kick for some time now, and Maeve wished he'd get over it.

He smiled at her thoughts. "If you'd like," he said, "I could dress as a sultan. I rather like the way I look in that jeweled turban."

Maeve sighed. "You would," she muttered. "Listen to me, Valerian—I encountered another of those creatures tonight. Benecia and Canaan found it wandering around All Souls' and brought it to one of their infernal tea parties."

Valerian winced. "What reprehensible creatures they

are." A mischievous look shimmered in his eyes. "Have you ever noticed what a tacky lot vampires can be?"

"I wouldn't talk if I were you," Maeve replied, tossing a telling glance toward the discarded turban. She put her hands on her hips to let Valerian know she would countenance no more nonsense. "We must do something," she said.

The other vampire spread his hands in a gesture of helplessness. "I seem to remember telling you exactly that," he said, as if saddened that modern manners had degenerated to a pitiable state.

"You might well have been wrong in suspecting Lisette," Maeve insisted. "All the same, the situation bears looking into. Where do you suggest we start?"

"We?" Valerian echoed, giving the word a rich and resonant tone.

"Damn you, Valerian, do not try my patience. It has already reached the breaking point!"

He swept his cloak around her in a patronizing gesture and crooned his answer into her ear. "Relax, darling," he said. "Valerian will protect you."

Maeve was still kicking and struggling when the two of them landed in a tumbling heap on the stone sidewalk outside London's All Souls' Cathedral. Maeve quickly discerned that it was the late twentieth century, and her fury at Valerian was tempered with a great sadness rooted in the fact that, in this time and place at least, Calder Holbrook did not exist. Except, perhaps, as a pile of moldering remains as ugly as the guests at Benecia and Canaan's tea party.

Valerian got to his feet first and offered a hand to Maeve. She slapped it away and stood under her own power, ignoring the curious glances of the few passers-by abroad at that hour.

Valerian started after one of the stragglers, in fact, and Maeve was forced to pull him back by his cloak.

"I haven't fed," he complained. It was a wonder to Maeve how he could look and sound imperious even when he whined.

"You should have thought of that before you squandered half the night playing sultan," Maeve snapped, dusting off her long dress and hooded velvet cape. She needed sustenance herself, but she could delay it for a while.

"Come," Valerian said, suddenly serious, taking her hand. "Let us see what other fiends wander the earth besides ourselves."

CHAPTER

Maeve was rapidly becoming an obsession.

Calder thought of her constantly, the woman he knew only by her given name. He wondered who and where and, indeed, *what* she was, and agonized over the distinct possibility that he would never see her again. Despite years of scientific training and a purely practical turn of mind, he felt certain she was not a mortal woman.

He fingered the pendant she'd left in his keeping; he wore it around his neck now, as faithfully as small children and elderly women wore religious medals. No, the mysterious Maeve was not an ordinary human, but she had not been born in Calder's imagination, either, as he had once feared. She was quite real, as real as this talisman she'd given him.

He stretched in his hammock, which he'd suspended between two birch trees behind the summerhouse on his father's estate, out of sight of the great house. Hands cupped behind his head, Calder reflected that it would be a mercy if he could just return to his work—the local hospitals were overflowing with wounded soldiers and victims of the current typhoid epidemic—but he had already pushed his normally sturdy body beyond its considerable limits. If he did not rest, he risked physical collapse, a state that would put him completely at his father's mercy.

Despite the leaden heat of that summer afternoon, Calder shivered. He would get through his confinement, and that horrific war awaiting him just beyond the gates of the magnificent house like a sleek and violent beast, simply by living from one moment to the next.

And perhaps, if he'd done anything right in his life, anything deserving of reward, he would see Maeve again and begin to learn her secrets.

Maeve looked up at the shadowy spires of the great cathedral with trepidation. It would be morning soon, she had not fed, and just being in that place brought all her fears of divine punishment surging to the fore.

"Where do we begin?" she asked in an unusually small voice.

Valerian was silent for a moment, thinking, then replied, "Lisette has to have some place to hide these revolting creations of hers during daylight. Surely they can't tolerate the sun any more than we can. If I were her, I would keep them in the old tombs beneath the cathedral—there's a nice irony in that, if she hasn't gone too mad to notice it."

Maeve glanced nervously toward the sky. She'd had a

brush with the dawn herself once and wasn't anxious to repeat the experience. "Let's hurry," she said, tugging Valerian toward the nearest entrance to the great church.

Valerian balked, suddenly tense. "Not so fast," he rasped. "I sense something. Lisette may be lying in wait for us."

Deliberately Maeve calmed herself. Valerian might be right; it would be like Lisette to bait them. Narrowing the blazing light of her consciousness to a pinpoint of concentration, she assessed the general atmosphere; yes, there was danger, but the vampire queen was nowhere about.

"Something else," Maeve said thoughtfully. "It's waiting for us in the tombs."

Valerian nodded. "Forewarned is forearmed," he said and proceeded toward the entrance.

With a trick of his facile mind, he sprung the lock on the heavy wooden door, shaped from oak trees that had probably towered in some dark northern forest well before his human birth. They entered, hesitated in the shadows, sensing the lurking danger.

Together the vampires proceeded through passageways and corridors until they found the inner door leading down filthy stone steps to the catacombs. The lock was forged of iron, rusted through, and the key had been lost so long that even the oldest priest would have no recollection of it.

Again, Valerian maneuvered the mechanism by his own brand of sorcery, but the task was more difficult this time. He was clearly tiring; like Maeve, he had not fed, and as the dawn neared, the deep sleep of all vampires surely tugged at the underside of his consciousness. For all that, he was insufferably bold.

"Do you think we don't know you're there?" he called

irritably, his voice echoing through the dark, dank chamber where only the moldering dead and the scurrying rats belonged.

Maeve braced herself as the door swung open on hinges that shrieked in protest. This was not just one thing lying in wait for them, but many, and the danger was immense. Still, she felt angry challenge, rather than fear, and made ready for any sort of battle.

"Come," Valerian snapped. "Show yourselves."

Although the enormous chamber was utterly void of light, Maeve saw clearly and knew Valerian did as well, for vampires functioned best in darkness. There was nothing to see, except for crypts and tombs and marble monuments of the sort Benecia and Canaan used for tables at their infamous tea parties.

The cavernous, dusty place, with its great curtains of spiderwebs, seemed suddenly to echo with tension, and Maeve focused all her being on the powers she'd honed since the night of her making.

A humming silence throbbed and rushed throughout the chamber, encircling Maeve and Valerian like invisible floodwaters, and in the next instant the attack began.

Their assailants were not the lumbering, corpselike vampires they'd encountered before, but great, raucous creatures, ravenlike beasts the size of humans.

Valerian had set himself to fight and began to flail against the things, when Maeve reached out to stop him, touching her fingers lightly to his forearm.

"Illusions," she said.

In that instant the fluttering, noisy onslaught ceased.

"Of course," Valerian confirmed in a rather sheepish tone. "Warlocks. How many?"

Maeve considered briefly. "Ten or twelve."

Valerian sighed. "Damn." He turned away from

Maeve, and she pressed her own back to his, preparing for the true battle. "If we end up in hell together," he went on, "please accept my apology for getting you admitted."

A soft, mocking laugh escaped Maeve. "Your apology," she marveled. "A rare gift indeed. And what a comfort it will be during an eternity of suffering."

The warlocks came at them then, from behind tombs and out of crypts, shrieking and clawing and assaulting both Maeve and Valerian with their greatest weapons, their minds.

Back to back, the two vampires fought for their lives, both well aware that if the warlocks overcame them, they would not leave them to recover on the cool stone floor of the mausoleum. No, if they lost the battle, Valerian and Maeve would be taken to some very public place and left there to smolder in the sun, as a gruesome warning to all other vampires.

Once, Valerian slipped to his knees—Maeve felt him slide gracefully down the length of her back and thighs—but he fought just as valiantly as a knight defending his queen.

"We should have fed first!" he sputtered.

Like her friend, Maeve fought on two fronts; she flailed her arms and kicked mightily, at the same time forming a mental shield to protect her mind from the assault of many others.

"Yes, yes," she answered Valerian impatiently. "I know. You *told* me so!"

It had been a mistake, shifting even a small part of her concentration from the warlocks to Valerian. One of the enemy got through at that precise moment; Maeve felt a tear in her consciousness, followed by a dizzying sickness.

In the next instant blunt teeth sank themselves into the side of her neck, and agony flashed from the wound into every part of Maeve's body.

"Be ye cursed, Vampire!" one of the would-be slayers shrilled.

Maeve had not experienced physical pain of this magnitude before, even while mortal, and the force of it stunned her, weakened her knees. She swayed, but felt Valerian surge upward to stand back to back with her again, to virtually support her with his own strength.

Hold on, he told her mentally.

In the next moment the attack suddenly ceased, and the abruptness of it was somehow like an added blow. Valerian whirled and took Maeve into his arms, holding her up.

One of the warlocks came slowly toward them, pushing back the hood of his black cloak to reveal the handsome, ingenuous face that was so typical of his breed.

"It grows late," he said with a smile. Neither he nor his companions were human practitioners of the old religion; they, like the vampires, had been born of some ancient curse, some misbegotten magic, and they too were immortal. "Soon the dawn will come."

"What is your business with us?" Valerian demanded, his embrace tightening around Maeve.

The warlock's dazzling smile intensified, and he spread his arms, in their drapery of black, wide of his body. "We wanted only to get your attention, Vampire— obviously, we could have destroyed you both if we'd wished it so." He paused, splaying his fingers and touching the tips together in a prayerlike fashion. All in all, he made a disturbing caricature of a holy man, with his reverent stance and flowing robes. "Hold your arguments," he told Valerian, thus proving that he was perceptive as well as theatrical. "There is no time. Carry our message to the Brotherhood of the Vampyre."

Maeve felt adrift in a deeper darkness than she'd ever known before; she could barely comprehend the warlock's words and would have fallen if Valerian hadn't been supporting her.

"There is a renegade among you," the creature went on calmly, "the female, Lisette. She makes vampires indiscriminately; mindless, bumbling ghouls who wander the earth murdering children."

Maeve could not be sure whether she actually heard Valerian's reply or only sensed it. Dawn was close; the need to sleep was pulling her downward, as was the injury.

"Since when do you mourn slaughtered humans, Warlock, be they children or the oldest of the old?"

"Your assessment is quite right—we don't give the proverbial damn about mortals, except for the amusement they provide. But the Warrior Angel cherishes them, as does his Master. Even now, Nemesis implores the highest courts of heaven to let him wage war on *all* unnatural creatures, not only vampires, but werewolves and witches and faeries and warlocks—all of us. He's been waiting centuries—nay, eons—for an excuse to wipe the earth clean of all immortals except his own angels, and your Lisette may well have given it to him!"

Valerian was weary, too; Maeve heard it in his voice, felt it in his large frame. "What do you want of us?" he asked.

"That is simple," the warlock replied. "Stop the female, Lisette, immediately. If you do not, then our kind will declare war upon yours, in the hope that by destroying every last one of you, we can win mercy from

Nemesis. Do not forget, Vampire, that we have an advantage over you—we can venture out into the daylight."

A vision entered Maeve's fevered mind; she saw black-cloaked figures moving through sunshine from one vampire lair to another, while the blood-drinkers lay helpless, systematically driving stakes through their hearts.

Valerian was undaunted, or at least he appeared so to Maeve. "Do not threaten us," he retorted. "We are not without superior powers of our own, and if you are wise you will remember that."

There was a general rustling, and Maeve fought the darkness even as she saw the first faint tinge of dawn shining beneath the ancient oaken door.

"They're gone." These two words, spoken by Valerian, were the last things Maeve heard before she sank into utter oblivion.

The warlocks vanished as quickly as they had appeared, for, although their leader had boasted of their ability to move about in the light of day, they were essentially creatures of darkness, like vampires.

Valerian had no time to consider them further, however, for dawn was imminent and he could already feel its molten fingers groping for him and for Maeve. He swept her up into his arms and hastened into the blackest regions of the crypt, found a chamber with a door, and dodged inside.

The sleep took him before he could set Maeve down, or even assess their surroundings—all Valerian knew, as he lost consciousness, was that he had found a place where the light would not penetrate.

•   •   •

Maeve awakened on a cold stone floor scattered with bones and crumbling mortar from the ancient walls, her head in Valerian's lap. The wound to her neck, inflicted by a warlock during the battle the preceding night, had already begun to heal, but she was weak with the need for blood.

Valerian woke up just as she was raising herself from his thighs. "So," he said and shrugged. "We shall live to hunt another night. Frankly I wasn't entirely sure the warlocks wouldn't come back while we were sleeping, armed with stakes and mallets."

Maeve's head spun; she wondered if she had the strength to hunt. "Think, Valerian," she said, somewhat peevish in her discomfort. "They want us to carry the message to the Brotherhood. Destroying us now would have defeated their purpose."

The magnificent vampire thrust himself to his feet and pulled a shaky Maeve after him. "We are not the only blood-drinkers who could spread the word," he pointed out with weary reason. "Come, let's find nourishment before we perish."

Fortunately for both Maeve and Valerian, All Souls' Cathedral was in an area of London that had degenerated into crowded squalor, teeming with small-time hoods, drug dealers, and pimps.

Spotting a smarmy-looking man in a cheap striped suit, leaning against a lamppost, Maeve raised the collar of her cloak higher, in order to hide the mark on her neck, and elbowed Valerian aside.

"You're on your own," she said. "This one is mine."

Valerian shuddered. "Yuk," he said.

"Beggars can't be choosers," Maeve retorted and sashayed toward the pimp. She saw, in the recesses of the man's mind, that he made a habit of picking up scared runaways in bus and subway stations, winning their confidence and then introducing them to prostitution.

As she approached, she felt an inexplicable need to see Calder Holbrook again; he was proof that decency and honor still existed in the world.

For now, however, Maeve had to play a part, for if she did not feed, she would perish.

She formed her mouth into a saucy smile, and the pimp straightened and looked her over with a practiced eye.

"You ain't no workin' girl," he said in a thick cockney accent.

Maeve laid her hands on his shoulders—he was wearing a worn drum major's coat, burgundy velvet with gold piping—and looked deeply into his eyes, his mind, his spirit. By the mental equivalent of flipping a switch, she shut down his brain.

He followed her mutely into the nearest alleyway, and there Maeve drank. For the first time since her making, she was tempted to take her victim beyond the point of death, and the realization worried her. While she felt none of her brother Aidan's sentimentality toward humankind—indeed, she was contemptuous of such attitudes—Maeve was not vicious; she took blood only to sustain her powers and remain immortal.

Restored and strengthened, Maeve left the procurer sitting in the alleyway, vacant and staring, with the seed of a moral awakening sprouting in his brain. Come the bright light of morning, this particular deviant would forsake the life of sin, move in with his poor mother in Manchester, and spend the rest of his days clerking in a series of small shops.

Valerian was waiting impatiently on the sidewalk when she reached it, pacing back and forth, his cape flowing behind him. His color was high, which meant that he, too, had fed.

"It's about time you came back," he snapped, stopping in the center of the walk, arms folded, glaring down at Maeve. He was, typically, completely unaware of what a spectacle he made, with his imposing size, his cape, and his haughty manner. Nor did he seem aware of the flow of pedestrian traffic moving around him.

"You shouldn't have waited," Maeve said, refusing to be intimidated. Valerian might be able to dominate other vampires, but she was different.

"We have to speak to the Brotherhood," he told her huffily. "Or has it slipped your mind that the warlocks are threatening to make war on all of us?"

"Of course it hasn't," Maeve replied pleasantly but in a firm tone. "It's just that there is something else I want to do first." She glanced at the starry sky with its tracings of clouds, for this was the vampire's way of measuring time. "I'll meet you at the stone monument where Aidan disappeared—two hours before sunrise."

"Maeve—" Valerian protested.

She did not give him time to finish speaking before she interlocked her fingers above her head and vanished, for there was a sort of sustenance her spirit needed as badly as her body needed the blood of mortals.

Maeve returned to the nineteenth century, her favorite for all its trials and shortcomings, and found herself on the steps of a summerhouse behind the Holbrook mansion in Philadelphia. There was a soft, warm rain falling, and Calder was standing with his back to her, his hands gripping the rail that encompassed the open structure.

He sensed her presence immediately, although Maeve had not made even the intimation of a sound, and whirled to face her.

He said her name as though it were holy, and in that moment Maeve did what she had sworn she would never do. She lost her heart to a mortal.

The realization left her stricken, for, even now, in the face of a love she knew was unceasing and eternal, she did not want to become human again, as Aidan had done for his beloved Neely.

For Maeve, then, this grandest and most powerful of all emotions was a sentence to loneliness without end. Overcome, she turned, there on the steps that glimmered with rain, and would have vanished if Calder had not grasped her shoulders from behind.

"Don't go," he pleaded hoarsely. "Please—stay. Just for a few minutes—just long enough to tell me who you are."

She faced him then, for she hadn't the heart to disappear from his embrace, and looked up at him, knowing that all her suffering was visible in her eyes. "Who do you think I am, Calder Holbrook?" she asked gently.

He had stepped out from under the summerhouse roof, and the rain wet his dark hair and turned his fine linen shirt transparent against his skin. "An illusion? An angel? Or perhaps a beautiful devil?" he mused gruffly. "I don't know, God help me. Nothing in my medical training, or in all my life before that, could have prepared me for this. All I know is that I think of you, and nothing and no one else, through every day and every night." He paused, pushed back his dripping hair in a gesture that was touchingly boyish, and then whispered, "Tell me what is happening here, before I go mad. I beg of you—*help me understand.*"

She wanted to weep. The truth was a crushing burden, and she knew he would not believe her. As a doctor, a man of science, Calder would find even the existence of blood-drinkers impossible to accept.

Nevertheless, she could not deny him an answer, or anything else for that matter, because he was too precious to her. "I am a vampire," she said, her voice soft but matter-of-fact.

Calder stared at her, and she saw that the color had drained from his strong face. "A drinker of blood?" he marveled, and the words were hardly more than bursts of breath.

Maeve nodded, while parts of her spirit trembled and collapsed beneath the weight of Calder's horror. "Vampires are immortal," she explained, all the while wishing she'd never let herself begin to care for a human being. "Without blood, however, we would perish in a way far more terrible than even you, with all your knowledge of battlefields, could ever imagine. We must avoid daylight at all costs, and we have special powers—the ability to travel through time, for instance."

Calder seemed unaware of the rain, which was coming down much harder now. "What do you mean, you can travel through time?"

She felt a stirring of hope because Calder had not bolted in revulsion or terror, but she was far too wise to let herself think he believed her. He was probably humoring her, as he might a mad person.

Only then did it strike Maeve that Calder's mind was closed to her; she could not divine his thoughts or feelings.

"I just came from the late twentieth century," she said, amazed, prodding gently with her thoughts and meeting with an impenetrable block.

To her surprise, Calder clasped her hand, led her into the summerhouse, and sat her down on a wrought-iron bench tucked into the cool folds of shadows. "Tell me—what sort of world exists—in that other place and time, I mean? Do they still make war? What advances have been made in medicine?"

For a long moment Maeve was too taken aback by his ready belief to speak. Then she whispered, "You don't think I'm insane or a liar?"

"You are not a mortal woman," Calder answered. "That much was clear from the moment I first saw you." He was wearing the pendant she'd given him during their last encounter, and he held it out for her to see. "It was only this medal, solid proof of your existence, that kept me from having myself admitted to the nearest asylum," he said. "Now—please—tell me about medicine and warfare in your century."

Maeve checked the sky, only too aware of her commitment to meet Valerian at the stone monument in the English countryside. When she gazed into Calder's eyes again, however, she wondered if she would ever be able to look away. "There have been tremendous advances in medicine—they can cure or control a lot of diseases that are fatal in your time. It is possible to immunize children against measles and diphtheria and many of the other illnesses that almost always end in death here. Surgeons are performing successful organ transplants there, and the infant mortality rate is a fraction of yours.

"War is very much a part of the modern world unfortunately. There are weapons capable of destroying the earth, and while the largest and most powerful nations are trying hard to get along, there are a number of small, fanatical factions that are not so willing to cooperate."

Calder absorbed her words for a long interval, one of his hands clasping hers. "Can you take me there?" he asked, finally, catching Maeve off guard with the last question she would have expected him to ask.

She shook her head regretfully. "Mortals cannot travel through time as yet, though you do have the propensity for it locked away somewhere in your brain. It is an ability that must evolve over many, many generations."

He looked so disappointed that Maeve's heart ached, but a moment later his countenance brightened again. "Can you bring me things from the future, Maeve—like medicine, or books about surgery and diagnosis?"

Maeve considered, knowing she should leave this man's side, once and for all, and never return and, at the same time, feeling infinitely grateful for an excuse to see him again. "I suppose there would be no harm in that. There's just one thing, however—it isn't wise to change the course of history, because one can never predict all the ramifications of even the simplest act. You could use the things you discover in twentieth-century books, but you must not teach them to others." She stood, unable to ignore the hour any longer, and Calder rose with her. She put her hands on the warm, supple flesh of his face. "I cannot stay any longer—there are matters that must be attended to."

"Will you be back?"

Maeve felt a pang, for she could not discern whether he wanted to see her again because he cared for her just a little, or because he wanted the books and wonder drugs she could bring from the future. "Yes," she said. "If I can return, I will."

Calder bent his head then and touched Maeve's lips with his own, and as brief and innocent as it was, the contact rocked her to the very center of her being.

Her gaze flew to his, searching for the revulsion she so dreaded, seeking Calder's horrified reaction to kissing a cold mouth. Instead of those things, however, she saw a certain reverence, unmasked affection, and, yes, a disturbing sort of curiosity—that of a scientist studying a unique specimen.

Filled with sadness and bliss, she reached up and touched his lips with three fingers.

"Good-bye," she said.

One moment Maeve was there, standing before him, pale and ethereally beautiful in the darkness, and the next she was gone.

Calder felt a bleakness unequaled in his memory; he wanted to be with Maeve, now and forever, but that was clearly impossible. He would wait, he told himself, as patiently as he could, and one night soon she would return to him.

He stood in the rain for a long time, remembering. Then he dropped the pendant down inside his wet shirt, to hide it from the curious gazes of his father and half brother in the same way he had always hidden his heart from the world.

Until Maeve.

The pattering shower turned to a downpour, but still Calder remained where he was, marveling, telling himself that Maeve could not exist, could not be what he knew she was. An immortal.

Finally Calder broke his stunned inertia and strode toward the house, where he was met by Prudence, the family's longtime housekeeper.

"Lord have mercy," that good woman fussed, seeing Calder's wet clothes and distracted expression. "I thought you had better sense than to be runnin' around in a cold rain! You want to die of the pneumonia, you foolish chile?"

Calder paid no attention to Prudence's ire, for the

affection between them was old and deep. "Send Perkins around for the carriage," he said, entering the big kitchen and heading straight for the rear stairway. "Tell him we're going to the Army hospital on Union Street."

Prudence followed her erstwhile charge as far as the newel post, her sizable body quivering with disapproval. The glow of the gaslights flickered over her beautiful coffee-colored skin, and her jaw was set at a stubborn angle. "You ain't goin' to no hospital at this hour," she ranted. "I swear this war of Mr. Lincoln's done somethin' to your brain. . . ."

The war had "done something" to Calder's brain, all right, and it had nearly broken his spirit and his physical strength in the bargain. Now, however, knowing there was a future, a time when miracles would occur in the realm of medical science, gave him new hope.

"Tell Perkins to bring along a slicker," he called back over one shoulder as he gained the upper hallway. "It might be a long night, and this rain isn't likely to let up."

"Mr. Calder!" Prudence bellowed after him. "You get back here—you hear me? You ain't well!"

Calder opened the door to his room, already stripping off his wet shirt when he crossed the threshold, thinking to himself that, contrary to Prudence's assessment, he was feeling better than he had in years.

CHAPTER

❊5❊

Maeve passed the following day not in her favorite lair beneath the London house, as usual, but in a dusty crevice behind the foundation of the Union Hospital. She'd known Calder was going there after their meeting in the summerhouse, and she had wanted to be near him.

Normally Maeve's slumber was untroubled by dreams, be they pleasant or unpleasant, but that time was different. The wards and even the passages of the old hospital were filled with the wounded and the dying. They were only boys, these soldiers, most of them so young that they'd never been away from home at all before marching off to battle.

Maeve did not hear their screams of physical pain, for suffering, however intense, is a temporal thing, meaning little in the face of eternity. No, it was their soul-cries Maeve discerned, the agonized protests of their spirits.

When she awakened at sunset, she was instantly aware of her mistake in coming to that particular place. With so many mortals in torment, it was only logical that the premises would be crawling with angels.

A surge of terror moved through Maeve as she raised herself, dusted off her clothes, and pressed her back against the wall of the foundation. What had possessed her to make such a dangerous error in judgment?

She listened, and waited. Now, with all her senses on the alert, she could feel the presences of companion angels, hundreds of them. Fortunately—and this fact, she thought, might well save her from certain destruction—they were not warriors, these winged messengers from heaven, but comforters. Their full attention was fixed on their charges.

For all of that, Maeve was trembling when she closed her eyes and willed herself away from that hospital and far into the future, where other challenges awaited her.

She fed on a mean drunk, who'd been on his way home from the pub with every intention of beating his wife for his own sins, as well as a bevy of imagined infidelities, and left him whimpering on a heap of trash.

Maeve found Valerian at the circle of stones, sitting patiently on a fallen pillar and blowing a haunting, airy tune on a small pipe.

"Well, then," the great vampire said with good-natured sarcasm, "you have at last decided to honor me with an appearance." He bowed deeply. "Welcome."

Maeve was still agitated by the foolish carelessness she had exhibited back in Calder's Pennsylvania. She'd never made such a mistake before, since the night of her making.

Valerian climbed gracefully down from his perch and approached. For the first time since her arrival, Maeve noticed that he was dressed as a seventeenth-century gentleman. He wore a waistcoat of the finest silk, along with kid-skin breeches, leggings, and buckle-shoes. His hair was tied back with a dark ribbon and lightly powdered.

"Going to a costume party?" Maeve asked with the merest hint of disdain in her voice.

Valerian smiled indulgently, using only one side of his sensual mouth, and dropped the musical pipe into a pocket of his coat. "I was indeed attending a festivity, of sorts, but since this is the way the French aristocracy always dressed during those glorious pre-Revolutionary days, I did not stand out from the other guests."

Maeve sighed. Valerian would always stand out from the other guests, no matter how carefully he chose his clothing, in her opinion, but to say so would only inflate his already monumental ego, and she wasn't about to do that.

"Where is the lecture?" she asked instead, sounding weary and dispirited even to herself. "Surely you expected me before this?"

Valerian shrugged. "I kept myself occupied in your absence," he said. "What were you doing—mooning over that mortal of yours? What is his attraction, Maeve—is it the fact that he spends most of his days drenched in blood?"

Maeve was instantly angry, though in truth, had she been in Valerian's place, she might have offered much the same question. She whirled away from the other vampire, restraining her temper, and then, after a few moments, turned back to face him again. "Calder is accustomed to blood," she admitted softly. "He's a doctor, a scientist, and it isn't revolting to him, the way it is to most mortals. Indeed, I imagine he knows, on some level, what a magical substance blood really is."

Valerian arched one eyebrow. "After all your grumblings about Aidan and his penchant for that human woman, Neely Wallace, I would never have expected this of you. You're smitten with a mortal, just as your brother was." He paused and touched her face lightly with curled fingers. "Nothing can come of this affection of yours, Maeve. Not, that is, unless you're willing to make the fascinating Dr. Holbrook into a blood-drinker."

Maeve gave her head a quick and slightly wild shake. "I won't risk that—you know how many vampires come to despise their makers. An eternity of Calder's hatred would be worse than Dante's version of hell."

"Do you hate me?" he asked with uncommon gentleness.

She looked at him for a long moment, then shook her head.

Valerian made a soft sound of exclamation. "Ah, well, that is a relief." He raised an eyebrow. "Still, the situation is dire indeed. I needn't tell you what a rare instance it is when a nightwalker puts the welfare of another before its own wants and pleasures—particularly when that other is mortal."

Trembling, Maeve nonetheless drew herself up and glared at Valerian in her most aristocratic fashion. "Enough talk of my personal affairs," she said, her voice icy with authority. "What of Lisette? Have you learned anything new? Has she made more of her deviant vampires?"

Valerian's smile was slow and insolent, and he had the audacity to touch the tip of Maeve's nose with a forefinger. "All vampires are deviant, my darling—don't ever forget that. Now, to the business at hand. Lisette is ranging far and wide, but from what I can discern, she has made her vampires only in this time period. Still, we must find her, before she strews the beasts throughout history. Surely you know without my telling you how the warlocks, not to mention Nemesis and his army of angels, would react to *that*."

"We'll start by approaching the Brotherhood," Maeve said in a tone that invited no disagreement. "Then, with or without their approval, we will hunt Lisette down and destroy her."

Valerian affected a sigh; it was one of his favorite forms of expression, especially when he was feeling martyred. "At last," he said. "You have grasped what I was trying to tell you all along—that both the mortal and immortal worlds are in desperate trouble."

Maeve could not disagree. The warlocks would not stand idly by while Lisette filled the earth with zombie-like vampires, and Nemesis was surely lobbying the highest courts of heaven for permission to make war. Should the battle actually break out, it would make the ancient tales of Armageddon sound like cheerful whimsy.

"I must change into something more fitting for an audience with the Brotherhood," Maeve said, looking down at her dusty gown and cloak and then focusing a critical gaze on Valerian's garb. "Although no costume could possibly be more in character for you, I do hope you aren't planning to approach the Vampyre Court dressed as a French aristocrat."

Valerian sighed again, and all the sufferings of the ages echoed in the sound. He splayed the fingers of one hand over the place where his heart should have been. "You wound me," he said, but there was a broad grin on his face. At Maeve's scowl he gave another sigh. "Very well," he agreed. "I'll meet you in the south garden on the Havermail estate. The Brotherhood's headquarters isn't far from there."

Maeve frowned. "Why not go directly to the secret chamber?"

"You don't just pop into the place," Valerian replied indignantly, tugging at one elaborately trimmed cuff and then the other. "These are the oldest vampires on earth, and we must use a degree of protocol."

"We could bypass them completely and handle the problem ourselves, I suppose," Maeve mused, resting her hands on her hips.

"Perish the thought!" Valerian said, and for once in his immortal life, he sounded sincere. "They'd never tolerate such disrespect!" There was a pause, then he leaned toward Maeve and peered into her eyes, narrowing his own. "You have fed, haven't you? You'll need your strength to deal with the old ones."

Maeve simply gave her companion a scathing look, raised her arms, and vanished.

She materialized in her suite in the London house, where she shed her rumpled, dust-splotched garments, washed her alabaster skin, and brushed dust and tiny stones from her hair. Finally Maeve donned a beautiful dress, made of shimmering red silk, with Irish lace trimming the cuffs and yoke, along with a matching cape.

Moments later she stood in the Havermails' south garden, where a long-forgotten marble fountain presided, nearly hidden under blackberry vines and wild roses. The statue in the center had once been lovely, an exquisite sculpture of a young Greek boy with a vessel in his arms, but now it was spotted with moss and bird scat, and a knee and elbow had been chipped away.

"Couldn't you have found a more dismal place for us to meet?" Maeve snapped when Valerian joined her in the garden. He stood upon a low stone fence, practically invisible for the brambles and scrub brush that had grown up around it.

He looked like the conductor of a great orchestra, or perhaps a movie vampire, in his rustling black cape and impeccably tailored tuxedo. "The whole of the Haver-mail estate is dismal," he said irritably. "They wouldn't have it any other way. Now, might we stop this quibbling, please—at least long enough to deal with the difficulties at hand?"

Maeve felt a degree of chagrin, though she would not have admitted as much. Because of her past relationship with Valerian, and the pain he had caused her with his cavalier ways, she invariably sought to rankle him. He was right, however—this was no time for childish jibes. There were true perils that must be overcome.

"Take me to the Brotherhood," she said quietly.

Valerian closed his cape around her, and, momentarily at least, she put aside her own powers and surrendered to his.

With dizzying quickness the two of them disintegrated, shot through space like a single beam of light, and reclaimed their normal forms inside a cave far beneath the surface of the earth.

"This is the place where Aidan became human again," Maeve said in a stricken whisper. She saw clearly in the dense blackness, and took note of the paintings of animals and primitive gods and goddesses on the walls.

"Yes," Valerian said hoarsely. He, too, seemed shaken. "The resurrection ritual was carried out here, in the central chamber." He took Maeve's hand and began leading her along the edge of an icy subterranean stream.

"If you've having any thoughts about becoming mortal so that you can live happily—not ever after, as in the fairy tales, but merely for the length of a heartbeat—you'd best reconsider. The Brotherhood has decided that no more vampires will be allowed to cross over after this—they've destroyed all written records of the rite and cleansed their minds of any memory of the chemical formula."

There were more paintings on the walls along both sides of the stream, and Maeve marveled at their pure definition and richness of color. The artists had been dead in the neighborhood of thirty thousand years, at her best guess, and yet their handiwork looked as fresh as if it had been completed that morning.

"I wasn't thinking of becoming mortal," Maeve bristled a few seconds after the fact. "I've told you before, I'm not interested in giving up my powers to sit and darn stockings in some man's parlor."

"Things have changed a bit since your time as a mortal, Maeve," Valerian pointed out dryly as they proceeded along the narrow path. "Modern women don't mend stockings, to my knowledge, much less gather or wash them. They work at their own careers and guard their independence."

"I would not wish to live in the twentieth century were I human again," Maeve said, sounding just a bit defensive even in her own ears. "I prefer the nineteenth, as you know. It's more gracious and elegant."

"And Calder Holbrook is there," Valerian said.

Before Maeve had to answer, a brilliant wall of sunlight appeared ahead, and both she and Valerian stopped, keeping to the shadows. Maeve stared in wonder and no little fear, for she had not looked upon such light in two hundred years and, had she stepped into it, it would have consumed her in invisible flames.

"Don't be afraid," Valerian said quietly, squeezing Maeve's hand. "It's only an illusion—the Brotherhood's way of guarding the innermost cave."

"What makes you so certain it's an illusion?" Maeve snapped. "There could be a crevice on the surface. . . ."

"Think," Valerian scolded with gentle exasperation. "The sun set less than an hour ago. How could that be daylight?"

Maeve felt foolish for the second time since she'd awakened in Calder's hospital and realized that it was full of angels, a vampire's most dangerous enemies, and her impatience with herself made her prickly.

"Do they know we're here?" she asked in a peevish tone.

Valerian glanced back at her over one broad shoulder. "Don't be a ninny," he said. "Of course they know. We'll wait here until they send someone out to meet us."

Maeve gazed upon the false sunlight, both fascinated and repelled. She did not miss the limitations of human life, the aches and pains and superficial joys that were always so quickly gone. She sometimes yearned for bright spring days, however, for azure skies, and fields of wildflowers and sweet grass rippling beneath a golden sun. . . .

Only moments had passed before Tobias appeared, walking straight through the light, smiling and un-harmed. He was one of the elders, a member of the ancient Brotherhood, and yet he looked no more than seventeen years old, with his slender, ladlike figure and youthful features.

"This way," he said. "The others await you."

Valerian started toward the light, but Maeve drew

back, afraid. Illusion or no illusion, sunshine was a terror to all vampires, as agonizing as the flames of hell itself, and she was wary.

"Did you see this—this barrier of sunlight, when you were here before?" she whispered to Valerian.

"No," he said, sounding mildly impatient. "What's the matter with you, Maeve? I've already told you the light isn't real—Tobias probably projected it from his mind."

"He's right," said the latter, standing only a few feet away now. "I manufactured the barricade in my imagination. Isn't it splendid?"

Maeve would not have described it so charitably, but of course she wasn't about to voice her observation aloud. "Lead the way," she said, determined to bring her fear under control. If she and Valerian were to succeed in their quest and stop Lisette, then she, Maeve, would have to face many more challenges. This was no time to allow her courage to fail.

She stood at Valerian's side, instead of cowering behind him, as she had done for the space of several humiliating moments. "That's a marvelous trick," she said, swallowing the desire to turn and flee. "Will you show me how to do it?"

Tobias shrugged. "Perhaps," he said. Then he turned and strolled back through the shimmering golden curtain.

Maeve rushed past Valerian, in a burst of bravado, and hurled herself through the barrier. Even though she knew the veil was an illusion, she was still surprised that there was no burning as she passed, and she was dizzy with terrified relief to find herself safe.

Valerian was next to her in an instant, a half-smile curving his mouth.

Annoyed at his smugness, Maeve drew herself up and then turned to look back at the golden curtain. It dissolved into a magical fog of shining dust and finally vanished entirely.

Maeve was impressed, and her mind was busy as she and Valerian followed Tobias through the twists and turns of the natural passageway alongside the stream. If Tobias could do such magnificent things as make walls of sunlight appear, then she, too, must possess at least the seed of that ability. . . .

What wonders might she be able to perform if only she knew the trick?

She was still pursuing that intriguing idea when suddenly the passageway widened into a cathedral-size chamber, filled with the light of burning torches. The stream meandered off in another direction, into the depths of the earth.

The Brotherhood was gathered, and they were an imposing lot, seated along the length of a long, exquisitely carved table as they were. They did not wear black capes or somber hooded robes, as Maeve had expected, but instead were clad in garb typical of various periods of human history.

The spokesman, a giant with a red beard and piercing blue eyes, seemed to be a Viking. As Tobias took a seat behind the table, the vampire with the fiery hair stood and rounded one end to face Valerian and Maeve squarely.

He merely nodded at Valerian, but studied Maeve with such concentration in his features that she began to grow uncomfortable. "You are the one," he said at last. "The one spoken of in our legends."

Maeve said nothing, for she was still not at all certain that she was "the one," nor was she sure she wanted to be.

"Our next queen," Valerian said smoothly with a grand

nod in Maeve's direction. His eyes twinkled as he registered her carefully concealed irritation.

Still, though she was simmering with denials, Maeve did not speak.

Valerian, as usual, was not at a loss for words. "We've come about another matter," he said formally, taking in the other members of the vampire counsel with a polite sweep of his eyes. "As you probably know, Lisette, in her madness, is making an undue number of blood-drinkers. They are substandard creatures, insensible and indiscriminate."

Maeve was listening, but she was also looking around the enormous cavern and wondering what thoughts had been in her brother Aidan's mind when he was here, undergoing the terrible transformation from vampire to mortal. Surely he had been afraid and, at the same time, full of hope.

The Viking brought her attention back to the matter at hand with surprising ease. "We despair of what Lisette is doing, of course," he said. "But we are weary, and we do not wish to govern any longer."

Valerian leaned slightly forward, as he always did when he was trying to make a point. "You cannot abdicate your authority now!" he hissed furiously. "Don't you understand? The warlocks are ready to wage war against all vampires if Lisette is not stopped, and even at this moment Nemesis impugns the highest authorities in the heavenly realm to let him unleash his angels upon all of us! If this happens, the suffering, both human and immortal, will be incalculable!"

The Viking spread his hands as if to say he could offer no solution, and turned to walk away.

Impulsively Valerian reached out and grasped the

ancient vampire's shoulder in an effort to make him listen.

The old one whirled, icy blue eyes shining with fire. "It is your battle, Arrogant One," he said, and then his gaze shifted to Maeve with all the sharpness of a fine-edged sword. "And yours. As for us, we want only to rest. Eternity has gone on too long for us as it is!"

Maeve shrank back a little, startled, as Valerian obviously was, that any living thing would actually yearn for death. Perhaps, she thought, she would feel that way herself after a few thousand years, but at the moment the idea made her shudder inwardly.

"If you refuse to help us," she said with dignity, "at least promise that you will not hinder us, either." Her gaze sought and found Tobias's face. "So be it," Maeve finished, when no member of the Brotherhood spoke up.

She wanted to go to Calder, to have what might be her last look at him before she found Lisette and engaged her in battle, but she brought her emotions under stern control.

The old ones stood and bowed—except for Tobias, who regarded her with an expression of curious concern.

Maeve turned and walked regally to the center of the chamber, well aware that only one choice was left to her.

For the sake of all other vampires, for her own sake and that of Calder and of Aidan, the two mortals in all creation that she loved, she must take charge, with Valerian, and find a way to stop Lisette. If she failed, the most savage and terrible war since the expulsion of Lucifer would break out.

Perhaps even then it was too late.

She regarded each of the old ones in turn, then clasped her hands together and vanished.

A moment later she was far away, as she had wished

to be. A cool night breeze ruffled the heather of a Scottish moor, and in the distance Maeve heard the crashing of the surf against rocks that had been part of some earlier earth.

Valerian was beside her, but before either of them could speak, Tobias arrived.

His voice was infinitely sad. "They plan to destroy themselves," he said, speaking, of course, of his friends in the Brotherhood. "They are so tired, and this modern time is foreign and confusing to them. They do not wish to survive."

Maeve caught hold of Tobias's sleeve; he was wearing a flowing white shirt, reminiscent of a pirate captain's, along with leggings and soft leather shoes. "What about you, Tobias? Do you want to die, too?"

He shook his head. "No, but I, too, am weary. I will lie dormant, for a century or so, and recover my strength. I'm afraid the battle does indeed fall to you, my friends."

Valerian made an angry sound, but Maeve had tender feelings towards Tobias. He had saved all their lives, once upon a time, her own, Aidan's, and especially Valerian's, and she owed him a tremendous debt.

"Rest easy," she said gently, taking his upper arms in her hands. "And when you awaken, please seek us out."

Tobias nodded, looking out of his young face with ancient eyes, and then he disappeared.

"Who would have thought they'd abandon us like this?" Valerian demanded when they were alone. "Great Zeus, Maeve—where do we begin?"

Again Maeve thought of Calder, and of Aidan and Neely, and her beloved housekeeper, Mrs. Fullywub. All their lives depended upon her, and upon Valerian, and Maeve would perish herself before she let any harm come to them.

"At the beginning, of course," she said with a bright carelessness she most certainly did not feel. "We must find Lisette and confront her."

Valerian was pacing back and forth in a patch of moonlit heather. He had been the instigator of the campaign against the queen, and now he was plainly terrified.

Which only went to prove that he was as smart as Maeve had always believed him to be.

"I last saw her the night before Aidan and Neely were married," he said.

Maeve was stunned; Valerian had not mentioned that encounter with Aidan, let alone with Lisette. *"What?"*

He stopped his pacing and tilted his magnificent head back, silhouetted against the bright, enormous moon. "I wanted to see Aidan once more, to say good-bye to him, so to speak, though of course he didn't know I was there. He was sleeping." Valerian's voice became choked and raspy. "He was so beautiful, and I loved him so much. And then she appeared—Lisette, I mean. She planned to make Aidan into a vampire all over again."

Maeve hugged herself, seeing the horrible vision in her mind's eye. Such an occurrence would have utterly destroyed Aidan—he would almost certainly have laid himself down in some open place and waited for the sun to rise and devour him.

"Lisette was strong," Valerian went on, his voice still sounding strangled, when Maeve didn't speak. "I tried to fight her, but she overcame me easily."

"What happened?" Maeve managed to ask after a long silence had stretched between them.

Valerian was weeping quietly at the memory, and Maeve wanted to touch him, to offer some small comfort, but she restrained herself. "She was about to change

Aidan, Lisette was. I cannot describe the agony I felt watching that, unable to help him . . ."

"Go on," Maeve urged.

"It seems that all mortals do indeed have an angel assigned to them," he finally said, after regaining his composure, "though I must say I wondered where the creature was when Lisette met Aidan the first time and changed him against his will."

"You saw an angel?"

Valerian nodded. "Yes—it was a spectacular being, full of light and power. Lisette fled in terror."

"Why didn't you tell me this before?" Maeve demanded, though her tone was still quiet and even.

"You were upset about Aidan's transformation as it was. Since the knowledge wouldn't have done you any good, I decided to make the accounting another time, when you were stronger."

Maeve turned her back to Valerian, arms folded, and stood regarding the gigantic moon for some minutes, dealing with a riot of conflicting thoughts and emotions. Finally she faced him again. "Aidan is gone from me," she said. "And the important thing is that he is safe, for the time being at least, and happy. The only point that should concern you and me is that Lisette has regained her strength, and is perhaps more powerful than ever because of her madness."

"Together," Valerian said, with a brazen confidence that was typical of him, "we have the power to destroy Lisette."

"I hope you're right," Maeve reflected. Lisette's age made her a formidable enemy, for with the passing of centuries came unpredictable abilities, traits that were not common to all vampires, but often wholly unique. It was rumored that one member of the Brotherhood, for instance, could walk freely in the light of day, and Maeve had heard of vampires who did not need to drink blood, and even of some who could travel between dimensions as well as centuries. The possibilities were disturbingly infinite.

Valerian was in full control of his dignity again. "What choice do we have," he reasoned, "but to try?"

"None," Maeve answered. "Do you know where Lisette is?"

He shook his head. "Others have told me that she strikes at random, and that she is able to veil herself from ordinary vampires."

"But we are not ordinary vampires," Maeve reminded him.

Valerian smiled. "No, my darling, we are not." He paused, and his countenance darkened again. "Still, we have expended considerable energy this night. In my opinion, it would be unwise to face Lisette now, though we might certainly seek her out."

Maeve nodded in agreement. "We will concentrate on her majesty, then," she said with quiet sarcasm, "and see where our thoughts take us."

"Yes," Valerian said. "But remember—be cautious. This is no time to show off."

Maeve gave the other vampire a wry look even as she raised her hands high and interlocked her fingers. "You're a fine one to lecture me about showing off," she said, but as she vanished, she was glad to know Valerian was with her.

CHAPTER
❈6❈

Valerian assembled himself a split second before Maeve managed the same feat, and he immediately uttered a curse.

Maeve looked around anxiously, getting her bearings. They were in the common room of an elite boy's school, she soon realized, tucked away in the quiet of the English countryside. One of the instructors, recently human but now a walking corpse, with bluish-gray skin and pro-truding eyes, came snarling from the shadows.

Flanking him were two smaller vampires, with fangs bared. Before their making, they had been ordinary schoolboys.

"Children," Maeve whispered in stunned despair. "Valerian, she's changed mere *children*."

"Have a care. Lisette may still be here somewhere," Valerian replied in a taut voice, "and there could well be other creatures like these prowling about." He stopped, strengthening his resolve, and then went on. "We'll have to destroy them, Maeve."

"I know that," she murmured as the erstwhile teacher and his now-vicious pupils encircled them.

"Great Zeus," Valerian muttered, "they're too stupid to know they're no match for us. Look at them—circling like sharks around a shipwreck."

Maeve shuddered. She had not anticipated having to kill child-vampires, and the prospect filled her with grief and fury. When she could, she would settle this grim debt with Lisette, but in the meantime there could be no question of her duty.

The schoolmaster lunged at Valerian with an earsplitting, unearthly shriek, and Valerian's responding shout of anger was far more terrifying.

"Bloody wretch!" he cried, after flinging the lesser creature hard against the nearest wall.

The two boys were staring hungrily at Maeve and making dreadful, slavering sounds. She felt no pity for these monsters, for they were beyond such tender emotions now, but she did despair for the parents and siblings who had loved them. They would never know, of course, what had really happened on this horrible night.

Valerian had, by this time, overcome his attacker and forced him down onto the cluttered surface of an antique mahogany desk, one hand clamped around the beast's throat. With another swearword, this one only murmured, he raised a sterling letter opener and plunged it into the other vampire's heart.

"Handy item, that," Valerian remarked, jerking the blade out of the creature's chest wall again and staring at it. It was bloody. "Do you suppose it's the equivalent of a silver bullet?"

Maeve had her hands full, what with two agile boy-fiends hurling themselves at her, and she snapped, "Oh, for heaven's sake, Valerian, will you stop babbling about the letter opener and help me?"

"Since heaven does nothing for my sake," Valerian replied, catching one of Maeve's assailants by the back of his collar and curving one arm around to stab him, all in a single swift motion, "I will do nothing for heaven's."

Maeve was distracted, though only for a moment, but in that time the other creature was upon her, biting and clawing, fierce as a winter-starved wolf. She flung him off and, since Valerian did not offer the sleek blade he'd used on the others, grabbed a decorative sword from its place on the wall and pinioned her mindless enemy in one ferocious thrust.

The corpse was now truly dead. Maeve withdrew the sword and watched as the thing's knees folded, and it toppled to the floor.

"We'd better see if there are others," Valerian said gently, putting an arm around her shoulders and turning her away from the scene. As they left the common room, he warned, "Remember—be on your guard, my friend. Lisette may still be about, veiling herself from our awareness."

There were no more victims, as it happened. Apparently the carnage of that night had been meant as a message—perhaps even a challenge.

Maeve and Valerian proceeded carefully through the school, room by room. They found a great many sleeping boys, warm and blessedly human, and several teachers, also unharmed. There was no sign of Lisette, but that meant nothing; she was the most treacherous of creatures and might loom up before them at any moment.

Eventually they returned to the common room where they collected the bodies of the vampires they'd destroyed earlier. The things were already shriveling, their flesh crumbling to dry, gray dust; the morning sun would reduce them to fine grains that would blow away in the first brisk wind.

"How will their disappearances be explained?" Maeve asked when she and Valerian had laid the unholy and now harmless trio out on the green grass bordering a rose garden.

Valerian shrugged. "Who cares?" he asked. "Let them broadcast the horror on every television and radio station in the world. Let the local police wonder. Such things make no difference to us."

"I care," Maeve insisted, nodding toward the school buildings. "One of those children is bound to stumble across these things and be marked forever by the discovery."

The great vampire lifted one eyebrow. "There it is again," he said in a tone of playful warning, "that Aidan-like tendency to worry too much about the affairs of mortals."

"Valerian, these are *children* we're discussing here. Surely even you have some shred of compassion for them."

He affected one of his sighs. "Very well—if we burn them, there'll be no trace of their bodies or clothes by sunrise. Wait here."

"I wasn't going anywhere," Maeve said peevishly. It had been a hellish night for her, and she wanted only to find a safe lair somewhere near Calder and sleep.

Valerian entered the nearest building through a pair of

French doors, returning momentarily with lighter fluid and matches. With uncanny calm, he doused the horrid evidence of Lisette's rampage and lit the dead creatures afire.

Within seconds there was nothing left of the vampires themselves or of their clothes, except for a few curling ashes. Neither the police nor the teaching staff nor the children would be able to discern that bodies had been burned here.

Maeve turned away, scanning the star-spangled sky, trying to take comfort from its constancy and beauty but instead feeling weary, and sick at heart over the events of that night. At last Maeve spoke aloud, but she was not addressing Valerian. "Where are you, Lisette?" she whispered, her voice taut with rage. "Show yourself."

There was a great rustling sound, like the wings of many enormous birds, and a sudden, high wind scattered the last few ashes over the grass and the flower beds.

"You might have consulted me," Valerian hissed angrily through the din, "before you issued a challenge!"

Lisette was at first a swirling blackness before them, an unreasoning hurricane of fury, bending the rosebushes close to the ground with her force. Then she solidified into a dark angel, at once breathtakingly beautiful and horribly unnatural. Her long auburn hair moved softly, as the furious wind died down, and she looked at Maeve with glittering, curious eyes.

"Who are you?" she demanded, holding herself with all the regality befitting her position as the oldest and most powerful female vampire on earth. "You resemble Aidan Tremayne."

What Maeve felt was not fear, exactly, but an excited sort of awareness. She was an equal to this creature, she sensed that, but at the same time she must be alert to every nuance, every shift of Lisette's body and mind.

"I am—or was—his twin sister," Maeve allowed. She took a step toward Lisette, and Valerian grasped her arm, tried in vain to pull her back.

Lisette laughed, and the sound was high and musical and utterly chilling. "Do you imagine that you can protect her from me, Valerian?" she demanded. "When last we met, at Aidan's bedside, I dealt with you as easily as one of these schoolboys." She gestured toward the still-dark and silent buildings. "Or have you acquired an angel to guard you, like Aidan?"

Maeve interceded before Valerian could reply, certain that he would have chosen brash and foolish words to do so. "I don't need Valerian or anyone else to look after me," she said. She narrowed her eyes, studying the vampire queen's perfect features and cloud-white skin. "I think I know the answer to this question, Lisette," she said, "but I'm going to ask it anyway. Did you change this schoolmaster and the two students?"

Lisette laughed again, and the sound must have soured the sweet dreams of a hundred boys, turning them to nightmares. "Yes," she said defiantly after a brief interval of studying Maeve, sizing her up. "I made the others, too."

"Why?" Maeve wanted to know. "It makes no sense."

Suddenly a storm raged around Lisette again, a tempest of her own making. "Do not try my patience!" she shouted. "I am the queen of all blood-drinkers, and I answer to no one, mortal or immortal!"

Maeve took another step forward. "You must stop this," she said, even though she knew there was no hope of persuading this most daunting of all vampires to show mercy. "The warlocks have threatened open warfare on

all of the dark kingdom if you persist in creating these
unreasoning creatures, and it is said that Nemesis will
unleash his armies of angels at any moment."

For the merest flicker of an instant, Lisette looked
uncertain, even afraid. Then she drew herself up and
lifted her arms from her sides, and the breeze caught her
voluminous black sleeves and made them look like
wings.

"Stop me if you can," she said. She looked Maeve up
and down with mad, beautiful eyes. "I look forward to
the challenge."

With that, the legendary Lisette glanced toward the
lightening sky, laughed again, and vanished into nothingness.

Valerian spat an exclamation, gripped Maeve by the
arms, and turned her to face him. "Do you know how
lucky you are that she didn't bind you to the ground and
leave you to broil in the light of tomorrow's sun?" he
rasped. "How could you be so stupid, so rash?"

Maeve drew back out of the other vampire's grasp,
straightening her sleeves. "She tried," she said. "She
tried to overcome me—I felt it—and I resisted her."

For a long moment Valerian searched Maeve's face,
his own expression solemn. Then, finally, he smiled and
said, "I was right. You *are* fated to be the new queen."

Maeve was in no mood for Valerian's self-
congratulations and I-told-you-so's. She knew the full
extent of the ordeal she faced now, for she had felt the
first tentative tugs of Lisette's power, and she was afraid.

"I must go—I will need to feed and fortify myself
before I do battle with the likes of Lisette," she said.

Valerian clasped her hands and looked deeply into her
eyes. "We're all depending on you, Maeve," he said
hoarsely. "And there is little time to lose."

Maeve only nodded. Then, after one last sad glance at the school buildings, she interlocked her fingers over her head and vanished.

She gathered herself into solid form briefly in London's Fleet Street, just long enough to purloin three newly published medical textbooks and a selection of drug samples from a surgeon's office.

She ended her journey in the wine cellar beneath Calder's family home in nineteenth-century Philadelphia, with the booty held close in her arms. After a few minutes of searching, she found a long-forgotten hidden passageway that probably dated back to the American Revolution and took refuge there.

The place was cold and dank, populated by spiders and skittering mice, but it would shelter Maeve from the coming sunrise and the bumbling discoveries of mortals, and it was close to Calder. Close enough, in fact, that she could feel the strong, steady beat of his heart in her own spirit. She set her treasures on top of an old whisky barrel and stretched out on the floor to let the vampire sleep overtake her.

At sunset Maeve awakened immediately, and she knew Calder was there, somewhere in the reaches of the great house towering above her, but she did not go to him straight away. First, she went to one of the scores of field hospitals near a battleground and fed, taking nourishment from dying soldiers and giving comfort and ecstasy in return.

She stopped to reclaim the medical books and drug samples before centering her thoughts on Calder and transporting herself to his presence.

He was standing at one of the windows in his spacious bedroom, the lace curtains billowing on either side of him as a rain-scented breeze blew in. While Maeve watched him, marveling at the perfection and strength of his strong arms, his powerful legs, and broad shoulders, she felt again that most treacherous of emotions—unconditional, unreasoning love.

"Calder." Even his name was sweet on her tongue, like the chocolates her father's solicitor had often brought when visiting her, as a human child, in that faraway convent.

He turned, his expression bleak, and silently held his arms out to her. It was an entreaty, as well as an offer of comfort, of sanctuary.

She thrust the things she carried into a leather chair and moved into Calder's embrace.

"What is it?" she whispered.

"I had pushed my emotions away," Calder answered, his breath brushing her temple, "into the farthest recesses of my soul, and you made me face them again. You brought them back, Maeve, and some of them hurt like hell."

She drew back a little way and looked up into his wonderful eyes. "So, then," she said softly, "you too were only pretending to live. Inside, where no one could see, you were really dead."

He nodded, pulled her close again very gently, and kissed her forehead, her temple, the hollow beneath her ear. "It's rather like freezing a hand or a foot—the numbness masks the pain for a time, but the healing process is agonizing."

Maeve felt a rising excitement as Calder held and caressed her, and that surprised her, even though she'd had tender feelings toward him from the first. As a rule, vampires mated only with other vampires, and then it was always a detached, mental sort of intercourse.

Now, to her amazement, Maeve wanted a different

kind of loving. She wanted to lie naked in Calder's bed while he touched and kissed her everywhere, and then give herself to him just as a mortal woman would.

She was instantly terrified, for, although such things had happened before—Lisette, for instance, had made love with Aidan while he was still a mortal—it was wildly dangerous. Other vampires Maeve had heard of, male and female alike, had become frenzied in lovemaking with humans, and had quite literally torn their lovers apart. She moved to pull away, but Calder did not release her.

"What are you afraid of?" he asked huskily. "Tell me."

"Myself," Maeve whispered, lowering her eyes. "I'm afraid of myself and—and of the revulsion you might feel if you touch me. I'm—I'm not like the women you've known, Calder—"

He curved a finger under her chin and lifted it so that she had to look at him. "I'm feeling a lot of things toward you right now, God help me, and revulsion isn't one of them." He bent his head slightly and touched his lips to hers. In the next moment, instead of withdrawing in disgust as she'd feared he might, he intensified the kiss, deepened it until Maeve's entire body was throbbing with sensation.

Nothing, not even her wild exploits with Valerian in the early years following her transformation, had prepared her for this onslaught of passion and pounding, relentless pleasure. As a vampire, Maeve felt everything a human woman would have, multiplied a hundred-fold.

It was terrifying.

Again she pushed away from Calder. He waited without speaking, letting his eyes ask the questions.

Maeve hugged herself. "Suppose I'm not—suppose I

can't make love the way you expect? I'm not a woman, Calder, I'm a vampire."

He smiled that heartbreakingly gentle smile of his. "I have no expectations, Maeve, and I'm not about to make judgments. Have you ever been intimate with a man before?"

She shook her head. "I was a virgin when Valerian changed me into an immortal." She looked away again, then forced herself to meet Calder's tender but steady gaze. "Vampires mate—even physically sometimes— but most often their lovemaking is mental. For all I know, I won't be able to respond the way a woman would."

Calder reached out and traced the outline of her jaw with one curved finger. "If that kiss was anything to go by, my love, you'll have no trouble responding. Tell me the truth—you're afraid of hurting me, aren't you?"

She felt the unvampirelike tears spring to her eyes even before they blurred her vision. "Yes—Calder, I'm far stronger than you are, simply because of what I am. I could lose control."

"You love me, don't you? As I love you?"

Maeve couldn't speak; she merely nodded. No man had ever told her he loved her before, and no vampire, either—except, of course, for Aidan. That was a different sort of love, since he was her brother.

Calder stroked her dark, silken hair with his hands, and she felt his gentleness seep into her, through her skin, where it melted the last of her resolve. "You would never do me harm," he said. "Never."

She went into his arms again and gripped the front of his fine linen shirt in her fingers, just to hold him close. "Kiss me again," she whispered, and he did.

This contact was even more electrifying than the first,

and Maeve was dazed by the extent of her yearning—it was a primitive and elemental thing, older than stardust. To prevent an intrusion by Valerian, or any other immortal, she cast a mental shield around that quiet room. After that, Maeve and Calder might as well have been alone on the planet.

When Maeve was bedazzled by kisses, and certain she could bear no more of the ecstasy they gave her, he withdrew gently and began removing her clothes. As those garments fell away, so did all Maeve's private heartaches and horrors. Nothing else existed except for the two of them, that room, and the passion they felt for each other.

By the time Maeve stood naked before Calder, and his clothes had joined hers, she had forgotten that she wasn't a flesh-and-blood woman, but an immortal.

Calder arranged her in the center of his bed and then lay beside her, admiring her, caressing her, murmuring soft words that made her long to be joined to him.

She knew a moment of fear when Calder bent his head to her breast, but as he tongued her nipple and took it into his mouth to suckle, all her self-doubts were lost in a pleasure so fierce, so keen, that it was nearly painful.

For a long while Calder simply loved Maeve, introducing her to a new universe of sensation. Then, when she was clearly ready, indeed nearly delirious with the wanting of him, he parted her legs with a gentle motion of one hand and mounted her.

Again she was afraid and was certain she would die if she could not take this man inside her in the same way a mortal woman would do.

He touched an index finger to her full lips to quiet her and whispered, "Shhh. It's all right." Then, slowly, cautiously, Calder entered Maeve's body in a single, gliding stroke.

There was no problem in receiving him, only in restraining her passion, which escalated to a feverish pitch as he began to move upon her. She cried out and clutched at his shoulders with her hands, and then, fearing to cause him pain, spread her fingers over his back.

"Move with me, Maeve," Calder said in a tender rasp. "It will be even better for both of us if you do."

She was breathless, even though she had had no need of her lungs in more than two hundred years, and she felt certain that if she'd had an actual, living heart, it would have burst in her chest. Obediently, with all the trust she had to offer, she began to return his thrusts.

The ecstasy was intolerable, consuming, and she shouted with it, aware even in her fever that it was an animal sound, wild, untempered by any constraint of humanity, but she could not keep herself silent. The noises she made, the small groans and whimpers and pleas, as well as the lusty cries, were all part of what was happening, interwoven with the loving itself.

Nor was Calder silent, as he approached some soul-sundering completion of his own. He moaned Maeve's name and, just when her body and indeed her soul exploded in a burst of glorious, brutal passion, he stiffened upon her and rasped some senseless plea to heaven.

Maeve continued to react helplessly beneath him for some time, her body seemingly independent of her mind, trembling and flexing in a downward spiral of pure joy. Even while this was happening, however, she watched Calder's face and feared that she'd killed him, for his eyes rolled back, and he was still and rigid as his warm seed emptied into her.

He finally collapsed beside Maeve, his head resting on her bosom, and she wept with relief because he was breathing, and she could feel his heartbeat through her own flesh.

She wound a finger in his soft, glossy hair as he slept. At last she understood why her brother had been willing to risk the very fires of hell to be with the woman he loved, to exchange his immortality for a short span of human years.

It wasn't just the physical joining—it was the vast universe of emotion that underlaid that need to be of one body, of one flesh, with the man she loved.

Dawn was beginning to light the sky when Maeve gently removed herself from beneath the weight of Calder's sprawling arms and legs and climbed out of bed. She dressed without waking him, knowing he would find the books and medicines she had brought for him, and bent over him to lay a kiss as soft as a fairy's whisper on his forehead.

Then, regretting the necessity of leaving as she had never regretted anything, Maeve took herself to her favorite lair, the one beneath the London house, and stretched out on the stone slab that awaited her there.

She had only moments to think, before the day-sleep of all blood-drinkers captured her and dragged her under, but it was long enough. She had done something irrevocable this night, something that might bring doom, but she had no remorse.

If she perished that very night and spent the rest of eternity among the damned, the glories Calder had fostered in her spirit, the joys he had taught her in his bed, would sustain her throughout.

Calder awakened slowly, groping toward the surface of consciousness, fairly drowning in the deep sense of well-being his lovemaking with Maeve had engendered in him. In the next instant he wondered if he'd imagined the entire encounter.

"You have a woman in here last night?" Prudence boomed, sending the door crashing inward with a motion of one large hip. She was carrying a breakfast tray, and her round face was full of wary disapproval. "I heard plenty of carryin' on, and me way down on the second floor, too. It's a wonder your daddy didn't march right in here with a horsewhip!"

Calder raised himself to a sitting position, the sheets covering him to the waist, and grinned groggily at the beloved housekeeper. "You've been in this house a lot of years, Pru," he teased. "You must know by now that my daddy is no moral giant himself. Any crusade he might mount on the side of virtue would probably collapse under the weight of its own hypocrisy."

Prudence set the tray down in Calder's lap with unnecessary force. "I don't see why you can't talk in plain and simple words like anybody else!" she fussed.

He chuckled as he lifted the silver lid of a serving plate and saw his favorite fried potatoes and onions beneath it, along with several strips of bacon and some toasted bread. "And here I thought you were my greatest admirer."

The housekeeper stopped herself from smiling, but just barely. "Go on with you," she huffed, waving a scornful hand at Calder. She lingered a few moments, perhaps hoping he would say more about his night visitor, but, of course, he did not. At long last Prudence heaved a great and martyrly sigh and left the room.

Calder's banter with the housekeeper had been mostly superficial; inwardly he was reliving the events of the night, pondering them in his heart, wondering if he wasn't insane.

He might have believed that if Maeve's pendant didn't still rest against his bare chest.

Just as he was finishing his breakfast—for the first time in weeks he ate ravenously—Calder noticed a stack of books and other, less recognizable items in a nearby chair. Excitement possessed him—Maeve had remembered her promise to bring medical texts back from the latter part of the next century.

He nearly sent his tray flying in his eagerness to bound out of the bed and cross the room. Reaching the chair, he simply stood there, naked and transfixed by the books and by the strange medicines. They were pressed into tablets, these drugs, and packaged with stiff paper on one side and some hard, clear substance he didn't recognize on the other.

Calder felt wonder as he studied those strange packets and no small amount of frustration with his own lack of knowledge. In the end he was able to identify only one of the compounds—morphine, the painkiller that was in such tragically short supply on the warfront.

Reverently he picked up one of the books and opened it to the copyright page. The publisher was William B. Finley and Sons, and the publication date was 1993.

1993.

Even though he knew the volume was real—it had weight and substance in his hands—Calder was still shaken. It had been—*would be?*—printed one hundred and thirty years in the future. He dressed, never taking his eyes off the book for more than a few moments, and kept it open on the washstand while he shaved. Unable to restrain his curiosity and his desire to learn, Calder stopped now and then to read a sentence or two.

By the time he was through grooming himself, he'd cut his chin and right cheek with the razor, but he didn't care, for he was in a state of quiet ecstasy. Maeve had brought him not just one medical book, but several, along with some of the miraculous concoctions of twentieth-century chemists, and he was greedy for their wisdom.

Bending close to his mirror, Calder touched one of the spots where he'd nicked himself, then stared curiously at the bead of blood on his fingertip. As he did so, he thought of Maeve, and of her wonderful powers, and began to speculate. . . .

CHAPTER
❧7❧

Maeve ached to go to Calder, to warm herself by the gentle fire burning in his soul, but her practical instincts warned her to be wary. It would be only too easy to bring him to the attention of other fiends—most notably, Lisette, though Maeve was by no means certain she could trust even Valerian.

Instead she fed in the seamiest part of London, near the docks, and tried to content herself with the fact that she and Calder were at least in the same century. Because she was building her strength and attempting to hone her skills, she took blood often. As always, Maeve was careful to prey only upon the deliberately evil, not on the merely misguided.

On her third night among seagoing rats, of both the

two-legged and four-legged varieties, Maeve encountered another vampire—one she had only heard of
before, but never actually met.

The female was from the fourteenth century, like
Valerian, and that made her old. She was, despite her
great age, as beautiful as an angel, with waist-length
blond hair, enormous eyes the color of spring violets, and
a sweet, heart-shaped mouth.

She took shape at the end of an alleyway as Maeve
was leaving another victim to sleep off his blood loss,
and she was a vision in a blue velvet gown trimmed in
exquisite handmade lace.

"You are Maeve Tremayne," she said in a voice like
the merest brush of fingers over the strings of a harp.

Maeve gave a cordial, if guarded, nod, for she recognized Dimity from Valerian's description, and she recalled that the beautiful vampire was rumored to consort
with angels. In some quarters of the dark realm, this was
considered mildly suspicious behavior; in others, it was
outright treason.

"Dimity," she said by way of acknowledgment and
greeting.

The other nightwalker tilted gracefully to one side, in
order to peer around Maeve and have a look at the
victim. "You chose well," Dimity said thoughtfully.
"This one is so foul-natured that even the devil would not
wish to keep him company."

Again Maeve nodded. She had, of course, assessed the
man before feeding from the vein in his throat. "Do you
have some business with me?"

Dimity smiled, clasped the rich velvet of her skirts in
both hands, and executed a half-curtsy. "Yes, indeed, my
queen," she said, and though she was plainly teasing,
there was a note of awe in her voice as well.

"Save your curtsies," Maeve said, approaching Dimity. She was cautious and full of amazement, for the other vampire seemed to glow with some inner light, the way creatures of heaven did. It was possible that this ethereal beauty was not a blood-drinker at all, but an angel. "I am not yet queen. Perhaps I never will be."

Dimity's delicate mouth curved again, into another, softer smile. "Oh, but you will," she said with certainty. "And you are wrong in what you're thinking about me. I am a vampire like you." She stepped forward and linked her arm with Maeve's. "Come," she said, her expression serious now. "We must talk."

Dimity led Maeve along the street, into another alleyway, and far back into the complexity of that London slum. Finally they came to a pair of cellar doors, beneath a place that seemed to be a second-rate mortuary, and even though Maeve was used to death, she shuddered.

The other vampire's laugh chimed like music, and she raised the heavy wooden doors as most immortals would—by a trick of her mind.

Dimity started down the stone steps, glancing back at Maeve over one shoulder. "Does it trouble you to know the dead rest here?" she asked, indicating the mortuary with a slight motion of her glorious head. "Who would understand better than you, the queen of nightwalkers, that they are mere husks, incapable of harm?"

Maeve didn't speak, though she was well aware that that didn't matter. Dimity could discern at least the shadow of her thoughts, as Maeve could hers. Dimity wanted to tender a warning, and it didn't take a genius to guess what it was.

For Maeve's part, she was recalling her brother Aidan's account of his making as a vampire, in the eighteenth century, when he'd lain in such a place as that morgue, cold as a corpse and unable to move the tiniest muscle. Those who had attended him had believed him dead, and though he had struggled to convey the fact that he was, despite all outward indications, very much alive, they had prepared him for burial.

Maeve, being Aidan's twin, as close to him as his heartbeat and his breath, had felt the ordeal herself, even as it occurred, and even after all that time, she had not forgotten the inexplicable, smothering terror. When Aidan had given an account of the experience, some weeks later, she had relived it with him. For that reason Maeve longed to be far away from this disturbingly familiar place.

Dimity continued into the cellar and then into another chamber, below that, a place lighted by the glow of scores of candles and quite comfortably furnished. There was an elegant Roman couch, where Dimity undoubtedly slept during the day beyond the reach of the sunlight, along with several comfortable settees and velvet-upholstered chairs.

There was even a painting on the wall, and it brought a sad smile to Maeve's lips, for it was a portrait of two elegant vampires, waltzing together. She knew without looking at the signature that this was Aidan's work, done many decades ago, when he was struggling to come to terms with what he was.

"Did you know my brother?" Maeve asked, her voice unusually thick.

"Only by reputation," Dimity answered, taking a seat in one of the beautifully upholstered chairs, kicking off her delicate velvet slippers and wriggling her toes. "He became a legend, understandably, when he traded vampirism for mortality." She winced prettily at the thought. "Can you imagine it?"

"No," Maeve admitted readily. The image of Calder nearly came to her mind, but she managed to keep it hidden. Or so she hoped. "But the life of a blood-drinker was torment to Aidan. He'd reached the point where he was ready to perish—even to risk the Judgment—rather than go on as he was."

"And he loved a mortal woman."

Again Maeve struggled to suppress thoughts of Calder, but this time she wasn't quite so certain of her success. "Yes," she said, staring at the portrait.

"And now you love a mortal man," Dimity pressed.

Maeve turned her back on the painting with rather a lot of difficulty, since it represented a connection with her lost brother, however indirect.

Dimity laughed and raised a finger to stop Maeve from speaking. "Do not worry," she said. "Your human lover is safe from me. Like you, I feed only upon the lowest of the low. Child molesters are my particular favorite, though I enjoy the sort of ham-fisted, drunken louts who like to beat their wives as well."

Only moderately reassured—for vampires were not, as a rule, creatures of their word—Maeve took a seat on a settee. "You are very good at veiling your thoughts," she said, "but I have discerned that you want to warn me about something. Please, tell me, although I believe I know."

Dimity arched one pale gold eyebrow. "You *are* powerful," she said. "I am an old vampire, and shielding my mind is one of my most distinctive skills."

Maeve leaned forward slightly. "Please."

Dimity folded her hands gracefully in her lap, and the candlelight flickered and danced in her fair hair. "I am acquainted with certain angels," she said after a few moments of deliberate silence. "They tell me that war is imminent—vampires will be purged from the earth, along with warlocks and werewolves—all immortals, in fact, except for those who belong in the ranks of Nemesis's army."

Maeve was not surprised, but she felt a tremor of terror all the same. "Because of Lisette?" she asked, although she knew the answer.

Dimity nodded.

Maeve thought frantically of Calder in this century and Aidan in the next. Even she, with all her gifts and powers, could not be in two places at once and protect both of them at the same time. "Where will this war be fought?" she asked.

"In all times and dimensions," Dimity replied. "Although every effort will be made to preserve mortals—as you know, the angels bear them unceasing affection—many will be wounded or killed in the fray."

Rising from the settee, Maeve went back to the painting, touched it gently with the palm of her right hand, and spoke very quietly. "Can it be stopped?"

"Yes," Dimity said doubtfully, and that single word flooded Maeve with relief. "But only if Lisette is destroyed within a fortnight. At the end of that time Nemesis will be given free rein."

Maeve turned to face Dimity again. Before, the threat of war had been only rumor, but now she had to accept it as fact. She knew with all the certainty of her being that Dimity was telling the terrible, unvarnished truth.

"How do you know these things?" Maeve did not wait for a reply. "Is it true what they say—that you keep company with angels?"

Dimity smiled, unruffled. "The answer to the second

question is also the answer to the first—I do have a special friend from that quarter. His name is Gideon, and he is indeed an angel. He told me."

Maeve had been shaken by Dimity's earlier warning, but she was also curious. "How can such a thing happen? I have always been told that angels are the most fearsome of all our enemies."

The golden-haired vampire raised one shoulder in a shrug. "Nothing is absolute," she said. "Gideon, like many angels, despises the vile creatures you and I feed upon, especially since the women and children who suffer are so often their particular charges. Angels, however, are not free to wreak vengeance, no matter how justified it may be—as you have seen, even Nemesis, the greatest of all warriors, must have the sanction of the highest realms before he can make war."

"That is probably as it should be," Maeve observed quietly. "If it were not so, you and I and a great many other beings would have been destroyed long ago."

Dimity's expression was one of mild agreement. "Perhaps."

A thought struck Maeve. "Would they take our side against Nemesis, these sympathetic angels?"

"Never," Dimity answered with gentle certainty. "They are loyal to heaven, first and always. When the line is drawn, they will stand with the uncounted legions who are their brothers and sisters."

Maeve might have sighed then, had she been human. "They couldn't save us anyway," she said.

Dimity shook her head. "No, it is true, they could not. Even if each of Nemesis's warriors stood touching another angel on all sides, over the face of the whole earth and upon the surfaces of all the seas, there would not be room for even a fraction of their true number."

The image practically overwhelmed Maeve, and the most dreadful thing was that she knew she hadn't even begun to picture the full size of the opposing army. If such a conflict came about, Calder and Aidan would both be wiped out in their separate centuries, and if that happened, even Maeve herself would yearn for death.

No, more than death. Oblivion.

"I have to stop her," she whispered, thinking aloud, feeling the truth of the situation for the first time. It was like some acid, eating away the marrow of her bones, working its way slowly, relentlessly, toward her soul. "I cannot allow this to happen."

Dimity's hand came to rest on Maeve's shoulder; until then, she had not been aware that the other vampire had risen and crossed the candlelit chamber to stand beside her.

Maeve raised her gaze to the shadowy ceiling. "Perhaps they are to be envied after all," she said in a hoarse whisper.

Again Dimity lifted an eyebrow. "And perhaps not. Remember, we don't know what actually becomes of them, after they shed those weak and pitiful bodies of theirs."

Standing, gathering her strength and her resolve for all that faced her, Maeve allowed a touch of sarcasm to creep into her voice. "Couldn't your friend Gideon enlighten you about that?"

Dimity was unruffled. "He knows the truth, of course, but to speak of it is forbidden—especially to us."

Maeve started toward the door, which was a high archway of stone. One would never have guessed, from the ringing silence of that place, that busy, raucous London lay above it. "Thank you for the warning," she said, pausing at the bottom step to look back. "I trust I will see you again?"

"I am your servant," Dimity said with another nod and a twinkle in her purple eyes. Then she sat down, calmly took an embroidery basket from a table next to her chair, and brought out her stitchery.

For a long moment Maeve hesitated. Then, knowing she had no choice, she turned and climbed the stairs, toward the ugliness and the glory, the love and the treachery, that awaited her.

She half expected Valerian to be there, on the surface, pacing impatiently, but there was no sign of him. Both disappointed and relieved, she stood in the passing crush of sailors and prostitutes, missionaries and thieves, staring up at the starry heavens and wondering why this terrifying, impossible task had fallen to her.

Maeve awakened with sudden violence, like a submerged buoy rushing to the surface, at sunset of the following day. She was filled with the sense of being watched, and looked wildly about for Valerian or Tobias, but she was alone in the chamber beneath her London house.

Her second thought was of Calder and all the horrors he would see and suffer if angels actually made war on vampires and other creatures. She had to protect him; she would not be able to think clearly, to track and destroy Lisette, if Calder wasn't at least reasonably safe.

She went upstairs, by normal means, drawing no more attention from her nineteenth-century servants than she ever had. Just then, a little sympathetic notice would have been welcome, and Maeve found herself missing Mrs. Fullywub, her housekeeper in the nineteen-nineties, who hadn't been born yet. Mrs. F. knew when and how to fuss over her mistress.

After grooming herself and donning a simple gown of royal-blue sateen, Maeve immediately took herself across the ocean to Pennsylvania.

She materialized just inside the great double doorway of the Holbrook mansion's main parlor and immediately regretted her impulsive entrance. Calder was there, standing next to the fire and brooding, but so was another man, thinner and shorter than Calder, perhaps a decade older. This second person was looking right at Maeve when she took shape, and his glass fell to the floor with a clink, spreading whiskey over the Persian rug.

The dropping of the glass made Calder turn, and when he looked at Maeve, the light in his eyes stopped all other thoughts. He came toward her, took her hands in his, and bent to kiss her gently on one cheek.

"My darling," was all he said, but those two words might have been an epic love poem, given the effect they had on Maeve.

"Who the devil are you?" the other man demanded, breaking the spell and causing Calder and Maeve to draw apart slightly. "And where did you come from?"

"Maeve," Calder said, his voice weighted with quiet irony, "may I introduce my half brother, William."

She smiled at William, even though he was bad-tempered and petulant, and gently closed down a major part of his brain. He sagged to the floor in a faint, and Calder, ever the doctor, was about to stoop to the other man's aid when Maeve stopped him.

"Your brother is neither ill nor injured," she said. "He will be all right in a few minutes, though he'll never have more than the foggiest memory of meeting me."

"He's my *half* brother," Calder stressed, smiling.

"William is a mean-spirited little jellyfish, quite deserving of whatever ill fate might befall him, but tonight I actually pity him. He has met you, only to forget the experience in the next instant. How sad that is."

Maeve remembered the reason for her mission, and the smile faded from her lips. "You must come with me, Calder—now, without asking questions."

She had not expected him to balk—Maeve was used to getting her own way—but Calder did resist, however gently. "I can't leave my patients," he said. "Or, for that matter, the experiments I've been performing in the laboratory at Union Hospital."

Maeve was exasperated. "I have no time to explain this to you now," she said imperiously. "After I have fed—"

"I'm not going anywhere," Calder interrupted stubbornly. He looked puzzled as well as recalcitrant. "What is this all about, Maeve? You've never behaved this way before."

She might have left him there, to face his fate, except that she loved him too much. While Nemesis could not attack for nearly two weeks, the warlocks were under no such compunction, and neither was Lisette, who might think it a great joke to make Calder into one of her witless monsters. It was absolutely vital that he be hidden away somewhere, at least until she'd had a chance to decide on a precise course of action.

Being in no mood to argue, Maeve laid a hand to Calder's forehead and caught his strong, solid frame in her arms when he sagged against her, temporarily unconscious. She saw William Holbrook raise himself from the floor and gape in horrified amazement as both she and Calder vanished into thin air, but she didn't worry, knowing he would forget.

Within moments, of course, the two of them were in Maeve's London house. It was still the nineteenth century, for mortals had yet to develop the faculties for traveling between time periods, and Calder had not yet regained his wits.

She laid him on the bed in her suite, smoothed his hair, and felt a mixture of sympathy and amusement as she imagined his reactions when he realized he was in England and not Pennsylvania. Unfortunately she needed to feed, and that meant there was no time to wait for him to come around and try to cushion the shock a little.

Maeve bent, kissed Calder's forehead, and disappeared from the room as quickly as she had arrived there moments before.

Soon she was on the waterfront, stalking the night's prey. She fed once, twice, a third time, feeling her powers grow with each infusion of fresh, vital blood. All the while, she waited for Lisette and wondered where Valerian was.

Several nights had passed since she had seen him and, under normal circumstances, Maeve would not only have been unconcerned by this, but relieved in the bargain. Valerian was a hopeless hedonist, totally devoted to his own pleasures and interests. Therefore it was not unusual for *years* to pass between their encounters, not to mention a few scant turns of the moon, while he indulged one or more of his complicated fantasies in some far-off and very exotic place.

This was different, however, for Valerian was well aware of the danger and urgency of the situation—indeed, he had been the one to bring it to Maeve's notice—so it seemed unlikely that he would have gone off on one of his tangents. . . .

Maeve slipped into an alleyway, closed her eyes, and

concentrated on Valerian. Within a moment an image formed in her mind: She saw the other vampire in the depths of some sort of pit.

The image came clearer as she focused her thoughts . . . the pit was an abandoned coal mine, somewhere in Wales. Slowly the story unfolded in her mind.

Three nights past, Valerian had been set upon by warlocks, outnumbered by the sneaking blackguards. They'd beaten him, torn his flesh with their talons and their teeth, and carelessly cast him aside, to be consumed by the next day's sunlight. Somehow, the legendary vampire had dragged himself to that forgotten mine, and found sanctuary in the cool darkness.

Heartsore, Maeve went to Valerian immediately, in that rat-infested hole in the stony, unforgiving Welsh ground, and gathered him up into her arms. He felt as light as a child, and she did not know, or care, whether that was because of his weakness or her increased strength.

Holding him, in quite the same way she had held Calder earlier, Maeve took her mentor to London, and the chamber beneath her house. There, she laid him on the stone slab where she so often slept, then took a blade from the pocket of her skirt and drew it across her wrist.

When the blood flowed, she held her flesh to Valerian's mouth, and slowly, tentatively, he took sustenance from her.

"What in the name of God—?"

Maeve started at the sound of that voice, for she had not sensed anyone's approach, and she was genuinely shocked when she looked up from Valerian's prone form and saw Calder standing only a few feet away. He was holding a lamp high over his head, and his face was white with horror.

"Calder," she said, stricken. But she did not take her wrist from Valerian's lips.

"What devilment is this?" Calder demanded. "First you bring me to this place against my will, and now I find you—I find you—" He stepped closer, his physician's curiosity beginning to take precedence over his shock. "What in hell *are* you doing?"

"This is my friend, Valerian," Maeve said evenly. "He is a vampire, like me, and as you can see, he has been sorely wounded. Blood is the only thing that will restore him, though I think it may already be too late."

Calder set the lamp down on a ledge nearby and took Valerian's right wrist into his hand, searching for a pulse. Of course, he didn't find one. He raised questioning eyes to Maeve's face. "What happened to him?"

"He was attacked by warlocks," Maeve answered, almost defiantly, because she knew only too well how outrageous the story would sound to a mortal. She sensed that Valerian had taken all the blood he could assimilate in his weakened condition, and she withdrew her hand and turned it palm up so that Calder could see it clearly in the light of the lamp.

He watched, obviously stunned, as the wound in Maeve's wrist closed before his eyes, leaving only a trace of a scar. That, too, would disappear with the passing of another sunset.

She waited while Calder absorbed the things he had just seen, and tried to deal with them in his mortal, if formidable, mind. No doubt the events of this night had been too much for him to take in.

When he met Maeve's eyes, however, she took heart,

for the pallor had left his face, and he was breathing at a
normal rate instead of in fast, shallow gasps.

"Is there anything I can do to help?" he asked.

Even though Calder was visibly calmer, Maeve was
still taken aback by his question. In his place most
mortals—even the bravest—would have been thinking
mostly of escape, of their own survival. "Valerian is not
human," she said after a long pause. "He is a vampire.
We are different anatomically from you."

Calder's gaze touched her, gently and with remem-
brance. "Not so different," he said softly.

Even in that dark place, with tragedy present, Maeve
felt a tender stirring inside. Calder had done more than
make love to her a few nights before—he had changed
the shape and substance of her soul.

It was Calder who was the first to speak again. "Let's
have a look," he said, stepping closer to the slab were
Valerian lay and handing the lamp to Maeve. "Hold this
for me, please. Although I suspect *you* can see in the
dark, I can't."

Maeve accepted the lantern and did as Calder had
asked.

Without taking his gaze from the unconscious Valerian, Calder pulled off his rumpled suit coat and tossed it
aside. "The next time you kidnap me, madam," he said to
Maeve, still not looking at her, "I hope you will do me
the favor of letting me fetch my medical bag first."

"Instruments will do no good," Maeve said, feeling an
overwhelming sadness as she looked down at Valerian.
Although he often annoyed and even enraged her, she
bore certain tender sentiments toward him, and it did her
injury that he had been the first real casualty of the
coming war. "I told you before. Vampires don't have

what you doctors call vital signs—we have hearts that do not beat and lungs that do not breathe."

"Hmmmm," said Calder, obviously not listening. He had opened Valerian's shirt and was examining the wounds thereupon. "Remarkable," he reflected, excitement rising in his voice. "He's healing so rapidly that I can see it happening—just as you did!"

Maeve closed her eyes for a moment as relief rushed through her. So they hadn't killed Valerian after all, those rampaging warlocks. He was coming back, getting stronger—his healing faculties were indeed remarkable, as Calder had termed them. Even for a vampire.

"You really thought he was going to die?" Calder asked, lifting one of Valerian's eyelids with a practiced thumb and peering into the glassy depths. "I thought members of your—species were immortal."

Valerian stirred slightly and made a muttering sound.

The word "species" had roused Maeve's temper just a little, but she stopped herself from indulging it. After all, it was true that vampires and mortals were not of the same genus. "Vampires can be destroyed," she said quietly, laying a hand on Valerian's forehead to soothe him as he struggled to regain consciousness. "Some of the lore is true, you see. A stake through the heart will finish us, and so will fire and the light of the sun." Her voice caught. "The blood of a warlock is a lethal poison, often fatal for us, and Valerian's wounds tell me he was infused with the stuff."

Calder shuddered. "What else?"

Maeve shrugged, but she felt despondent. Now he would begin to feel repulsed by her, and by the world she lived in. Calder had seen too many of the realities of life as a vampire. "There is nothing else, as far as I know."

Valerian had at last gained the surface of awareness,

and with a shake of his head, he raised himself onto his elbows and narrowed his eyes at Calder.

Calder stared back at him, with interest but not fear.

"Who the deuce is this?" Valerian demanded, in the booming and imperious voice of old. His gaze shifted, flashing with accusation and ill temper, to Maeve. "Are you mad, bringing a mortal here?"

"Incredible," Calder muttered, surely seeing, as Maeve did, that the last of Valerian's wounds had knit themselves together.

"Explain!" Valerian thundered, turning to Maeve again.

Maeve would not be intimidated—especially by Valerian. "Your manners are insufferable," she said, and although her tone was lower than Valerian's had been and much more moderate, it carried an unmistakable warning. "Kindly remember that I am not required to explain anything to you."

Valerian subsided a little, but he still looked petulant. "This is the mortal lover," he said with a theatrical sigh of realization. "I should have known from the first."

Calder watched Valerian with amazed fascination and said nothing.

Maeve had long since set the lantern aside, but now she grasped its curved handle and handed it to Calder. More misgivings stirred in her as she considered the possible meanings for the doctor's fascination—the most alarming of which was that Calder might see her, and Valerian, as specimens to be studied. "We have things to do," she said to Valerian. "Are you well enough to wage war?"

CHAPTER

Calder followed Maeve and her strange friend slowly up the winding stone staircase that led to the main part of the house. The place was as dark as a deep well, and if not for the flimsy light of the lantern he carried, he would have been completely blind.

Maeve and the other vampire were silent, and yet Calder knew they were communicating; he could feel their unspoken words flowing like a river, just beyond the edge of his understanding, rapid and urgent and angry.

He supposed at least some of the discussion concerned him, but at that point Calder didn't care. He was still struggling to come to terms with what had happened to him during the course of that evening.

He'd been standing in his father's parlor, he clearly remembered that, thinking about the war that was tearing his country apart, and William had been there, too, hectoring him about something. Then Maeve had appeared, in that dramatic way of hers, and Calder had been so glad to see her that he hadn't really thought beyond his joy.

After that she had transported him here, to this vast, elegant and vaguely spooky house, where he suspected she meant to hold him prisoner.

Calder objected to that on principle, even though he was sure she believed she was protecting him from some mysterious peril. He wasn't an inanimate object, and he wouldn't be swept up and whisked off to faraway places on Maeve's whim.

Yes, he decided, as they gained the main floor of the dark, empty house, Maeve would have to take him back to his real life straightaway. He had patients to look after, wards full of them, thanks to the war, and then there were the medical books she'd brought him from the twentieth century. Practically every spare moment had been spent poring over those volumes, though free time was rare in his life, and on some level of his being he'd been sorting and assimilating the knowledge the whole time, waking and sleeping.

Maeve's friend turned his leonine head to glare at Calder in brazen assessment. For the first time since the three of them had left the cellar, the vampire spoke in audible language. "I say he'll be nothing but trouble," he told Maeve. "Furthermore, as you might expect, I'm long overdue for a feeding."

Maeve glided between them, and Calder's feelings about that were immediate and mixed. On the one hand, he was insulted that any female should think he needed physical protection, and conversely, he was relieved because he knew Valerian would probably have devoured him had Maeve not been there to intervene.

"Lay a hand on him," she said evenly, her backbone rigid, "and I will kill you for it, Valerian. I swear that by the heart that beats in my brother's breast."

There was a short, thunderous silence, during which the two vampires glared at each other in unspoken challenge.

Then, with a contemptuous sweep of his eyes and a dismissive and patently arrogant gesture of one hand, Valerian subsided. "He's probably anemic anyway," he said. An instant later he simply vanished, leaving not so much as a wisp of vapor in his wake.

Calder immediately turned Maeve to face him. "Time for some explanations, my love," he said, his hands still resting on her shoulders. "First of all, why did you bring me here?"

The expression in her eyes, which were alight with fierce pride, implored him to understand, to trust. "You are in the gravest of danger—we all are. I must keep you safe, within these walls, until it is past. For the time being, I can say no more than that."

Calder drew in a great breath, thrust it out again in a raspy, exasperated sigh. "You didn't seem to think I was particularly safe a moment ago, when you stepped between me and your friend."

"You weren't," she conceded. "You needn't worry, however—Valerian won't do you any harm now. He knows I meant what I said about killing him."

Calder shook his head, and a grim chuckle escaped him. "I've never been defended by a woman before—at least, not in that way. It's going to take some getting used to."

Maeve straightened her shoulders and raised her chin a degree. "I am not a woman," she reminded him. "I am a vampire, and whether you like it or not, I am far stronger than you."

In truth, Calder didn't know whether he "liked it or not"—he was attempting to digest an already complicated reality. "I want to go back to my own life, Maeve. The change was too abrupt, and there are things there that need doing."

She shook her head, and an infinite sorrow showed in her wide eyes. "I can't oblige, my darling," she said. She raised one cool, graceful hand and laid it against his cheek. "I love you so that it grieves me to refuse you anything, but I cannot do what you ask. You will simply have to occupy yourself here and trust me until I can take the time to explain fully."

They were in the kitchen, and, despite the strangeness of the situation, Calder was suddenly hungry. He went to a wooden icebox, worked the brass latch, and opened the door. There was a platter of cold chicken inside.

He was devouring his second piece when he spoke again. "All right," he said, amused at himself because he sounded as though he thought he had a choice in the matter, which he plainly did not. "I do indeed love you, Maeve Tremayne, and I will trust you. All the same, I am a man, with a life and responsibilities, and you cannot simply pick me up and haul me from continent to continent the way a child drags a rag doll from one room to another. You have twenty-four hours to convince me that I belong here, and at the end of that time I want to go back. I will book passage on a ship if you refuse to take me there by means of your hocus-pocus. Agreed?"

She regarded him with those sorrowful eyes, taking a long time before she replied. "I can promise you nothing,

Calder, except that I will perish myself before I will see harm come to you." She came a step nearer, and this time it was she who laid her hands on his shoulders. "I must go. Amuse yourself as best you can—there will be plenty of food because the servants are all human—but please don't venture outside this house, no matter what the temptation."

Calder lifted a drumstick and started to wave it in protest, but in the space of an instant Maeve was gone, and he was alone in that enormous, echoing kitchen. Even with the gaslights burning, the place seemed bleak and dark without her.

He sat down at a long trestle table, where there were benches instead of chairs, and tried to steady himself, to catch up with reality. Calder might have thought he was hallucinating, but the experience was undeniably solid, and the proof of that was all around him.

After an interval of gathering his strength, as well as yearning for a double shot of brandy, he raised himself to his feet. If he couldn't get an explanation from Maeve, then perhaps he could find one by exploring.

Calder found the brandy he wanted in a cabinet in the main parlor and poured a generous portion into a cut-glass snifter. Then, carrying the drink in one hand and a small kerosene lamp in the other, he set out on his private expedition.

The first floor alone was vast. There was a ballroom with floors of gray marble, three massive chandeliers, and mirrors for walls, as well as a formidable library, a gallery, two parlors, servants' quarters, and various nooks and crannies where perfectly ordinary things were stored. On the second level of the house was Maeve's bedchamber, where Calder had awakened earlier in the evening, completely bewildered and suffering from the headache of a lifetime. He'd wondered wildly where he was and how he'd come to be there, connected it all to Maeve, and then gone in search of her.

That was when he'd found her in the cellar, with one seemingly fragile wrist pressed to Valerian's lips.

Calder decided to think about that later, and continued his tour of the house.

It was on the third floor, in a huge chamber with high slanted ceilings and towering mullioned windows, that Calder found what he believed to be the heart of Maeve's home. There, in that solitary place, stood an ancient weaver's loom, with a half-finished tapestry spilling from one end.

The light of the moon flowed unobstructed through the great arched windows, and Calder set aside the lamp, having no need of it. He examined the loom first, and then the weaving itself.

It showed a woman's delicate slippered feet, the skirts of her gauzy dress, a scattering of pale rose petals and autumn leaves on the ground. Behind the figure of the woman was a low stone wall, but Calder could make out nothing more because the rest of the image had not yet been woven.

He stood for a long time, looking at the partial scene, feeling a strange urgency to understand. He knew the work was Maeve's and that it was important to her, but the meaning of the thing, like so much of her life, was a mystery.

Calder finally turned away from the tapestry and crossed the bare wooden floor to the windows. Beyond them lay London, a scattered tangle of light and darkness, good and evil, joy and sorrow.

London.

He took out the watch his mother had given him, one

long-ago Christmas, flipped open the case, and narrowed his eyes to read the numerals. The watch had stopped, and he was too distracted and too tired to work out the difference between American time and British; it was enough just to comprehend that he'd been taken from that place to this one in minutes or even moments.

It was incredible.

Terrifying.

Fabulous.

Calder finished the brandy and turned the snifter thoughtfully in one hand. What would it be like to possess such powers? To travel through time and space so easily as ordinary mortals moved from their front parlors to the post office or the grocer's?

Was it possible to go backward in time, as well as forward? To the terrible period preceding his daughter Amalie's death, for instance? Could that tragedy be undone somehow, or even prevented?

Uncomfortable with the turn his thoughts had taken, Calder reined in his imagination, picked up the lamp he had set down just inside the door of Maeve's private refuge, and left the room.

The brandy was taking effect, and he was weary. He returned to the second floor, entered one of the guest suites, and collapsed, fully clothed, on the bed.

Calder immediately tumbled headlong into a fathomless sleep, but after a little while he began to dream of Amalie. He saw the five-year-old chasing butterflies in a sun-spangled meadow, her laughter riding softly on the breeze.

He called to his child, shouted her name over and over again, but she couldn't hear him. It was as though an invisible wall stood between them, transparent, eternal and utterly insurmountable.

Calder sat bolt upright, prodded awake by a stabbing sense of grief, and felt the wetness of tears on his face. "Amalie," he whispered hoarsely.

"Your child?" Maeve's soft voice did not startle him, even though he hadn't known she was there. She stepped out of the shadows to lay a cool hand on his forehead.

Calder nodded, full of a misery that was at once ancient and brand-new, and even though he suspected that Maeve knew all about Amalie, despite her question, he answered readily. "She was five."

Maeve sat down on the bed beside him and gathered him close in her arms. He realized in that moment of bittersweet tenderness that she was everything to him— goddess and lover and comforter—and the weight of the love he bore her was terrifying.

"What happened?" she asked, although she knew all the secrets of his heart, and although dawn, her most vicious enemy, was already tingeing the darkness with the first faint strains of apricot and crimson. Calder was well aware that Maeve had tendered the question only because she knew he needed to answer it, and he loved her all the more for her charity of spirit.

"My wife, Theresa, fell in love with an old friend of mine and left Amalie and me behind. Secretly I blessed the bastard for stealing the woman before she drove me mad with her sniveling and her petty concerns, but Amalie was a child, hardly more than a baby, and she missed her mother." A memory came back to haunt Calder then; he saw Amalie standing at one of the windows on either side of the door of the town house they'd rented in Philadelphia, her face pressed to the glass, waiting for Theresa to come back. "She was listless, Amalie was, as though her spirit was dying. She fell sick about the time of the first snow, and by

Christmas she was consumed by fever. She developed spinal meningitis, and when the new year came, she was gone."

Maeve pressed her dry cheek against his damp, beard-roughened one. She didn't speak—indeed, there was no need for that, for Calder knew her feelings as though they were his own.

He put his hands on either side of her smooth and unbearably beautiful face. "Go now," he said. "The sun will be up soon."

She turned her head slightly, kissed the palm of his right hand, and nodded. Then, without another word, she rose and left the room, her movements graceful and unhurried, and when she was gone, Calder believed for a few moments that she wasn't real at all, that he had only dreamed her.

Valerian lay in bed beside Isabella, a saucy mortal who was one of his favorite companions, and marveled.

It was morning. All his instincts told him this was so, even though the light could not reach into that hidden place, tucked away beneath the oldest part of Madrid.

He waited for the trancelike sleep to suck him under, just as it had at dawn every morning for nearly six hundred years, but nothing happened. He was wide awake, full of energy and ideas and questions.

Could he stand daylight, for instance? He considered testing the theory, then decided not to push his luck. This was no time for impulsive moves.

Wait until Maeve heard about this, he thought, settling back against the pillows with a self-satisfied smile. Even she, with all her power, had never managed such a feat.

Isabella stirred, rustling the sheets, and opened one of her lovely dark eyes to peer up at him. She knew Valerian

was not made of flesh and blood as she was, though he
had never, in the course of their long association,
explained the exact specifics. They had met often,
always at night and always in places where the rays of
the sun could not reach. In the past, however, Valerian
had invariably awakened her well before dawn and
escorted her back to the world she knew.

She reached out and made a twirling motion on his
belly with the tip of one index finger. "It is morning," she
observed in soft Spanish. "And you have not sent me
away."

Valerian wanted to shout with joy, but at the same time
he was frustrated because he couldn't tell another vampire about the miracle. Not until nightfall, at least, for all
but a select few were asleep in their lairs.

"*Sí,*" Valerian responded with a smug smile. "It is
morning, and you are still here." When night came, he
would stand with Maeve against the warlocks and the
unpredictable Lisette, but for now he would remain
where he was—safe in the bowels of the great Spanish
city, under layers of brick cobblestones, dirt, and rocks.

She smiled mischievously. "You do not wish me to
hurry away?"

"No," he said, turning onto his side to look deeply into
her eyes. He could almost hear her warm, rich, vital
blood coursing beneath the flawless surface of her flesh,
and he felt a wounding thirst. He bent his head, kissing
her throat, and she gave a crooning whimper, never
guessing how she tempted him. Her pulse throbbed
beneath his lips, a sweet torment, and Valerian relished it,
as he always relished the forbidden.

Perhaps just a taste . . .

"Valerian." The feminine voice jolted him; he whirled
to see Lisette standing at the foot of the rumpled bed. She

looked like a beautiful witch, fresh from the pages of a storybook, in her high-necked satin gown, with her rich auburn hair tumbling almost to her waist. "Did you think you were the only vampire who could be abroad while the sun was up?"

"Go," Valerian whispered to Isabella in a hoarse voice, all but shoving her from the bed.

Lisette watched with amusement as the naked woman scrambled for her clothes, trembling and casting quick, frightened glances in Valerian's direction.

Miraculously Lisette allowed Isabella to escape, but when she turned her attention on Valerian again, he saw the hatred in her eyes and remembered the last time he'd seen the other vampire.

They had stood face to face on either side of Aidan Tremayne's bed, while he slept, unknowing and vulnerable, between them. At that time Aidan had been newly human—he had risked everything, even his immortal soul, to be changed back into a man—and Lisette had meant to transform him again, to rob Aidan of his hard-won humanity. The idea had been all the more ironic for the fact that she had been the one to condemn Aidan to a life he hated in the first place.

Valerian had moved to defend Aidan, one of only two mortals he had ever loved with honor and purity of heart, but Lisette had been much stronger and rendered him virtually powerless. Had it not been for the intercession of another, she would have succeeded in making Aidan into a vampire again.

It was the ease with which she'd overcome him that Valerian recalled most vividly at that moment. He was indeed afraid, but he wasn't foolish enough to show that. He would deal with Lisette in the same way an old snake charmer in India had taught his students to deal with cobras—by keeping calm and making no sudden moves.

"We meet again," he said, rising slowly from the bed, making no effort to hide his nakedness. He reached for his clothes—doeskin breeches and a loose silk shirt with no buttons—and donned the trousers unhurriedly.

Lisette was watching him with a troubled, curious expression. "I will not destroy you immediately," she mused aloud. "I have uses for you, as it happens."

"I'm delighted to hear it," Valerian responded in the most cordial of tones, pulling the shirt on over his head. "Did you know there may be a war because of you and those damned brainless creatures you've been making?"

"War? With whom?"

Valerian pretended to sigh. "None other than Nemesis himself, I'm afraid. Then there are the warlocks—"

"I don't care about angels or warlocks!" Lisette interrupted, spitting like a cat.

"That's because you're quite mad," Valerian answered as pleasantly as if he'd been chatting with a pretty prospect in some elegant vampire's drawing room. He ran the fingers of both hands through his love-mussed hair and smiled indulgently. "You really ought to put yourself out of all this misery, poor darling. I'd be happy to oblige by driving a stake through your shriveled little heart."

Lisette glowered at him for a long, tense moment, then erupted in a burst of musical laughter. It was not a melodious sound, of course, but something better equated with a funeral dirge. "Great Zeus," she said. "You've never lacked for balls, Valerian, I'll say that for you, even if you *are* the most self-indulgent, arrogant, and impulsive vampire on the face of the earth."

He executed a mocking half-bow. "At your service," he said. Then, in the desperate hope that his other powers had gotten stronger when the mysterious change had occurred that made him able to function during the daylight hours, he fixed his thoughts and energies on a place far away.

It was rather like flinging himself at a rock wall with all his strength, he discovered in the next instant, when the impact of Lisette's opposing wishes slammed into him from every direction.

Valerian slipped to one knee, dazed by the intangible blow she'd struck, but soon raised himself back to his feet.

"No more of your foolish tricks," Lisette scolded coyly, almost crooning the words. She came to stand before Valerian and wound a lock of his hair around one index finger. "You are a splendid creature. How sad I will be to destroy you." Her whole countenance darkened as her mood and expression changed. "Make no mistake, Valerian. This time no one will save your miserable hide. This time you will perish, as you should have months ago, when I bound you to the earth in that old cemetery behind that beloved abbey of yours to await the sunrise."

Valerian did not allow himself the shudder that threatened as he entertained *that* memory. Lisette had caught him in a state of great weakness, and staked him out in a neglected graveyard. Aidan, still a vampire then, had been her real prey; Valerian had been little more than bait. Had it not been for Maeve's timely arrival, and that of Tobias, both he and Aidan would have been roasted like pigs at Easter.

"If you think you can draw Maeve into a trap by holding me prisoner," he said in tones of contemptuous reason, "you are misguided as well as mad. She has no great love for me, and even if she bore me the utmost tenderness, she is entirely too cunning to fall for such a silly trick."

Lisette looked and sounded disturbingly sane, which was, no doubt, only another indication that her mind was as diseased as her spirit. "You are right—Maeve Tremayne loves another, a mortal, and most devotedly, too. She came to help you after your little episode with the warlocks, however, and she will appear again."

For once Valerian was not thinking of his own difficult position, but of the singular vulnerability of Maeve's cherished mortal. He still didn't really care what happened to Dr. Calder Holbrook, late of Philadelphia and Gettysburg, but Maeve's happiness mattered to him. In fact, it mattered far more than he would ever have guessed.

"Tread carefully, Lisette," he warned in his soft, smooth snake-charmer's voice. "Maeve is no ordinary vampire." He smiled in his most irritating fashion. "Don't say I didn't warn you, darling. Your day is over. You're out of your league with her."

"Enough," Lisette snarled, raising her arms from her sides. In the next instant Valerian lost all conscious awareness.

"Damn that vampire," Maeve murmured, tapping one foot. "Where is he?" She'd tried focusing her mind on Valerian, a technique that had always worked before, but this time no image came into her head, no whispered warning or cry for help.

"Aren't all vampires damned?" Calder asked dryly. They were in Maeve's front parlor, where gaslights flickered and popped, and night was thick at the windows.

"That isn't funny," Maeve snapped, pacing now.

Calder leaned against the huge mahogany desk that served Maeve in that century and the succeeding one as well, his arms folded across his chest. He needed a shave, and his dark hair was rumpled from repeated combings with his fingers.

"Twenty-four hours have passed, my love," he said with gentle solemnity. "As delightful as I find your company—and rare though it is—I still want to go home."

Maeve looked at him and ached. "I'm sorry, that's impossible."

What he said next rocked her to the center of her being. "Then make me a vampire, Maeve," he suggested quietly. "Give me the powers you enjoy, and the immortality."

She stood still, staring at him, stunned and brimming with conflicting emotions. On the one hand, she wanted to make Calder a blood-drinker, like herself, and keep him at her side forever. On the other, she recollected only too well how Aidan had hated Lisette for changing him. In Calder's case, after all, the alteration would be irrevocable.

"I couldn't bear it if you despised me," she whispered.

Calder approached her, looking honestly puzzled, and laid his hands lightly on her shoulders. "I could never do that," he said. He sounded sincere, but he didn't really understand what he was facing.

"Before, when you said all vampires were damned," she began miserably, "you were very close to the truth. Becoming an immortal means wagering your soul against an eternity in a fiery hell, Calder. It means that you can never walk in the sunlight again, and that many years would pass before you could get through even a single night without taking blood. In fact, my darling, being a vampire means living forever—and forever is a very long time."

He bent his head and touched his mouth to hers. "Would you watch me get old and die instead?" he asked, after giving her a kiss so gentle that it nearly broke her heart. "Damn it, I don't care how long eternity is—and I don't mind the other things, either—not if I can be with you."

She studied him uncertainly, weighing his words in her mind. She had never changed a human into a vampire before, and the decision was not one she could make easily—especially when someone she loved so desperately was involved.

She recalled his great love for his lost daughter and felt a new level of sadness. "There would never be any children," she said. "Vampires mate, but they do not reproduce."

Calder curved a finger under her chin, and Maeve tried to probe his thoughts, but as before, she had no success. The love she bore this man seemed to function as a barrier between his mind and her own.

"I would have liked having another child," he said quietly. "I won't deny that. But given the choice between marriage to a mortal woman and all that entails, and the adventure of living with you, there is no contest. I love you, Maeve, and it's you I want."

His words warmed Maeve's heart and at the same time wrung it painfully. For the first time in her two centuries as a vampire, she missed mortality and all its sweet, if temporal, joys.

"I must go," she told him after a moment of struggling with her emotions. "Please, darling—trust me, and do as I ask. Stay here until I come back."

He nibbled at her lips, tempting her to stay, and she

decided to punish him with a very special kind of pleasure. "All right," he conceded, with a heavy sigh. "I'll wait. But don't be long, because I want to make love to you."

She smiled mysteriously and straightened his collar. "When I return tomorrow night, I will show you more of my magic."

A twinkle lit his eyes, though there was frustration there as well, and sorrow. "What sort of magic?"

Maeve ran her fingers lightly down his chest and made a circle around his belt buckle. "You'll see," she said. Then she stood on tiptoe, kissed the slight cleft in Calder's chin, and vanished.

CHAPTER
❧9❧

Maeve did not like leaving Calder unguarded, for even in that house, where few vampires and even fewer warlocks would dare to venture uninvited, he was a target. Still, the day of Nemesis's revenge was drawing nearer with each passing moment, and her instincts told her that skirmishes between vampires and warlocks were breaking out all over the planet. On top of that, every night when the moon rose there were more of Lisette's creatures to contend with.

Powerful as she and Valerian were, Maeve reasoned, they wouldn't be able to handle the entire situation alone. They might go after Lisette personally, but other vampires and even warlocks, if they could be enlisted, would have to be sent out to battle the corpselike wretches she continued to create.

Maeve fed twice, within the space of an hour, near the London docks, and still there was no sign of Valerian. Her irritation with him began to turn to concern. Normally, of course, she would have been able to track the other vampire's thoughts, or at least pick up on his whereabouts, but things were far from normal.

She hurried distractedly along a crowded roadside, pondering. Likely as not, Valerian was simply being his usual thoughtless and undependable self, playing sultan in a harem or pretending to be a gunslinger in some saloon in the American West. She was probably worrying needlessly.

Still, Maeve couldn't shake the uneasy feeling that Valerian was in trouble again. After all, the last time he'd disappeared, she'd found him lying at the bottom of a mine shaft, half dead of a warlock attack.

One way or the other, she must find the unpredictable vampire or tackle the job of destroying Lisette on her own.

"I wouldn't if I were you," a feminine voice said.

Maeve turned her head and saw that Dimity had fallen into step beside her. She was carrying a dulcimer, and Maeve could hear the faint hum of the strings in the night breeze.

"You wouldn't go after Lisette if you were me?" Maeve retorted with grim impatience. "Well, then, can you offer a better suggestion? In less than two weeks Nemesis and his legions of angels will be turned loose, and the situation with the warlocks and Lisette's vampires gets worse every night."

"You'll need Valerian's help—as well as mine and that of every other vampire you can manage to recruit."

"I can't find Valerian," Maeve said in frustration. Drunken sailors, men who hadn't been within a furlong of a bathtub in months, were stopping in the street to stare at Dimity and Maeve, their eyes glittering with lust and speculation. "Concentrate, Dimity. See if you can pick up an image or something. I've tried, but there's nothing."

Dimity stepped into an alleyway, and, of course, Maeve followed. While she watched, the angelic blond vampire closed her blue eyes and fixed her thoughts on Valerian.

More sailors gathered at the mouth of the alley, leering, plainly getting ideas. Neither Maeve nor Dimity paid them any attention for, as mortals, they were no threat.

"I see a dark-haired woman with beautiful brown eyes," Dimity said after several moments. "She's in Spain—Madrid, I think. I'm sorry, that's all I can determine."

"Isabella," Maeve murmured. Usually she didn't keep track of Valerian's many and varied playmates, but she knew about this particular mortal because he had told her once in a moment of candor. The woman was a simple soul, he'd said, though beautiful and possessed of a fiery spirit; she worked in a cantina, serving wine and ale.

Dimity cast a glance toward the growing crowd of sailors, and her sweet mouth formed a smile. "It would seem that we have admirers, you and I," she said.

Maeve curled her lip in contempt. "You can have the lot of them," she replied. "I'm going to find Isabella and ask if she's seen Valerian. In the meantime, I would appreciate your help."

"Anything," Dimity answered as the little cluster of men started toward them. She smoothed her hair and skirts, as though intending to waltz with each one in turn, instead of feeding on their life-blood and then tossing them aside like chicken bones.

"Spread the word to as many vampires as you can that there will be a ball at my house tomorrow night, immediately after sunset."

Dimity inclined her lovely head in agreement. "As you wish," she said.

Maeve hesitated for a few moments, watching as the first misguided sailor reached out a grubby fist to grab a handful of Dimity's silky blond hair.

The magnificent vampire made a snarling sound and tore into her would-be assailant like a tigress. The man screamed, probably more from terror than pain, and his companions turned to scramble toward the relative safety of the street.

It did them no good, trying to flee, Maeve noted with a certain grim satisfaction. Dimity had worked some mental trick, thickening the air around them until it was like invisible quicksand, and though they ran, their efforts took them nowhere. They had surely planned a savage rape, but they had expected to be the hunters, not the prey.

By Maeve's reckoning, having to deal with Dimity was no less than the blackguards deserved; she clasped her hands together and vanished without giving the matter another thought.

She found Isabella alone in the back room at the cantina, polishing copper mugs. The woman started violently at Maeve's sudden appearance, crossed herself, and murmured a rapid petition to the Holy Mother.

"Don't be afraid," Maeve said in unhesitating Spanish. One of the talents she'd acquired upon becoming a vampire was an ability to learn languages and indeed memorize the histories of whole societies, simply by paging through books on those subjects. "I mean you no harm. I'm Valerian's friend and I want to know if you've seen him."

Tears brimmed in Isabella's dark, thickly lashed eyes. Maeve could glean no real information from the woman's brain because the poor creature's emotions were in absolute chaos.

"He was killed by a witch!" Isabella sobbed after several false starts and so much blubbering that Maeve wanted to shake her. "We were—together, Valerian and I. *She* came—" Again the mortal paused and made the sign of the cross with a swift, practiced motion of one hand. "She appeared out of nowhere, just as you did. Valerian told me to go quickly—*Madre de Dios*, I ran for my life—and I did not look back." Isabella stopped to draw in a great, snuffling breath, then lifted her apron to her face and wailed, "He is dead! I know he is dead!"

"Stop it!" Maeve said firmly, her mind already racing. It wasn't hard to figure out who the "witch" had been. The question was, what had Lisette done with Valerian? "I want you to take me to the place where all this happened. Right now."

Isabella mopped her face, now puffy and tear-streaked, on the apron. "I c-cannot," she said balefully, interspersing her words with hiccoughs. "It was a secret. Valerian worked some spell to take me there."

"But you must know where it is, if Valerian sent you away on your own when the witch came," Maeve insisted, speaking more moderately this time. She was worried about Valerian, of course, but beneath her fear ran an undercurrent of pure annoyance. If the vain creature hadn't been so occupied with his pleasures, he might have sensed trouble in time to protect himself.

Instead, he'd quite literally been caught with his pants down.

If Valerian managed to survive this latest escapade, Maève thought furiously, she would probably kill him herself.

"It was dark," Isabella said, shaking her head. "I was afraid. I remember only that it was the oldest part of the city, and that there was a cemetery nearby, a forgotten place where all the stones were crumbling."

Maeve gave a soft exclamation of frustration, composed herself, and spoke again. "If you see Valerian before I do, please tell him that Maeve Tremayne is looking for him. This is important, Isabella, so make certain it doesn't slip your mind."

"I will remember," Isabella said with an indignant sniffle. "This is not the sort of experience one forgets."

Maeve smiled. "I suppose not," she agreed. Once again she vanished, arriving moments later in the heart of Los Cementerio de Los Santos y Los Angels, the graveyard Isabella had mentioned.

A cool wind tossed Maeve's dark hair as she stepped up onto one of the ancient, sinking crypts and scanned her surroundings. *Valerian!* she called in the silent language that could be heard in other times as well as other places, but, as before, there was no answer.

She was concentrating on finding the love nest where Lisette had surprised Valerian—it was almost surely underground—when the sound of hoarse, wordless whispers began all around her. The noise came from behind every crypt, every broken headstone, growing louder and louder.

Maeve kept her composure, even when the warlocks began to appear, one by one, seeming to take shape from the shadows themselves. They wore hooded cloaks that hid their faces and rustled as they made a large circle around her, these ancient and deadly enemies.

She might have fled, for she had the power to transport herself anywhere in the known universe, but her pride would not allow it. Besides, instinct would have taken her straight to Calder, and the warlocks would surely follow.

"What do you want?" she shouted, in order to be heard over the incessant, thunderous whispering.

It stopped, that grating sound, as suddenly as it had begun. One of the warlocks stepped forward to look up at Maeve, who stood regally atop the old headstone, like a queen on a dais.

The creature pushed back his hood, revealing a head of brown hair and a face as fetching as any angel's. The beast looked human, even to the discerning eye of a vampire.

He inclined his head in a polite gesture of greeting and actually smiled. "Allow me to introduce myself, Your Majesty," he said, and to Maeve's surprise there wasn't so much as a hint of derision in his tone or expression. "My name is Dathan, and I speak for the covens."

Maeve did not ask how many covens; she knew this being was a leader among his kind, with much power. "I am no one's queen," she said coolly. "There is no need to address me so formally." She narrowed her blue eyes and folded her arms. "But perhaps you were mocking me?"

"Never," Dathan replied with watchful geniality. His hair and eyes were brown, and his face had a look of impossible innocence. It was as if he were really an altar boy, turned warlock only an instant before by the spell of some evil magician. "A counsel was held, and we have decided to ask for an alliance between vampires and warlocks—albeit a temporary one."

Maeve was suspicious, and she could discern little from the friend's mind because he was uncommonly powerful in his own right. "An alliance? Why should we trust you, we who do not trust our own kind?"

"Our mutual survival depends upon it," Dathan reasoned. "There are already warrior angels moving among the mortals—scouts and spies preparing the way for war. Need I tell you, gracious queen, that we cannot win against such enemies?"

Precisely because her courage was flagging a little, Maeve raised her chin. "I am well aware of that," she said.

"Our only hope lies in destroying the vampire called Lisette," Dathan went on moderately. "We left this task to you and your heedless friend, Valerian, and—please excuse my directness—we have not been pleased with the results."

Maeve's considerable pride was nettled. "Perhaps if Valerian had not been set upon by warlocks, poisoned and then left for dead, we might have succeeded sooner." The large, rustling circle of cloaked figures drew tighter as each one stepped forward a pace. "I warn you"—she paused and then raised her voice so that it would carry—"*all of you*—that I will be taken only at great cost to you. The first to fall will be your leader, Dathan."

There was an angry murmuring in the ranks, but Dathan silenced his followers almost immediately, simply by raising one hand into the air.

"I have told you, my queen," he said to Maeve a moment later, "we mean you no harm. We want only to ally ourselves with you, with all reasonable vampires, until the danger is past."

Maeve raised an eyebrow. "And then?"

Dathan smiled his endearing, altar-boy smile. "Should

we be fortunate enough to survive, I'm certain our separate factions will return to their old enmity. Our differences are deep-seated, after all, and our feud is so ancient that no one seems to remember how it began. It is time for a meeting between vampires and warlocks."

"I will consider your proposal," she conceded warily. She swept the circle of cloaked creatures up in a single eloquent glance. "Come alone to my house in London, at midnight tomorrow, and I will give you my decision."

The warlocks began to mutter and stir again, and Maeve knew the consensus of the crowd would have been to take their chances and make an attempt at tearing her apart, had Dathan not been there.

"Enough," that warlock said sharply, and his eyes glittered with fury as he assessed his minions. "Go now and do not trouble this or any other vampire before the agreed time has come!"

They vanished, moving noisily into the night, like a pack of crows flapping their wings, but Dathan lingered.

He reached up to offer Maeve his hand, and after only the briefest hesitation, she accepted it and let him help her down from her perch on the headstone of some long-dead and probably forgotten Spaniard.

"Until midnight tomorrow," Dathan said smoothly. Then he lifted Maeve's hand to his lips, brushed her knuckles with the lightest of kisses, turned, and walked away to become a part of the darkness that claimed his soul.

And her own, Maeve thought glumly. Again Calder's image filled her mind, and again she despaired because he had no glimmer of what it meant to be an immortal.

She would return to him, she decided, for the night was almost over and she had no choice but to seek shelter. She was discouraged that she had made no more progress in finding Valerian.

Perhaps, just as the mortal, Isabella, had said, that august vampire had finally met his end. It wasn't impossible that he'd gotten himself destroyed, considering the foolish risks he undertook in his constant pursuit of pleasurable adventure. And that would certainly account for the fact that she was unable to link her mind with his as she had always done before.

Glumly Maeve lifted her hands above her head and took herself home to London and to Calder.

She found him in the library, surrounded by stacks of books and voluminous notes. He started when she appeared before him, and a heavy tome tumbled to the floor.

He rose, his grin revealing irritation as well as genuine welcome. "I wish you wouldn't just pop in out of nowhere like that. It's unnerving."

"What would you have me do?" Maeve inquired, short-tempered because she could not find Valerian and because a devastating war was imminent. "Arrange for someone to blow a trumpet announcing my arrival?"

Calder sighed. "We can't go on like this, Maeve. I'm a doctor, and back home the hospitals are brimming with wounded soldiers. I cannot hide here any longer, no matter how much danger I might be in."

Had she been a mortal woman, Maeve might have given way to tears at that moment, so great was the pressure she was under. The paradoxical nature of their situation threatened to tear her apart; she loved Calder entirely too much to hold him prisoner in that house and too much to let him go out and face perils he couldn't begin to comprehend.

He saw that she was wavering. "Make me a vampire," he said quietly.

She stared up into his eyes, searching his very soul, seeking some shred of understanding. The dawn was near; she could not tarry much longer or she would be badly burned, perhaps even devoured, by the first apricot-gold light of the sun.

"Why?" she whispered, tormented. "Why do you want this?"

Calder didn't hesitate; she knew he'd given the matter a great deal of thought. He'd had a lot of solitude since coming to Maeve's house, after all. "I want the power," he said plainly. His thumbs moved on her shoulders, caressing, reassuring her. "Even more, I want to be with you always. I want to sleep when you sleep, and for your battles to be my battles, too."

Maeve rested her forehead against his strong shoulder for a few moments before gazing up at him again. He looked gaunt, tormented, and more earnest than she'd ever seen him. "You don't know what you're saying," she told him sadly after a few moments had passed. "There is going to be a war, and Valerian is missing, and tomorrow night I must meet with the leader of the warlocks—"

"I'm no stranger to war," Calder broke in. He'd sensed the coming of the sun, too, and taking Maeve's elbow, he began escorting her through the house, toward the cellar door. "I've been up to my elbows in bleeding, dying soldiers for three years. As for Valerian—"

"Never mind him," Maeve said impatiently. "I know your American war is a terrible one: I would not presume to minimize the suffering or the significance of such a thing. But the conflict I'm speaking of would destroy the world as you know it, Calder. Though the battles would take place between angels and those who move in darkness, like vampires and warlocks, human beings would necessarily be caught up in the fray. It would make your war of states look like a playground scuffle between children.''

They had gained the cellar, and Calder moved unerringly toward the door of the hidden chamber, the place that had once been a secret from all mortals, even those who had lived and worked in Maeve's house for years. "If this apocalypse comes about," he said reasonably, "then I'll not escape it anyway. I might as well be at your side, with at least a chance of being some help to you.''

Maeve lighted a candle, for Calder's sake. She, as always, could see plainly in the dense darkness. "That is a noble, if foolish, argument," she said wearily, seating herself on the edge of the stone slab where she would sleep in the same way a mortal woman might sit on the side of a bed. "There are still other considerations, however." Her words were coming more slowly now, and they were slightly slurred. "Once you make this decision, you will never be able to undo it and go back to being a man. You might come to hate me for changing you.''

Calder laid her down, as gently as if she were a tired child, and took one of her hands into both his own. "That's what you really fear, isn't it? That I'll grow discontented with the life of a vampire and then despise you for making me into a nightwalker in the first place. It won't happen, Maeve. I'm not an impulsive man. I've thought this through. For our sakes, yours and mine, and that of a great many suffering mortals, I want to be changed.''

Maeve could no longer keep her eyes open. She

tightened her fingers around Calder's for a moment, then sank into the fathomless sleep that awaited her.

Calder sat with Maeve for a long time, until the candle flickered wildly and guttered out, in fact. During that bittersweet interval, he held her seemingly lifeless hand and wept for all that might have been, all that would never be.

Then, partly by groping and partly by memory, he found his way back to the main part of the cellar, where thin London sunlight came in through narrow windows at the ceiling level.

Leaving Maeve would be the hardest thing he had ever done, but if he could not be what she was, if he could not serve and protect her, and share her life to the fullest extent, then leave her he would. He'd book passage on a ship—even though he had no money, his family's credit was good in virtually any part of the world—and God help him, once he left, he'd never look back.

But what agony he would feel, remembering her, missing her, cherishing her. He had not dreamed, even in the poetic passion of his youth, that it was possible to love another as deeply as he loved Maeve.

Still, he was a doctor, first and foremost, and to him life was a sacred thing. To waste that most precious of all gifts was the greatest sin a mortal could commit. And this was no life he was living now; he was cowering, like some hunted creature, while the minutes and hours allotted to him were passing by, unused.

In the meantime, patients were suffering and dying. *His* patients.

He would wait no longer; he must *do* something, he must stop the waste.

Having spent several days in the Tremayne house,

Calder had gotten to know the servants a little. They all regarded him with bafflement and no small amount of fear, and he thought he detected a smidgeon of pity as well. Obviously they were not used to having members of the household underfoot during the daylight hours, either.

"I'll need the carriage, if there is one," Calder said to the butler, Pillings, a beanpole of a man who said as little as possible but always made sure the newspapers were brought in and the fires lighted.

"You'll want to shave and change your clothing, sir," Pillings replied. "I believe Mr. Aidan Tremayne's garments would fit you. And I daresay he wouldn't mind making you the loan of a razor as well."

Calder knew Pillings was referring to Maeve's brother, the vampire of legend, the only blood-drinker in history to have turned mortal again. It was a safe bet, however, that Pillings didn't know Tremayne in quite the same context as that.

"Thank you," Calder said, looking ruefully down at his own rumpled garments. "I came away from home rather quickly, not to mention unexpectedly, and had no chance to pack a valise before I left."

"Quite," said Pillings in a noncommittal tone, giving a little bow before starting up the main staircase. "I will see that the appropriate items are brought to your rooms, sir."

Half an hour later Calder was freshly groomed, and a sleek black carriage drawn by four matching gray horses awaited his bidding. The driver greeted him by touching the handle of his driving whip to the brim of his hat, and Pillings insisted on opening the door for Calder and lifting down the portable step inside.

"The offices of the London-New York Bank, please,"

Calder said to the driver before climbing into the carriage.

The driver nodded and touched his hat.

"The mistress won't like this, you know," Pillings confided at last, so tall that he could look straight in through the carriage window. One of his temples was throbbing, and Calder deduced from the man's state of controlled agitation that he'd been wanting to protest the idea from the first and had only now worked up the courage to do so. "She gave express orders, she did, that you were not to leave the house for any reason."

Calder hoped his smile was reassuring, and that it didn't reflect the annoyance he felt at being cosseted and caged like some exotic bird, or the terrible, clawing grief that bruised his heart. "Don't fret, Pillings. I'll be happy to bear the brunt of Miss Tremayne's fury—if indeed she ever finds out that we conspired to ignore her instructions."

At that, the driver cracked his whip in the moist, cool air, and the carriage moved forward, wheels rattling over the cobblestones, leather fittings creaking.

Reaching the bank, Calder arranged for a transfer of funds from one of his own accounts in Philadelphia. Even there, an ocean away from his own country, the Holbrook name was influential enough that strangers would advance pound notes against it.

Leaving that establishment, he went to the wharf, where he booked passage on a ship leaving for New York the following morning. If he and Maeve could not agree on a course of action when they spoke that evening, he fully intended to be aboard the vessel.

After that Calder visited a shop where men's clothing was sold ready-made, and purchased enough garments for the journey, which would take ten days to two weeks.

Provided, of course, that Maeve didn't give in and change him into an immortal, as he wanted her to do.

Eventually Calder returned to the Tremayne house, where he was greeted with no little relief by Pillings. He enjoyed a lengthy luncheon in the library, while Pillings and the footman carried his purchases upstairs and stowed them away in his rooms.

When he'd finished his meal, Calder paced, impatient. It would be hours before Maeve awakened, and even then he might not see her. She was an unpredictable creature and might start off on one of her adventures without bothering to speak with him first.

The thought filled him with frustration and loneliness. Every moment, every hour away from her side, was like a wound to his spirit.

He could go to the chamber belowstairs and wait there, holding her hand, until she opened those beautiful, impossibly blue eyes of hers, but he was afraid of drawing attention to her. Calder knew little about vampires, but he had gleaned, both from things Maeve had said and from an obscure book on the subject that he'd found on one of the library shelves, the worrisome fact that a blood-drinker was never more vulnerable than when it lay sleeping.

At that point Maeve was utterly unable to defend herself. He could not risk having one of the servants follow him, or worse, some supernatural being. He had no idea who—or what—might be watching with interest the events taking place in this household.

The thought only deepened his wish to be a vampire himself, to share Maeve's fate, be it damnation or an eternity of walking the earth. He didn't care, as long as he could be with her.

At sunset, while Calder was having tea beside the fire

in the sitting room off his bedchamber, Maeve appeared before him, her form seeming to knit itself from the very ether.

She took in the boxes of new clothes with a sweep of her eyes, then stood frowning down at him, her arms folded.

Calder rose from his chair, out of good manners, yes, but also because he'd felt like an errant schoolboy sitting down, looking up at her, awaiting his fate. "What have you decided?" he asked quietly.

He saw an infinite sorrow in her eyes and knew her answer before she spoke. "I will not be the one to damn you, Calder. I cannot sever the invisible cords that bind you to your Creator."

He did not attempt to argue, for he could see that she'd made up her mind. He was sick at his soul—his very heart seemed to crumble within his chest—and he would not allow himself to think of being parted from her, inevitable though it was, because he could not bear the knowledge.

"Tonight," she said before Calder found the strength to speak, "you will see other vampires firsthand. I will show you what dreadful creatures they can be."

Calder was shattered, but he was also intrigued, for he was first and foremost a scientist, and he was more than curious, he was greedy for whatever knowledge of vampires he could garner. "How?" he asked simply.

Maeve smiled, but her eyes were liquid with mourning, for she knew he would not stay and await her brief appearances, warming himself on the hearth like a lapdog. "There will be a vampire ball," she said. "Right here, in this house, this very night. Will you be my escort, Dr. Calder Holbrook?"

CHAPTER
❧ 10 ❧

Maeve's guests began arriving at approximately ten-thirty that night. Most were vampires, ruddy from recent feedings, but Calder noticed a surprising number of mortals, too. These brave, or perhaps reckless, souls were artists mostly, and writers; curious people, like himself, fascinated by the nightwalkers.

All were ushered into the great ballroom, where gaslights flickered softly, their glow dancing golden in the polished mirrors that lined the walls. At the far end, on a dais, a small orchestra played Mozart.

Glancing at the butler, Pillings, who was unruffled by this grand and innately horrible affair, Calder realized that he'd been wrong, thinking the other man didn't know that there was something very different about the mistress of this house. Pillings obviously understood that the majority of that night's visitors were not human.

"Why didn't you tell me you knew?" Calder said in a low voice after making his way to the butler's side.

Pilling's manner was smooth and rather smug. "Because I couldn't be certain that *you* did, sir."

Calder smiled, though he felt raw inside, and broken. Maeve had made her decision; she would not turn him into a vampire, and since she wanted him to stay in London, where she could protect him, she probably wouldn't agree to transport him home by means of her strange magic, either. All of which meant that he would be traveling back to America by ship and leaving Maeve behind forever.

The prospect of being parted from her filled Calder with a grief the like of which he had not felt since those torturous days, weeks, and months following his daughter's death. All the same, there was no question of staying. He would have died for Maeve but, ironic as it was, he could not live for her—not if it meant enduring an insipid, sheltered existence. As it was, he felt like a tame mouse, caged, running round and round inside a wheel.

Just then Maeve came to his side. She looked magnificent in a voluminous gown of purple velvet, the skirt decorated with crystal beads that glimmered like frost over clean snow. She might have been mortal, except for the pale, extraordinary perfection of her skin and the restrained energy she exuded with every movement.

Calder looked down into her eyes and felt himself tumble, then free-fall, headlong into her very soul, where he would doubtless be a prisoner forever, even if he never saw her again. "How can I leave you?" he whispered raggedly.

Maeve laid one slender, elegant hand to his cheek, and
her touch sent a charge through his system. Then,
silently, she linked her arm with his and led him the
length of the ballroom and out through a set of French
doors. They stood then on a terrace, under a glittering
arbor of stars.

"Perhaps it's better if you go away," she said coolly,
but Calder wasn't fooled. He heard the sorrow in her
voice and felt it throbbing in her soul, the counterpart of
his own mourning. "Better if you have no memory of me,
or of what we've shared together—"

"Wait a minute," Calder snapped, unable to hide the
note of desperation that reverberated through his whole
being. "What do you mean, 'if I have no memory of
you'? Surely you can't—" He paused, realizing that
Maeve could do virtually anything she wished. "You
wouldn't—take that, the most precious gift I've ever
been given!"

She looked away for a moment, then faced him
squarely again. "One night soon, when I can bear it," she
began evenly, "I will return to the precise instant when
you first saw me, outside that church at Gettysburg. I will
adjust that moment, make myself invisible to you, and all
that came after will be undone."

Calder felt his eyes go wide. "No!" he protested in a
hoarse cry.

Maeve nodded sadly. "I should have done it days
ago."

He shoved one hand through his hair and turned away
to stand at the stone railing of the terrace, looking out
over the rooftops of London. "I can't endure it," he said.

He felt her hands come to rest on his shoulders. "It's
for the best, darling," she said.

Calder whirled, putting his arms around her slender

waist, pulling her close to him. "What about you?" he demanded, and although he sounded angry, what he really felt was wild, raging despair. "Will you remember?"

She regarded him for a long moment. "Briefly," she replied. "Then, after a while, our time together will seem like a lovely dream, the kind that comes just as one is waking from a pleasant sleep."

"You can't do this," Calder rasped. "You can't!"

Maeve's gaze was steady. She tugged at the chain around his neck, brought the pendant from beneath his collar, lifted the necklace over his head, and dropped it into her bodice. "I can, my darling," she said gently. "And I will. For your sake, as well as my own. Perhaps, by the grace of the One who cherishes all mortals, you will be protected from the evils that surround you now." She took his hand. "Come now—let us dance together while we can. Then I will take you home to Philadelphia and your wounded soldiers."

He swallowed hard, knowing it would be useless to argue the point, that night at least, and finally nodded. Even so, he could not, would not accept Maeve's decision without a fight.

Inside, among the pallorous, beautiful ghouls, they danced, two lovers doomed to be parted so completely that soon, too soon, they would not even remember each other.

Midway through the evening a family of vampires arrived. Maeve explained that they were the Havermails, Avery and Roxanne and their offspring, Canaan and Benecia. The smaller pair were, in some ways, the most chilling of all the fiends Calder had seen that night, for although their eyes were ancient, they were trapped forever in the bodies of little girls.

Calder shuddered in Maeve's embrace as they waltzed. "And you were aggrieved that we'd never have children," Maeve jested. Although she was plainly teasing him and her eyes were mirthful, Calder knew her sorrow was as fathomless as his own.

At eleven-thirty Maeve called a halt to the dancing and stood on the dais, in front of the orchestra, to address her guests.

Her voice was at once gentle and full of authority. She told the crowd about a vampire called Lisette, who had been creating blood-drinkers at random. They were mindless, inferior creatures, she said, and because of them the angels were ready to make war on all night-walkers, not only vampires, but every supernatural being.

Calder listened in fascination as Maeve went on to say that the warlocks were outraged over this situation. Either the vampires would have to join forces with their age-old enemies, to destroy Lisette and defeat her growing army of ghouls, or the warlocks would make war on all blood-drinkers. Their hope was that, by wiping out vampires, the warlocks could appease the warrior angels and their commander, Nemesis, and thus avert their own destruction.

A stir rose in the gathering, and then one of the macabre child-vampires stepped forward. She was small and blond; Benecia Havermail, Maeve had called her.

"Where is Valerian?" she asked in a clear voice. "Can we not depend on him to lead us? He is the oldest and most cunning vampire of us all."

Maeve seemed to grow before Calder's weary eyes, to loom taller and more imposing. She was terrifying to see, in her beauty and her power, and yet he knew he'd never loved her more than he did at that moment, when he first realized that she truly was royalty.

"Valerian has disappeared," she answered without hesitation. "And even you, Benecia, should know better than to expect leadership from him. Furthermore, he is *not* the oldest blood-drinker—Lisette and the members of the Brotherhood of the Vampyre are ancient compared to him."

Benecia subsided a little, though she didn't look happy about it. Calder imagined encountering such a creature on a dark sidewalk some evening, in the thin light of a gas-powered street lamp, and shivered.

"Tonight," Maeve went on, "Dathan, a warlock, will come to this house. He seeks a pact between our kind and his, a temporary truce. His suggestion is that we band together, blood-drinker and warlock, long enough to destroy our common enemy."

An elegant-looking male vampire with dark hair and eyes stepped forward. Like the other guests, he wore formal clothes, but there was an air of refinement about him that went deeper than appearances. "Are you suggesting that we trust those creatures?" he asked of Maeve. "Warlocks have been our greatest foes from the beginning. What is our assurance that they won't turn on us, that this isn't some sort of trick?"

Murmurs of agreement rose from the crowd, but Maeve silenced the lot with a single sweep of her eyes.

"Your question is a reasonable one, Artemus," she said to the elegant male, "but this is a desperate time and it calls for desperate measures. Keep in mind, all of you, that we have more fearsome enemies than warlocks— angels. And they will descend on us in legions, these beings, unless we stop Lisette and destroy her minions. It will take all our strength to accomplish such a task, and that of the warlocks as well."

Calder was mesmerized, having forgotten his own

despair for the moment. Maeve had spoken of the approaching cataclysm and stressed that all their circumstances were dire indeed, but he had not guessed the true scope of the situation. Incongruous though it seemed, the matter was one of life and death for immortals.

Roxanne Havermail stepped forward, to stand next to Artemus. She, too, was beautiful, but, like her daughters, she made Calder's skin crawl. "If Lisette is sent to face the Judgment, there will be no queen. Is that not so?"

A collective groan followed her words.

Roxanne bristled. "Well, if there's going to be an election or something, I think I should be considered." She cast an accusing glance in Maeve's direction. "I am eminently suited to be queen, it seems to me, since I've been around much longer than certain upstarts I could mention."

"Yes," muttered a short, squat male vampire in a bottle-green waistcoat, breeches, and a ruffled shirt, who stood within range of Calder's hearing. "Roxanne has been around, all right. Around the block."

The female's gaze sliced to her critic's face in an instant; she had heard him plainly, even though a considerable distance lay between them. "You may keep your fusty old opinions to your fusty old self, Clarence Doormeyer," she said, and Doormeyer actually quailed.

Having dispensed with her detractor, Roxanne turned back to Maeve, hands resting on her hips. "Well? Will I be queen or not?"

"There will be no dominion for you to reign over," Maeve responded reasonably, "if we do not stop Lisette in time to appease Nemesis and his armies."

"We have something to say about who is queen, it seems to me," put in a male dressed in the garb of a seagoing brigand. The remark started another uproar.

Maeve raised both her hands in a graceful command that there be silence. There was. "Such matters need not be decided now," she said.

Roxanne went back to stand beside her vampire husband, looking disgruntled and unhappy. Apparently she'd expected a coronation on the spot.

"What will I tell the warlock, Dathan, when he comes to me tonight to ask for our decision?" Maeve went on, and even though she didn't raise her voice, there was a note of steel in it that brooked no further nonsense. "Do we stand together against this threat, or do we scatter like frightened hens and perish at the hands of angels?"

For a moment the room seemed to rock with a sort of silent thunder. Then Artemus spoke again.

"I say we have nothing to lose by allying ourselves with Dathan's followers, and our very lives to gain. What other choice do we have? Shall we allow angels to take us, and find out firsthand what special hells their Master has set aside for the doubly damned?"

Silence reigned again, then Canaan Havermail spoke up in her sweet, horrid, piping voice. "Suppose it's all a lie?" she offered, glaring at Maeve. "Why should we trust this one? Perhaps she is weak, like her brother." Her unholy eyes sought and found Calder in the crowd, and he felt his spirit shrink before the magnitude of her evil. "Here is the proof. Maeve Tremayne consorts with mortals!"

Maeve's fury, though contained, was nearly tangible. Calder feared that she would explode and that when she did, the mirrored walls would shatter and the marble floor would undulate with the force of it.

"Look around you, Canaan. There are any number of mortals here," she said. "I am not alone in finding them diverting."

Diverting. The word sliced into Calder, sharp as a scalpel. Was that what he was to Maeve—a plaything, a curiosity, a diversion? He pushed the feeling aside to consider later.

Just then, the doors to the terrace burst open, as though they'd been struck by some great, silent wind, and all heads turned.

Calder felt his heart pound in a combination of excitement and fear.

In the next instant a creature as lovely as any angel of the highest realms appeared in the opening. She was female, with flowing golden hair, eyes the color of bluebells, and a sweetness of countenance that was truly remarkable.

Calder glanced at Maeve and saw that she was watching him, a pensive expression on her face. It gave him hope, though precious little, to think she might be jealous of his attentions.

"It's Dimity," someone whispered close behind Calder. With reluctance he shifted his gaze from Maeve, who was more poignantly beautiful to him than any angel could ever be, to watch this new drama unfold.

Dimity did not speak, but instead stepped aside to make room for a second entrant. This creature was male, and he seemed to blaze with some fire of the soul. He was so tall that he had to lean down as he stepped through the doorway from the terrace, and when he lifted his head again, Calder saw that his eyes were as black as polished onyx. His hair was fair, like Dimity's, and he wore medieval garb, leggings and a tunic. He carried a magnificent sword with a jeweled hilt.

Calder was drawn toward him, and the wild thought crossed his mind that this was the legendary Arthur, King of Camelot, founder of the Knights of the Round Table.

He soon realized, however, that everyone else in the room, with the exception of Maeve and the vision called Dimity, had retreated.

"Do not be afraid," the lovely female said in a voice as soft as a summer shower. "Gideon has not come to do harm to any of you, but to relay a message."

Calder saw Maeve move to approach the giant, Gideon, and he followed, wanting to be at her side whether the outcome of the confrontation be good or ill.

"What are you?" he asked baldly. Gideon's person shone so brightly that Calder had to squint.

Gideon smiled. "I am a Comforter," he said. "A Guardian." His wondrous features became solemn. "What are you doing here, Mortal, with these blood-drinkers?"

Calder stepped a little closer to Maeve. An angel. God in heaven, this creature was an *angel*, albeit without wings, robes, harps, or halos. The experience was remarkable, even after encountering vampires. He tried to answer, but no words came to his mind, and no sound to his lips.

Dimity linked her arm with the angel's. "Do not try the poor human, Gideon," she said in a tone of good-natured scolding. "He has the gift of free will, just like the rest of us."

Calder found his voice; he had to answer, for his own sake and for Maeve's. "I'm here because I love Maeve Tremayne."

"You must indeed love her," Gideon replied. "More than your own soul, in fact."

"Yes," Calder answered.

Maeve laid a hand on his arm in an unspoken command that he be silent. "What is your business with us?" she asked Gideon.

"I've come to warn you all," he said in a clear voice, "for I feared that you would not believe Dimity if I sent her in my stead." The angel paused, perhaps formulating his thoughts, perhaps translating them into words lesser beings like humans and vampires could understand.

"Why would you, an angel, an *enemy*, want to help us?" Benecia Havermail demanded.

It was Dimity who answered. "You heard what Gideon said. He is a Comforter and a Guardian—it is his task to look after one particular mortal. That mortal, a child, has been sorely abused by people who should nurture and protect him. I, and some other vampires, feed on the likes of that little one's tormentors, and certain of the angels appreciate that. They, you see, are not permitted to take vengeance on human beings, no matter how grievous the offense."

Finally Gideon spoke up. "Mind you, one and all, that I have no sympathy with those among you who feed on the blood of innocents." He laid one great hand to the hilt of his sword, and Calder saw his muscles tighten as he gripped it. "Such vampires should be shown no more mercy than their victims have known!"

"What message do you bring?" Maeve asked, and although there was no fear in her voice, Calder had seen her glance quickly at a small timepiece hidden beneath a ruffle on the bodice of her gown.

"Listen well, one and all," Gideon began, and though he spoke quietly, the words reached into every corner of that enormous room. "I come at the order of my commander, Nemesis. He bid me tell you that if the renegade vampire, Lisette, is not stopped, he will destroy each and every one of you, with pleasure, and that even the darkest corners and crevices of hell itself will not hide you from his wrath."

Calder felt a communal shudder move through the room, and he was afraid himself, but his fascination had not lessened. Had anyone told him that such creatures as these actually existed, he would have dismissed that person as mad. Now, here he stood, watching as the light and the darkness confronted each other.

Having spoken, the great angel turned and walked away, bending low again as he passed through the doorway onto the terrace, and, after a quick nod to Maeve, Dimity followed him. The doors closed with a crash behind them.

A moment later Maeve's ballroom erupted with the terrified chatter of vampires who faced an enemy they could not hope to defeat.

"Silence!" Maeve shouted, and, reluctantly, the others obeyed her, though it seemed to Calder that the air fairly crackled with the force of their fear, outrage, and frustration. "What else must happen before you are convinced that our only hope is to rally our forces, join ourselves with the warlocks, and bring Lisette down like the rabid animal she is?"

No one spoke or even moved. Even Pillings, or perhaps *especially* Pillings, stood motionless and stricken, watching Maeve.

"If you stand with us, come forward," she said, stepping up onto the dais again and indicating an area in front of it. "If you do not, leave now."

Still, for what seemed like the longest time, no one moved. Then all the mortals, except for Pillings and Calder himself, headed toward the door, followed by a few sullen vampires. The others gathered, as Maeve had bid them to do, looking up at her with expressions that ranged all the way from fearful reluctance to unbounded admiration.

Calder watched in wonder as she dispatched groups of vampires to other parts of the world, where they were to do all in their power to find and destroy Lisette's creations. When the long-case clock in the entryway chimed twelve times, however, she left her followers and strode toward the front door.

Calder was right behind her, even though he knew instinctively that she didn't want him there.

Reaching the massive door, she swung it open, and on the step stood another visitor. He wore a black cloak and pushed back the garment's yawning hood to reveal a head of shining brown hair and an innocent, boyish face.

This, Calder knew, was Dathan, the warlock Maeve had spoken of earlier, and the newcomer greeted her with a single word.

"Well?"

"We will join forces with you," Maeve said in a cool, reserved tone. It was plain that she didn't relish the prospect of dealing with warlocks any more than her colleagues did, despite the fact that she had offered the suggestion herself.

Dathan inclined his head in a cordial nod. "Very well," he said. "All that remains is for you and I to plan our strategy."

Maeve looked back at Calder over one slender shoulder, and he saw a fathomless grief in her eyes. "Yes," she answered distractedly. "That is all that remains."

Calder felt a chasm open between them, a vast, eternal one, and some part of him died in that instant.

Dathan spoke again, and his words wrenched Maeve's attention back from Calder. "We have word of your friend, Valerian."

At that, Calder turned away, for there was no love lost between him and Valerian, and he frankly didn't care what predicament that vampire might be in. His mind was full of the terrible, splendid things he'd seen and heard that night, while at one and the same time his heart was breaking.

In his rooms he gathered his things together and began packing them neatly into the trunk he'd purchased that day. He wanted to weep, but that release, which would have been so welcome, was denied him by his own long-standing habit of stoicism.

Although he waited, Maeve did not come to him that night.

Maeve spent the remainder of the dark hours with Dathan, laying plans to find and destroy Lisette. She did not allow herself to think of Calder, indeed, she could not afford the indulgence, for there were so many things to be decided.

According to Dathan, Valerian was alive, though he was indeed a captive. Lisette almost certainly planned to use him as a weapon or a pawn, and for the moment there was nothing Maeve could do about that.

Just minutes before sunrise, she went to Calder's rooms and found him sprawled across his bed in his clothes, sleeping as deeply as a child. Maeve lay down beside him, wrapped her arms around him, and thought of the great house in Philadelphia.

In moments they were there, on Calder's bed, and he was still asleep, though his rest was fitful now and probably haunted by dreams.

Maeve kissed his forehead and then, with only seconds to spare, vanished, assembling herself inside a small space a dozen feet beneath the surface of the earth. There she settled, in that gravelike place, into the vampire sleep.

• • •

Calder awakened suddenly, his body drenched in sweat, and sat bolt upright. He was stunned to find himself in his own bedroom in the Philadelphia house, bathed in the light of a late-summer sun.

He blinked, terrified that his time in London, and Maeve, and the vampire ball, were all just fragments of some feverish dream. He was still trying to discern between reality and illusion when the door of his room flew open and William burst in.

"Where the hell have you been?" his brother snarled, storming over to the side of the bed and gripping Calder's shirtfront in clenched fists.

Calder threw William's hands off and stood up. "What the devil do you care?" he countered, just as furiously. He groped for the pendant Maeve had given him and found it gone.

William paled, but with fury not fear. He knew, in some part of his withered little soul, that Calder would never do him actual physical harm, because it would have been a violation of his personal code of honor.

"It's Father," William said. "He's taken sick, and the doctor says he's dying. He's been asking for you, though I can't think why he'd make the effort. He must know, as I do, that you don't give a damn about him now any more than you ever have!"

Calder had believed himself to be utterly without sentiment where his father was concerned, but this news shook him, distracted him from the mysteries Maeve had brought into his life. "Is he here, or did you have him taken to the hospital?" he snapped, already halfway to the door.

"Father would never set foot in a hospital," William snapped. "Besides, there isn't a bed to be had because of this damn war. You ought to know that better than anyone."

Calder ignored his half brother, wrenched open the door, and strode down the hallway to his father's bedroom. He found the old man sitting up, though he looked smaller, as the dying often do, as if his body were crumbling in upon itself.

Bernard held out one hand imploringly and croaked Calder's name.

Calder realized, with shattering suddenness, that the little boy who had loved and idolized his father still lived, tucked away in some part of his psyche. His own caring struck him with the force of a meteor, and tears sprang to his eyes.

"Papa," he said, clasping the offered hand in both his own and brushing his lips once across the knuckles. He started to pull away. "I'll get my bag—"

"No," Bernard protested. "Don't—go. I want you to listen. I'm sorry, Calder, so sorry—for all the things I did and—all the things I should have done—and didn't. I loved you, and—I loved your mother. But I didn't have your strength—none of us did. Not your mother—not Theresa or Amalie—not William. You were always so—impatient, so in-intolerant."

Calder's shoulders heaved as grief assailed him for the second time in twenty-four hours. A sob tore itself from his throat. He could not speak.

"Rest, Papa," William said from the other side of the bed. It seemed to Calder that his half brother's voice came through a pipe or tunnel, from somewhere far off. "Don't try to talk."

"I've made my peace with you, William," Bernard said quite clearly. "Go now, and let me do the same with your brother."

Calder sat down on the edge of Bernard's deathbed, still too overcome to utter any of the words that crowded his heart and throbbed in his throat.

His father spread one surprisingly strong hand behind his son's head and pressed him close, into his shoulder. "Forgive me," he pleaded again. "Forgive me for not being the man you are."

In the next moment Calder felt the old man's spirit leave his body like warm vapor rising into the air. It was as simple, and as complex, as that, and having witnessed the phenomenon a hundred times before did nothing to lessen its impact.

He drew back, looked into the familiar face, and saw empty, staring eyes. Gently, with practiced fingers, Calder lowered his father's eyelids.

Regret filled him, regret that he had waited so long to face and accept the love he'd always borne for this man. He sat there for a long while, keeping a lonely vigil, and only when Prudence came in, sometime later, did Calder stand and move to the window where he stood staring out at the sunlit courtyard below.

"He's gone," he said quietly.

Prudence wept and wailed and began to pray, and it seemed to Calder that, for all her noisy suffering, she was better off than he was. She knew how to release her emotions, at least, while he'd carried his own around like the carcass of an albatross.

It was really no wonder, Calder thought numbly, that he'd lost everything and everyone who had ever mattered to him. He did not know how to love.

CHAPTER
❧ 11 ❧

"You made his life miserable, you know," William said in a wooden voice as he and Calder stood in the formal parlor that afternoon. The undertaker and his assistant were upstairs, in their father's room, preparing the old man for viewing and subsequent burial.

Calder was still dazed, by his experiences in London with Maeve, by the death of his sire, and by the realization that he had indeed loved Bernard Holbrook, faults and all, despite his own utter conviction to the contrary. He squeezed the bridge of his nose between his thumb and index finger. "Spare me the discourse on my shortcomings as a son," he said wearily, looking out the window. "I'm well aware, believe me, that I might have been a little more tolerant."

" '*A little more tolerant*'?" William repeated furiously. The last time Calder had glanced in his direction, his half brother had been standing next to the mantel, brooding over a glass of bourbon. "You crucified him daily with your damnable contempt, your self-righteous assumption that he didn't want to be better than he was. The man craved your respect and affection, God help him, every day of your life, and you withheld those very things!"

Calder closed his eyes tightly, for nothing possessed the power to wound quite so deeply as the truth. While he regretted some of the choices he'd made, and bitterly, he'd dance with the devil before apologizing to William.

"Are you through?" he inquired with biting politeness.

He heard the musical explosion of glass shattering against stone and turned at last to see that William had flung his drink onto the hearth. "No, *God damn you*, I am not through! My father is dead, and his suffering was compounded by your arrogance and insensitivity!"

"What do you expect me to do?" Calder asked reasonably, his voice as cold as his manner. "Resurrect him? Turn back the clock to the time he was driving my mother to despair, perhaps, and decide that it was all right for him to break her heart with his women? Declare that, after all, 'boys will be boys'?"

William's handsome if faintly ineffectual face went ruddy with anger. "You bastard! I want you to say you're sorry."

"Apologize to you?" Calder rubbed his chin, which was stubbly with a day's beard-growth. "Never. I've done you no wrong, William."

William's features contorted. "Haven't you? That's my father lying up there with embalming fluid in his veins! If it hadn't been for you, he might still be alive!"

"I won't take the blame for his death," Calder replied.

"He came down with pneumonia and couldn't rally his strength. I had no part in that."

"You *robbed* him of his strength!" William insisted, and Calder began to fear that if his half brother did not contain his temper, he would burst a blood vessel. "Papa expended all of it, worrying that you had finally vanished forever. He might have used that fervor to cling to life!"

Calder shook his head and sighed, too weary and too stricken to be diplomatic. "Damn it, William, open your eyes—you just accused Father of wasting energy, yet your hatred for me and your petty jealousy are eating you alive!"

William turned away then, lowered his head onto the arm he'd braced against the mantel, and gave a choked sob.

Calder started toward him, realized there was nothing he could say that would give the other man comfort, and stopped himself. Nothing less than his younger brother's complete humiliation would satisfy William, and Calder wasn't willing to supply that.

Prudence rushed in just then, eyes swollen from weeping, carrying a broom and dustpan. She glared accusingly at Calder and William in turn, and bent to sweep up the shards of glass littering the hearth. "Land sakes," she huffed. "A body'd think you two could keep civil tongues in your heads at a time like this, but no—here you are, bellowin' at each other—and with a dead man in the house, too."

William lifted his head, seething with abhorrence, and flung a scalding stare in Calder's direction, at the same time straightening his perfectly tailored coat. If he'd heard Prudence's admonition, or even taken note of her presence, he gave no indication. "You've destroyed this entire family," he said. "How I wish your whore of a mother had died before ever giving birth to you!"

Calder took a step toward his brother, his voice deceptively quiet. "I know you're suffering, William, and I'll abide your insults because of that. If you value your hide, however, you will not refer to my mother again, except in the politest of terms. Do you understand me?"

Prudence stepped between the two of them, her great, warm girth quivering with outrage, a dustpan full of broken crystal in one hand and a broom in the other. "If I has to take a buggy whip to the both of you so's you'll behave respectful-like, that's just what I'll do! This ain't no time to be workin' out your brother troubles."

Despite Prudence's words, which made a great deal of sense, Calder still wanted to slam his fist into William's smug, haughty face, and he expected that his half brother was thinking similar thoughts about him. He breathed deeply, purposely relaxed his hands, and turned away, intending to return to the window and his private musings.

William made that impossible by spitting defiantly, "Stay out of this, old woman. This is my house now, and I'll speak to this bitch's whelp in any way I choose."

Calder crossed the space that separated him from his sibling in two strides. Ignoring Prudence's fluttering fury, he grasped the lapels of William's suit coat and hoisted him onto the balls of his feet. "Nothing will appease you but an opportunity to draw my blood, it would seem," he hissed. "Well, then, so be it." He flung his brother free, and William scrambled, his face purple with anger, to keep from losing his balance. "We'll settle this out back," Calder finished.

William nodded, spun on his heel, and headed for the door. Calder was right behind him, but Prudence waylaid him by gripping his elbow, with surprising strength, in one large black hand.

"That man up there didn't deserve to have his only sons brawlin' in the backyard like a pair of drunken field hands, no matter what his failin's might have been!"

Calder's head felt light, and he saw the familiar parlor and the woman who had comforted him from childhood through a shifting haze of red. "On the contrary," he rasped, "my father pitted William and me against each other from the first." He wrenched his elbow free of Prudence's grasp. "This is *exactly* what dear Papa always wanted, to see the two of us fight like roosters until one left the other bleeding in the dust. And you know it as well as I do."

Great tears welled in Prudence's eyes. "Don't do this," she pleaded. "William's hurtin' something terrible, him bein' so close to your papa, and he ain't right in the head."

Calder shoved splayed fingers through his rumpled hair. "I'm sorry, Pru," he said gruffly. "I would do anything in the world for you, anything except run from my brother."

He heard Prudence weeping as he moved along the hallway leading to the rear of the house and the yard beyond it.

William was standing in front of the summerhouse, waiting, his jaw hard with conviction, his eyes flashing. He'd already taken off his coat, draping it neatly over the back of a wrought-iron bench, and was in the process of rolling up his sleeves.

"I half expected you to disappear again, little brother," he taunted.

Calder wore no coat, and no gold links bound his cuffs to his wrists. He pushed up his sleeves, one at a time, ashamed of the wicked joy he felt at the prospect of doubling up his fists and pummeling William into a whimpering pulp. "You knew better," he said with a grim smile. "Of course, you can still save your worthless ass by taking back every rotten thing you've ever said about my mother. If you don't, I'm going to stuff parts of you down every gopher hole on this property."

William faltered slightly, but he didn't relent. On the contrary, he poured salt into raw, gaping wounds. "Did you know she ran away with another man, the night she died, your sainted mama, just the way your wife did years later?"

Calder felt cold and sick, as though some evil creature, some dragon of the invisible realms, had opened its mouth and spewed forth its vile, frigid breath. "Enough," he said, all but strangling on that single word.

His half brother smiled, resting his pale clerk's hands on his hips. "Oh, no, Calder," he said. "That wasn't nearly enough. You're going to hear the truth about your mother, the beautiful Marie, at long last. She was leaving Papa the night she died in that carriage accident, running away with a lover, just the way your wife left you. And, like Theresa, Marie was abandoning her child as well. She didn't want you, Calder."

Calder laughed, actually laughed, though bile scalded the back of his throat and he really believed, in that moment, that he could kill his half brother without compunction. "You're lying, about all of it," he said. "My mother died of a fever. And she would never have abandoned me—never. If you're looking for a way to make my blood boil, brother, you'll have to do better than that."

William made a contemptuous sound. "Fool. They brought Marie home after the accident, and she never regained consciousness. Papa only told you she was suffering from a fever to save your precious feelings— ask old Dr. Blanchard if you don't believe me. She'd broken every fragile bone in her body in the wreck, and they carried her here to die. The truth was, she'd been whoring with some second cousin of hers. They'd conceived a bastard, Marie and her sweetheart—she lost the poor little creature, of course, only hours before she passed on." He sighed philosophically. "That was for the best, no doubt."

Calder's knees felt weak. In his mind he heard Marie Holbrook's lilting voice singing a lullaby, felt her hands tucking the blankets in around him, knew again the brush of her lips across his forehead. "You're a liar," he said.

William went on as though Calder hadn't spoken. "Personally I've always wondered if *you* weren't the by-blow of one of Marie's many admirers," he said. "Papa was in his late forties when you came along, remember, and he hadn't sired a second child by my mother or, to my knowledge, any of the paramours that came later."

Because William's assertions challenged some of his most basic beliefs about himself, because he sensed a grain of truth in them, Calder was shattered. "Suppose you're right," he said in a low, raw tone of voice. "Let's assume my mother was indeed a tramp, and I was sired by one of her lovers. Why did you wait until now to say these things, when you've obviously hated me for so many years?"

William indulged in a slow smile, even though he had to know he was about to take a trouncing from a younger, stronger man. "Papa wanted to pretend you were his. You were everything he would have asked for in a son, you see. Isn't that ironic? You, Calder, were the prodigal, always running off to some far country, or landing yourself in the middle of this damnable war. You tormented him, and he loved you for it, *cherished* you for it." He paused, took a deep breath, and tilted his head back to search the azure sky for a few moments. "Obviously I couldn't tell you the truth. I would have been disinherited for my trouble."

Calder ran a hand over his face. The fight had not even begun, and William had already defeated him, already broken him. "Can you prove any of this?"

"Of course I can—if I hadn't, you would be able to discount everything I've said on grounds of petty jealousy and spite. I have letters addressed to the lovely Marie, as well as some she'd written herself but never had a chance to post."

"I want to see them," Calder said. He was reeling inwardly, fighting for balance. He turned and moved away, toward the house.

William would not leave matters at that. Instead he came after Calder, grabbed him by one shoulder, whirled him around so that they stood face to face.

"You've already won," Calder said grimly, shoving a hand through his hair again. "What more do you want?"

William didn't bother to answer, he just flung his right fist at Calder, who saw the blow coming and blocked it by raising one arm. He was baffled, for a few moments at least, by his brother's insistence on provoking him, for *this* was truly a fight William couldn't win. Then, in a blaze of revelation, Calder realized that William *wanted* the pain, needed it to expunge demons of his own.

Closing his hand, Calder brought his knuckles up hard under William's chin. The punch connected; William's teeth slammed together, and a tiny bubble of blood appeared at the corner of his mouth.

"Is that enough?" Calder demanded, clenching his teeth. He almost missed the uncontainable anger he'd felt only minutes before; now he was numb. There was no fury inside him, no joy or sorrow. Nothing. "Or do I have to beat you senseless?"

William threw another punch, and this one was more accurate. He caught Calder square in the center of his solar plexus, forcing the air from his lungs.

Adrenaline surged through Calder's system, though his emotions were as dead as the man who had sired him. He hurtled into William headfirst, as he'd done many times as a boy, when his brother had tormented him until he lost control. The difference was, William was no longer bigger and stronger than Calder.

The conflict continued from there, fairly equal at first, and Calder reveled in it. He got as much pleasure, in fact, from taking punches as he did from throwing them. While the battle raged, he did not have to think about the impossible, fantastical situation with Maeve, the loss of a father he had not known he loved, and now this second, and somehow more wrenching, forfeiture of a mother he had adored.

Finally, his own face bloody and his knuckles bruised, Calder sent William to the ground with a right cross, and William did not rise. He half lay, half sat, one shoulder braced against the edge of a garden bench, breathing hard and deep. His eyes were blackened and nearly swollen shut, and yet there was an expression of redemptive bliss on his face that made Calder want to tie into him all over again.

He turned and stumbled toward the house.

The undertaker and his helpers had brought Bernard's body downstairs by that time; he was to lie in state until the next morning, when there would be a formal ceremony, followed, of course, by burial.

Capshaw, the mortician, assessed Calder's rumpled, grass-stained clothes and bleeding face with undisguised disdain. He and the old man had played poker together, among other things, and there had been a certain grudging friendship between them.

"You haven't changed," the undertaker said, reaching into the fancy mahogany coffin his helpers had brought in to straighten Bernard's ascot.

Calder forced himself to the side of the long library table that had been moved into the parlor to support the casket and the sizable man reposing inside. He curled his fingers around the side of the coffin, heedless of the small bloodstains he left on the white satin lining, and stared down into the pale, still face of his father.

Or the man he had always believed was his father.

"Was my mother leaving him, the night she died?" he asked, mindful of the words only after they had left his mouth. It was a question Capshaw might well have the answer to, since he was close to the family and had probably prepared Marie Holbrook's broken body for the grave.

The undertaker cleared his throat. "This is no time to be discussing—"

Calder raised his eyes, locked his gaze with the other man's. "Damn you, *just tell me*," he rasped.

"Yes." Capshaw sighed the word, sending it out of his mouth on a rush of air. "Yes, Marie was leaving Bernard. And don't devil me about it, Calder, because that's all I'm going to say. Perhaps you don't have any respect for the dead—perhaps you've become hardened to it, seeing so much destruction on the battlefields—but I do.

Bernard was a good friend to me, and I won't see his death turned into a parlor theatrical!''

Calder studied his father's cold, marblelike face, as if expecting to see some answer written there. Then he turned and moved away, walking slowly, like a man entranced, toward the main staircase.

He took refuge not in his room, but in the nursery where he had slept and played as a child. It had been kept much as it was, in the hope, Calder supposed, that there would be other children after the disastrous loss of Amalie.

One of her dolls was still seated in a miniature rocker next to the fireplace, as if waiting for the little girl to come back and claim it. Calder touched the toy as reverently as if it were some holy object, a belonging of Saint Paul or even Christ, then wrenched his hand back.

He'd lost everything, he realized. His life with Maeve— soon, even the memory of her would be gone, thanks to her macabre magic—his child, his father, his illusions that there had been one person in his life—Marie—who had loved him selflessly, even his own identity. Calder no longer knew who he was.

It would have been a mercy if he'd been able to weep then, or curse the heavens, but he was still without feeling. His was a dead soul, entombed in living flesh.

Presently Calder returned to his own room.

He wasn't surprised to find a packet of letters resting on his bedside table, tied with faded ribbon. Beneath them were a few miscellaneous pages of expensive vellum, still faintly scented with his mother's perfume, their edges crumbling with age.

He left them long enough to go to the washstand and cleanse the blood and dirt from his face and hands. Then he carried the letters to a chair near the window and hunched there, stretching out his long legs, to read.

The loose pages told him all he needed to know; Marie Holbrook had indeed been leaving her husband for a lover, and she made no mention of her son.

Doubtless, he'd been nothing more to her than an inconvenience, despite the soft lullabies he remembered, the gentle nurturing, the tender words. Had Marie lived, then he, Calder, would have been as bereft as his own child was, years later, when Theresa abandoned her.

He laid the letters aside, closing his eyes, willing Maeve to come to him, willing her to be real.

In her cool, dark burrow, deep beneath the surface of the ground, Maeve stirred in her vampire sleep, but she did not awaken until sunset. She was aware of Calder's desperate summons the moment she opened her eyes, but she paused before going to him. She and all blood-drinkers were at war, and she could no longer follow every whim.

Lisette was clever, and she would like nothing better than to take Maeve prisoner. The ancient vampire was mad, but she wasn't stupid; she surely knew that the rebellion would fall apart without its central players, and she had already taken Valerian.

So Maeve waited, there in her hidden pit, until full consciousness returned. She felt a terrible thirst and knew that it must be slaked first thing. She could not risk weakness now, any more than she dared take impulsive chances.

She assembled herself in a faraway field hospital and fed on a dying soldier, obliterating his agony and his fear, making his passing one of ecstasy. Like the others, he mistook her for an angel of mercy, and blessed her, and

Maeve wondered who the true monsters were—creatures like herself, or the mortals who orchestrated war.

After that, Maeve's head was clear, and she felt strong. Before setting out to search for Valerian, and thus, Lisette, she took herself to Calder's room in the family mansion.

He was slouched in a chair, unshaven, his hair and clothes mussed, drunker than a lord. Maeve went to his side, sensing the presence of death in the house, as well as rage and sorrow and, worst of all, hopelessness.

She touched his hair. "Calder."

He opened his eyes and looked at her, and even in that very disheveled state he was so beautiful to Maeve that she wondered how she could ever wipe out all memory of the love that had grown between them. She only knew that she must.

He groped for her, drew her down onto his lap. "I was beginning to think even you were a lie," he murmured, burying his battered face in her hair, which fell loose around the shoulders of her blue woolen cape.

"Tell me what's happened," Maeve said gently, placing light kisses on each of his bruised cheekbones. "Please."

Calder released the story in agonized increments, telling how he'd adored his mother, and believed in her, and found out only today that she'd deceived him, that her devotion had been nothing more than pretty pretense. He produced the crumbling pages, penned by her own hand, and Maeve felt his grief move in her spirit, like a child in a womb, as she read the telling words.

She thought, too, of her own mortal mother, a laughing, beautiful, and completely scatterbrained tavern maid. She'd lived in the eighteenth century, had Callie

O'Toole, and gotten herself pregnant during a flirtation with a wealthy English merchant named Tremayne. Maeve and her twin brother, Aidan, had been the result of that liaison.

Maeve tilted Calder's head gently back and examined his wounds. "I could find out," she said, the idea coming to her only as she voiced it.

"Find out what?" Calder asked. He was more sober now, more focused.

She smoothed his hair. "About your mother. I could go back to that night, Calder. I cannot change history, that's entirely too dangerous, but I can find out whether she really meant to leave you. The question is, can you deal with the truth?"

He considered for a moment, his arms around her waist, drawing her closer. "There's no need of that, Maeve. I'm a grown man—I'll learn to accept that I've mourned a fantasy mother all these years. God knows, I've had enough practice at learning to accept unpleasant realities."

Maeve knew that he was right, but she also knew that emotions weren't governed by logic. Understanding what had happened to him, accepting it, would not spare Calder the pain of disillusionment. And there was always the chance that his suffering was based on a lie.

She rose from his lap and stood straight and tall. "When did it happen, your mother's accident?"

Calder murmured a date, his reactions slowed by the liquor he'd consumed earlier, then thrust himself to his feet, groping for her. "Maeve, wait—"

She closed her eyes and concentrated, ignoring Calder's protests, and when she opened them, she was standing on a sidewalk in front of that same house, but it was nearly thirty years earlier.

A storm was brewing; the wind was high and the sky dark. Maeve wrapped her cloak more closely around her, even though she did not feel the chill. She focused on the woman she sought, and was transported inside the great house, into a nursery.

There candlelight flickered, and a low fire burned on the hearth. A slender dark-haired woman sat on the side of a child's small bed, her narrow shoulders slumped. She was dressed in traveling garb, a simple dress, bonnet, and cloak, and as Maeve drew nearer, she realized that Marie Holbrook was weeping.

It was the sight of the child, however, that stunned Maeve to the core of her being. This was Calder, her love, the one man she would have considered spending all eternity with, as a little boy.

He was sound asleep, his dark hair tumbled over his forehead, his thick lashes brushing cheeks still plump with youth and innocence.

As Maeve watched, Marie bent and kissed the boy Calder's forehead lightly. He stirred and murmured something, but did not awaken.

"My baby," Marie whispered brokenly. She rose from the edge of the mattress with reluctance, and Maeve saw her in profile, saw the gleam of tears on her cheek, catching the light of the struggling fire. "Good-bye."

No, Maeve thought, closing her eyes for a moment. *Don't let it have happened this way, please.*

Lightning blazed beyond the leaded windows of Calder's room, and thunder threatened to burst the sky, but still he did not awaken.

Marie turned, half-blinded by obvious grief, unaware of Maeve's presence because Maeve had willed it so.

Maeve was confused; the woman didn't appear to be leaving her child willingly, and yet she did not bundle him up and carry him away with her, as a thousand, nay a million, other women would have done in a like situation.

She followed Marie into the hallway, where a young, thin, eager-looking lad awaited. Maeve guessed accurately that this was William, the difficult half brother Calder had mentioned, and she felt a surge of fury even before the youth spoke.

He flung himself away from the wainscoted wall to stand behind Marie, and his very being seemed to bristle with hatred. "Leaving so soon, Marie? Why don't you take your brat with you?"

She whirled, the fiery Marie, and slapped William hard across the face. "You know," she whispered. "Damn you, *you know* why I have to leave him—because no matter where we went, your father would hunt us down and tear Calder from my arms. I would die before I'd see that happen!"

Strangely prophetic words, Maeve thought sadly, watching from a little distance away. Marie Holbrook would indeed die, and soon; her accident was probably only minutes away.

It was a mercy, then, that the doomed woman had been forced to abandon her child. If she hadn't, Calder would surely have been killed, too, or at least crippled.

Maeve was still dealing with the mental images that idea produced when suddenly William grabbed at Marie, wild-eyed, shaking with some unholy passion. "Why did you waste yourself on that old man?" he rasped, speaking, no doubt, of his own father. "What do you see in this lover, this cousin of yours? Don't you understand that *I* can love you as no one else ever could?"

Marie struggled in the youth's grasp, her eyes bright

with fury, despair, and fear. "William, let me go! This instant!"

At that moment a door closed heavily downstairs, and then a younger Bernard Holbrook started up the stairs. His handsome face was contorted with angry confusion.

"What in the name of hell and all its demons is going on here?" he demanded.

Marie was still fighting to free herself, and it was all Maeve could do to keep from interceding. No matter what transpired this night, she must not meddle, for the ramifications would creep into the years ahead like vines, dividing and dividing again, changing the future in myriad unpredictable ways.

William raised his voice to an unnaturally high, thin pitch, and his fingers bit into Marie's shoulders as he tightened his grip on her. "She was leaving you, Papa!" he cried. "Your *wife* was running away, but I stopped her!"

The expression on the elder Holbrook's face was one of wounded bewilderment. "Release your stepmother, William," he ordered, hurrying up the stairs. "Have you taken leave of your senses?"

"*Bitch*," William whispered, and then he flung Marie from him. She struggled to regain her balance, a look of startled horror on her face, and then tumbled not down the stairs, but over the railing that edged the uppermost landing. She did not scream as she fell, and there was no sound after her body struck the marble floor below, except for William's rapid breathing and the tick of the long-case clock on the first landing.

Bernard broke the silence first, with a choked sigh. "Good God," he cried, scrambling, groping his way back down the stairs, like a man blinded. "Marie! Oh, dear God help us, *Marie*!"

CHAPTER
❦ 12 ❦

"Oh, Marie," Bernard Holbrook whispered brokenly, kneeling beside his wife's motionless body, there on the marble floor of the entryway. He took her limp hand and smoothed the knuckles with a circular motion of his thumb. "Marie—"

Maeve followed, still invisible to both William and his father, as the former moved slowly down the stairs. Above, in the nursery, the youthful Calder slept, heedless of the fact that his life had just been altered forever.

"Will she die?" William rasped when at last he'd reached his father and the stepmother he had clearly both loved and despised.

"I hope not," Bernard said in an agonized whisper. "Dear God in heaven, I hope not." Tears gleamed in his eyes. "All the servants are out, so you'll have to go for help. Get Dr. Blanchard, quickly!"

William lingered, clenching and unclenching his fists, his collar wet with perspiration. "But what if she dies?" he asked. "They'll say I killed her. I'll hang or spend the rest of my life in prison—"

Bernard stroked Marie's pale forehead with a tender motion as she stirred and murmured, trapped beneath a crushing burden of pain. The older man spoke with quiet determination. "I know you didn't mean for this to happen, William. And you are, after all, my son. I will do whatever I must to protect you."

William's look was hot with contempt and totally void of pity as he glared down at the unconscious Marie. "She was nothing but a whore," he said. "She even tried to lure me to her bed—"

The elder Holbrook closed his eyes tightly for a moment, and a crimson flush climbed his neck to throb in his face. "Enough," he growled. "Get the doctor before I change my mind and hang you myself!"

At last William turned and hurried toward the door, but the expression on his face was hard with a hatred terrible to see, even for a vampire.

Maeve drew nearer, soothing Marie's internal suffering as much as she could by means of her thoughts, but she dared not show herself.

Bernard was weeping quietly, pressing Marie's small hand to his mouth. "Oh, darling," he pleaded. "Forgive me."

Marie stirred again and moaned softly. "Calder," she said in the merest shadow of a whisper. "Help him— William will—kill him—"

A ragged sob escaped Bernard. "No, my darling—I

promise you, Calder will be safe. Please, Marie—were you truly leaving me?''

"Yes," Marie said. Her eyes were open now, though there was a faraway light in them, as though she looked beyond Bernard, beyond the walls of that grand house, beyond the stormy night sky. She felt no pain, for Maeve had mentally deadened those places inside Marie that measured suffering.

"Why?" Bernard said, although he must have known.

"I wanted—needed your love—you wouldn't give it." Marie's gaze shifted, then locked with Maeve's. The vampire saw quiet acknowledgment in the woman's eyes.

It didn't surprise Maeve that Marie could see her, while she was invisible to both William and Bernard. The dying could often discern shapes where the living saw only thin shadows, or nothing at all.

After that, Marie closed her eyes and lapsed into the enfolding warmth of a coma, one from which she would never recover.

Bernard kept his vigil at his wife's side, smoothing her hair now and then, or stroking the curve of her cheek. Presently William and the doctor burst into the foyer, along with two men they must have recruited along the way.

The doctor, a diminutive man with a balding pate and blue eyes as fierce as those of a Viking, dropped to one knee to examine Marie. In a soft voice he said, "You'd best prepare yourself for a loss."

Marie was carefully placed on a long panel of mahogany, the extension piece from the huge table in the dining room, and carried upstairs to her deathbed by the two strangers.

When those men had gone, and Dr. Blanchard had

joined William and Bernard in the study, Maeve was present, too, a part of the night, listening and watching.

It was there, in Bernard Holbrook's august study, that the story of the carriage accident was concocted. A wrecked coach would be easy enough to produce, they agreed grimly, and from that night forward they would all swear that Marie Holbrook had met with tragedy as she fled her unhappy marriage.

Maeve's feelings were mixed as she left the study for the nursery upstairs, where the boy who would become the man she loved more than life itself lay sleeping. He was beautiful, that child, with his mother's coloring and his father's strength of features, and she stood watching him as long as she dared.

Gazing at him, Maeve mourned her lost humanity bitterly, if briefly. This sleeping child was the mirror image of the little ones she would never be able to give Calder, despite the staggering depth and breadth of her love for him.

It would be difficult to go back to that future time, where her cherished one awaited her now as a grown man, and tell him the whole truth. He was bound to be furious with William for causing Marie's death, even though the act had been committed more by negligence than intent, and he would hate his dead father all over again, for engineering and then perpetuating a lie to protect his elder son.

Maeve crept close to the bed, brushed the slumbering child's tousled hair with the lighest pass of her fingertips, indulged in the futile wish that she could somehow spare him the suffering he faced, and then took herself ahead in time.

Calder was keeping a vigil in the main parlor, where

his father lay in state, a pale, solemn figure, grand even in death.

"What happened?" Calder asked when Maeve appeared at his side.

She took his hand and drew him away from the casket and the husk of a man inside, toward the glow of the fire. There was no other light in the room, but for that and the shimmer of the summer moon.

She said the most important thing first, and she said it gently. "Your mother didn't want to leave you, Calder—it broke her heart, in fact. All the same, she couldn't stay with your father, and she knew there was no place she might take you where Bernard wouldn't find you. She wanted to spare you the trauma of being pulled from her arms by some sheriff or detective and taken away again."

Calder closed his eyes, absorbing what Maeve had told him. Then he laid his hands on her shoulders and said hoarsely, "There's more."

She nodded and then, slowly, as tenderly as she could, she explained how Marie had really met her death that night—how William had flung her from him, in a fit of thwarted passion, and she'd fallen over the rail at the top of the staircase. How Bernard had staged a carriage wreck and told everyone that Marie had sustained her fatal injuries in the accident.

Calder's face, already bruised and abraded from the altercation with William earlier in the rear garden, tightened with rage as he listened. Maeve began to fear that he would go straight to William's room, drag his brother from his bed, and kill him with his bare hands.

Maeve's worry did not stem from the possibility that William Holbrook might be the next to lie in a coffin in that very parlor; it was the knowledge that Calder would be hanged for the act that troubled her.

"Let me take you back to England," she pleaded softly when the sorrowful tale had been told and a few moments of silence had passed. "You'll be away from this place, these people——"

Calder turned from her abruptly and strode toward the center of the house, and Maeve went after him, forgetting to use her vampire powers, hurrying as a mortal woman would.

Instead of climbing the stairs, however, Calder turned up the gaslights in the massive foyer and stood on the exact spot where Marie's shattered body had struck the hard, cold floor. As he looked up at the rail of the highest landing, Maeve knew he was imagining the whole terrible scenario, assimilating the fear his mother must have felt as she fell, the blinding pain that would have assailed her at impact.

"Calder." Maeve said his name quietly, laying calming hands on his broad, tension-corded shoulders. "Let it be over now. Forgive your father and brother and go on."

He whirled, his face as cold and hard as the polished marble beneath his feet. "Forgive them? That would mean saying they were right in what they did!"

Maeve shook her head, very human tears gathering in her eyes because looking upon Calder's torment was far worse than bearing her own had ever been. What treacherous business it was, this loving another being so completely, so hopelessly.

"No, darling—that isn't the case at all. Forgiving won't change what Bernard and William did—it's not something you'd be doing for them, but for yourself. Don't you see? You'd be rolling back the stone that keeps you inside your tomb."

Calder's smile was rueful and bitter, utterly void of tenderness or mirth. "That sounds like an angel's reasoning to me," he said. "Have you been consorting with Gideon, like Dimity?"

She rested her forehead against his shoulder for a moment, coping with the inner tumult of loving this man, then looked up at him, her hands resting on his chest. Beneath her right palm his heart thumped, pumping the substance that sustained them both, though in very different ways, of course.

"Whether spoken by a devil or an angel, the truth is the truth," she said wearily. "Hating your father and brother will serve no purpose but to sap your strength. Now—will you come away with me? Please?"

He averted his gaze for a long moment, then looked directly at Maeve again. "I can't," he said in a voice gruff with desire and regret. "Unless I can share your life—every part of it—then it's better if I stay here. When I was in London, I was hardly more than a house pet. I can't live that way."

Maeve knew he was right, and she nodded woodenly. Although leaving Calder behind was torture, she had no choice—there was a war being fought in her world, as well as his. The night was passing, and she had yet to find Valerian or confront Lisette. "I love you," she said, desperate to retain some link between them.

He leaned forward and kissed the top of her head. "I know," he said. "And I certainly love you. But it appears that we're a star-crossed pair if ever there was one. Even Romeo and Juliet can't equal the tragedy of our romance."

Maeve's heart splintered within her. She wanted to deny his words, wanted it with everything in her, but she couldn't. Again, he was right. "I'll make you forget me soon," she said raggedly. "But just now, during this terrible time, I need for you to love me consciously, willingly."

"It's all right," Calder said. "Kiss me good-bye, darling, and go on about your deadly business."

She shook her head again, stepping back. The temptation to give in to her own selfish desires and make Calder into a blood-drinker, like herself, was overwhelming. She couldn't afford to forget, even for a moment, that if she transformed this man, she would also seal his eternal damnation. From the moment of change, his soul would belong to darkness.

"I don't trust myself to kiss you," she said, feeling as though she would shatter into pieces, crushed between her passion for Calder and the purity of the love she bore him.

He laid his hands to either side of her face, his thumbs stroking her cheekbones. Then he offered a familiar plea. "Make me a vampire, Maeve. Make me like you. Can't you see that there's nothing here for me anymore? That there is no reason for me to go on living as a mortal?"

Maeve's temper flared. "There is every reason!" she cried. "You're a doctor, and there are human beings suffering in hospitals, on battlefields—"

He silenced her by moving the pad of one thumb across her mouth. "I would be able to relieve far more of that suffering if I had powers like yours," he said gently. "As it is, I can do very little, except watch my patients die in agony, or worse, survive, in the kind of pain that can only produce madness."

She hesitated, wavering, swayed by Calder's argument and by the fact that she wanted him near her, now more than ever. Then, however, her prior convictions won out.

What were a few score years spent as a mortal, compared to an eternity of hellfire?

"Good-bye," she said, and then she raised her hands high, closed her eyes, and vanished.

The warlock, Dathan, was pacing when Maeve met him at the agreed place, the stone monument in the English countryside that had figured so prominently in her experiences. Aidan had died to the life of a vampire and been resurrected here as a mortal man, and she and Valerian had met within the druids' circle many times, to argue and confer.

"Where have you been?" the warlock demanded, the night wind catching his dark cloak and causing it to flow behind him.

"I had business to attend to," Maeve said stiffly. "And kindly remember that I don't have to account to you— about anything."

Dathan's strangely beautiful countenance softened, but only slightly. His eyes were still feral and sharp, missing no physical nuance of emotion or intent, no matter how minor. "We will not serve our purposes by arguing," he said finally. "My forces, because they can move about in daylight, have destroyed a vast number of Lisette's vampires with stakes and fire. She herself still eludes us, however."

"We'll find Lisette when she wants us to find her," Maeve said with weary certainty. "What of Valerian? Is there news of him?"

Dathan looked impatient for a moment, as though he'd rather not trouble himself with the likes of that particular, and undeniably controversial, vampire. Then he sighed like a suffering saint and said, "She's taken him to a place we cannot reach."

Maeve stiffened. "Back in time," she mused aloud as the realization struck her. "Back to a period before my death as a human, so that I cannot reach him."

Dathan nodded. "We warlocks cannot travel between decades and centuries, the way you blood-drinkers do, so we can be of no assistance in this matter. Far better if we simply put all thought of the unfortunate Valerian behind us and concentrate on the business at hand. Time is slipping away, remember. The forces of Nemesis will be on us soon."

Turning away, Maeve stepped up onto the curve of a fallen pillar and stood gazing at the dark plain that stretched away to the horizon. She knew well that time was sorely limited, and that the effort to destroy Lisette would neither stand nor fall because of Valerian. Still, he was the one who had given Maeve the dubious yet cherished gift of immortality. It had been he who had shown her her new powers and taught her to use them. He who had loved her once, in his own way, and introduced her to passion.

No matter what came of it, she decided, gazing up at a star-splattered sky, she could not abandon Valerian. She would have to find a way to help him.

When she turned to face Dathan again, she saw that he had divined her thoughts, and he was coldly furious.

"Come," he said in a charged but otherwise even voice. "Let us seek the troublesome Lisette and move to destroy her."

Maeve assessed the sky. "It will be morning soon. I cannot tarry much longer."

Dathan looked violently impatient. "Then shift yourself to the other side of the world, where the light won't reach."

His reasoning was simple, and it wasn't as though the

option hadn't occurred to Maeve many times since her making as a vampire. Some blood-drinkers, however, had experimented with the technique and never been seen again.

"It would be logical," she reflected, "for Lisette to do that. It's evident that she can move about during the day, from what Isabella said about Lisette's sudden appearance in her and Valerian's love-nest that morning. But I doubt our queen has progressed to such a point that she can endure the full glare of the sun."

"Exactly," Dathan said. "Let us go there—to China—and search for her."

Maeve turned, looked down into the warlock's handsome face in surprise. "You can do that? Travel so far, simply by the power of your mind?"

"Of course we can," he replied with exaggerated politeness. "Did you think we had no magical powers?"

Maeve went to stand facing him, on the stony, much-trampled ground. The druid stones were obviously a popular meeting point for humans, too, though only the most intrepid would venture there at night. "Let us see what powers you have," she challenged coolly. "Just as dawn arrives, we'll take a little journey together."

They waited, side by side, cloaked in silence and private musings, until the first glow of pink and apricot rimmed the horizon. Then, like a fledgling swimmer plunging into deep water, Maeve thrust herself into the unknown, the darkness on the opposite side of the globe.

At first, dazed by the swiftness of the trip and the energy it required, Maeve could not discern where she was. She knew only that Dathan was beside her, and that he supported her with a chivalrous arm around her waist.

After a few moments Maeve's head cleared. She had not been stricken by the distance, she knew, but by the avoidance of the vampire sleep that would normally have claimed her just then.

"Fascinating!" Dathan remarked, looking down into a moon-washed pit, where dozens of life-size bronze soldiers marched in formation, accompanied by life-size horses and chariots. The excavation had clearly been abandoned for some time, and Maeve knew intuitively that there were hundreds, perhaps thousands, more of these ancient sculptures buried all over China.

Maeve marveled, but not at the industry of a long-dead civilization. No, it was her own ability to resist that all-encompassing sleep that amazed her. It was probably these reflections, she would conclude later, that prevented her from sensing the impending attack.

They came out from behind every soldier, those terrible, blood-drinking corpses Lisette had made, making a shrill sound that was part shriek and part groan.

Dathan muttered an exclamation and tensed beside Maeve, and she knew that if he'd had a sword, he would have drawn it.

"Great Zeus," he rasped, "there are hundreds of them!"

Maeve nodded, a half-smile forming on her lips at the prospect of challenge. "It would be my guess," she said, "that we have found more than this army of blathering creatures."

"What?" Dathan demanded, bracing himself as the creatures scrambled out of the pit and began lumbering toward them.

"Lisette is here," Maeve said calmly.

In the next instant a geyser of blue-gold light exploded in the center of the pit full of statues, and as the glow solidified into a female shape, looming some twenty feet off the ground, even the mindless army stopped and stared.

Maeve applauded. "Very impressive," she called as the shape became Lisette, dramatic and horrible in a gauzy gown that caught the night wind.

"Are you insane?" Dathan hissed, as the bluish light of Lisette's countenance played over both their faces.

"Perhaps," Maeve said, taking a step forward to stand at the precipice of the pit. "If you can summon your warlocks, you'd better do it now. Otherwise, you and I are doomed to a terrible end that might well have a beginning but no finish."

Dathan shuddered, the way a mortal would have, and whispered back, "Don't be naive. I don't have to send for my armies—I brought them with me."

Maeve did not look over her shoulder; indeed, she did not shift her gaze from Lisette's shimmering form. Still, she could feel the warlocks now, gathering in the darkness behind her and Dathan.

Their presence, while reassuring, was by no means a reprieve from Lisette's vengeance, however. She was possessed of spectacular powers—that much was obvious—and her army of brainless marvels would fight tirelessly at her command, not out of any such unvampire-like trait as loyalty, of course, but because she controlled them so completely.

"You are bold, Maeve Tremayne," Lisette said in an earsplitting and yet strangely sweet voice, looming there in the darkness like the angel of death.

Oddly, Maeve thought of a movie she had seen once, during one of her reluctant visits to the twentieth century—a tale containing an alleged wizard, who had projected a terrifying image to frighten visitors away. All the time he'd been hiding behind a curtain, pulling levers and twisting dials, a nervous, fretful little man with no magical powers at all.

"Yes," Maeve agreed. "Some would even say brazen. Show me your true self, Vampire. I am not misled by this theatrical trick of yours, though I must say it's memorable."

The creature that Lisette wanted them to believe was herself undulated with furious, beautiful light, and a continuous shriek of rage filled the night, loud enough, piercing enough, to shatter the very stars themselves.

Suddenly the banshee-like cry shaped itself into words. "Kill them!" Lisette screamed, and her troops, mesmerized only a moment before, began their stumbling, awkward advance again.

Battle erupted all around Maeve and Dathan, but they were in the eye of the storm, at least temporarily, for the warlocks came out of the night to meet the vampires and engage them in bitter combat.

Unearthly shrieks rent the air as warlocks were cut down by the vampires' superior strength and, conversely, blood-drinkers were infused with the poisonous blood of their enemies.

Maeve concentrated on Lisette, whose image still hovered above them, shining and huge, and her thoughts transported her to a niche in a sheer cliff overlooking the battleground.

There Maeve found the vampire queen, no bigger or more daunting than she was herself. Lisette looked disconcerted for a moment, but then, with a scream of madness and outrage, she flung herself at Maeve.

They fought, the two vampires, snarling like panthers battling over a kill on some African steppe, tearing at each other. Maeve felt herself weakening, felt the vampire sleep threatening her, and redoubled her efforts, knowing that if she did not win this battle she would be left in the open to face the ravages of the morning sun.

Just when Maeve believed she could not continue, that the disastrous sleep would swallow her, however, Lisette turned to vapor and vanished.

Maeve collapsed against a wall of the shallow cave. She was alone, and gravely weakened, and if she did not feed and rest in a dark, safe place, she would be lost. She tried to transport herself back to her lair in England, but the effort failed. She clutched her middle and slid helplessly down the side of the cave to the ground.

She heard the battle going on and on outside. Evidently, when Lisette had fled—if indeed that had been her intent—she had not chosen to take her horrid soldiers with her.

Maeve's head lolled, and she thought of Calder, and then of Aidan and Valerian. This was the ironic end of it all, then, she reflected, with a strangled sound that might have been either a laugh or a sob. She was wounded, the dawn was inching slowly, inexorably, toward her, and her only hope of rescue was a band of warlocks—*warlocks*, who six months ago, even six days ago, had been her implacable enemies.

She had almost lost consciousness by the time the din ceased, and she could feel the first light of dawn creeping into the cave, finding her with its acid fingers, tearing at her injured flesh.

Then—surely it was only a dream—strong arms lifted her, and she felt a rushing sensation, and the burning stopped.

Maeve opened her eyes slowly, fearing to find that Lisette had come back for her, and brought her as a captive to some place of temporary safety. She found, instead, that she was inside an old crypt—there was no telling what country she was in—and Dathan was with her.

He smiled, though his blue eyes were as cold as ever, and held a golden goblet to her lips. "Drink," he said.

Maeve knew the chalice contained blood, the substance she most needed and that, at the same time, most repulsed her. She hesitated, quite sensibly, for this supposed gesture of mercy might well be a ruse. Dathan might be offering her the poison that flowed through his own veins, or those of one of his multitude of followers.

"Take it," he ordered gently, reading her mind. "It's low-grade stuff—we stole it from a refrigerator in a nearby hospital—but there's no warlock taint to fret about."

Maeve's choices were limited, since she could not regain her strength, or indeed even survive, without ingesting blood. She decided to take the risk and let the stuff flow in through her fangs, completely bypassing her tongue.

When the chalice was empty, she sank back onto silken pillows and regarded Dathan with questioning eyes. Her wounds had already begun to mend, closed by the cool, healing darkness and her own mystical powers, but she was frightfully weak.

"You saved me," she said with emotion. "Why?"

Dathan narrowed his eyes at her and sighed again. He would have made an excellent martyr, it seemed to Maeve.

"Not out of anything so misguided as mercy," he finally replied with a shrug. "We cannot achieve our objectives without you."

Maeve tried to rise, but Dathan pushed her back down again.

"Wait," he said. "You must have more rest and more blood. You will be of no use to us without your strength and your powers."

"None of that will matter," Maeve argued, "if our time runs out and Nemesis is unleashed with his sword of vengeance."

Dathan did not look quite so desperate or despairing as he had in times past. He shoved a hand through his thick, maple-brown hair. "We can conclude by the events of last night, I think, that Lisette's new lair is somewhere in the region of that excavation."

Maeve nodded in full, if reluctant, agreement. "How did your warlocks fare against those monsters of hers?"

"Like your encounter with the queen," Dathan answered, "it ended in something of a draw. We fought until dawn was imminent, and then the opposing forces fled, of course, to escape the light. That was when I found you on the floor of that cave—until that moment I thought you'd deserted us."

Had Maeve been mortal, she would have flushed with annoyance and outrage. "Do you believe me to be such a coward? Think again, Warlock—I have as much courage as *ten* witches!"

Dathan laughed and handed her the chalice again; it had been refilled and brought back by a cloaked creature Maeve had glimpsed out of the corner of her eye. "And as much pride, I vow," he said. "Drink up, Mistress Tremayne. I fear we have many frightful adventures still ahead of us."

CHAPTER
❈13❈

Somehow Calder passed the night without awakening William and throttling him, and with the morning came a drizzling rain and a steady stream of visitors. Like crows in their black garb, the mourners passed by the casket single file, peering inside to see how death suited Bernard Holbrook.

All morning and all afternoon they came, the grieving, the curious, the indifferent, the relieved, and the secretly pleased. They ate hungrily of the food Prudence and her small staff had prepared, and speculated among themselves about Calder and William and the bruised state of their faces.

Calder hated every moment of that interminable day and dreaded the one to follow, for that would bring the funeral, the eulogies, the grim and final business of burial. To him, the world looked dark, and it was difficult to believe that the sun would ever shine again.

After the last of the sorrowful callers had left, Calder and William accidentally found themselves alone in the large dining room. William took a piece of smoked turkey from a platter and bit into it, regarding Calder through swollen eyes.

"We'll have the reading of the will tomorrow, after the ceremonies," the elder brother announced, reaching for another piece of meat.

Calder shrugged. "I don't give a damn about that," he said.

"Good," William replied. "Papa was closeted away for hours one day, just last month, with his lawyers. I recall that he was especially exasperated with you at that time, so don't be surprised if you find yourself in the street, with nothing to live on but that pitiful stipend the army pays you."

Although Calder's stomach rebelled at the very sight of food, he knew only too well that he would not be able to think clearly or function well in an emergency if he did not eat. He went to the long table, against his will, and filled a plate, taking slices of turkey and ham, some potato salad, and a serving of Prudence's famous fruit compote. Then, by a deft motion of one foot, learned in boyhood, he drew back a chair.

He paused for a few moments, regarding the food he'd taken and envying Maeve because she didn't have to trouble herself with the stuff at all. As he took up his fork, Calder raised his eyes to William's face.

"Take it all," he said, only a little surprised to realize that he meant it. "Take the money, take this goddamned mausoleum of a house, take the illustrious Holbrook name and the power that goes with it."

William blanched, his fingers tightening over the back of a chair. Plainly he hadn't been expecting Calder's acquiescence, but another fight instead. "You can't be serious," he said.

Calder ate a few bites of ham, chewing each one thoroughly, before answering. "You murdered my mother," he said at last. "And that old man lying in there with his eyelids stitched together covered up for you. As far as I'm concerned, if I never see you or this place again, it will be too soon."

Sweat beaded on William's upper lip. "I killed Marie? Where did you get such an idea?" he demanded hoarsely, pulling back a chair of his own and collapsing into it. "And why is it that you can't speak of our father with some semblance of respect, even now?"

"I loved him," Calder conceded. "But respect is another thing. As for my mother's death, well, you might say I have a way of looking into the past."

William's hand trembled visibly as he reached for a carafe of Madeira and then a wineglass. "I didn't lay a hand on her," he said.

"You're a liar," Calder replied, still eating. He knew his calm manner was unnerving his brother, and he was pleased by the fact. "She was going to leave this house, and our esteemed father, and you intercepted her. There was an argument, and you gripped her by the shoulders. She struggled, and you wouldn't release her—until you thrust her away from you in a moment of fury. That was when she tumbled backward over the railing and fell twenty feet to the floor of the foyer."

William had managed to pour wine, but his subsequent

attempts to raise the glass to his white lips failed because he was shaking. "Pure fantasy," he said.

Calder stared at him for a long, purposely disconcerting interval. "It happened just that way," he insisted quietly, "and we both know it. Kindly don't insult me with your denials."

After casting a yearning look at his wine, William wiped one forearm across his mouth. "If you really believe this—this delusion, then why haven't you tried to avenge Marie's death?"

Calder smiled grimly. "There has hardly been time for that," he said indulgently. "Still, we're young, you and I," he added with a shrug. "There's no rush."

At last William made a successful grab for his glass and raised it tremulously to his lips. After a few audible gulps, his color began to return, and he was steadier. "Is that a threat?"

Again, Calder shrugged, reaching for a platter and helping himself to some of Prudence's cold rice salad. "It might be. Then again, it might not. To be quite frank, I haven't decided how I'll deal with you." He chewed thoughtfully for a few moments, swallowed, and then gestured at William with an offhanded motion of his fork. "Rest assured, though, that I *will* deal with you."

William swallowed the rest of his wine and reached for the carafe while he could. "You don't scare me," he said, though his manner and the pallor of his complexion gave the lie to his words.

Calder smiled again and continued to eat.

That night he waited for Maeve to come to him, prayed that she would, and finally she appeared. She was as ethereal as a spirit, and throughout the magical encounter that awaited him, he feared he was only dreaming.

Without a word she slipped into bed beside him, encircling him in her soft, strong arms. She kissed the underside of his jaw and sent shivers of forlorn desire rushing through his system.

"Maeve," he whispered.

She touched his lips with an index finger to silence him, then trailed kisses down over his chest and his belly. His manhood surged upright in response, and he drew in a harsh breath when she touched the tip with her tongue.

Calder groaned and arched his back, completely in her power. He whispered a plea, and she granted his wish, consuming him, and he writhed in a fever of passion and need. At the last possible moment, she moved astride him, and took him deep inside her, and rode him while his body buckled beneath hers in the throes of triumph. She muffled his ragged shout of release by laying one cool hand over his mouth.

"I love you," he told her when their encounter was over, and she lay beside him, close and slender and solid. "Please, Maeve—don't leave me. Don't work your sorcery and make us forget each other—I can't bear the prospect of that."

She leaned over him and kissed his mouth, but lightly, brushing his lips with her own. Still she did not speak, but in truth there was no need of it. Everything she was thinking and feeling was plain in her dark blue eyes.

Calder's vision blurred as he looked up at her, and he touched her smooth cheek with an index finger. "So incredibly beautiful," he marveled in a whisper, certain he would perish with the loss of her. He wasn't sure, in fact, that he himself would exist at all, without the knowledge and memory of Maeve Tremayne.

Maeve smiled at him, the expression full of sweetness and sorrow, and then removed herself from his arms, from the warm tangle of the bedsheets. Once again she was wearing the soft, gauzy gown she had shed earlier to enter Calder's embrace.

He gave a low, despairing cry and stretched out a hand to her, but between one heartbeat and the next, she vanished.

Calder wept, though he did not make a sound, well aware that Maeve had made up her mind to destroy their love, to tear it from the universe by its very roots.

For the first time in his life he wanted to die.

Perhaps, he thought later, when he'd composed himself a little, she had already begun the mysterious process that would erase her from his memory, and him from her own. Perhaps he would awaken the next morning, or the one after that, with no recollection of the beautiful vampire who haunted his soul, as well as his mind and body.

Even though he knew the transition itself would probably be painless, the prospect of it was the purest torture.

Calder tried to reason with himself. Undoubtedly he would simply go on with his life, treating his patients, perhaps meeting another woman, marrying, fathering a houseful of children. The war, God willing, was bound to end soon, and the sundered land would begin to mend itself into some new and better nation.

No, it wouldn't be a bad existence, and he wouldn't know the difference anyway, wouldn't know what he was missing any more than the corpse of his father, still lying in a wash of candlelight in the parlor, could comprehend that life was going on without him.

Still, for all the dangers and all the terrible things he would see and probably do, Calder wanted to be with Maeve. And yes, he wanted to share her fantastic powers, too, but only because they would enable him to help his patients in ways that were impossible then. He could travel into the future, for instance, into the late twentieth century, the era to which the mystery of time had progressed, according to Maeve, and learn even more about the art of medicine than the miraculous textbooks had taught him. He would be able to bring that knowledge back to people who suffered, along with chemicals, pills, and serums that could kill pain without making the heart race the way morphine did. Vaccinations that would protect small children who in his own time were cruelly felled by maladies such as measles, diphtheria, and whooping cough . . .

He drifted off to sleep, and morning took him by surprise. Confused, uncertain if Maeve had come to him during the night or simply worked some trick of the mind on him and created the illusion of herself.

By rote, Calder washed and dressed and went downstairs to the dining room, but even as he filled his plate at the sideboard and went to the table, his thoughts were muddled. He was not aware of William's presence until his brother spoke.

"Calder."

William had taken a seat at the head of the table, but he wasn't taking breakfast. A hot cup of coffee steamed before him, and he poured rum into the brew as Calder looked at him in cold silence.

William was flushed now, his eyes feverishly bright, like those of an animal approaching the last stages of rabies. "I think you should go away," he said. "To Europe, perhaps, or maybe out West. I'm sure Papa left you enough money to make a new start."

Calder pushed back his chair, dropped his fork to his china plate with a deliberate clatter, and stood. "You've waxed generous, all of a sudden, even reasonable. Why is that, William?"

His brother started to answer, choked on his own words, and began again. "I want to be fair, that's all."

"You want to be fair," Calder repeated softly in a marveling tone. "Of course you do. And General Lee wants to hand all of Dixie over to Mr. Lincoln, tied with Union-blue ribbons." His voice hardened. "Damn it, do you take me for a fool? You'd murder me in my sleep if you thought you could get away with it!"

William closed his eyes tightly for a moment and swayed in his chair. He didn't speak again as Calder turned and strode out of the room.

Valerian sat in the cool, dark dungeon, knees drawn up, back pressed to the dank stone wall behind him. Had his captor been anyone other than Lisette, he'd have escaped easily, but her power was as strong as it had ever been—perhaps stronger, in that peculiar way of diseased minds. It was her magic that held him; the chains and bars and heavy iron doors were just for show.

He sighed, ran one hand through his mane of chestnut-colored hair, and wondered what Maeve and the others were doing, two hundred years into the future in the nineteenth century. It was just possible, he thought with a scowl, that Maeve was glad he was out of the way or, worse, that she hadn't even noticed that he was gone.

Valerian thrust himself to his feet, which were half buried in the fetid straw covering the floor. Rats and mice and a variety of other vermin populated the stuff, rustling and scurrying in the darkness.

"Lisette!" he shouted, his voice echoing in that enormous, lonely tomb of a place. "Damn you, show yourself!"

There was no answer, of course. Lisette had simply dropped him here, sometime in the middle of the seventeenth century, and it was entirely possible that she planned to let him rot. That would probably be a more effective, and more twisted, form of torture than anything else she could have devised.

In the distance he heard a creaking sound and the terrified blathering of a mortal.

Valerian closed his eyes and at the same time tried to shut the sound out of his ears, repulsed and shaken by it, but his efforts were futile. Until that night, he'd been sustained by animal blood, inferior stuff that barely kept him conscious. Now, plainly, Lisette or one of her several lieutenants had apparently decided to serve up a feast.

No doubt he, Valerian, was being fattened up for the kill.

A vampire called Shaleen, a dark-haired minx of a creature Valerian had never encountered before his imprisonment, appeared in the arched doorway of his cell, gripping a half-starved, flea-ridden mortal by one arm.

The boy was dressed in rags, all bones and filthy in the bargain, and he blinked in the darkness, all the more terrified because he could not see the fate that awaited him.

Shaleen, who was beautiful and eminently sane, unlike most of the ludicrous creatures Lisette surrounded herself with, curled her lip contemptuously and flung the unfortunate, blubbering human down at Valerian's feet.

"Here," said the other vampire, quite uncharitably. "Your dinner."

Valerian ignored the pitiful creature groveling in the rancid straw, at least for the moment, and fixed his attention on Shaleen. "Did Lisette make you into a blood-drinker?"

She studied him with insolent brown eyes. Her hair, a lovely caramel color, tumbled to her waist, unbrushed, with a thistle entangled here and there. "No," she answered. "Did she make you?"

Valerian's making was a memory he cherished, and he had never shared the experience with another being, not even Aidan or Maeve. "No," he replied shortly as the mortal clutched at his clothes, begging in incoherent phrases for mercies that were not forthcoming. "Why do you stay here? Why do you help her?"

Shaleen smiled. "I'm a new vampire. Lisette is teaching me her magic—I'm going to help her rule, after she destroys Maeve Tremayne once and for all."

Valerian laid a hand on the mortal's head, stroking him in consolation, the way he might have done with a whining dog. Using the oldest magic he knew, he numbed the poor wretch's mind, thus calming him. "Surely you're not foolish enough to believe it will be easy to stop Maeve? Her powers are as great as Lisette's—perhaps greater, because she isn't mad. Furthermore, Maeve has fate on her side—she is the blood-drinker of legend, the one who will overthrow Lisette."

Shaleen's lovely face hardened, only for a moment and almost imperceptibly, and yet in that time Valerian discerned that she had fancied *herself* to be that vampire. In her heart of hearts, she was plotting against Lisette, planning to supplant her.

Valerian smiled. "You are very ambitious indeed," he said. He let the smile fade, for he had not lived so many centuries without learning a few things about dramatic effect. "You are also foolhardy. Lisette will recognize your duplicity, and when that happens, the worst sinner in hell will be better off than you."

She raised her chin in defiance, did the beautiful and treacherous Shaleen, but there was no hiding her fear, not from Valerian.

"Help me get out of here," he said softly in his most persuasive voice, one that had lured many a mortal and not a few vampires into his web. "Your plan cannot succeed, little one. Lisette is too suspicious, and much too powerful, to fall for such bumbling deceptions as yours."

He saw her waver, sensed her indecision, but then she withdrew into the doorway.

"Lisette warned me about you," she said accusingly. "She said you were a better liar than the devil himself, and twice as charming, and she was right. Enjoy your supper, Valerian."

With that, Shaleen went out, shutting the great door behind her, and Valerian looked down at the whimpering, half-conscious, pathetic excuse for a human clinging to his leg. Gently he bent, grasped the lad by his painfully thin shoulders, and drew him to his feet.

"Don't be afraid," he said in the tenderest of tones as he gazed deeply into the terrified blue eyes of his next victim. "I promise you will feel only the keenest pleasure, and no pain at all."

Valerian bared the fragile throat, found the warm, sweet place where a full vein pulsed just beneath the skin, and sank his fangs in deep. Bliss flooded him as he drank, and he felt the specimen tremble in his hands and beneath his lips, not with pain but, just as Valerian had promised him, with an almost unbearable ecstasy.

•   •   •

Maeve was a little distracted; her thoughts kept straying to Calder. She was torn between guilt—she had tricked him, after all—and the hope that, by making him believe she'd been with him earlier in the night, by projecting an image of herself into his mind, she had afforded him a measure of comfort. . . .

She strained to catch hold of what Dathan was saying and pulled herself back into the conversation.

". . . as far as we have been able to discern, the time of his captivity is the middle of the seventeenth century. . . ."

"The seventeenth century?" Maeve echoed, round-eyed, seeing that one of Dathan's warlock spies had brought in a scroll. Closer examination proved that Lisette herself had penned a description of Valerian's exact whereabouts on the crumbling parchment. The message itself, of course, was intended to taunt Maeve, to challenge her. "That's before my birth as a human—and I can go back no farther than my death."

Dathan arched an eyebrow. "Are you so certain? After all, you thought you couldn't escape the vampire sleep, either, but you did exactly that when we traveled to China."

Maeve nodded thoughtfully. More than ever, she wished Valerian was here—he knew about these things. Once, in fact, in an effort to help Aidan find the secret of transforming himself from vampire to mortal, Valerian had actually ventured back beyond his own mortal lifetime. The trouble was, the effort had nearly destroyed him, and he'd been incapacitated by the resultant weakness. Time was running out, and Maeve couldn't afford the long recuperation her friend and mentor had needed.

On the other hand, the war with Lisette was going to be much more difficult, if not impossible, without

Valerian's counsel and moral support. Furthermore, if he perished in the skirmish ahead, then any victory, however sweet, would be tarnished by the loss of him.

Dathan paced. "Surely," he snapped, "you are not thinking of gallivanting off into some other century simply to rescue that worthless Valerian!"

"Your opinion of my friend does not concern me," Maeve said coldly.

"Perhaps it will," Dathan retorted, "if I tell you that we are watching your beloved Calder Holbrook, far away as he is. We can and will take him hostage, Maeve, if you do not listen to reason!"

Maeve trembled with both shock and fury. Stupidly perhaps, she had not expected a threat to Calder to come from this quarter but instead from Lisette. "Here and now," she said, and the even meter of her own voice surprised her, "I make this vow. If you lay a hand on Calder, I will flay you alive and serve you to the devil on a dozen different platters."

Dathan drew back slightly and raised both hands, palms out, in a jaunty gesture of conciliation. "That's a very colorful threat," he said. "And I assure you, I'll keep it in mind."

Maeve narrowed her eyes and leaned toward him. "See that you do, Warlock," she replied. "And keep this in mind as well: I make *promises*, not threats."

Although his eyes snapped with rage, Dathan did not press the matter further. Maeve, for her part, was not in the least reassured, for if she should be felled, as had nearly happened in China, Calder would be left completely unprotected.

Rising from the couch where she'd reclined and then sat, Maeve straightened her gown and ran splayed fingers through her long, loose tresses. "I will send Dimity to

check on Valerian," she said quietly, and no nuance of
the preceding argument showed in her countenance. "She
is medieval, like him, and may be able to reach that time
in history without danger to herself."

"Fine," Dathan said, his eyes still glittering with
controlled fury. "That will free the two of us to seek out
Lisette and make yet another attempt to finish her."

Maeve nodded distractedly. She was not thinking of
Lisette, or even of Valerian, but of Calder, far away in
Philadelphia. She should make another trip back in time,
she knew that, to the night when he'd first seen her, in
that grisly churchyard at Gettysburg, where the dead and
maimed had been laid out in endless rows. Once there,
she would blind Calder to her presence, as she should
have done in the first place, and in that moment his
attachment to her would be undone.

Knowing what needed doing and actually tackling the
task were two different things, however, and Maeve was
not anxious to destroy Calder's memory of her. Selfish as
it was, she needed the certainty that he loved her, that he
wanted her, that he would recognize her if she came to
him.

None of those things would be true from the instant
she changed history and, for all practical intents and
purposes, she'd be alone in eternity once again.

She left Dathan, in his underground hiding place
somewhere in the French countryside, and sought out the
vampire Dimity.

Maeve found the other blood-drinker haunting London's seedy dockside area, as usual, and they fed together
on a pair of deserving louts before retiring to Dimity's
graciously furnished cellar to confer.

There, seated in comfortable chairs and cheered by the
light of a lively fire in the grate, Maeve told Dimity that

Dathan's warlocks had learned where Lisette was keeping Valerian. Dimity nodded when the explanation was through and said she'd attempt a visit to his cell. If possible, she promised, she would find a way to release him.

"I could not ask for more," Maeve said, rising. After offering a quiet thanks, she took herself away and met Dathan in another part of London, one where sleek carriages rolled past through the fog, carrying passengers who would never have believed that such creatures as vampires even existed.

"I'm certain Lisette is in China," Dathan said without preamble, falling into step with Maeve as she passed a street lamp glowing with sickly blue-gold light.

Maeve took her time answering. "I've been thinking about that," she said. "It's possible, you know, that she's found herself another, safer lair. She has to be aware that we'll look for her in that same area."

"She is reckless," Dathan argued, and it was a statement Maeve could not refute. Lisette *was* reckless, making dramatic appearances, taking captives, spawning those dreadful creatures in defiance of the entire supernatural world.

"We'll try again," she agreed with dignity.

Dathan nodded, satisfied that he'd swayed Maeve to his way of thinking. "Shall we meet just before dawn, then, at the circle of stones?"

"I will be there," Maeve said, and in the next instant she realized that the warlock was no longer beside her. In fact, he was nowhere in sight.

She shrugged and set out to feed a second time. In the hours to come, she would need all the strength she could muster.

●   ●   ●

Dathan idled the rest of the night away in a backstreet tavern, nursing a mug of bitter ale, and watched in detachment as a variety of monsters came and went.

Oh, yes, there were vampires among the revelers, mostly new ones, heedless of the dangers of prowling places they did not know, and one or two warlocks came in as well. Still, it was among the human beings that Dathan found the greatest number of fiends.

He marveled to himself that mortals frightened their children, and each other, with tales of witches and warlocks, vampires and werewolves, while some of the vilest things in all of Creation lived next door to them, or up the street, or just down the road in the next village. And those beasts were not supernatural at all, but other humans, with beating hearts, brains throbbing with mysterious electrical impulses, and, supposedly, souls.

He sighed, lifted the copper mug to his mouth, and drained its contents in one final swallow. Then, suddenly sensing something different in his surroundings, he rose from his bench at one of the trestle tables, tossed a coin down to pay for his refreshment, and went outside into the summer night.

In the street, which was muddy and fouled with spittle and manure, Dathan stopped, sensing rather than hearing the strange, rhythmic chatter of several beings. He smiled, raising the hood of his cape so that his face was hidden in shadow, as well as his hair.

He was being stalked.

Dathan meandered into the nearest alley, drawn there by the vibration in his senses. They awaited him in that dark place, six drooling fiends, newly dead and starved for blood. Any blood.

Lisette's friends were too stupid and too greedy to

know of the ancient enmity between their own kind and the warlock.

He pushed back his hood and bared his sleek, white neck to them, and they stumbled toward him, making that odd and frantic murmuring sound he had heard before. He waited, and pretended to flinch when the first one fastened on him.

Infusing a vampire with the venom that flowed through his veins was a ferocious pleasure to Dathan, to all warlocks, and he felt a sweet tightening in his groin as a second monster pushed aside the first to drink.

Dathan allowed that, but ecstasy left him weak and distracted, and those were indulgences he couldn't afford. The poison took effect, and the first two vampires dropped, writhing, to the filth-strewn ground. He killed the other four by a more flamboyant method, one he had not yet exhibited to his reluctant comrade, Maeve Tremayne.

Narrowing his eyes, murmuring an incantation far older than the pillars of Stonehenge, Dathan produced a spontaneous burst of fire. It consumed the vampires, and he watched them twist and flail within the flames, in their gruesome dance of death.

Before the grudging truce, Dathan had consigned many blood-drinkers to the same fate, and he would have destroyed them all if he'd been able; immortals of equal power could, of course, resist his curses. How strange it was to be in league with Mistress Tremayne, when at any other time in history the two of them would have been sworn enemies!

Reaching the street, Dathan raised his hood again, then paused to look back into the alleyway. There was no light, for the fire he'd ignited was a spiritual one, and no screaming, for the vampires' cries could be heard not by the ear, but only by the most sensitive souls.

Most humans had not reached that level of conscious-ness, and so it was that the passers-by on that London street did not even pause, let alone rush into the alley to watch in their customary helpless fascination while the vampires burned.

Calder stirred uncomfortably in his sleep, dreaming of a night nearly thirty years before. In that dream, he was six years old again, and his mother was still alive, sitting on the edge of his bed, stroking his hair with a gentle hand, saying her tearful farewells.

The boy he had once been opened his eyes, something Calder had not done in reality, and reached up to wrap his arms around Marie's neck. "Good-bye, Mama," he said into the fragrant softness of her neck.

She embraced him, this other Marie, and he felt her tears on his face. Then she stood and walked toward the open doorway, never looking back, yet not seeming to see the young, dangerously passionate William hovering ahead of her. Waiting.

Calder, still trapped in the dream, thrust himself out of bed and ran into the hallway. He'd screamed a warning, putting all his strength into the effort, but not a sound had come from his throat.

He watched, in horror, as William and Marie argued, saw his half brother grab his mother by the shoulders and shake her, heard his father's stern order to let her go. Then, cold as a corpse, paralyzed with fear, Calder had watched as Marie tumbled over the stair rail.

It was torment enough, seeing that horrid spectacle once, but the scene kept repeating itself, over and over again, with a slow, macabre grace.

Calder thrust himself back to the surface of consciousness, unable to bear it any longer, only to feel his heart lurch at the sight awaiting him.

William was standing at the foot of the bed, hardly more than a shadow in the thick darkness, so still that he might have been part of the furniture. As Calder stared at him, still half-asleep, still half-entangled in his nightmare, the clouds that must have covered the moon moved on, flooding the room with an eerie silver light.

A fragment of that light caught on the nickel-blue barrel of the dueling pistol clasped in William's hands.

"I'll say you were killed by robbers," he said in an odd, strained voice, "rebel deserters who broke in looking for gold and whiskey. Everyone will believe me, just like before."

Calder dared not move, either slowly or suddenly. "Put down the gun," he said in a low, even voice. "They *won't* believe you, William. This is murder, and you'll surely hang for it."

He might not have spoken for all the response he received.

"I hope you burn in hell," William said, and then light blazed from the pistol's barrel. There was an explosion, though Calder couldn't tell whether it had come from within himself or outside, and then there was only darkness.

CHAPTER
❧14❧

William watched dispassionately as Calder sank back against his pillows, a strangled, gurgling sound coming from somewhere deep inside him. In the moonlight William made out the torn place just below Calder's right nipple, and saw the matting of dark chest hair turn slick and crimson with blood.

The elder brother moved to turn up the lights, the dueling pistol dangling from his left hand now, resting hot against his thigh, burning right through his trouser leg.

There were murmurings in the hallway, and sounds of rushing this way and that, but William felt no urgency, no fear. Smiling grimly, he drew up a chair next to Calder's bed and sat down to watch him die.

The world, he told himself, would be better off without the likes of Calder Holbrook—if indeed he was entitled to the surname at all—just as it was better off without tramps like Marie.

Calder was unconscious, but even then he struggled, and a muscle in William's jaw tightened. Perhaps, he reflected coolly, it would be necessary to reload the pistol and fire a second bullet. This time the barrel would be pressed to Calder's throbbing temple.

"Maeve," Calder choked, though he had not roused. "*Maeve*—"

The bedclothes were sodden with blood now, William noted with satisfaction. Surely no one could lose so much and still live.

He settled back in his chair, undisturbed by the continued noise beyond Calder's bedroom door. It might as well have been another country, that hallway. Another world.

William relaxed, stretching out his legs and crossing his booted feet. "I don't suppose anyone will believe that story I made up about robbers," he mused aloud, half to himself and half to Calder.

Just then Prudence burst in, massive in her nightdress and wrapper. "What's happened in here—" she began, but then her eyes found Calder, and she gave a weeping scream and trundled to his bedside. "Sweet Jesus in heaven, you done shot him!" she cried. "You done murdered your own brother—"

William sighed as Prudence tried to staunch Calder's blood-flow with the corner of her wrapper. She was wailing in despair all the while, and when a cluster of other servants jammed into the doorway to gawk, she shouted for someone to get a doctor, and after that a constable.

Meanwhile, a storm was rising outside, and the wind rattled the sturdy leaded windows in their frames.

"I did the right thing by killing him, Prudence," William said calmly. "He's a bad seed—evil, just like his mama was. You'll come to see that, all in good time."

Prudence left her patient long enough to round the bed and snatch the dueling pistol from William's limp grasp. "You gone crazy, that's what," the housekeeper said wetly. "You gone plum out of your mind!"

She stormed back to Calder and laid the dueling pistol on the other nightstand.

"What made you do such a thing, Mr. William? Ain't there been enough grief and sufferin' in this house over the years?"

William didn't mind answering the question. In fact, he was certain that, once he had, no further explanations would be required of him. He looked at Calder, whose flesh was pallorous and gray—except, of course, where the blood soaked him—and could not disguise the hatred he felt.

"I stayed here, all those years, and learned the banking business. I did what Papa wanted, always. I put aside my own wishes, my own dreams, to honor his." William felt his very soul contort within him; it was an ugly pain. "Calder here was the prodigal, fancy free, and his briefest appearance in this house was cause for killing the fatted calf. Still, fool that I was, I believed Papa appreciated my sacrifices, that someday I would be rewarded for my loyalty. And what happened? Papa left everything to Calder—the house, the bank, the fortunes we made together. All of it was Calder's, except, of course, for a pittance of an income earmarked for me."

"Dear Jesus, save us," Prudence muttered. She'd taken off the wrapper now and made a bandage of sorts, but

William knew her efforts were hopeless. The white flannel she pressed to the wound was already turning scarlet. "You had no call to do this—Mr. Calder would have done right by you. I don't think he even wanted this old house, nor much money, neither."

William recalled the things Calder had said earlier, in the family dining room. He *had* claimed that he didn't want any of their father's bequests, but William hadn't believed it then and he didn't believe it now. How could anyone fail to want all that surrounded him, and with the full measure of his soul at that?

Monumental as it was, his father's final betrayal wasn't the whole reason for what William had done. Somehow Calder had found out the truth about the night Marie died, and he'd sworn revenge. However mild his tone, Calder had meant what he said. He would have dogged William to his very grave, making him wonder, making him sweat.

William offered none of that to Prudence, though, for she had always favored Calder over him, just the way Bernard Holbrook had done.

"You hold on, precious," Prudence was murmuring close to Calder's ear. "You just hold on—don't you go off nowheres. I won't have you dead and hauntin' this place, and always gettin' underfoot when I'm tryin' to get my work done!"

William closed his eyes as the muscles at his nape clenched.

The constable and an army doctor arrived at the same time.

"It was him," William heard Prudence say, and of course he knew without looking that she was pointing a finger in his direction. "He done shot his own brother. And over money, too."

William was hauled, none too ceremoniously, to his feet, by the redheaded, blue-eyed policeman. "Afraid you'll have to come away with me, Mr. Holbrook," the big Irishman said.

The doctor had already torn off his suit coat and begun working over Calder.

"It's hopeless," William told him pleasantly as his hands were wrenched behind him by the Irishman and bound with heavy iron cuffs.

The physician spared him one scathing glance and returned to his futile efforts.

Lisette's lair, a beautifully appointed tomb intended for some ancient and very important Chinese personage, was empty.

Maeve examined everything—the pyre, made entirely of ivory and inlaid with twenty-four-karat gold, the chests brimming with treasure, the many jade carvings. The mummified being for which the crypt had been created was gone, but in an anteroom she found horrible evidence that Lisette had spent time here.

One of the mortal lovers for which she was so noted, a handsome young man, sat upright in a chair, dead. He looked more like a wax statue than a corpse, and on a small table before him rested a cup and an exquisite porcelain teapot.

"It would seem the poor lad died under sociable circumstances, at least," Dathan observed. "I'll wager there isn't a drop of blood left in him."

Maeve shivered as a spider crawled out the spout of the teapot and scurried across the tabletop to perch on one of the corpse's gray fingers. "There's no need to give an accounting," she said. "I have eyes of my own and I can see what's happened here."

Dathan sighed. "At least he didn't get himself turned into one of those vile creatures Lisette has been plaguing us with these past weeks."

It was a small consolation to Maeve. This young man, whoever he was, reminded her of Aidan. He'd had friends and a family, no doubt, and he'd been allotted a share of too-brief, precious years to live and laugh beneath the sun. Lisette had robbed him, carefully and indiscriminately, of a gift stemming from the very heart of the universe.

"He must have displeased her somehow," Maeve said sadly. She laid one hand on the lad's shoulders and was sickened to feel it crumble like dry clay under the fabric of his well-tailored waistcoat.

"Do you think she'll return?" Dathan asked. "Perhaps we have only to wait for her here."

Maeve shook her head. "No—I'm afraid it won't be so easy as that. Lisette is through with this place—she wanted us to find it, find her dead lover, and be frustrated."

"Well." Dathan heaved out a heavy sigh and thrust one hand through his hair. "Her plan certainly worked."

Maeve was looking at the corpse, now leaning ludicrously to one side because of the damage to his shoulder. "She seems to favor these dark-haired, blue-eyed lads, the younger and more good-natured and gullible the better. My brother, Aidan, was her lover for a while, before she turned him into a vampire, and there have been many others. A striking number of whom were of similar appearance, now that I think about it." She stopped and fixed her gaze on Dathan's grim face. "Have you any warlocks in your army who resemble this poor wretch?"

A light went on in Dathan's eyes, one of irritation. "A

number of them," he confirmed quietly. "You want to trap Lisette, lure her by placing one of my more winsome followers under her nose. Brilliant, except that she'll undoubtedly recognize him for a warlock at first glance."

Maeve raised an eyebrow and then explained patiently, "Vampires recognize warlocks by reading their minds, so to speak. If the warlock in question can be made to believe he is a man, then blood-drinkers will accept him at his own estimate."

Now Dathan looked intrigued and thoughtful. "You're aware, of course, that you've just given me a powerful tool with which to deceive vampires, once this current calamity has been thwarted and things go back to normal?"

"Which means that you owe me something in return."

"What?" Dathan asked, moving out of the mortal's eternal resting place and into the main part of the tomb. He busied himself pocketing gold bracelets and strings of pearls taken from one of the chests while Maeve framed her reply.

"I want you to teach me the incantation that enables you to start fires," she said finally.

Dathan looked at her over one shoulder. "I would be a fool to do that. You could teach it to your vampires, and they'd use it against us."

"I would share it with a select few," Maeve countered. "And you have my word that it would be used against your kind only in self-defense."

"Your word," Dathan mocked, slamming the lid of the chest he'd been looting. "The word of a vampire is hardly something I hold in esteem."

Maeve could feel her strength fading. She sat down on the edge of the ivory pyre where Lisette had probably passed many days. "I have told you one of our secrets. I have trusted you with my very life—you've had numerous opportunities to drive a stake through my heart while I slept. If I can trust you that much, then you can surely give me the same consideration in return and teach me one small incantation!''

Dathan crossed the room and lifted Maeve into his arms. "No sleeping here, princess," he said with grudging affection. "Our intent is to surprise Lisette, not be surprised by her. Think of someplace in England, someplace dark, and I'll be with you at sunset."

Maeve was exhausted, her head lolling against Dathan's shoulder, but it wasn't England she fixed in her mind, but America. In fact, she focused on Pennsylvania and the dark cellar beneath Calder's house.

Reaching that place, she crouched behind stacks of dusty boxes and crates and closed her eyes.

Only then, when she was helpless, did images of Calder dying come to her mind. She saw him bandaged, lying unconscious in his bed upstairs, his skin bluish from the loss of blood, but there was nothing she could do. She was trapped, mired, in the deepest, darkest part of her own mind.

All during the coming day, immersed in the vampire sleep, vivid pictures came to her, like scenes from a dream, and she heard him calling her name. Calling it over and over again, the voice growing fainter with every passing moment, and more hopeless.

The rain went on throughout the night and the morning, casting an added pall over the circuslike ceremony at Bernard Holbrook's graveside. Word of the shooting in the Holbrook mansion had gotten out fast, and folks had come from every corner of the city, whether they'd known the dear departed or not, to stare and speculate.

God knew, the undertaker thought disgustedly, it would be years before folks stopped chattering about how one brother had shot the other one in his bed, while their dead father lay downstairs in his coffin, and how William Holbrook had been brought to the funeral in handcuffs.

It was a damn pity, all of it, though there was *one* redeeming element in that ugly situation. Poor Bernard was at peace, and he'd never have to know that he'd spawned a murderer.

Not that Calder Holbrook was the kind of son a man relished having, either. He'd been stubborn his whole life through, that boy, tormented by things inside him that no one else could see, and he'd broken his father's heart on more than one occasion with his cussedness.

The undertaker sighed. Well, Calder was barely clinging to life; that was a fact, for he'd been to the house and seen the young man lying in his bed, unconscious, with half the blood in his body drained away.

Like as not, there'd be another funeral in a few days, and when they hanged William Holbrook, still another.

It made a man wonder, that it did. Bernard Holbrook had worked hard all his life, and if he hadn't always been completely ethical, well, a fellow did what he had to do to make his way. And now it was all gone, blown apart like a house built of matchsticks struck by a high wind.

When sunset came, Maeve bolted upright.

All thoughts of Lisette and the impending disaster of war with the angels were barred from her mind. She cared for nothing and no one but Calder, and she transported herself to his room immediately.

He was indeed dying, just as she had seen in the awful visions while she slept, and his soul had already left his body, bobbing at the far end of the long silver cord that attaches the two, ready to break free. When that happened, Calder would be truly dead, for once the cord is severed, there is no returning.

A heavy woman in simple calico sat next to the bed, weeping quietly, but she did not look up when Maeve approached on the opposite side because she could not see or hear her.

Maeve looked with despair upon her lover and found in the murky shallows of his brain the events that had brought him to such an end. William Holbrook had crept into the room with a dueling pistol, stood at the foot of the bed, and shot his only brother, intending to kill him.

She would go back, she decided, to the night before, when this travesty had taken place, and undo it. She would kill William if she had to, to prevent this from happening.

When Maeve tried to transport herself, however, her efforts were blocked. In a fury of urgency and despair, she tried twice more, and twice more she failed.

She needed no explanation for what had happened, for Valerian had explained such matters to her long since. Sometimes, for unknown reasons, time travel simply wasn't possible.

Maeve gave up on the attempt to change recent history and instead concentrated on turning herself into a mist, pervading Calder's being, lending him strength. For a while she was truly a part of him, as close as the breath in his lungs and the thready beat of his heart. Then, suddenly, the shimmering silver cord contracted, wrenching his spirit back into its prison of flesh and blood. The sheer force of the event drove Maeve outside of him again.

The housekeeper, probably sensing that something

was going on in that room that she couldn't see or hear, grew restless, folded her hands, and began to pray under her breath. Her words were like liquid fire, pouring over Maeve in waves, but Maeve did not flee.

No matter what she had to suffer, she wasn't going to leave Calder.

She huddled in a corner of the room, in the shadows, and presently the housekeeper yawned and went away.

Maeve made herself solid again and hurried to Calder's side, taking one unresponsive hand into both her own. His spirit had retreated again, straining at the invisible tether, trying to escape the pain.

The best and most unselfish thing to do was let Calder go, let him return to his Maker and be received in that place where she could never venture, and she loved him enough to do just that.

She raised her hand to her lips and brushed the knuckles with a kiss as light as the pass of a feather. "Good-bye, my darling," she whispered. Then she rose and turned away, and would have departed forever, except that he spoke to her.

Not with his lips, but with his mind.

Maeve. The name was an entreaty.

She whirled to stare at him, waiting, her whole being suspended. Her soul cried out silently to his, begging him to stay.

Help me.

Maeve was in agony. *I am helping you, darling. Look for the Light, and follow it.*

You are the light.

No! Don't you see? I am the darkness.

Don't leave me, Maeve. Don't let me die.

She took a step closer to Calder, standing at his

bedside. Without another word, she lay down beside him, covered him in her cloak, and thought of London.

If there was a way under heaven to save Calder, besides turning him into a fiend, like herself, into a being who would one day hate her for her trouble, Maeve vowed she would find it.

Dimity was out of practice when it came to time travel, and she made several abortive efforts before she landed herself in the middle of Valerian's cell.

The place was rank, and a half dozen frail-boned, ragged humans slept in a pile in the corner, like puppies huddling on a cold night. All of them were alive, but they would need to consume a great deal of calves' liver before their blood could truly serve them again.

"Valerian?" Dimity said, annoyed, placing her hands on her hips. "Show yourself!"

He appeared suddenly, directly in front of her, and made her jump backward with a little cry of fright.

"What the—?"

Valerian's grin was a bit wan, but just as audacious as ever. "Sorry," he said, though he plainly wasn't. "It gets boring, being stuck away in a rat's nest like this one, so I've taken to practicing my magic."

Dimity looked around the gloomy cell. "Well, it's no palace, of course, but it could be worse." She nodded toward the pile of rags and flesh in the corner. "At least Lisette's kept you well fed, and you don't look as if you've been abused—only neglected."

Valerian drew himself up to his full and haughty height at that point and glared down his patrician nose. "She's been fattening me up like a Christmas goose," he said, "and I'll thank you not to minimize my sufferings until you've been through a similar ordeal yourself."

She affected a sigh. "All right," she conceded. "If you want my sympathy, you have it. Now, are you through with your travail, or would you like to enjoy it a little while longer? If you're quite satisfied that you've undergone sufficient agony, then let's discuss getting you out of here."

Valerian flushed, a sign of recent feeding more than anger, and narrowed his eyes at her. "You are a most caustic individual, for one who avails herself to the favors of angels."

Dimity glared. "And you are a hardheaded, arrogant idiot," she retorted, standing her ground. She was not acquainted with Valerian, although she'd often heard of his exploits, but she had encountered plenty of creatures just like him, both human and immortal. She knew only too well that if she allowed it, he'd run roughshod over her. "Do you wish me to rescue you, or leave you here to rot?"

The legendary vampire was plainly furious, and no doubt his pride was injured as well. After all, he'd been captured by a vampire of the feminine gender, and now his only hope of salvation was in the hands of yet another female.

Dimity smiled. A little humility was good for the soul. "Well?" she prompted.

"All right," the great Valerian snarled. "*Yes*, of course I want to get out of here—I feel like a mouse shut up in a shoe box! But how do you propose to achieve this magnificent feat? Have you grown more powerful than Lisette and failed to mention the fact heretofore?"

Dimity rolled her eyes. "Lisette grows careless. There are weaknesses in the mental barrier she's put up around you, or I wouldn't have been able to get in." She crossed the room to the heavy iron door and fixed her gaze on the ancient, cumbersome lock.

"There's no point in attempting *that* old trick," Valerian said. "I've tried to move that lock a hundred times, and it won't give."

A smile came to Dimity's lips as the works splintered inside the lock under the force of her thoughts. "I guess you just didn't try hard enough," she said sweetly. "Who's guarding you?"

Valerian's exasperation was plain, but so was his relief. "A conniving, back-stabbing little chit named Shaleen," he said. "I like her."

Dimity swung open the door and stepped into the stone passageway beyond. "You would," she replied. "Come along. I've found this whole experience a little enervating, frankly, and I'd like to get back to London and my beloved nineteenth century in time for an extra feeding."

" 'I've found this whole experience a little enervating,' " Valerian mimicked sourly, following her along the hall. Dimity imagined it would be quite some time before he got over his pique at being saved by a lesser vampire. "You haven't saved me yet," he said aloud, reminding her that he was an old blood-drinker, like herself, and a skilled one.

"You're right," she replied diplomatically. "Let's try to be civil to each other, shall we? After all, we're both up to our necks—if you'll forgive the expression—in trouble."

As if on cue, a shape rose up ahead of them in the corridor, with a soul-splintering shriek.

"Please," Valerian said contemptuously.

For one terrible moment Dimity thought the creature confronting them was Lisette itself, and that Valerian had further sealed their doom by mocking her, but a closer inspection revealed the little spitfire Valerian had mentioned before, the fledgling called Shaleen.

"Step aside," Dimity ordered quietly. "You must know, naive as you are, that you haven't the strength to prevail over two mature vampires."

Shaleen seemed to wilt, until she looked like what she'd been before her making, a scrap of a girl who'd never had enough love or food, enough of anything, in the whole brief span of her mortal life. "I want to go with you," she said. "The queen will stake me out in the courtyard to burn in the daylight if she comes back and finds that her prize captive has escaped."

Valerian nudged Dimity from behind. "She'll make a handy soldier in our present trouble, with that fiery spirit of hers."

"I suppose you want to be her tutor," Dimity said dryly. "I don't think you're going to have the time, though. Maeve seems to think she needs your help to prevail against Lisette."

There was a scrabbling sound behind them, and Dimity whirled, as did Valerian, to see the pale boys creeping out of the cell and groping their way along the wall in the other direction.

Shaleen pushed between Valerian and Dimity to stop them, but Valerian caught her arm as she passed. It was then that Dimity got her first glimpse of the peculiar nobility that was as much a part of the fabled vampire beside her as his blatant hedonism and his deft sarcasm.

"Let them go," he said.

Shaleen's face was a study in angry confusion. "But why? Why did you suffer them to live? It's not as though they matter at all—"

"Everything matters," Valerian said, his voice firm but

kind as well. "Now, come with us. We blood-drinkers have far weightier things to contend with than a pack of anemic beggars and thieves."

Shaleen cast another greedy glance after the victims she'd no doubt gathered herself for the prisoner she both feared and admired, but then she slipped off in the other direction, leading the way.

"There's a weak place, here," she said finally when they came to a little chamber at the end of a virtual rabbit's warren of twists and turns. "It's how I get in and out with the lads for this one's supper." She nodded her tousled head in Valerian's direction. "Herself didn't want him to have no supper, you know, but I couldn't stand to think of it."

Valerian grinned and reached out with one graceful hand to muss the girl's hair, and she beamed at this attention.

Dimity was impatient. "Come," she snapped, raising her arms. "Lisette might return at any moment, and I for one do not want to be invited into her parlor for tea."

Valerian found Maeve in the echoing chamber on the uppermost floor of her London house, working feverishly at her loom. The tapestry had lengthened considerably since he'd last viewed it, but the vampire took no time to examine it again. Instead he stared, confounded, at the bloodless, near-dead mortal lying on a pallet beside the towering windows, awash in moonlight.

"Calder Holbrook," he muttered, both irritated and confused.

Maeve whirled, for she hadn't sensed his presence, and in looking at her Valerian knew why. She was almost gaunt, and there were enormous shadows under her eyes.

"Valerian," she half sobbed, half whispered, and ran to him.

He enfolded her in his arms, this vampire he had made more than two hundred years ago, and for the first time wished that he'd left her alone that fateful night. At least then she'd have been spared whatever cancerous grief was devouring her now.

"Look at you," she said, her sunken eyes too bright as she took in his splendid tunic of dark gold velvet and the sleek leggings that matched. "You look like a duke or an earl."

"I've been in a sixteenth-century mood of late." The explanation was inane, in light of the suffering he saw in Maeve. "What has happened?" he demanded in an urgent whisper, glancing once again at the mortal still lying senseless on his pallet. "I beg of you—tell me how to help you!"

CHAPTER
❖15❖

"The last thing this world needs is another vampire," Valerian said, the frown he'd worn throughout Maeve's explanation still in place. He glanced thoughtfully at Calder, who stirred on his deathbed, just beneath the surface of consciousness. "On the other hand, the soul in question is his own. If he wants to be a blood-drinker, then it seems to me that he has the right to make that choice."

Maeve had been over the same arguments in her own mind, with tedious attention to detail. In fact, the dilemma had tortured her, sapped her strength and dulled her wits—all this at a time when she most needed all her powers.

She looked at Calder, one hand over her heart, and

whispered, "He'll hate me for it someday, just the way Aidan hated Lisette."

Out of the corner of her eye, Maeve saw the great vampire wince—though not, she was sure, at the mention of Lisette, but that of Aidan. He had loved her brother, she knew, with a poetic poignancy that transcended simple sex, vampire or mortal, and it was likely that he still cherished those feelings.

"That's a selfish argument," Valerian observed gruffly. He crouched beside Calder's pallet and touched his waxen face with gentle fingers. "How have you kept him alive this long?"

Maeve hesitated before revealing her terrible secret. "I've been giving him blood—just small infusions of it—in the hope of sustaining him until he rallies from his own strength."

Valerian's magnificent features tightened, and his eyes flashed. "The process is already begun, then," he said in a brusque whisper. "Great Zeus, Maeve, it's a miracle he hasn't become one of those wretched *things* Lisette has been plaguing us with!"

She swayed under the shock of the older vampire's words and gripped the framework of one of the tall windows to steady herself. "*What*?"

Kneeling now, Valerian bared Calder's throat with one hand, all the while gazing up at Maeve with fiery frustration in his violet eyes. "You've never wanted to make a vampire, to my knowledge, so I saw no reason to explain the process." His thumb stroked the fragile skin over Calder's jugular vein gently, almost caressingly, as he spoke. "There is no halfway measure, Maeve. Vampires can give blood to each other, but it is very dangerous with humans. How do you think Lisette made those dreadful creatures of hers? By subjecting them to only part of the process! It's the very reason they have no logic, no individuality, but only unrelenting, terrible hunger."

Maeve covered her mouth with one hand to stifle a cry of pain at what she might have done to Calder. "Why didn't I just let him die?" she pleaded. "Why?"

"There is no time for self-recrimination now, my darling," Valerian scolded, but with the utmost gentleness. "Steps must be taken to rectify what you've done—if not, he'll become an enemy, one we'll have to destroy."

She sank to her knees at the foot of Calder's pallet, watching with both hope and horror as Valerian bent over the love of her immortal life and began the transformation. She wanted to look away a hundred times, nay, a thousand, as the vampire emptied Calder of his blood, but that would have been a form of disloyalty, of cowardice. So she kept her terrible vigil.

Calder was, for all practical intents and purposes, dead during those moments before Valerian sunk his fangs into that fragile flesh again and restored the blood, changed.

At last Valerian thrust himself away from Calder, a gleam of some unholy satisfaction in his eyes, and rose gracefully to his feet. "Now," he said, "if this fledgling wishes to hate anyone for his transfiguration, let him hate me."

Maeve stood and moved around to the side of the pallet to look down into Calder's face. He was still asleep, but the lines of suffering were smoothed away by some inner magic even as she watched. He seemed larger somehow, his body harder and more powerful.

"We'd best move him to a safer place," Valerian

suggested with a sigh. "He cannot bear the sunlight any more than we can."

Maeve nodded, closed her arms around Calder, and willed the both of them to the dank gloom of the secret part of the cellar were she herself reposed. Valerian, a showman at heart, was there before them and in the process of lighting the candles.

"What will happen now?" Maeve asked when Calder had been settled comfortably on the slab. She had had no experience with the making of vampires, as Valerian had pointed out earlier, and did not remember anything helpful about her own metamorphosis.

"The transformation has already begun, of course," Valerian said. "He's lying there, wide awake and cognizant of everything we say and do, but unable to communicate in any way." He moved to Calder's side, touched his shoulder with that same tenderness he had exhibited before. "Do not worry, fledgling," he said gently. "Do not struggle. In a day, or perhaps two, you will be completely functional."

After a moment of thoughtful silence, Valerian turned his attention to Maeve. "I would suggest, my love, that you leave your darling in the care of another vampire, one less vital to our cause, and join the rest of us in the effort to save ourselves."

Maeve nodded, though the reluctance she felt at the idea of abandoning Calder, especially now, was a keen sorrow in itself. "Yes, you're right, of course—but who can we trust?"

"Trust?" Valerian smiled grimly and arched one eyebrow. "Why, no one, Your Majesty—perhaps not even each other. Still, I know of a fledgling who is most anxious to endear herself to me—a thought should be sufficient summons." With that, he closed his eyes, and an instant later a young, brown-haired snippet appeared in the room with an unceremonious crash, toppling several crates and boxes.

"What the bloody hell?" she screeched in a voice that made Maeve want to put her hands over her ears. The new arrival focused her spritely brown gaze on Valerian, then a glorious smile spread across her smudged face. "Oh, it's you, then!"

Valerian shook his head. "Yes, it's me. Where are those pretty clothes I gave you, chit? And how do you manage to stay sooty as a chimney pot even after a washing?"

The young vampire looked chagrined and, at the same time, very pleased that Valerian had taken notice of her in any way. She would have blushed splendidly, had she been a mortal creature; instead, she simply turned to Maeve and executed an awkward curtsy.

"Pleased to make your acquaintance, mum," she said.

"This is Shaleen," Valerian explained with a smile in his eyes.

Maeve smiled herself, for the first time since before Calder's shooting. Valerian was the most ferocious of vampires and, some said, the most ruthless, and yet he loved playing the mentor. Now that she thought of it, Maeve could not remember a time when he hadn't had some fledgling under tutelage—herself, for instance, and Aidan, and others too numerous to name.

"How do you do?" Maeve said grandly, extending her hand to the feisty little spitfire and hoping she wasn't making a mistake in abandoning Calder to her care.

"Enough of the social refinements," Valerian snapped, suddenly impatient with the whole proceeding. "There is a war on, in case you've both forgotten." He gestured toward Calder. "This one has just been changed. We'll be wanting you to look after him, stand guard, so to speak. You've had experience with that, now haven't you?''

Shaleen quailed a little under Valerian's fierce glare, but then she made a visible effort to muster her pride and succeeded to a degree. "I'll look after him, all right. Won't no mortals come and stake him, I'll see to it personal—"

Valerian closed his eyes for a moment, a study in impatient grandeur. "We are quite convinced," he said sternly.

His apprentice subsided, chagrined. "Well, then," she murmured, dragging a crate over for use as a chair and taking up her post beside Calder, "I'll just button me lip, then, won't I?''

Maeve's amusement ebbed as she thought of leaving Calder, especially in so fragile a state, but she knew she must not tarry. She went to the other side of the slab where her lover lay, opposite the bristly, determined Shaleen, and bent to kiss his mouth.

"I'll be back soon, darling," she whispered. "Please don't be afraid."

"Great Zeus," Valerian snapped, gesturing wildly with one arm toward the greater world beyond that cellar, "we're about to be overrun by legions of avenging angels! Must we dally in this dusty pit all night?''

Maeve laid her ear to Calder's chest, hearing no heartbeat, feeling no rise and fall of breathing, and knew an infinite sorrow, as well as joy. They would be together for eternity, if they were fortunate, rich with power and full of strength, and yet Calder's soul had been stolen this night, and she'd been a party to the theft.

She felt Valerian's hands come to rest on her shoulders, gentle, elegant, and firm. He spoke quietly.

"There can be no looking back now, Maeve. It'll turn

you into a pillar of salt, like Lot's wife, and rob you of all your power."

She turned, looked up into his dark purple eyes, and nodded. "You're right," she said.

Valerian took her hands in his own, and they raised their arms high, in a graceful, simultaneous motion, and then they vanished, Shaleen's parting words echoing in their ears.

"Coo, mate!" she cried, no doubt elbowing Calder in the ribs at the same time. "Did you see that?"

Lisette gave a snarling shriek of outrage when she found Valerian's cell empty, and the new vampire, Shaleen, gone as well.

Fools! Did they truly believe they could escape her so easily? Why, when she found those two she'd bind them to trees and burn them, like Joan of Arc at her stake, as a lesson to all vampires!

She dropped to her knees in the fetid straw, clutching her middle, as the troublesome weakness struck her. It was that rebel Maeve Tremayne's fault that she suffered now—Lisette had not been the same since their battle in that cave, far away in China.

She'd been sorely tried in that confrontation, and injured, and she had had to console herself by lying in her crypt beneath the cellar of her villa on the coast of Spain for several days and nights, with two captive mortal lovers to sustain her.

Even now, curled up in the straw of that miserable castle in the north of Scotland, a bleak spot abandoned even in Bonnie Prince Charlie's day and naught but a ruin in modern times, Lisette smiled at the memory of the pleasures she'd taken.

First, she'd prowled the city in her carriage, finding

one luscious boy and then another. She'd taken them to her villa, gotten them drunk on wine bottled before their great-grandfathers were born, and then taught them passion, one by one.

Finally she'd taken them, sated and senseless, to her hiding place deep beneath the floor of the cellar, and slept, waking only long enough to feed off one or the other.

They'd been dead when she left them, both of them, for she hadn't wanted to go to the effort of making the poor lads into vampires.

She frowned, recollecting another experience.

She'd selected Aidan Tremayne for her favors, one night beside a seventeenth-century road, and taught him ecstasy so keen that each of their trysts had left him dazed and drunk with pleasure. Eventually she'd given her cherished Aidan the ultimate gift, immortality, and he'd thanked her by calling her cursed, by hating and reviling her.

Lisette raised herself, both hands braced against the filthy carpet of straw. That, she thought bitterly, was why she'd turned no more of her lovely boys into nightwalkers. They were just too thick to comprehend, those ungrateful creatures, that they'd been translated from mere clay to virtual gods.

A strange exhaustion felled her, and she dropped to the floor again, overcome by the need to sleep. She would find Valerian and the miscreant, Shaleen, later, along with a fine-looking mortal lad to nourish her. In the meantime, though, she'd just rest a little while.

Calder was awake, inside his hardened husk of a body, just as he'd heard Valerian assert earlier, but he could not so much as twitch a muscle or force the weakest murmur past his lips.

He tried to piece together his shattered memories, in an effort to make sense of what was happening, but he remembered only two things at first—William firing the bullet that had in effect killed him, and the terrible, fiery elation he'd known when Valerian had drawn the very blood from his veins and then given it back again, forever changed.

He groped forward mentally, and more came to him. Things were definitely falling into place.

He, the late Calder Holbrook, was now a vampire, an immortal creature with the power to travel through time and space at will. Granted, he wouldn't be able to go backward very far—Maeve had told him once that a blood-drinker could venture only so far as the instant following his own death. Since this had occurred so recently, there was no point in going back.

Still, the future was his. As soon as he was able to move, he would go forward to the final years of the twentieth century and begin soaking up the knowledge he craved. He would soon understand all the newest surgical techniques, know how to mix chemicals into miraculous drugs. Then, *then* he would return to his own century, and save as many of the soldiers, as many of the suffering children, as he could.

Calder's thoughts returned, as he suspected they always would, to Maeve. He knew, even in his distracted state, that he was somehow tethered to her, and he blessed the fact. She would be the center of his life, the sunshine he must now foreswear, the light he warmed himself by, now and forever, world without end, amen and amen.

He tried again to move, and again found the effort to be futile.

Valerian pervaded his mind, that imperious and arrogant vampire whom he had mistrusted and disliked from their first encounter. Like it or not, Calder reflected, with a sigh of the spirit, a bond existed between them now. In a very real sense, Valerian had sired him into the new and exciting life that lay waiting, just ahead.

He struggled, eager to regain consciousness and begin that life, and felt a cool hand come to rest on his forehead, one so small that it might have belonged to a child.

"There now," a youthful, feminine voice chided, "just lie still and don't be so impatient. You'll be prowlin' the night soon enough, I'll wager, and a pretty fellow you is, too."

Calder felt the forces of his changing body trying to overcome him, push him under the dark, glimmering surface into oblivion. They wanted to get on with the business of transformation, those forces, and Calder hadn't the strength or the will to counter them.

He relaxed his roiling emotions, soothed his tempestuous mind, and went under.

The old manse was tucked away in the English countryside, long-deserted, overgrown with vines and ivy, almost certainly purported by the locals to be haunted, and Maeve could see that Valerian loved the place on sight. It would, she supposed, appeal to his macabre sense of humor to make mysterious lights appear in the windows on occasion and send out the odd bone-chilling shriek just for the sake of drama.

Dathan stepped out of a shadowy, cobwebbed corner, seeming to form himself from the particles of dust and darkness that made up the night. He raised his arms, causing his cloak to spread like wings, and grinned.

"Perfect, isn't it?" he asked cordially, though Maeve immediately sensed the chilly wariness that had sprung up between the warlock and Valerian.

Valerian nodded, his jawline unusually taut. "All it needs is a bubbling cauldron and some cackling crones," he said evenly.

Dathan laughed, but the sound had a jagged edge. "Stereotypes," he scolded. "You don't sleep in a casket, do you, Vampire? Nor, I trust, would a necklace of garlic put you to flight."

Maeve interceded, worried by the growing tension. Dathan and Valerian would be no good against Lisette and her forces if they were battling each other. "Stop it," she said, stepping between the pair and laying a calming hand to each of their chests. She gave Valerian a warning glance, then turned to look into Dathan's unreadable eyes. "Why did you summon us here?"

The warlock smiled indulgently, every inch the suave country host, but Maeve was not misled. Dathan was about as warm and welcoming as one of those twentieth-century knives—switchblades, she believed they were called.

"I have something to show you—" he said, shifting his gaze to Valerian's glowering countenance only after stretching the moment to very uncomfortable lengths. "—both."

Beyond the crumbling stone walls of the manse, in the luxurious, black-velvet darkness of that isolated place, something howled.

Maeve and Valerian exchanged a quick glance as they followed Dathan deeper into the old cottage.

No owl, that, Valerian observed in a mental undertone

that somehow crept beneath Dathan's level of awareness.

I know you'll protect me, Maeve teased in response.

They had entered what had probably been a parlor at one time, and even though they could all see as clearly as cats, Dathan went through the formality of lighting the nubs of tallow spilling messily from an old candelabra.

Maeve took in the chandelier, draped with dust, the worn organ that only the mice played now, the stained and peeling wallpaper, and imagined the ghostly forms of a dozen long-dead vicars moving about, colliding with each other.

"A very colorful thought," Valerian commented with quiet amusement, making no effort to keep the conversation private this time. "Rather like that attraction in Disneyland."

Dathan cast a scathing glance at the clearly unwelcome vampire towering beside Maeve, and then clapped his hands together with brisk authority.

Immediately two warlocks entered the room from deeper inside the house, the dining room probably, escorting a young man between them.

Both Valerian and Maeve cried out, in despairing shock, for this enchanted wretch was their Aidan, the one they had both loved and lost.

Valerian found his voice first. "What have you done to him?" he rasped, springing forward as if to free the poor captive from the warlocks' hold. He whirled on Dathan, grasped his flowing shirt in both hands, and wrenched him onto the balls of his feet. "God damn your black soul, *what have you done?*"

"It's all right, Valerian," Maeve said gently, for after the first shock she'd realized that, however perfect the resemblance, this was not her brother. She ventured close and touched the seemingly frozen, breathtakingly handsome face tentatively. "Aidan is far away and quite safe. This is only someone who looks like him."

Dathan shook himself free of Valerian's grip, his eyes glittering with a suppressed thirst for vengeance, and nodded. "Very astute, Your Majesty. This is Llewellyn, one of our own. We've tampered with his mind a bit, as you suggested, and when he comes out of this stupor we've so mercifully induced, he'll believe with all his treacherous little heart that he's mortal."

Valerian looked confused, and started to speak, but Maeve stopped him by reaching out to grasp his forearm.

"Ingenious," she said.

"What is the purpose of this?" Valerian demanded, exasperated.

Maeve walked around Llewellyn, studying him in amazement. If it hadn't been for the connection between herself and her twin brother, she would have believed this creature, this warlock, to be Aidan—sweet, stubborn, *human* Aidan.

"Smooth your feathers and think for a moment, Vampire," Dathan said. "How do you believe Lisette would react, were she to encounter our brilliant creation?"

Maeve sensed the quickening in Valerian as, at last, he made the connection.

He muttered an amazed exclamation and peered into the exquisitely molded face of the warlock who would, when fully conscious again, wholeheartedly believe himself to be an ordinary man.

"Did he look this much like Aidan Tremayne in the beginning," Valerian wondered aloud, "or did you alter him somehow?"

Dathan sighed, as if weary of silly questions. "There was a resemblance—rather faint really. We accentuated it, knowing of the lovely Lisette's special fancy for Tremayne. Now the question is, how do we draw her notice to our lad here?"

Valerian flung a testy glance at the warlock. "And I was so certain that you'd thought of everything."

Dathan seethed but, with visible effort, managed to control his temper. "If that were so," he replied in a strange, purring growl, "then we'd have no need of you, would we, Vampire?"

Valerian took a step toward Dathan, and again Maeve moved between them.

"Once Lisette has taken the bait and poisoned herself with the blood of this lovely warlock," she said, "the two of you may feel free to ravage each other. In the meantime, everything we hold precious is at stake, and our only hope is to work together!"

"Take the lad to Spain," Valerian said moments later in a hoarse, grudging whisper. He named an obscure village. "Lisette has a villa there, on the coast. Wherever she is, she's attuned to that place, and she'll sense his presence and come to him."

Maeve stared at him. "You knew of this villa, and yet you said nothing?"

Valerian shook his head. "I had forgotten. Seeing Llewellyn here brought back memories."

It was plain enough that the memories in question involved Aidan, but Maeve didn't pursue the subject because it was so obviously personal.

"To Spain, then," Dathan said, clapping his hands again.

After Llewellyn had been led to the entrance of an especially lively cantina, Dathan broke the spell that had rendered him catatonic, using a brief incantation.

"Hello, George," the warlock said, offering his hand to the lad.

The young man blinked, and then his eyes cleared and he smiled. "Hello," he said, shaking Dathan's hand. "Do I know you?"

The sight of that smile, an eerily exact duplicate of Aidan's, wrenched Maeve on the deepest level of her being, and she suspected Valerian's reaction was quite similar.

"We were acquainted once," Dathan said, stepping back. "Well, I won't keep you—you're obviously bent on meeting friends."

George nodded happily. In their clever, mysterious way the warlocks had evidently provided him not only with a new identity, but a past as well. Furthermore, they had altered the memories of several mortals to include him. "I don't believe I got your name," he said cheerfully.

"Not important," Dathan said, turning away.

George stared after him in bafflement for a moment, and Maeve feared that the trick had not worked after all, that the youth remembered being a warlock. If that were so, Lisette would not be deceived.

Then Maeve shifted her consciousness, the way she generally did instinctively when warlocks were around, and the signal from George's mind came through loud and clear. He believed he was a man, and, therefore, he transmitted that belief to everyone and everything around him.

Valerian gripped her arm and hustled her away into the darkness. "Much as we might like to hang around and watch," he explained rather tersely, "Lisette will pick up on our presence and smell a trap if we do."

He was right, of course.

Maeve turned to him when they were well away from the cantina. Dathan and his companions had already vanished, probably for the same reason Valerian had mentioned. "What do we do now?"

"We wait," Valerian said, plainly as irritated by the prospect as she was. "We wait and hope that Lisette bites into our lovely warlock's jugular and subsequently chokes to death on his blood."

Maeve was frowning, worried. "It might not be fatal, you know," she said. "When Aidan fed on a warlock, he was very ill, but he survived."

"I remember," Valerian said somewhat gruffly. Talk of Aidan always made him either restive or testy, or both. "Even if she does not glut herself with the poison, in her greed Lisette will be seriously weakened. We will close in then, destroy her, and send her ashes to Nemesis along with our most eloquent pleas for mercy."

He glanced up at the starry sky and smiled wanly. "Do you suppose Dathan would mind if I explored that delightful old manse?"

"As if you cared whether he minded or not," Maeve retorted, amused, eager to feed and then return to Calder. She would send Shaleen away, lie beside her beloved on the slab, and join her dreams to his. "Good-bye for now, my friend."

Valerian bent and kissed her forehead lightly. "Farewell," he responded, and then he was gone.

Damn, but he's good, Maeve thought, still awed by the other vampire's theatrical flair.

She raised her arms, then, smiling, and took herself to her favorite hunting grounds—the seediest part of London, where the lowest of the low prowled the night, scheming, indulging in their deliberate evils.

She was drawn to a dark, stinking attic of a dockside

pub, a place even rats and fleas would hesitate to frequent. There a drunken man had cornered his wife, demanding the few pence she'd been able to scrape together while he'd been at sea.

Maeve knew in a moment that the woman had been beaten half senseless for her trouble, and her wail was pitiful to hear. "Please, Jack—don't 'urt me no more—I needs the money for the babe that's comin'—"

The lout drew back one booted foot to kick his fallen wife, and outrage surged through Maeve, as hot and sour as bile. She gave a snarling shriek, one fit to wake the dead, and flung herself at the brute, who raised meaty hands to shelter himself.

The woman, whimpering with terror, having no way of knowing that she would not be next, scrambled for the ladder at the edge of the loft.

Jack's blubbery, unshaven face was white beneath a layer of filth. "Saints in 'eaven," he rasped, *"what sort of devil are ye?"*

Only an instant later he found out exactly what sort.

When his mates from the pub below came scrambling up the ladder to see what poor Mary had been blathering about, they discovered old Jack in a heap, near dead, and him with two bloody holes in his neck in the bargain.

CHAPTER
❧16❧

The cellar where Maeve had left Calder was empty.

Wild panic seized her. Had Lisette, or some other fiend, found him and stolen him away?

Frantic, Maeve searched the room and found Shaleen dozing behind a crate of antique china.

The little hoyden was barely conscious—dawn was so near—but she looked up at Maeve and blinked.

"What happened?" Maeve demanded, crouching and grasping the child's bony shoulders. "Where is Calder? *Where is he?*"

Shaleen scrambled to her feet, visibly struggling against the inertia that overcame most vampires with the approach of sunrise. "He's gone, mum, that he is—and it's been a long time now, too! I tried to stop him, but he wouldn't be stopped—he's a strong one, he is. Why, he came off that slab like a cannon shot!''

Maeve felt herself succumbing to the catatonic sleep and knew there was no point in resisting it. Her terror and despair increased even as she began to lose consciousness—there were so many things Calder didn't know, so many dangers.

Calder had escaped his keeper easily, for he'd been full of strength when he awakened, half wild with curiosity and excitement.

Five minutes after bolting from Maeve's cellar, he stood on a busy street corner in twentieth-century London, watching in amazement as magnificent horseless carriages rushed past, displacing the night air, making an extraordinary din. There were plenty of people about, too, streaming out of clubs and theaters, strangely dressed and chattering about unfamiliar things.

He was delighted, confounded, awed by his own powers and by the wonderful new world that surrounded him.

A place, he admitted to himself, grimly amused, that he knew absolutely nothing about.

He began to walk, following a high, wrought-iron fence. Beyond it lay a graveyard, the marble stones pristine in the moonlight, the grass well kept. He remembered the sensation of William's bullet entering his chest, and a silent celebration stirred inside him because he was still alive.

Calder smiled as he strode along, reflecting now on the fact that Maeve had evidently come to the house in Philadelphia and collected him, prior to his transfiguration. He wondered what poor Prudence and the others had made of his mysterious disappearance.

Presently Calder began to feel a tightening inside himself, a need for sustenance, but he had no idea how to stalk prey. He knew very little, as it happened, except that he could not survive even the briefest encounter with sunlight.

Calder walked for hours, just looking in wonderment at the strange mix of new and old that was London. He was in the vicinity of Maeve's grand house, which he presumed was still in her possession, when a glance at the sky warned him that it was time to find shelter.

He let himself onto Maeve's property by a side gate, begrudging every moment of awareness he would miss by lapsing into the comalike slumber he could not hope to escape.

He found a narrow cellar window, dislodged the grillwork that covered it with a single wrench of his arm, and crawled through the space, whistling softly under his breath. Perhaps once he got the knack of being a vampire, he would discover a way for blood-drinkers to remain awake in the daytime, or even a means by which they could endure the full glare of the sun.

After all, he speculated, reaching out and pulling the iron grillwork back into place, he was a scientist. He might dissect one of those bumbling creatures Maeve and Valerian were so concerned about, after it was dead, of course, and learn a great deal about the inner workings of all vampires.

The prospect filled him with excitement.

Humming softly to himself, Calder found the very chamber he'd left earlier, and he could see immediately that it had not been in use for some time. Odd, he thought, loosening the collar of the shirt he'd awakened in, well over a hundred years in the past, that Maeve didn't seem to favor this bustling, energetic century. It was like a carnival, rife with noise and color; he wanted to see and do everything, to take it all inside him somehow and possess it.

He stretched out on his slab, the same one he'd abandoned only hours before, and yet *decades* before, to go exploring, and considered the paradox of time. How deliciously ironic to be lying there in the cellar, in the very place he was missing from in the nineteenth century.

Sleep overtook him before he could make sense of the enigma.

The day must have passed quickly, for when Calder opened his eyes, it was as if he had just closed them. He felt a violent thirst, a growing weakness, and an unrelenting desire to continue his explorations.

He let himself out of Maeve's house by the same method he'd used to enter it—he crawled through the cellar window—and was nonplussed to find Valerian waiting for him, arms folded, his expression dour.

"Do you know," that august vampire began in a deceptively smooth, even voice, "how foolhardy it was to go rushing off into the world on your own like that?"

Calder felt only mild chagrin, and that was because of the worry his abrupt departure might have caused Maeve. He hadn't wanted to hurt her, and yet the drive to try out his new being had been irresistible.

He began to walk away and would have opened the gate and passed through if Valerian hadn't caught him by the back of his coat and brought him up short.

Calder's temper flared; he bristled and opened his mouth to tell Valerian to go to hell, but thought better of it when he looked into those fathomless violet eyes.

"You have much to learn," Valerian said quietly. "We'll start with passing through solid objects, and then you'd better take your first feeding."

Calder swallowed his formidable pride and nodded. He had trained a number of younger doctors during his career, but there were a great many vital things he didn't understand about this new existence. For the first time in years he would have to play the part of the apprentice rather than the master.

Valerian affected a sigh, then began his instruction.

Calder was so taken with the mechanics of dissolving himself and passing through gates and walls and trees that his mentor finally had to remind him that there were other tasks that must be accomplished in the space of that night.

The finer points of stalking and feeding came next, and a lesson on the proper method of time travel as well. Valerian took Calder to a place he couldn't help recognizing—a field hospital—but this was clearly a later conflict than the one he remembered so vividly.

"World War II," Valerian explained as Calder tried to adjust himself to the sights and sounds of suffering so intense, so terrible that he could barely take it in, even after all the practice he'd had in his own century. "These are German soldiers, technically the enemy, since you were an American, but the pain is the same."

They moved, unseen except by those nearest to death, among the rows of canvas cots.

Calder whispered a horrified exclamation as he looked upon some of the wounds. "What happened to these men?"

"I'm afraid warfare has advanced significantly since your time, Doctor—in this particular period, they used a lot of poisonous gasses and, of course, they were capable of dropping bombs from airplanes."

"Airplanes?" Calder hadn't come across the word in his brief exploration of modern London.

"Flying machines," Valerian answered in a distracted tone. "I'll show you later. In the meantime, you must choose one of these poor, suffering louts and draw from him the blood you need to survive."

Calder had been awash in blood since his first day of medical college and he had gotten past the stage of revulsion long ago. It was medical stuff, blood, full of mystery and power—he believed that with his whole heart. Still, the prospect of drawing on a patient in such an intimate way was abhorrent.

Valerian spoke quietly, standing close behind him. "Trust me," he said. "Your—victim, if that is indeed the correct word, will feel no pain. On the contrary, his agonies will cease, if you choose for it to be so, replaced by that same sense of ecstasy you felt when you underwent your own metamorphosis."

Calder glanced back at the other vampire uncomfortably. He didn't like being reminded of the joy his conversion had brought him, because he had yet to sort out its meaning. He certainly felt no physical attraction to this enigmatic creature who had given him everlasting life, but neither could he deny that he had known indescribable bliss during their unholy communion.

The elder vampire smiled—he'd probably discerned Calder's thoughts—and moved past him to stroke the pale forehead of one of the fallen soldiers. The boy opened his eyes, stared up at Valerian in baffled adoration, and murmured something in German.

Calder recognized the word for *angel,* since he'd had some training in the language while studying to become a physician. He recalled, of course, how Maeve had moved among the wounded at Gettysburg, bestowing her strange mercies, and how the dying soldiers had seen her as a creature of heaven.

"Like this," Valerian said gently, his gaze locked with the rapt, too-bright stare of the lad lying on the rickety cot. Then, to demonstrate, he bent over his welcoming prey, punctured the artery with his fangs, and fed.

When he straightened, Calder was stricken by the singular beauty of his tutor's expression; his countenance seemed to glow, his skin appeared translucent. Tenderness shimmered in his eyes, along with the most brazen glint of satisfaction.

The "victim" lay still, plainly dead, his slender young body slightly arched, as if frozen in the first throes of some sweet passion. He stared, peering straight into the very heart of heaven, it seemed, and his flesh was like ivory, backlit by the flame of an inner candle. His smile was beatific and so tranquil that Calder averted his gaze, feeling that he was intruding on some very private moment.

Calder felt a variety of emotions, as well—anger, frustration, pity, awe, and strangely joy. Still, he had never gotten used to death, its peculiar loveliness be damned, and his most basic instincts urged him to fight against it until the last.

Valerian gestured silently toward another cot, where yet another man-child lay, his once splendid body ruined, his mind fogged with the horror of seeing behind the glorious facade to the true nature of war.

By this time Calder was ravenous, and he knew he could put off the sacrilege no longer. He spoke softly to the soldier, smoothing his hair as he had seen Valerian do, as he himself had done with other dying children, in another war, another time, another life.

He wept inwardly as he bent over the bruised throat, found the pulse point, and plunged his fangs through the thin but stubbornly resistant flesh.

Calder tensed, bracing himself for utter revulsion, but to his surprise the nourishing blood did not flow over his tongue, but through the short, needle-sharp teeth that had once been ordinary incisors. As the stuff raced into him, he was electrified with a pleasure so brutally intense that for several moments he feared it would destroy him. He started to withdraw, in fact, then felt Valerian's hand come to rest lightly on his back, urging him to continue.

When it was over, when he'd felt the life force as well as the pain and terror leave the boy, Calder rose and turned away, ashamed. Paradoxically, for he was well aware that he could hide little or nothing from Valerian, he did not want the other vampire to witness his disgust.

Or his rapture.

Graciously Valerian said nothing, but only went on to another cot and fed again.

Calder could not bring himself to follow suit, even though he yearned to experience once more the inexpressible jubilation that was only then receding, a tide of sweet fire raking his soul as it ebbed away. He left the hospital tent by ordinary means and stood gazing up at the stars for a long interval.

Presently Valerian joined him, and by tacit agreement they returned to twentieth-century London and Maeve's grand house.

Much to Calder's delight, she was waiting there in the formal parlor, pacing back and forth along the edge of the marble hearth. Her hair fell free in wild curls, and she wore tight-fitting denim trousers and a black blouse of some stretchy fabric that clung to her curves.

"Where have you been?" she cried furiously when she realized that Calder and Valerian were there.

Wisely Valerian faded into mist and took himself off to some safer and no doubt more cordial place.

Calder made no attempt to hide his admiration or his curiosity. "I'm sorry you were worried," he said in all sincerity, for he truly loved this glorious being, and even the bliss of feeding for the first time could not compare to the splendors he'd known in her arms. "I was impatient to see what it was like to move about as a vampire."

Maeve's temper seemed to subside a little, though her eyes still flashed with sapphire fury. "There are so many dangers," she sputtered, running the fingers of one hand through her lovely tangle of hair. "Warlocks, angels— the sunlight. And sometimes time travel can go wrong, and it's impossible to return—"

He gripped her shoulders. "I'm safe," he said pointedly, touched by her concern. If anything, the transformation had deepened his love for Maeve, and the emotions she stirred in him were almost too splendid to be endured.

She flung herself at him then, wrapping her arms around his neck and murmuring, "I was so afraid—"

Calder stroked her back, warmed by her love, nourished by it. He laughed hoarsely and held her a little away from him. "What about these scandalous clothes of yours, Maeve Tremayne? What manner of devilment is this?"

Her smile was tentative but genuine. "This is how twentieth-century women dress," she said. "If they choose to, that is. They have a lot more to say about a great many things than their ancestors had."

He took her hand, lifted it over her head, and twirled her about as he had seen dancers do. "Trousers," he marveled. Then he held her close again and kissed her. "I must say, I like the way they look on you."

Calder felt Maeve tremble in his arms, and he kissed her again before saying, "I love you."

Her blue eyes glistened with a sentiment equal to his own. "You taught me to mate as humans do," she said softly. "Now let me show you how vampires give each other pleasure."

Calder pretended to be shocked. "What? Do twentieth-century women seduce their men so boldly as that?"

Maeve touched his mouth with one finger, and with that single gesture effectively set him ablaze with the need of her. "Who cares what they do?" Her eyes, tender before, were smoldering with forbidden knowledge now. "I am a vampire, not a mere woman, twentieth century or otherwise. Come with me, and I will show you passion you have not even imagined."

He did not resist her; indeed, Calder doubted that he could have done that, even if he'd wished to do so. He gave her his hand and then felt himself dissolve, felt his very soul plunging through space. Then, just as abruptly, he was whole again, and they were alone in an upstairs chamber, a vast room that he remembered as Maeve's studio.

She'd brought him there after the shooting, and sometimes when she was working at her loom, unaware that he was conscious, he had watched her for a moment or two before slipping under again.

He moved to draw her close and kiss her once more, but she drew back, smiling and shaking her lovely head, like a mischievous nymph bent on luring him into some enchanted place.

"You're thinking of the human way of lovemaking," she scolded softly. "I want to show you how vampires mate."

Had he still had need of his lungs, or of air, Calder

would have drawn a deep breath at that moment. As it was, he simply watched Maeve, struck dumb by her terrifying beauty, and by the depth of his love for her.

She kept her distance, watching him with those magical eyes, too far away to touch him, and yet he began to feel the lightest of caresses. It seemed to him that fingertips brushed the sensitive place beneath one of his ears, made circles around his nipples, whisked ever so slightly across his mouth.

He moaned and moved to reach for Maeve, but she kept herself just out of reach. In the next instant he began to feel her touch in more intimate places, across his belly, the small of his back, along the insides of his thighs.

Calder gasped with pleasure, but Maeve silenced him with a soft "Shhh" and proceeded to tease the length of his staff. He was completely in her power then, as effectively restrained by his own desire as he might have been by iron manacles.

His clothes were not physically removed—they seemed to melt away like thin ice under a spring sun—and not only was Calder's body bared to Maeve's attentions, but his soul as well.

He whispered an exclamation, a plea, and then felt her touching him everywhere, inside and out, even though physically she was still well beyond his reach. Her mouth drew at his nipples, not one, but both, warm and wet and greedy. At the same time, impossible though it was, her tongue traveled the length of his shaft and teased the tip until he cried out in a ragged, glorious, despairing voice.

Maeve showed Calder no quarter that magical night, as she initiated him into yet another vampire mystery. She was a gentle but relentless conqueror, having him thoroughly, again and again, until it all culminated in one cataclysmic, soul-rendering release.

He lay trembling on the cool, hard floor when she'd finished with him, depleted and yet more fantastically alive than ever before. When his emotions would allow him to speak, he whispered, "It's a good thing you didn't do that when I was mortal, love. I might have died of the pleasure."

She laughed softly and came to lie with him, her own body naked and sleek and glowing in the moonlight pouring in through the tall windows. She took him into her arms and kissed the hollow at the base of his throat. "There are more terrible ways to die," she observed, nestling close.

He stroked her breast, in the human way, and draped one of his legs across hers in a possessive gesture. "Why are you tarrying here with me, Maeve?" he asked, his tone gruff with his love for her, and the sudden knowledge that even eternity can be a fleeting thing. "Has the war been won already?"

Maeve raised herself onto one elbow, her hair a silken mantle in the moonlight, and gazed sadly into his face, as if to memorize every feature. "No, my darling," she said, tracing his mouth with the tip of one index finger. "The war hasn't been won."

Calder asked no more questions, sensing that, for Maeve, this was a time out of time, a place of refuge and restoration. "I think I like the human way better," he said.

She looked puzzled. "Of making war?"

He gave a raspy chuckle and held her close against him, his chin resting on the top of her head. "No, sweet—of making love."

Maeve drew back to study his face. "Why?" she asked, sounding stricken. "Don't tell me you didn't feel pleasure, Calder Holbrook, because I know—"

Calder smoothed her tousled hair. "I felt more than

pleasure," he assured her gruffly, "more than ecstasy. But when mortals make love, they touch, they become one being, if only for a little while. I want that for us."

Her bewildered expression gave way to one of mischievous delight. "Before I decide that one is better than the other," she purred, "I would want you to take me the way you would take a human woman."

He turned her gently onto her back, this beautiful, complex fiend, and gripped her wrists, pressing her hands gently to the floor, just above her head. Then he mounted her, and she parted her silken thighs slightly, her dark blue eyes glittering in the darkness.

"Observe," he teased in a scholarly tone, and glided inside her with one long stroke. Within moments they were both wild with passion, rolling over the smooth wooden floor, first one taking command, and then the other.

The finish of their lovemaking was simultaneous, apocalyptic, a collision and a fusion.

Lisette sensed trouble, but she was intrigued rather than fearful and allowed herself to be drawn back to nineteenth-century Spain, back to her villa beside the sea.

She slept through the day, conserving her strength for battles she knew were coming, and had her carriage and horses brought around only moments after the sun had set. She would feed, of course, but for the time being she would make no more vampires, special or otherwise—to do so would be foolhardy, for her powers seemed to be waning. While she was sure the effects were temporary, she certainly didn't want another confrontation with Maeve Tremayne at this juncture.

Just the thought of that treasonous creature filled

Lisette with fury—she would destroy the rebellious vampires, all of them, and in ways so horrific that tales of them would be told for millennia—but for now she had more immediate concerns. She must coddle herself, feed well, and engage in her favorite diversion— seducing young, firm-muscled mortals, drawing badly needed strength from their unbridled passion.

The carriage rattled its way through sleepy streets and into the small seaside district, where a cluster of cantinas provided lively entertainment for visiting sailors and young noblemen alike.

One particular place drew Lisette, and while she was wary, it was not a new sensation. Over the centuries she had become expert in locating likely prospects—the scent and heat of their rich, sweet blood invariably drew her, even from great distances.

She signaled the driver to stop by tapping at the roof. Manuel was a slow-witted dolt who had—unknowingly, of course—provided Lisette with sustenance on several occasions, when it was inconvenient to hunt far afield. His saving grace was that he never asked questions, even though a great many strange things took place in the villa.

Lisette alighted without waiting for assistance and, clad in a flowing gown of blue silk and a white mantilla made of the finest lace, swept boldly into the cantina that had drawn her attention from the carriage.

Her entrance caused a gratifying hush among the celebrants—even the flamenco dancers stopped to stare—but Lisette did not offer so much as a nod of acknowledgment. Her gaze swept the crowded tavern, seeking the one who had summoned her back from her travels, however inadvertently.

Lisette uttered a small cry when she found him—

Great Scot, he was the very *picture* of Aidan Tremayne—studying her speculatively through narrowed blue eyes. He displaced the dancing girl from his lap, and the colorful ruffles of her petticoats swished as she flounced angrily away.

"Aidan," Lisette whispered brokenly, even though she knew quite well that this mortal was not her lost love, but only someone who looked like him. Still, it was a very attractive quality, an unexpected and welcome bonus.

Silently she summoned him, and he rose from his chair, frowning with bewilderment, to obey. No one else in the place moved nor, it seemed to Lisette, whose senses were suddenly hyperalert, even breathed.

She laid one white hand to his face, felt the lovely rush of vibrant blood beneath his flesh, the warm firmness of the muscles. "Come with me," she said. Then she took his hand, as though he were a child, and led him out of the cantina into the balmy, starlit splendor of a Spanish night.

"What is your name?" she asked when they were settled in the carriage and she'd smoothed the lines of bafflement from his wonderful face with a gentle hand. Even as she spoke she cupped his masculine parts through his trousers, to make the terms of the game clear, and to give him a foretaste of the ecstasies ahead.

His breathing was raspy, and a fine sheen of perspiration glimmered on his forehead and upper lip. Lisette was gratified to see and feel that he was aroused, eager for her.

"Jorge," he said in soft Spanish.

Lisette preferred English. "George," she said, dragging her fingers along the soft, thin fabric of his breeches, from the top of his muscular thigh to his knee, then back again.

George moaned as Lisette opened the buttons of his breeches and reached inside to stroke his straining shaft with expert fingers, and she was both pleased and touched by his reaction. It had been much the same that other night, long before, when she'd found Aidan Tremayne walking alongside an English road. He, too, had been a lusty young man, welcoming Lisette's skilled caresses, groaning softly as she attended him in various ways and showed him things he'd yet to experience with a mortal woman.

She maneuvered George so that he lay on his back, draped over her lap in delicious abandon, and then just sat admiring him for several moments, thinking what a splendid creation he was.

He writhed with pleasure, the lovely mortal, while Lisette taught him a few basics. Somewhat to her own surprise, she felt a deep tenderness toward the fragile creature, rather than the greedy lust that was usually at the root of such escapades.

Almost gently, Lisette brought the beautifully sculpted human to a satisfactory release. Then she simply stroked and admired him, from head to toe, for the work of art he was, as the carriage bounced and jostled over cobbled streets.

"She took the bait," Dathan said, rubbing his hands together in triumph and delight, when Maeve and Valerian joined him in that splendidly spooky old manse under its blanket of ivy and various vines. "Even as we speak, Lisette is playing her vampire games with our own beguiling 'George.'"

Maeve's attention was wandering; she was preoccupied with Calder, who had chosen to remain in the twentieth century, where they had made such tempestuous love. He was a new vampire, she reminded herself fitfully; he needed time to explore his powers.

Valerian nudged her. "He's fine, your fledgling lover," he said as directly as he would have if Dathan hadn't been there, listening intently. "Stop worrying."

Maeve glared at him for a moment to let him know she didn't appreciate his lack of sensitivity, then turned to Dathan. The warlock stood with arms folded, smirking a little.

"I want you to teach me that fire-starting trick now," she said.

Dathan only pretended to be taken aback by the request, but his glance at Valerian a moment later was genuinely uncertain. The towering vampire glowered at him in quelling silence.

Finally Dathan relented. "All right," he conceded grudgingly. "I will share the incantation. There is no guarantee whatsoever that the magic will work for vampires, however."

"We'll take our chances," Maeve said firmly. She'd betrayed an important bit of blood-drinker lore in letting Dathan and the others know how vampires recognized other supernatural creatures, knowledge that could be used against her kind, and she wanted something in return.

Dathan repeated the chant—the words were from some ancient language, eerie, and more like music than speech.

Maeve attempted the incantation and the simultaneous shift of consciousness a number of times before she mastered it and set a pile of old newspapers burning on the grate.

Valerian, that inveterate show-off, succeeded on the first try.

CHAPTER
❦17❧

The soul-cries of sick children all over nineteenth-century London seemed to ride on the night breeze and rise from the pavement itself. Overcome, Calder sagged against the brick wall of an ink factory and pressed his hands to his ears to shut out the terrible din. Since he was not hearing the sound, but feeling it instead, the gesture was fruitless.

"Maeve," Calder murmured like a man in delirium. "Valerian. Help me—show me what to do."

There was no reply.

Calder pushed himself away from the wall, wavered, and then gathered all his inner forces. No doubt this was a private ordeal, a rite of passage.

The suffering of the children pressed upon him from

all sides, and the helpless feeling that assailed him was
not unfamiliar. He had known this same frantic need to
be more than he was, to be in a hundred places at once,
as a mortal, moving among the wounded Rebels and
Union soldiers he had attended in America.

Focus. The word came soft and insistent, like a
whisper at his shoulder, and Calder had heard it often
while Valerian was introducing him to his vampire
powers.

Calder started to take a deep breath, realized that his
lungs were fossilized within him, having no need of air.
He smiled grimly and, as passers-by began to look at him
with wary curiosity, straightened his coat. The sorrow of
the children was as loud as ever, but he was beginning to
cope with it, just as he had coped with the screams and
moans of his patients in field hospitals and government
wards back home.

Focus.

Calder found a single thread in all that tangle of noisy
misery and grasped it with his mind. Then he allowed it
to lead him down an alleyway, past a graveyard and a
park, into a tenement.

There the horrid music of death and pain was so
pervasive that Calder could barely withstand it, but he
pressed on, whispering Valerian's word to himself like a
litany. *Focus, focus, focus* . . .

The ribbon of consciousness led Calder to an impossibly small room in the back of an enormous, dark, and
filthy building. One pitiful wad of tallow lit the stinking
chamber, though of course Calder did not need its light to
see the pale, spindly boy lying on a dirty pallet beneath
the window. A crust of molded bread lay within the
child's reach, and he watched with large, haunted eyes as
a rat nibbled delicately at the last of his food.

The boy looked straight at Calder, then without a word turned his attention back to the rat. The lad's history flooded Calder's mind, unbidden; he knew his name was Tommy, that he'd been on the streets alone since he was five years old, surviving by picking pockets and stealing food from trash bins and occasionally from street stalls and shops. His mother, who had loved her baby very much, illegitimate though he was, had been a simple country maid, drawn to London by dreams of going on the stage. Instead she'd had to sell her favors to buy bread and milk, and one night she'd been strangled to death by a client who hadn't wanted to pay.

Calder closed his eyes for a moment, grappling with the horrid images. When he had, he kicked at the rodent; the belligerent creature hesitated, then scampered away.

"What do you want?" the lad asked listlessly in a thick Cockney accent, his eyes narrowed. "You're not from 'round here, now are you—not with those fine clothes of yours."

"I'm a doctor," Calder said thoughtfully. "What's your name?" He asked the unnecessary question in an effort to put the lad at his ease.

"It's Tommy," the child said, trying to raise himself, and failing. "I ain't got no money to pay a doctor, so you'd better just take yourself out of here."

"I have no need of money," Calder answered distractedly, touching the pulse point beneath Tommy's ear. In that instant an image of the child's anatomy exploded into Calder's mind in rich and vibrant color, shining with clarity. Tommy was suffering from a respiratory infection; treating it would be fairly simple, by twentieth-century standards—the prescription was good food, rest, and antibiotics.

Unfortunately Calder's bag, which contained the modern medical supplies Maeve had purloined for him, as well as a few Valerian had collected for sport, was back at the Philadelphia house.

Tommy raised himself onto his painfully thin elbows and with effort demanded, "Why are you lookin' at me that way? You ain't plannin' to saw something off me, are you?"

Calder chuckled and then lifted the child gently into his arms. He could not carry Tommy through time, but space was another matter. He would take him back to Philadelphia and treat his illness. Calder knew a woman there, a widow robbed of three sons by that monstrous war, who would gladly look after the lad.

"No," the doctor answered belatedly, though Tommy had already guessed that he was safe, for he rested lightly in Calder's arms without struggling. "I'm going to take you on a little journey. Hold on tightly now and don't be frightened."

Tommy's eyes widened even farther. "My gawd, governor," he whispered, "you ain't an angel, are you? Tell me I ain't dyin'!"

Calder smiled sadly. "I'm no angel," he said. Then he closed his eyes and thought of that gloomy house in Philadelphia, where there had been so much pain and trouble and treachery.

The place was dark when Calder and Tommy arrived, moments later. The stair railing was draped in black bunting, and there were mourning wreaths everywhere.

Tommy was in a state of shock; nothing in his brief and difficult life had prepared him for traveling halfway around the world in the embrace of a vampire.

"Shhh!" Calder said when the child would have cried out in amazement. He didn't want to encounter Prudence or any of the other servants; they would be terrified.

Obediently Tommy nestled close against Calder's coat. He was weak, after all, and very sick, and he soon lost consciousness.

Calder treated him with an injection of penicillin, wrapped the wraithlike body in woolen blankets, and fixed his mind on the presence of Ellen Cartwright, the middle-aged widow he'd met in the hallway of the army hospital.

Mrs. Cartwright was downstairs in the parlor of her small but sturdy house when Calder arrived. He settled the sleeping Tommy in a warm bed, summoned the good-hearted widow upstairs with a thought, and stepped back into the shadows.

The lady appeared within moments. Her face filled with mingled joy and concern when she saw the fragile child resting in the bed of her youngest, Albie, who'd fallen at Vicksburg.

"My gracious!" Mrs. Cartwright cried, taking Tommy's hand, blissfully unaware of the vampire looking on. "Where did you come from? Who are your people? My heavens, look at you—you're nothing but skin and bones!"

Smiling, Calder allowed himself to fade. He would return, of course, to give Tommy doses of the medicine he'd need to recover. Mrs. Cartwright could be counted upon to do the rest.

This one was not nearly as smart as Aidan Tremayne had been, Lisette observed to herself as she studied the beautiful, exhausted mortal sleeping in the tangled sheets of her bed. They'd had little opportunity for conversation, of course, but a quick scan of George's brain had revealed a distressing degree of mediocrity.

He had none of Aidan's talent for art, for one thing, nor

did he possess his predecessor's poetic spirit and capacity for all ranges of emotion.

Lisette smiled. As far as she was concerned, all these factors were to George's credit—she had no need of another rebellious, troublesome lover, but an obedient companion, one fair of face and countenance, would be another matter entirely. And this one was certainly able to give her the pleasure she craved; he had a seemingly limitless ability to satisfy her.

It might be a comfort to have someone like George at her side, loyal and pretty and stupid, all of a piece. She could pretend he was Aidan if she wanted—she'd done exactly that while they were engaged in passion—and train him to be the perfect consort.

George stirred in the silken sheets, and Lisette smiled fondly and then glanced toward the window. Dawn was still hours away; there was time to enjoy her new toy thoroughly before submitting to the vampire sleep. The slumber would claim her this day, she knew, for although she was often able to evade it, the effort sapped her powers.

She slipped back into bed beside him, began to stroke his belly, muscled even in slumber, and tease his lovely staff back to life.

Yes, Lisette thought as George awakened, gripping her bare, slender hips and moving her so that she was astraddle of him, this one would do quite nicely. She would make him a vampire, of course, because watching him age was a prospect too dismal to consider, and after she'd destroyed the rebels, they would create other, more tractable blood-drinkers to serve as their court, and reign over the new dominion.

Together.

George plunged into Lisette, and she threw her head

back and uttered a sound like the cry of a panther,
deliberately forgetting, in her need and her ardor, that
part of what had attracted her to this insatiable mortal
was a sense of danger.

"It isn't wise," Valerian protested as he and Maeve
moved along the dark river, deep beneath the ground,
that led to the secret chamber of the Brotherhood of the
Vampyre, "arriving uninvited and unannounced like
this."

Maeve made a soft sound of exasperation. "Since
when have you troubled yourself with such trivia? These
are the oldest, most powerful vampires on earth. They
were present when Lisette was transformed from a
woman to an immortal. We've got to convince them to
help us, or at least tell us if she has any weak spots."

Valerian's irritation clearly hadn't waned. He was
uncomfortable in that dank, hidden place, Maeve knew,
but not because he was afraid of ghosts and goblins, or
even the Brotherhood itself. No, the cave unnerved him
because it hadn't been his idea to venture there, and
because he had kept a helpless vigil in that very place, in
the earliest and probably most horrifying stages of
Aidan's transformation from vampire to mortal man. "Do
you really believe they're going to point out Lisette's
Achilles' heel, if indeed she has one? After all, she is *one
of them*. In telling you how to destroy the mad queen,
they'll also be giving you the prescription for their own
destruction!"

They were deep inside the cave now, but no sentinel
barred their way, as Tobias had the last time they visited.
No illusion of sunlight formed a barrier to protect the
inner sanctum.

Maeve's spine prickled with an eerie premonition;

some shock awaited them, and she tried to prepare herself.

They proceeded into the great chamber where the Brotherhood had held court since Atlantis itself had crumbled into the sea, both silent, both tense.

"Great Zeus," Valerian whispered when they spotted the remains of those ancient vampires, macabre shapes, part charred flesh and bone, part collapsed into naught but pale gray cinders. Obviously the members of the Brotherhood had submitted willingly to their fate, for they lay in a precise row, most with their horrible ashen parodies of arms crossed over their chests.

Maeve recalled Tobias and the others speaking of the old ones' desire to be at rest, once and for all. She had not really believed him; the idea of wanting death, of seeking it out, was so foreign to her that she'd had no frame of reference.

Now, faced with the reality, she felt overwhelming grief.

"Tobias?" she whispered, looking for him among the ruined bodies, unable to recognize his familiar, lithe shape.

"He's not here," Valerian said calmly. He crouched beside one of the vampire corpses and frowned. "Who could have performed this execution?" he mused aloud. "And how could they have lain so still, and yet tolerated the agonies of burning?"

Maeve stayed back, trembling slightly. She had not known these creatures well, nor even held them in particular esteem, but they were the first of her kind ever to exist—ancestors, in a way. "Perhaps they were dead *before* the fire was set," she suggested.

Valerian looked up at her, his violet eyes distant as he

pondered Maeve's suggestion. "Perhaps," he finally agreed, rising to his full height.

"Could Lisette have done this?" Maeve asked.

The other vampire shook his head. "Even she would not have dared such a travesty. No, this is the Brotherhood's own work. They wanted oblivion and rest."

Maeve looked again at the horrible figures so neatly arranged on the chamber floor. "Enough to risk the Judgment of Heaven itself? Enough to face the possibility of hellfire?"

"Evidently," Valerian confirmed. "What I wouldn't give to know what they're experiencing right now. Is it nothingness or damnation?" He indulged in one of his pseudo-sighs. "Let's look around a little. There may be scrolls, or treasure."

It was then, as they began the search, that Maeve gave voice to what they were both thinking. "The task of destroying these old ones must have fallen to Tobias," she said. "Isn't it likely that he would have taken any written record of their secrets when he left?"

"We'll find out, won't we?" Valerian asked, sounding a bit impatient.

"Where do you suppose he is? Tobias, I mean?"

Valerian lifted the lid of a tarnished brass and copper chest and peered inside. "He has probably gone underground to rest. I seem to remember that Tobias wasn't quite so enamored with the idea of giving up the proverbial ghost as the others were." He paused. "Come here. I've found something."

Maeve left off opening other chests and casks, all of which had proved to be empty, and joined Valerian on the other side of the chamber.

Inside the chest were a number of parchment scrolls, carefully tied with shriveled, dirty ribbon. When Valerian touched one of the papers, the corner crumbled into dust.

Feeling a strong sense of excitement, along with a niggling, quiet terror, Maeve drew closer and focused her mind on the contents of those rolls of ancient paper. Opening and reading them in the ordinary way would obviously have destroyed them.

At first she couldn't understand the words that flashed into her mind, for they were not only foreign, but archaic in the bargain. When she concentrated, however, the meaning began to come to her.

Recorded there, by some vampire scribe, were the deepest secrets, sufferings, and philosophies of the Brotherhood.

"'The truth is ironic,'" Valerian read aloud, his graceful hands clutching the edge of the chest as he, too, scanned the writings with his mind. "'It is mortals who will live forever, while all blood-drinkers and other unnatural creatures must one day pass over into death.'" He raised himself to his feet and turned to look deep into Maeve's widened eyes. "I guess the joke is on us."

Maeve's attention was drawn back to the treatises inside the chest. "There are other things here," she said in a thoughtful tone. "They lied when they claimed there was no longer a means to change a vampire back into a mortal—the necessary combination of chemicals is recorded here. And they knew, these vampires, how to start fires with their minds, in much the same way Dathan did—"

Valerian stepped back to allow Maeve to move closer to the scrolls, gesturing her forward, his voice gruff with emotion. "Absorb the magic," he said. "You are the true queen."

Maeve hesitated for a few moments, then knelt, as Valerian had done earlier, and spread both her hands out above the parchments, as inscriptions she had already divined instructed her to do. A breath of fire seemed to consume her, and then the knowledge flowed into her like a continuous charge of electricity. She took in secrets and formulas older than the pyramids, and the experience, far from being a sublime one, was shattering. When she had secreted it all away within herself, she used her thoughts to set the dusty scrolls ablaze.

"What the hell—?" Valerian burst out, exasperated, looking wildly about for some way to douse the flames. Of course, there was none. "Why did you do that?!"

Maeve rose slowly, still half entranced. "It was part of the pact," she said, knowing Valerian would not understand—not yet, at least—and unable to fully explain. She had consumed the knowledge of the vampyre, but she had yet to assimilate the majority of it.

Valerian gripped her shoulders, turned her to face him. "We're doomed, aren't we?" he rasped. "Tell me!"

She was still under enchantment, but she sensed the other vampire's desperation and struggled to answer. "Not necessarily," she said in the tone of a mother lulling a frightened child to sleep. "We have choices—more choices than you and I have ever dreamed."

"Go on!" he pressed, giving her a gentle shake.

Maeve shook her head. "Don't plague me about this now, Valerian—I cannot yet speak of it in any sensible fashion, and there are some things I must never say." She turned and looked sorrowfully at the burned remains of the old ones, laid out so neatly, like fallen soldiers gathered from a battlefield. "They perished willingly," she said. "They possessed the power to make themselves burn from the inside, at temperatures so high that the process was over in an instant."

Valerian took her hands in his, gentler now that some of his panic had passed. "What now?" he whispered.

"I must rest," Maeve replied. "It's all like—like a maelstrom inside me—"

A moment later, she collapsed in Valerian's arms.

After he'd left Tommy with Mrs. Cartwright, Calder returned to the grand house where he had died by his brother's hand. There was nothing he wanted from that place or from those people who normally populated it, and yet he needed to put a figurative period to the brief, troubled sentence that had been his mortal life.

He had fed early in the evening, and thus was at the height of his strength when he assembled himself in a shadowy corner of the main parlor of the Holbrook mansion. Before, he had been careful to stay upstairs, out of the flow of normal activity.

Only a few feet from where he stood, a newspaper reporter and the chief of police were conferring over strong coffee laced with brandy. Prudence lingered at a little distance from the two men, taking theatrical swipes at a lamp with her feather duster.

"God knows," the chief of police, and old friend of Calder's father, was saying, "there was no love lost between William and his younger brother, but William couldn't have stolen Calder's body because he was in jail."

Prudence shook her head almost imperceptibly, and in a blinding flash, Calder knew what she was thinking as well as if the thoughts had taken shape in his own mind: These fools were doing a lot of talking, but they were really just covering the same old well-trodden ground. Furthermore, they were no closer to figuring out what had really happened the night Calder disappeared.

I'm all right, Pru, Calder told his old friend silently. *Don't worry about me.*

Prudence started as if somebody had poked her lightly with the prongs of a pitchfork and cast a wild look around the dimly lit parlor, but Calder made sure she didn't see him. She was superstitious, he reminded himself, and even a glimpse of him, lurking in the corner where the gaslight didn't quite reach, might keep her awake nights for years afterward.

She looked at the chief and the reporter, who were still making inane attempts at figuring out what was going on in that house, noted that they hadn't sensed or heard anything, and bolted from the room.

Calder watched fondly until she'd vanished, then transported himself to the jail cell where his brother William sat on the edge of a rusted iron cot, despondency evident in every line of his elegantly slender body, his head in his hands.

Veiling himself from his brother's conscious awareness, if not that deeper, more mysterious part of the mind, Calder stood leaning against the bars of the cell, his arms folded.

Each place he visited, he'd recently discovered, had its own nuances and messages and meanings woven right into the ether itself. In London he had felt the pain and despair of the children; here in America it was the suffering of the soldiers and their families. . . .

Calder shifted his thoughts to the matter at hand. William would not actually hang, he discerned, since no body would ever be found, and he would not be tried and sent to prison.

The immediate future unfolded before Calder's eyes, like a neatly written letter.

William was to be released on bail, put up by

Bernard's faithful attorneys, in just a few days. Before he could ever be taken before a judge, Calder saw as plainly as if the actual events were being played out in front of his eyes, William would consume a scandalous amount of bourbon and fling himself over the very railing Marie had tumbled from years before. He would break his neck in the fall.

Looking upon William while he still lived stirred strange emotions in Calder, not the least of which was pity. His half brother was not evil; he was merely weak. His fatal flaw had been nothing more than an unceasing longing for the very distinction he lacked. He'd craved the notice of others, especially Bernard, but tragically his own mediocre personality had rendered him all but invisible.

Calder laid a hand on William's shoulder, knowing all the while that the poor wretch would not feel his touch, or even sense his presence. As always, William's attention was turned inward, and he was unable to perceive Calder as Prudence had done.

Good-bye, he said, *and may God look upon you with compassion.*

With that, Calder left his murderer, the last living member of his family, to his fate and willed himself back to the beautiful house where so much tragedy and heartbreak had taken place. Not wanting to see the place as he knew it, but as it would be, he moved forward in time to the twentieth century.

He was mildly surprised, standing on the cracked sidewalk in the night and staring at the wreck of that once-grand house, to see its degeneration. Certainly no one in the Holbrook family had survived to live in it and pass it down, but Bernard, having been a far-sighted soul, had made provisions for even that. The mansion would be held in trust indefinitely.

Calder stared, feeling an expected pang of regret as he noted that the roof had caved in in places, and the windows had been broken out as well—including the fine stained-glass one that had once graced a medieval cathedral. The pillars supporting the roof over the veranda had long since fallen and disintegrated. The grounds, once manicured, were a tangle of weeds, the roses had gone wild decades ago, and the marble fountain that had once given a certain Grecian glory to the loop of the grand driveway was a ruin, marred by the lewd lettering of vandals.

He rested his forehead against a rusted iron rail of the fence, forgetting to veil himself as Valerian had taught him to do, too engrossed in his own despair to realize he was not alone.

"Personally, I think they should tear it down," a blustery male voice said. "It's an eyesore—brings down the value of the other estates in this area."

Calder looked over his shoulder and saw an older gentleman with bright blue eyes and an abundance of white hair. He was dressed in the garish fashion of the late twentieth century, his trousers plaid, his shirt open at the throat. With him on a leash was a golden retriever that made a whimpering sound and backed away from Calder until the strip of leather would allow it to go no farther.

"What happened to this place?" Calder asked. "It used to be one of the finest houses in Philadelphia."

"Hush, Goldie!" the mortal scolded, but the dog would not be soothed. It knew Calder was no ordinary human, even if its master didn't, and began to leap and plunge desperately at the end of her tether, until the old man could barely restrain her. "They say it used to be downright grand," he finally replied. "But there was some kind of trouble here, a long way back. What it all comes down to is, people started saying the place was haunted, and the rumors stuck. Why, when I was a boy, we wouldn't even *look* toward this house, for fear of being sucked right in and gobbled up by the ghoulies!" By this time the dog was going wild; Calder silenced the animal with an elementary mental trick. The beast's owner stared down at it for a moment, confounded, then finished up his discourse with, "You from around here? I don't recall seeing you before."

Calder smiled sadly. "I've been away for a while." He released Goldie from her spell, and she immediately started barking and pulling at the leash.

"Don't know what's gotten into this mutt," the old man fretted. He nodded in friendly farewell and allowed the dog to pull him on down the sidewalk, calling back with a laugh, "Have a care you don't get yourself bewitched or something!"

"Bewitched," Calder echoed with a somber chuckle. What an understatement.

He looked at the old house for a while longer, remembering—for not all his recollections were unhappy ones, of course—and then turned to walk away.

Valerian was leaning against the nearest lamppost, arms folded, a disapproving expression on his face. "There you are," he said, as if he'd conducted a long and weary search. In truth, Calder knew, the elder vampire had simply fastened his thoughts on his troublesome apprentice and willed himself to his side.

Calder felt a sudden stir of alarm coil itself in his chest, like a snake. "Maeve," he said, stepping closer to

Valerian, who still lounged against the modernized lamp-post. "Is she all right?"

Valerian arched an eyebrow. "What do you care?" he intoned. "You are hardly an attentive lover, the way you keep rushing off all over time and creation."

The alarm Calder felt intensified and was joined by a dull, pulsing throb of guilt. "Damn you, Valerian, what's happened to her?"

Valerian smiled, but there was a glint of bitterness in the expression, plainly directed at Calder himself and not Maeve. "You are right to be frightened, fledgling," he said coldly. "Maeve truly became the queen of vampires on this very night, when all the knowledge of the old ones was imparted to her, but the weight of it may crush her. She lies dormant, even now."

Calder forgot himself, forgot the other vampire's vastly superior powers, and grasped the lapels of Valerian's beautifully tailored velvet waistcoat in both hands. "*Where*?"

With pointed grace, Valerian freed himself. "For her sake," he said in a low, smooth voice, "and for her sake alone, I will not burn you like a stalk of dry grass for your insolence."

"Where is she?" Calder repeated, subsiding only slightly. Perhaps foolishly, he cared nothing for his own safety, but only Maeve's.

Valerian took his time answering, first straightening his coat and smoothing the lapels Calder had crumpled. "Have you forgotten everything I taught you?" he asked. "Simply think of Maeve and will yourself to be at her side."

Calder *had* forgotten in his anxiety. He scowled defiantly at Valerian, then closed his eyes and permeated himself with Maeve's image.

Moments later Calder found himself, and Maeve, in a vast, echoing chamber that looked like a medieval dungeon. The place was lit by hundreds of flickering candles, and Maeve lay in the center on a long table draped with velvet, like Sleeping Beauty awaiting her prince's kiss.

Her flesh seemed translucent in the candlelight, and the faintest of smiles touched her lips. Calder had seen that serene expression many times—on the faces of mortals who had died with clear consciences, after rising above their pain.

He took up her hand, kissed the knuckles. "Maeve?"

She did not respond, of course, or even stir.

It was only then that he noticed Benecia and Canaan, those horrible vampire children, sitting nearby in ruffled dresses, hair all in curls, swinging their feet. They smiled at him, in unison, but the glitter in their flat eyes was patently savage.

"If Maeve doesn't wake up," they said simultaneously, chilling Calder on some level far beneath his conscious reach, "then Mama will be queen, and we shall be princesses."

Calder glared at them. "Get out of here, you little demons!"

They leaped off their chairs then, fangs bared, making a hair-raising sound that was at once a snarl and a shriek. Calder braced himself for attack, but before they lunged, Valerian materialized, blocking their way.

"Go dig up a grave or something," that vampire said, waving a hand.

Benecia and Canaan looked sullen, to say the least, but they drew in their fangs and vanished.

Calder glowered at Valerian, even though—or perhaps *because*—his creator had just saved him an ugly experience. "What took you so long?" he asked, only then realizing that he was still grasping Maeve's hand, and that his grip was not only possessive, but desperate.

Valerian sighed, as long-suffering as a martyr about to be burned at the stake. "I had forgotten how trying a fledgling's insolence can be," he said. His gaze fell on Maeve then and turned tender in the face of an instant. "I had hoped she would respond to you. Misguided though she may be, she loves you very much."

Calder felt very human tears burning in his eyes as he looked down at Maeve. He had neglected her in the excitement of discovering and exploring his new powers, and he had never felt more remorse than he did then.

"Forgive me," he whispered, not caring that Valerian could hear.

Valerian stood on the other side of the slab. "Come back to us if you can, Maeve," he said with a strange mixture of gentle urging and sternness. "We need you if we are to survive. Nemesis's angels are nearly upon us."

There was not so much as a flicker of an eyelash from Maeve.

"How did this happen?" Calder demanded, as if knowing could make a difference, or somehow undo whatever it was that had brought Maeve to lie there on that slab, unmoving, unresponsive.

Valerian gave a complicated explanation, speaking of vampire corpses and a natural chamber far beneath the earth and a chest full of crumbling scrolls. Maeve had somehow absorbed the contents of those ancient parchments, all the knowledge the old ones had brought with them from Atlantis and gathered since. He finished with another brisk injunction for Maeve to wake up and resume her duties as leader of the vampires.

"Leave her alone," Calder said distractedly. "Just leave her alone."

He bent and rested his forehead lightly against Maeve's, and that was when he felt the spiritual storm raging in and around her. She was struggling, fighting some internal battle on which everything outward hinged.

Calder raised himself and, clasping both her hands tightly in his, willed his own strength into her, without stint or reservation. He grew weak and swayed on his feet, ignoring Valerian's orders to stop.

Maeve heard Calder's voice above the howling tempest within her own being. She struggled toward him, reaching and straining, and finally letting him lead her.

Then she felt the inrush of vitality, as if she were feeding on the mysterious ambrosia that sustained all vampires. She felt him grasp her somehow, and pull her upward with all his fledgling power.

She opened her eyes just in time to see what price Calder had paid to help her. His face was waxen and strangely gaunt, and as she watched, her joy and relief turning now to horror and regret, his eyes rolled back, and he toppled across her, completely spent. Perhaps even dead.

Maeve screamed a protest as Valerian clasped Calder's shoulders and gently pulled him away. She was still weak, and her efforts to sit up were futile.

"Valerian," she pleaded. "Tell me—I beg of you—is he—gone?"

The other vampire's voice was hollow. "I don't know," he answered. "I can't make a connection—"

Fear shot through Maeve and propelled her off the slab. She stood beside it, trembling, and saw Valerian kneeling on the floor where Calder lay, unmoving. She had never seen that terrible stillness in any other vampire, not even the dormant ones she'd occasionally stumbled across when she was abroad and looking for a temporary lair.

She closed her eyes, trying to link her mind with Calder's, but like Valerian, she failed. She could not sense her lover's spirit or his formidable intelligence.

"He did this for me," she said in despair, dropping to her knees. She took his hand and called to him silently with all the force and substance of her soul. And then she felt it—a spark, then a flicker of life, somewhere inside him.

Maeve bent closer and brushed his still, waxen lips with her own. "Come back to me," she told him. "I love you, and I need you—"

Valerian must have felt Calder's spirit rallying as well, for he gave a soft, joyous exclamation.

Calder grew stronger, and then stronger still. Finally, after what seemed like an eternity, he opened his eyes, stared blankly for a few moments, and then gave Maeve an insouciant wink.

With a strangled sob, intertwined with a burst of laughter, Maeve leaned down again and kissed him full on the mouth. "Don't you ever do anything like that again!" she said as his lips formed a smile against her own.

She knew when Valerian left them alone, and was grateful.

Still kneeling, Maeve laid one hand to either side of Calder's face, full of exaltation and love and fury that he'd nearly left her forever. "What happened?"

With considerable effort Calder raised himself onto his elbows. "Nothing," he answered thoughtfully. "All I saw was darkness. My awareness kept shrinking until it was only a pinpoint." He reached up, entangled his fingers in her hair, and tugged gently. "Then I heard your voice, and I followed it back."

Maeve's eyes burned with tears. "You were foolish to expend all your strength that way. Why did you do it?"

He strained upward to give her a nibbling kiss. "You know why," he answered hoarsely.

She did know, and it made everything worthwhile—all the suffering that lay behind her, and all the perils waiting ahead.

Calder Holbrook loved her.

CHAPTER
❧18❧

The knowledge that the old ones were gone came to Lisette as she dreamed in her secure chamber beneath the Spanish villa, and although she had long ago parted company with the Brotherhood, she felt their loss. One, Zarek, had been her childhood sweetheart and later her husband, when they were both still mortal, of course. She had left him behind soon after they became vampires, for Zarek had been something of a philosopher, and he had not approved of the way Lisette used her powers.

She stirred on her cool marble slab, vaguely aware of the luscious mortal moving about abovestairs, helping himself to her chocolates, her brandy, and probably her money as well. She felt mild amusement; when George became a vampire, he would no longer have use for such

human comforts. Let him enjoy them while he could, for
soon she would be introducing him to much keener
pleasures.

One of the first things she meant to do, she reflected,
floating just beneath the surface of wakefulness, where
mortals and vampires alike are awash in dreams, was
change George's name. She must choose something less
pedestrian and more suitable—Raoul, perhaps, or Julian,
or Nikos . . .

It wasn't unusual for blood-drinkers to eschew their
former identities completely, of course. She herself had
done just that, shedding her mortal name, Cassandra, and
abandoning her profession. Like the other old ones, she
had been a doctor and a scientist.

Those ancient memories tugged at her now, pulled her
back toward that time lost in mist, like the currents of
some vast, unseen river. She reasoned that she was prone
to reverie because Zarek and the others were gone, and
she was virtually alone in the firmament. In any case, she
made no effort to resist but instead allowed herself to
drift slowly back, and back, and back . . .

Atlantis.

The doomed continent was real to Lisette, not the
nebulous legend it had become in modern times, a green
place with gently rolling hills and a curving mountain
range edging its northernmost coasts. There were many
lakes and rivers on the great island, and animals peculiar
to it, curious and beautiful creatures that were lost in the
great cataclysm.

Standing mentally on the stony shore of her homeland,
Lisette put aside the certain knowledge that everything
she looked upon was mere illusion, every stone and stick
of wood, every grave and temple. All of it had fallen into
the sea so long ago that there was no one to remember,

save herself and possibly one other now-dormant vampire, the untrustworthy Tobias.

Lisette gave herself up to the joy of homecoming and climbed a grassy slope to look out over the impossibly blue seas. A fine, cool mist touched her skin and awakened that winsome mortal girl, the forgotten one who'd lain hidden within her all these thousands of years.

Lisette was no longer Lisette, but Cassandra, or Cassie, as she was called by those who loved her. She was young and beautiful, mortal and free, blessed with one of the finest minds in all Atlantis.

Cassie sat in the fragrant grass, drawing up her slim, strong legs and wrapping her arms around them. She did not fit the classical image of the Atlantean, she knew— she wore no toga or sandals, no wreath of leaves upon her head.

No, Cassie wore cutoff blue jeans and a skimpy summer top. She listened to rock music and lived in a split-level house, and her government was experimenting with weapons of terrifying power—bombs and missiles detonated by a process of turning atoms in upon themselves.

Cassie lay back on the grass, gazing up at the azure sky, her long auburn hair spread out around her. She tried not to worry about the tests her father and his colleagues, all top scientists, were conducting, but she knew too much for comfort.

Looking upon her younger self and at the same time gazing outward through that child's eyes, Lisette felt a terrible grief. Cassie was as lost as if she'd gone under the sea with the rest of Atlantis's population, including her father and mother and sisters and brothers.

Despite the pain of bereavement, Lisette was wont to

leave this vision of her doomed homeland. She lingered, watching as Cassie grew into Cassandra and married Zarek, her handsome lover. They had joined the secret society, a group of renegade scientists, young and old, who had stumbled on a formula they believed would slow the aging process.

The potion not only met that objective, but also lent the experimenters incredible powers. They could travel vast distances, even to other continents, on the strength of a thought. They could read the minds of others and veil themselves from the notice of ordinary people and, sometimes, even from each other.

The magic had a dark side, but it wasn't discovered until weeks after the members had imbibed the wonderful medicine that made them as strong and intelligent as gods. They developed a penchant for human blood—and soon learned, to their unending horror, that they required the mysterious vitality of the stuff to function. What began as a mere aversion to the light of the sun became a violent and extremely painful reaction. Finally the blood-drinkers found themselves succumbing to a deep, comalike sleep during the day.

They had become fiends, and they named themselves *vampyres* for a terrifying winged creature that existed only in the heart of the continent's southern jungles.

All the other members were alarmed, having foreseen none of these complications despite years of calculation and experimentation—except for Cassandra. She gloried in her newfound powers, honed them, and enjoyed the unspeakable bliss that always swept over her when she consumed the wine of the gods, the ambrosia that was blood.

She and Zarek, happy newlyweds only a few months before, began to argue violently. An antidote to the original potion was concocted, and Essian, the founder of the society, volunteered to sample it.

In return for his bravery, Essian received a horrible death. He aged while his colleagues looked on in fear and revulsion, wrinkling, caving in upon himself, his flesh drying out until it crumbled like dust. Still, he lived, a rotted corpse, as vile as something dug up from a grave, his eyes peering out of a skull, his screams of terror shrill and echoing.

After witnessing such an atrocity, volunteers for other experiments were not forthcoming. The Brotherhood of the Vampyre was formed, and Cassandra, who had taken to ranging over the whole of that hemisphere in search of victims and playmates, was tolerated but not, as the name of the fellowship indicated, really included.

She was not on Atlantis the night the accident happened, but in a village that would become Athens, battling with Zarek, who wanted to live quietly as a scholar, instead of wandering the earth with her, while the two of them explored their magnificent powers.

While these vampires argued their cases, the land of their birth trembled on the brink of disaster.

A power station had been built over a fault line, the vampire Tobias reported later. When the first explosion occurred, it set off a chain reaction of other blasts, violent enough to shift vast geological plates far beneath the surface of the land. There were quakes, and great fissures formed, snaking out in every direction. Tidal waves lashed the continent from every side, and volcanoes, long believed extinct, erupted all over the once beautiful land. In a matter of days Atlantis had cracked like an eggshell and literally fallen to pieces.

The people and the visible continent were gone, swallowed. The earthquakes continued for weeks, however, and great walls of sea water struck lands thousands of miles away, wiping out other civilizations as well.

Zarek and the others had been grief-stricken, holing up in a cave with primitive paintings of animals and birds on the walls, lying dormant for centuries. Cassandra, unwilling to waste a moment mourning a time and place that no longer existed and would never exist again, except in fairy tales, changed her name to Lisette and set about forgetting all that had gone before.

Now, lying prone and dreaming in her villa on the coast of Spain, the ancient vampire wept—for Zarek and the others, for Atlantis, and, most of all, for herself. Only now, when it was too late to stop the Brotherhood from choosing death, did Lisette realize that they'd all been interconnected in some mystical, inexplicable way. With the passing of her colleagues, Lisette had been diminished and perhaps had even died a little herself.

Far away, in a different land and century, in a vault beneath a forgotten grave, another ancient one lay slumbering. His was a deeper trance than Lisette's, dark and rich and vital, meant to last for months or even years.

Tobias also dreamed and remembered and grieved for his lost brothers. There were times when he regretted his decision to choose the healing sleep instead of death, but there were still too many mysteries on this plane of existence, troubled as it was, too many puzzles and possibilities he could not bring himself to abandon.

One night, in five years, or fifty, or three hundred—he was so old that he no longer needed blood to survive— he would stir, leave his burrow beneath the moldering bones of some English dowager, and venture abroad. When that time came, he hoped to encounter the magnificent Maeve Tremayne again, and Dimity, the enigmatic blood-drinker who consorted with angels, and even that most exasperating of vampires, Valerian.

Ah, Valerian. Fascinating creature, even if he *was* irritating. Tobias knew much more about him than anyone else did, including, perhaps, Valerian himself. Yes, indeed, that vampire's story was rich and complex, crying to be told.

Tobias settled himself deeper into his private enchantment and turned his thoughts to his own happy mortal youth, spent long ago and far away, in a verdant land overlooking a sapphire sea.

Maeve found Calder in the late twentieth century, a time she despised for its busyness and crass, materialistic orientation, just an hour before dawn. She was weary from warfare, for Lisette's creatures were spawning others like themselves, helter-skelter, and for every ten she and Dathan and Valerian and the others managed to destroy, it seemed a hundred others cropped up. Although there had been no further communication with Nemesis's forces, the deadline was mere days away, and the Warrior Angel, seeing the mindless vampires multiply, absorbing innocent mortals into their ranks, was surely straining to fight.

For a few minutes Maeve just stood there in the shadows of the famous medical college's library, watching as Calder took volume after volume from the shelves, absorbing the material as quickly as he could flip through the pages. He was greedy for knowledge, the way most vampires were greedy for blood, and that troubled Maeve.

Despite Calder's declarations of love, and his heroic sharing of strength when she'd needed it so badly, Maeve still had her doubts about his motives. She wasn't sure, in fact, that Calder himself truly understood them.

At last he sensed her presence and turned to smile at her in the comforting darkness, at its richest now that dawn approached. He slid the volume he'd just scanned back into its place and came toward her.

"I'm sorry," he said, taking her hands, bending slightly to kiss her cheek. "I was supposed to meet you in the circle of stones—"

Maeve smiled and touched his face tenderly, wanting to memorize it with the tips of her fingers as well as her eyes. "But you became so engrossed in your studies that you forgot," she finished for him in tender exasperation. "Did you even remember to feed?"

Calder kissed her lightly on the mouth, and Maeve felt the same pleasant shock she always did. "Oh, yes," he answered finally. "I am at the height of my powers, fledgling though I am. Would you like me to show you?"

She nodded, almost shyly, and, by tacit agreement, they took themselves to their new secret lair, the wine cellar of the now rundown Holbrook mansion in Philadelphia. There they made love in the vampire way, with Calder putting Maeve through the same demanding paces she had so often required of him, and again in the mortal fashion. This time Maeve was the aggressor, kneeling astride Calder's hips, riding him hard, taking him deep inside her and holding him there until he cried out and arched beneath her.

At last they slept, limbs entangled, on the old, scratched trestle table that was their vampire bed.

"I want to give you a new name, my darling," Lisette purred to her mortal lover only minutes after sunset.

They were on the terrace of her villa, overlooking the warm, star-splashed Spanish sea.

George enjoyed a hearty dinner of roast pheasant and new potatoes, among other delicacies, while Lisette perched on the stone rail, letting the soft breeze dance in her hair and in the delicate folds of her gown.

"I like my own name," George said, licking his fingers.

Lisette felt a surge of temper, but brought it quickly under control. There was no need to worry about this one; he wasn't clever enough to give more than the occasional amusing ripple of trouble.

"It doesn't suit you," she told him moderately, reaching out to touch his lovely ebony hair. Like silk it was, fine and glossy, sliding smoothly between her fingers.

He looked up at her with impudent blue eyes, Aidan's eyes, and Lisette's heart tumbled a few times before catching itself. "What would suit me?" he asked in Spanish, chewing as he spoke.

His manners were atrocious, Lisette reflected, but she didn't care about that, either. He would suit her purposes just fine, poor manners and vacuous brain notwithstanding.

She gazed upon him thoughtfully for a few moments, a finger to her chin, even though she'd long since decided that he would be called Nikos. "Have you noticed anything—well—*different* about me, darling?"

Nikos, formerly George, settled back, draining a glass of the finest Madeira in Europe before answering, "You are always gone when I awaken in the morning."

Lisette smiled to herself. "Is there nothing else?"

Nikos frowned beguilingly. "You are unusually strong for a woman, and your skin is like iridescent stone when the moonlight strikes you."

She leaned to trace the underside of his jawline with one fingertip, then slid it slowly down the length of his throat and into the dense, dark hair matting his chest. It was pleasant and diverting to watch him squirm in his chair, already wanting her.

"Would you like to live forever?" she asked, unbuttoning his silk shirt to the waist.

Nikos made a throaty sound of surrender as she worked his belt buckle easily and opened his trousers. "Yes," he rasped.

Using her mind and not her hands, she began to stroke and tease Nikos, until he was bucking in his chair and, at the same time, groping for her.

She withheld herself, although she wanted to be ravished by the eager young brigand as much as he wanted to ravish her, at the same time intensifying his arousal with ruthless skill. "Would you like to be just as you are tonight—young and hard and full of fire—for the rest of eternity?" she whispered close to his ear.

He groaned, and Lisette knew what he was feeling because she was inducing those sensations that made him so feverish and fretful. "Yes—*damn* you, Lisette—what are you doing to me? I feel your hands cupping me—I feel your lips, your teeth, and it's as if I'm about to be swallowed—" His words fell away as he gave an involuntary cry of savage need. "By the saints, I beg of you, give me mercy—"

But Lisette was not inclined toward mercy. She compounded the battery of sensations, toying with his nipples, laying a wreath of kisses on his hard belly, squeezing his powerful buttocks and lifting him, driving him deeper and deeper into his own senses.

The one thing she denied him was satisfaction.

Finally she pushed him to the point of madness; he

rose from his chair and overpowered her—or at least, she let him think that was what he'd done. He tore her clothes away, cleared the table with a sweep of one arm, and hurled her down onto the surface, taking her with deep, angry thrusts.

Lisette's release was instantaneous and violent. She pitched beneath Nikos's plunging hips, arching her back and crying out in animal ecstasy as he punished her for her teasing.

He was not satisfied with once, however—that was one of the things Lisette loved about Aidan—no, she must remember, this was *Nikos*—he was insatiable, just as she was. Thus, he turned her on the table, so that her buttocks touched his groin, and put himself only a little way inside her, just far enough to drive her wild with wanting him.

He fondled her breasts as she begged, denying her in a low, murmuring voice, telling her that she was his and his alone, that he would have her when he was ready, and no sooner than that. He told her that she was a beautiful whore, pinching her nipples lightly and giving her another inch of his staff when she pleaded, and said what she needed was a proper hiding, and he had a good mind to give it to her.

Lisette moaned, desperate, despairing, delighted. It was this explosive pleasure that gave her such tremendous power.

"What do you want, little whore?" Nikos whispered, caressing her breasts, weighing them in his palms, chafing the nipples with his thumbs. "Tell me what you want."

She gripped the edge of the table. "You," she wept. "I want all of you—oh, please—I want it all . . ."

Nikos teased her some more, venturing a little farther

inside her—but only a little—then withdrawing until he had almost left her completely. While he subjected her to this sweet torment, he pretended to ponder her request.

Lisette was certain she would perish, she wanted him so badly, and when he suddenly thrust deep inside her, she shouted with avaricious lust.

Nikos told her what a brazen wench she was, behaving in such a way, actually begging to be taken, making her whimper and whine, grasping her hips and holding her when she would have increased the tempo by thrusting herself against him. Finally, however, he lost control of his own need and pounded against her with greater and greater urgency, greater and greater violence, until they were fused by the heat of their fury, completely joined, each jerking against the other in instinctive surrender.

"You are a very naughty boy," Lisette said minutes later, when she had gotten down from the table and collected her shredded gown.

Nikos pulled her close and bent to kiss her lightly on the side of the neck. "I think I'll take you that way from now on," he said in a husky whisper. "Like a stallion, mounting his mare."

Lisette was weak with satisfaction, and yet she felt her intimate places heating again as he talked on and on about all the sweet, sinful things he wanted to do to her, weaving his lover's spell.

Only when Nikos had draped her roughly over the wide stone railing of the terrace and put her through all the same exquisite little torments again, only when she was buckling against him in the throes of brutal pleasure, did she wonder—just fleetingly—how a mere man could so bewitch a great vampire like herself.

Dimity was waiting when Maeve and Calder came up from the cellar at the setting of the sun and into the kitchen where Calder had eaten as a boy, well over a hundred years in the past.

Maeve was slightly troubled that the other vampire had found them so easily; she had made every effort to veil herself and Calder in the hope that they would sleep in safe anonymity.

"What is it?" Maeve asked.

"The angels have come," Dimity said. "They are encamped everywhere, waiting to attack us. Gideon says that Nemesis himself has come from the higher world to participate in the greatest purge since the war in heaven!"

Maeve felt chilled and cast a quick glance toward Calder. He was strong and brave and most willing to fight, but he was a fledgling, his powers were new to him, and he was unskilled at wielding weapons of the mind. If he tried to aid in the cause, the results were likely to be disastrous, for himself and for other vampires.

"There is more," she said, looking Dimity straight in the eye once again.

The angelic nightwalker nodded. "Yes. Nemesis wants to see you, Maeve. He's issued an order that you are to come to him this very night."

Even as a mortal child Maeve had been intrepid, walking the high crumbling walls of the convent where she grew up, running away with a caravan of gypsies on one occasion. She'd battled Lisette herself and lived through the terrible pain of losing her brother, but this was by far the greatest challenge she had ever faced.

"What is my assurance that I won't be taken prisoner?" she asked quietly, raising her chin.

Calder erupted in sudden protest, leaving the falling mantel he'd been attempting to right and rushing to her side. "You can't seriously be *considering* such a thing—"

Maeve used her superior powers to render Calder mute, though only temporarily, knowing that reason would not reach him.

Dimity answered Maeve's question as if Calder hadn't spoken at all. "You have Nemesis's word. The promise of the high angels cannot be false, you know that."

"Yes," Maeve said as Calder struggled to speak, glowering at her, knowing she had somehow frozen his vocal cords. "Where is Nemesis to be found?"

"Gideon said you are to go to All Souls' Cathedral in London and wait. You will be contacted."

Maeve nodded as Calder made furious strangling sounds and grasped her arm as if to restrain her. She turned her gaze to Dimity. "Look after him," she said, meaning Calder, and the other vampire nodded, her lovely eyes wide with sympathy.

Forming an image of the cathedral where she and Valerian had been attacked by warlocks, Maeve raised her hands slowly over her head and vanished. Calder could not cry out to her, it was true, nor could he follow with Dimity using her considerable might to restrain him, but Maeve felt his protest in the center of her soul all the same.

He would not soon forgive her for restricting his freedom again.

Maeve kept to the twentieth century, knowing that angels preferred the current moment to all the past combined.

The graveyard of All Souls' was not empty—here and there a derelict slept, curled up behind some headstone or monument, and all the benches were occupied as well.

Maeve scanned the place with a quick sweep of her thoughts, finding naught but mortals who would sleep until morning, and more mortals who would sleep until Gabriel sounded his trumpet. A Dante-like picture came to her mind of wavering, vaporous souls rising from all the graves to be judged by their Maker, and she shivered.

"Quite a dramatic image," a male voice said.

Maeve spun, taken by surprise, and looked upon the countenance of a tall, powerfully built angel. He was dressed in modern clothes, a tailored suit, an overcoat of the finest wool, a white cashmere scarf.

"Nemesis," she said, half in greeting, half in awe.

He actually smiled, and Maeve noted that he wasn't handsome in the standard sense, though if she managed to survive this night, she knew she would never forget a single detail of his features. He had brown hair, attractively shaggy, and green eyes; like Gideon, he shimmered with the light of a kingdom that could only be reached by traveling inward.

"At your service," he said with a slight bow of his head.

Maeve's awe began to give way to suspicion, annoyance, and plain ordinary fear. "I didn't expect you to be quite so courtly," she said.

"And I didn't expect you to be beautiful," Nemesis replied smoothly. He sighed. "Unfortunately, neither my manners nor your loveliness has anything whatsoever to do with the business at hand."

He began to stroll along a stone pathway, and Maeve kept pace. The mortals around them slept on, unaware that their fate, as well as that of vampires and warlocks and all other immortals, was being decided.

"What do you want?" Maeve finally dared to ask.

Nemesis seemed amused by her bravado, even a little

taken with it. "Surrender," he answered in a cordial tone. "Nothing less than the complete surrender of every evil creature walking the night."

The idea was foreign to Maeve, but she had others to consider besides herself. "What would happen then? If we gave ourselves up, I mean?"

"You would be cast into the pit, where you could do no more harm," Nemesis answered, as calmly as if they were two humans deciding whether to have biscuits with their tea or scones with jelly.

Maeve shuddered.

"You'll end up there either way, you see," Nemesis went on with quiet, terrible reason. "Surely you realize that you cannot resist legion upon legion of angels."

She nodded but was careful to hold her head high. "Of course we know that," she replied. "Our hope is to stop Lisette and bring her to you. She is the guilty one, after all."

"Every last one of you is guilty," Nemesis argued pleasantly. "Even if you do destroy this devil's spawn, this Lisette, why should I let you go on?"

Maeve thought fast. "Because if there is to be a kingdom of light," she said, "there must be a kingdom of darkness to balance it. You protect your Master's beloved mortals, you guide and teach them, but it is the so-called evil creatures who make them strong by giving them adversity to resist."

Nemesis was quiet for a moment, thoughtful. Then he gave a low, bone-shaking burst of laughter. "You are smart, Vampire—like your father, Lucifer."

She stopped, furious. "I'll thank you not to credit Lucifer with siring me—I've never met him, let alone sat at his feet to learn evil magic as you seem to be implying. Before I became a vampire, I was *created*—by the same God who made you."

The great angel glared at her for a moment, but then it seemed to Maeve that something in his bearing softened ever so slightly. "There is no time to argue semantics, child. I urge you again—surrender, and bring your dark followers with you."

Maeve shook her head, wondering if she was being brave or just foolhardy. "No, Nemesis," she said. "I will bring you Lisette, and then I will storm heaven itself with pleas for mercy. If you do not grant us clemency, perhaps your Master will."

"Such a waste," the warrior said, his eyes sad as he looked down into Maeve's upturned face. "You would have been a fine angel." With that, he shook his head once in apparent sorrow, turned, and walked away into the night.

CHAPTER
❧19❧

Cobwebs swayed in gray scallops from the great chandelier in the entryway, but for the time being, Calder was not concerned with the condition of his erstwhile home. Although his voice had been restored, he was still as much a prisoner as if he'd worn chains and manacles, and the fact outraged him.

"Maeve is only trying to protect you," Dimity, his jailer, remarked distractedly when he'd joined her in the parlor. She was standing beside the time-ruined harpsichord, running one finger over the keys.

Damn, but he hated the way they could look straight into his mind, Maeve and Valerian and Dimity. Was he to have no private thoughts at all?

"Not until you learn to veil them," Dimity replied as if he'd spoken, smiling that angelic smile.

Calder made yet another futile attempt to crash through the unseen barrier Maeve had erected around him, around this memory-haunted house, and it left him feeling as though he'd been struck by a train.

He collapsed into a dusty chair, rubbing his temples with a thumb and forefinger.

"Stubborn," Dimity said, turning back to the harpsichord, drawing eerie music from it. If the sound was heard by mortals, there would soon be a new spate of rumors about the spooky old mansion.

"I am Maeve's mate," he muttered. "I belong at her side—*especially* when she's in danger."

Dimity drew back the spindly-legged bench and sat down to experiment further with the harpsichord. "You would only be a liability to her at this point," she said, her attention mostly focused on that mouse-eaten old instrument. "Perhaps later, when you've learned to use your powers more proficiently—"

"Damn!" Calder bellowed, bolting from his chair and startling Dimity, who jumped and then turned to look at him over one beautifully shaped shoulder. "No one, not even Maeve, will rob me of my personal liberties—I will not endure it!"

"It seems to me," Dimity observed diplomatically, smoothing her brown silk skirts, "that you haven't much choice in the matter, at least for the moment."

Calder went to the warped, filthy mantel, which had once shimmered and smelled pleasantly of the oil Prudence used to polish it, and gripped it with both hands. His head was lowered, and his pride, like the exquisitely expensive mirror that had once hung over that fireplace, was in shards at his feet.

"You're right," he said hoarsely after a long pause. "I have no choice—now. But tomorrow night, or the next one, or the one after that, I will be free. And love Maeve though I do, with every grain and fiber, with everything that makes me who I am, I will not sacrifice my freedom of choice to her whims." Calder turned, knowing his bleak decision lay naked in his eyes, unable to hide the torment he felt. "I'm going to leave her, Dimity, if we survive this present trouble. I'm going to venture out on my own and learn the things I need to know, and work out just what sort of a vampire I mean to be."

Dimity's lovely face reflected both misery and understanding. "It will kill Maeve to lose you," she said softly. "She does love you, you know. Her passion is a part of her, as much so as her powers, even her soul."

"I feel exactly the same way about her," Calder replied grimly, "but that isn't enough. I need my right of choice, and Maeve's trust, as well, and she needs those same things from me." He paused, shoving a hand through his rumpled hair. "I don't think either of us is capable of giving them—not willing."

Slowly, gracefully, Dimity rose from the harpsichord bench and came toward him. "Maeve would give you anything," she whispered. "Anything."

"Except the holy right of deciding my own fate for myself," Calder replied. He escorted Dimity to a round table where his father and William had once played games of chess, the winning of which had been inordinately important to both of them, and drew back a chair for her.

When she was seated, Calder sat across from her and folded his hands on the rain-warped, dirt-covered tabletop.

"Since we apparently have considerable time at our

disposal," he said, "tell me about yourself. How were you made, and when? Were you changed against your will, or did you give your consent?"

Dimity laughed good-naturedly. "I see you haven't studied vampire etiquette yet," she said. "It is very rude to ask a blood-drinker about her making—the topic is a sore spot with so many of us."

Calder was undaunted. He had never worried much about protocol in his human life, and he didn't plan on doing so as an immortal. "Is it a sore spot with you?"

Dimity shook her head, as if amazed and a little scandalized by the bluntness of the question, but there was a mischievous light in her blue eyes. "No, actually—it isn't. I became a vampire by my own choosing, in the late fourteenth century . . ."

It was silly, Lisette decided, as she watched Nikos parading back and forth in front of her, showing off his expensive new velvet coat and doeskin breeches, to deny herself the pleasure of creating a prince consort for even one more night.

She thought of the process of changing a mortal into a blood-drinker and felt a rush of dark desire, almost as compelling as the passion Nikos could so easily stir in her. With him, she would bring the full extent of her powers to bear, and the experience would be exquisite for both of them—no more of those clammy corpses, quickly made and left to their own devices.

Lisette shuddered and then put the vile creatures out of her mind.

Oh, yes, she would take her time with Nikos. She would give him the powers and the prowess of a pagan god and teach the little scoundrel all—make that *some*—of the glorious skills and tricks she'd acquired throughout century upon century of adventuring.

She rose a little unsteadily, for she'd been feeling a strange sensation since the Brotherhood had perished, as if she were being pulled down and down into some black morass of the spirit.

"Come, darling," she said, holding out one alabaster-white hand. "It is time to give you the gift."

Nikos arched an eyebrow, but he understood the word *gift* only too well and was plainly intrigued by it. He came to her, in his lovely tight breeches and his fitted coat, and it was all Lisette could do not to gobble the delicious creature up the way some mortal women did chocolate.

She told herself there would be time for that later—all of eternity, in fact—and raised her hands to his sturdy shoulders.

"Do you trust me?" she asked softly.

He laughed, a delightful scamp of a lad, so hard and warm and beautiful, and for the briefest moment Lisette doubted her own plans.

"Of course I do not trust you," Nikos replied, grinning, so engaging and sweet that Lisette's heart threatened to crumble within her. "You are like me—you think only of your own wishes, your own pleasures. When you find another lover that you like better, you will abandon me."

Lisette smoothed his hair and spoke softly, hypnotically. "Oh, but that is not true, Nikos," she said. "I will never leave you, and you will never leave me. Not ever."

He looked puzzled; his grin faltered a little, and a shadow of bewilderment moved in his Aidan-blue eyes. "How is this possible?" he asked. "We are flesh and blood. We must grow old, we must die."

She took enormous delight in contradicting him, in

heightening that delectable confusion in his eyes. She shook her head and murmured, "We can live forever."

He seemed troubled now and moved to step back from her, but she took his shoulders in a grip calculated to be inescapable but also without pain, and would not let him go.

"What madness is this?" he whispered, and the flush of emotion under his warm, pliant skin made Lisette half wild with hunger and blood-lust. "No one lives forever!"

She calmed herself, made soothing, murmuring sounds, as a mortal mother might do for a child, pushed Nikos into a chair, and perched lightly on his lap. "Vampires do," she said, inwardly tensed for his reaction.

Instead of flying into a temper, Nikos laughed. He was scoffing at her, and that was worse, in some ways, than a storm of petulance would have been. "Vampires!" he mocked.

Lisette showed her fangs, both delighted in his recoil and despaired because of it.

He tried to throw her off then and escape her, but Lisette, by her own reckoning at least, had indulged him long enough. She took his head in her hands, as she had done so often before, but this time she was not gentle. No, this time a slight, quick motion of her wrists would have broken his neck.

"Do not resist me," she said in a crooning voice. "I will destroy you if you do."

The sound of Nikos's heartbeat seemed to fill the whole room with a pounding, steady *thumpety-thump, thumpety-thump*, and his beautiful eyes were wide with horror and, even then, disbelief.

The rushing of his blood, audible now, drove Lisette into madness. Her control was gone, and she bared Nikos's delicate throat and sunk her fangs into the vein, drawing on him greedily, nearly swooning with the ecstasy of their intimate communion.

Nikos cried out when she took him, stiffened slightly, then went utterly limp beneath her.

Lisette was moaning inwardly as his blood flooded her own empty veins, and she began to rock against Nikos, the pleasure so savage she almost couldn't bear it. She nearly forgot that if Nikos died in her arms, she would not be able to complete the transformation. Should that happen, he would be lost to her forever.

It was actually painful to draw back from that continuous, buckling euphoria. She expected Nikos to be waxen—she'd so nearly drained him—and certainly unconscious. Instead he was gazing at her with eyes too old and too wise for the face of a lad of some twenty years. . . .

At that moment the suffering began. It was as though there were small, vicious fish inside her, tearing at her vampire flesh, at the atrophied organs that should not have been sensitive to pain.

Lisette shrieked in rage at Nikos's betrayal as well as in the agony of being poisoned; this was no mortal lad, no innocent lover and playmate, but a warlock!

Even as she screamed and clutched at her middle, she saw the knowledge of his own identity returning to him, the awareness. That was how he had fooled her, her pretty Nikos—he himself had not known who or what he was!

Now his foul blood was burning Lisette's insides like acid; she fell to her knees, still shrieking like a wild jungle cat caught in a trap, and, clutching the rungs of a ladder-back chair, pulled herself upright again. Through a red fog of misery and the most primitive fury, she saw

Manuel, her mortal carriage driver, loom uncertainly in the doorway for a moment.

She reached out to him, desperate; he crossed himself and fled.

Nikos, for his part, had risen to his feet, and he was backing away from her, not fearful, but repulsed. There was even a hint of mockery in his eyes, the blackguard. If it was the last thing she ever did, she would see him suffer for that effrontery, as well as for his efforts to murder her.

Lisette struggled to remain conscious; the sun would rise soon, and in her weakened state she knew she could not survive its rays. Then, like a distant bell pealing somewhere far off in the Spanish countryside, she heard Maeve Tremayne's voice.

Come to me. Let us finish this.

Maeve, the enemy. The usurper. This was her doing, this betrayal, this physical and spiritual torment. A surge of hatred raced through Lisette's system, strengthening her.

She saw Nikos, laughing at her now, taunting her, but she could not hear his voice. No, all she heard was Maeve calling to her, calling and calling.

She could not tolerate the humiliation of looking upon her betrayer another moment, and she wanted Maeve Tremayne to suffer. Oh, how she wanted that traitor, that Judas, to suffer!

Gathering all her strength, which was greater than it might have been because of her rage, Lisette closed her eyes and willed herself to Maeve's presence.

Lisette took shape on the low rise behind the circle of stones, framed by the light of the moon, and Maeve readied herself for the battle of a lifetime. Unlike

Valerian and Dathan and the others, she did not believe that the ancient one was already defeated.

"She is magnificent," Valerian whispered, clearly awed, as they all watched Lisette raise her arms gracefully against the dark sky, a shimmering angel of hell, to summon her multitude of followers.

They began appearing, those dreadful walking corpses, a score here, a hundred there, bumbling and stupid and deadly in their unheeding obedience.

Dathan, who had been prepared for this confrontation, called to his own warriors, and they came out of the thin shadows, silent and ominous, anonymous in their hooded cloaks.

The vampires, Maeve noted with nervous irritation, were seriously underrepresented. It would serve them all right, she reflected, Benecia and Canaan and the other cowardly ones, if she left them to Nemesis without even *trying* to defend them.

Maeve looked up into Valerian's eyes, seeing sorrow there, and fear, and then into Dathan's. He smiled at her and nodded his encouragement.

"Maeve Tremayne!" Lisette called in her hollow, unholy voice. She loomed on the hillside like a living flame, her pain palpable in the cool night air.

Taking up her skirts, Maeve answered the summons, and the two of them stood facing each other on the line of the hill.

"Why have you done this to me?" Lisette rasped, more dangerous in her suffering, rather than less. Her eyes were enormous in her gaunt face, and sunken. "Why? To save a lot of ungrateful blood-drinkers from the just vengeance of heaven?"

Maeve felt a strange urge to reach out to the other vampire, even though it would be like trying to touch a she-wolf caught in a trap, and wisely resisted it. "I have not done this to you, Lisette," she said reasonably. "It is by your own recklessness, your own treachery, that you've come to this end."

Lisette swayed, but at the same time Maeve could feel power emanating from the creature, pulsing and throbbing like another entity, an ominous reflex that might function even after the wounded vampire had died.

She gave a snarling shriek and stumbled toward Maeve, who stood her ground even though she was mortally afraid.

Then she heard Valerian, just a few feet behind her, his voice as smooth and even as velvet. "You are the rightful queen, Maeve," he reminded her.

Calder's voice joined Valerian's and, although Maeve dared not turn to look, she knew that he, too, had come to her somehow, and she blessed him for it, and drew strength from his presence.

"I love you," he said gruffly, and it seemed to Maeve that there was a certain sorrow in the tone and texture of those precious words. "Be strong, beautiful Maeve."

Dimity spoke next. "We are depending on you," she said softly but firmly. "The weak and the strong, the good and the evil, all of us."

Lisette screamed again and started past Maeve, delirious now, like a wild animal in the last stages of hydrophobia. Her thoughts were clear; before she collapsed, she would kill as many of the rebels as possible.

Maeve stepped in front of her then, and the mental struggle that had been brewing for centuries finally began.

There was a great, ferocious sweep of invisible fire, encompassing Maeve, smothering her with its heat, singeing her marble-like flesh. She endured, and called upon all the things she'd learned from the scrolls of the Brotherhood, and the sky itself thundered with the power of her command.

Lisette dropped to her knees, then struggled back to her feet again. At her back Maeve heard the chilling sounds of combat as the warlocks and the handful of courageous vampires engaged the sharklike beasts formed and shaped from madness itself.

Maeve did not wait for Lisette to attack again, but struck ruthlessly herself, crushing the other blood-drinker to the soft, fragrant ground, bringing the weight of all the stones in the circle to bear upon that one ill-fated creature.

Lisette wept—it was a frantic, mindless sound—and, rolling onto her back, raised herself up onto her elbows.

Again Maeve was moved toward foolish mercy, but again she resisted. Never taking her eyes from Lisette, holding the wounded one to the ground with the power of her mind, Maeve raised a hand in the agreed signal, and Valerian came forward.

He gave Maeve the stake and mallet they'd brought for this very purpose.

"You mustn't lose your courage now," he said, reading her mind again, seeing the pity she felt for Lisette. "And you must not turn from this task."

Maeve hesitated for a moment, then nodded and accepted the instruments of death. She took a step toward Lisette, who made a whimpering sound and tried to crawl away.

"Do not be deceived," Valerian warned, staying close. "She is a beast, fit only for the bowels of hell. If your positions were reversed, she would not hesitate to finish you!"

It was all true, Maeve knew that, but knowing did not

make the duty before her any less distasteful. She trembled a little as she advanced on Lisette, thinking of Calder, of Valerian, of Aidan and his lovely mortal, Neely—all their fates were in her hands, and she must not falter.

Maeve dropped to one knee in the dew-laced grass, placed the point of the spike directly over Lisette's heart, and raised the mallet. After only a moment's hesitation she struck the first blow.

The stake pierced Lisette's papery flesh, and she shrieked in pain and in fury, and Maeve trembled, but she raised the mallet again. And again.

Lisette screeched and struggled, and Maeve watched in horror as the dying queen's beautiful face went gaunt, then turned to dust and crumbled. Finally only a skull remained, but with Lisette's blue eyes peering out of the charred bone, glowing with unholy fire.

The screams echoed through the night long after the staring eyes had turned to cinders and dissolved.

Maeve knew triumph, but she was shaken and sick as well. She knelt in the grass, still clasping the mallet, chilled to the center of her soul.

After some time had passed, Calder gripped her shoulders from behind—she would have known his touch anywhere, for it always reverberated through her like the toll of a great bell—and drew her to her feet and away.

Maeve watched, spellbound and horrified, until Lisette, half corpse and half skeleton, had disintegrated into a pile of ashes, a ludicrous parody of the human shape. The stake protruded from between those discolored ribs, and the mallet fell, forgotten, from Maeve's fingers.

A shout of victory made her turn at last and look first

into Calder's solemn eyes, then at the battlefield beyond. When Lisette had ignited herself, in the same way the members of the Brotherhood had done in their death chamber far beneath the ground, she had also destroyed her followers.

The grassy clearing was covered with grayish-white forms, and as she watched, the wind came and spread them over the grass, and only the warlocks were left— the warlocks, and the few vampires who had been willing to stand behind Maeve in her time of greatest need.

"The dawn comes!" one vampire cried.

Calder and Valerian collected Maeve between them, sheltering her with their larger bodies, and she felt herself dissolve into particles. Moments later she was in a dark place, as cool and welcoming as a grave. When her dazed eyes adjusted, she realized they had brought her to a chamber beneath the circle of stones itself.

At one end of the small cellar was an altar, probably druid, so old that it was crumbling. Valerian stood before it and executed a truly regal bow.

"My queen," he said.

Maeve was lying in Calder's arms, and she was definitely grateful for that. "Get up," she snapped. "I am nothing of the sort!"

Valerian laughed and spread the fingers of one graceful hand over his chest. "Anything you say, Your Majesty," he replied.

Maeve closed her eyes, inexpressibly weary, and let her head rest against Calder's shoulder. "Leave us," she commanded, "and find a lair of your own."

He obeyed, that troublesome, beloved vampire, dissipating into smoke with a finesse only he could have managed.

Maeve lifted her mouth to Calder's, and he kissed her

hungrily, furiously, and with unutterable despair. There was no time for lovemaking, however much they might want each other, for the sun was about to spill its light over the countryside above.

They lay entwined, Maeve and Calder, in the rubble of the old religion, and let the vampire sleep take them.

There were no dreams, at least not for Maeve.

When she awakened at sunset, Calder was already sitting up beside her, looking upon her with despair naked in his eyes.

"You're leaving me," Maeve said, certain that this was not reality, but merely what mortals called a nightmare.

Calder nodded once and reached out to caress her cheek lightly, with just the tip of one finger. "It will be better for us both," he said hoarsely. "I love you, Maeve—more than I ever dreamed I was capable of loving—and I understand that you've held me prisoner only to protect me. Still, I cannot be subject to your will, no matter how benevolent."

Maeve swayed, horror-stricken. It was real.

For an instant Maeve wished that she'd died in battle the previous night instead of Lisette, but her instinct to live was perhaps her strongest trait, and it prevailed.

She raised her chin. "I see."

Calder looked away. He was already withdrawing from her, even though they shared that small chamber. He started to speak and then stopped himself.

"We could change," she suggested tentatively.

His gaze returned to her face; his eyes smoldered with dark conviction. "Never," he said. "You are too strong, and I am too stubborn." He paused to sigh, and the sound was filled with heartbreak. "I wanted to be your true mate, your equal, but now more than ever I know that isn't possible."

Maeve closed her eyes. "But you are my equal."

"No, darling," Calder said gently, shaking his head. "You are the vampire queen, and I am a fledgling."

She was really losing him. It was unbearable, incredible, after all they'd been through. And they loved each other so much!

"How did you convince Dimity to bring you to the circle of stones last night?" she asked, needing to back away from the heart of the situation for a few moments, to gather the scattered pieces of herself and try to fit them back together somehow.

"I didn't," he said. "I sensed the danger you were in, and I guess my desire to be at your side was greater than your power to keep me away. I thought about you, and I was there."

"How do you intend to live without me?" Maeve asked in all seriousness. "How shall I live without you?"

Calder left her side, rose to his feet, and dusted off the legs of his trousers as a mortal man might do. "I suppose we'll see each other, now and then," he said, taking care not to look at Maeve. "In time we'll forget."

She shook her head. "When the last star collapses into dust, my darling," she said softly, sorrowfully, "I will still love you."

"Don't," he said, turning away. "Please. Just let me go."

"That's not so easy," Maeve replied, standing, laying her hands on his broad back where his shoulder blades jutted beneath his flesh. "I love you, Calder. I need you. Don't you care enough to forgive me, to try to understand?"

He turned then and looked down into her eyes. "It would only happen again and again—your trapping me somewhere every time you thought I was in danger—

until I came to despise you as my jailer! The only thing
we can do is end it now, before we're both destroyed!"

With that, Calder disappeared, but his words echoed in
Maeve's mind.

Before we're both destroyed.

"Too late," Maeve said softly. Then, with no one to
see, no one to lend comfort, she buried her face in her
hands and wept. She had won so much in that final battle,
and lost everything.

Nemesis was waiting in the graveyard of All Souls'
Cathedral three nights later when Maeve arrived. He
might have looked quite ordinary, in his conservative
overcoat, with that simple but frightfully expensive black
umbrella unfurled against the chilly rain, except for the
luminous quality that came from inside him.

Looking upon this magnificent creature from a little
distance, Maeve could see why the great masters had
graced their painted angels with halos and bright auras.
They must have been aware, some consciously, some
unconsciously, of their own heavenly guardians and
comforters.

She wondered if she'd had a guardian angel as a child,
and what he or she was doing now, when his or her
services were no longer required.

Or were they?

Nemesis smiled his cordial, benevolent smile when at
last she stood facing him, feeling the fiery heat of his
aura. "You did have a guardian, you know," he said.
"Every mortal does."

Maeve covered her trepidation with bravado, for
something about this powerful, mysterious, implacable
being made her feel as defenseless as a child. "Fat lot of
good it did me," she retorted somewhat testily. Losing

Calder had made her even more reckless than usual; she had so little to lose.

The warrior angel chuckled, and the sound was throaty and rich. "We are not infallible creatures," he explained, and Maeve thought it was rather generous of him, considering the circumstances. "Sometimes we make mistakes."

The rain pattered on the roof of All Souls', the gravestones, and the ancient walkway that had been worn smooth by the passage of generations of saints and sinners. Maeve looked directly into the angel's eyes and felt a strange, entrancing peace.

She shook it off. "Then perhaps you will be more understanding of the errors of others," she said. "We have destroyed Lisette as you probably know, and all but a very few of her vampires—which are being gathered by my friends at this moment."

Nemesis regarded her steadily, revealing none of his thoughts or emotions—if indeed angels had such things. She honestly didn't know.

"A great deal of damage has been done," he said.

"And there will be more still," Maeve reasoned boldly, flying blind, "if you unleash your forces on the dark kingdom. Granted, you'll eventually prevail, but we will fight you, you may be sure of that, as long as we have the strength to raise our swords."

"Insanity," Nemesis replied. "You cannot win!"

"No," Maeve agreed calmly. "We cannot. But remember this, Warrior Angel: We, the warlocks and vampires, have met your demands, and we plead without shame for peace. If you refuse us, and thousands of mortals die in the resulting fray, whose fault is that? Yours or ours?"

CHAPTER
❧20❧

Maeve did not have to seek out the Warrior Angel to hear his final decision; she was in her studio, working feverishly on the tapestry she had yet to properly study, when he appeared in the center of the floor.

There was less fanfare than she would have expected of one of the most powerful angels in heaven, but she was startled all the same. Somehow all Valerian's abrupt entrances had not quite prepared her for this particular surprise.

She let go of the shuttle and stepped down off the high stool, her eyes wide. Everything depended on this meeting—everything. Either heaven was satisfied that Lisette had been stopped and her minions destroyed, or the end was upon them all.

Nemesis, who wore a good nineteenth-century-style suit, including the tight celluloid collar, did not immediately speak or even look at Maeve. He went, instead, to the tapestry, now spilling, almost complete, from the back of the loom, and examined it thoughtfully.

"What does this image mean?" he asked after a long and, for Maeve, difficult silence.

Maeve had not looked at the tapestry in weeks, although she had worked the shuttle often in moments of intolerable stress. She felt stupid for not being able to answer the question—her pictures were never planned, they simply came out through her fingers—and they were often prophetic. She rounded the loom to stand beside Nemesis, and what she saw brought a small, strangled sound to her throat.

The tapestry showed herself, in a flowing dress, holding a lush bouquet of ivory roses. Some of the petals had drifted to the ground, which was covered in leaves of brown and gold and crimson, and behind her was a low stone wall, perhaps waist high. Sitting on the wall, with the casual grace so typical of the vampire, was Calder. He was smiling back at Maeve, who wore an expression of radiant joy, but it wasn't those things that moved Maeve. It was the beautiful, dark-haired child, perhaps a year old, who sat laughing on Calder's shoulder, small, plump arms reaching out to Maeve.

A child.

She laid her hands almost reverently on her stomach. A child? But that was impossible—no vampire in all of history had ever given birth.

Nemesis, probably weary of waiting for Maeve's long-delayed answer to his original question, had by then divined the meaning of the tapestry for himself. He reached out and touched the likeness of the little one with the gentlest brush of his fingers.

Maeve gazed up at him, in wonder and fear, because everything in that tapestry, every dream it represented, was in his hands. "Please," she said hoarsely. "Tell me what has been decided."

He heaved a great sigh and turned to look down on Maeve with a peculiar combination of sympathy and love and reluctance. "Were it up to me," he said, "I would still purge the earth of all night creatures— vampires, warlocks, werewolves, all of those things. But, alas, it seems there is some truth to that theory you expressed before—the Master feels that you have your place in the scheme of things." He was studying the child again, an expression of troubled amazement on his face. When he turned to meet Maeve's eyes once more, he said, "You will live and fulfill your destiny, and if you are to be destroyed, then it will have to be by one of your own kind."

Maeve felt a great surge of joy, closely followed by an equally powerful rush of fear. "This infant—" Her words fell away, and she laid a hand to Calder's woven image and then the baby's.

Nemesis heaved another sigh. "One of their poets said it—'There are more things in heaven and earth . . .'"

"But vampires do not have children," Maeve mused, as much to herself as to Nemesis, "and certainly I would never transform a mortal child. . . ."

"This infant *will* be mortal," Nemesis said, frowning at the tapestry again. "Perhaps conception occurred before Dr. Holbrook was transformed."

Maeve was in a daze. There would be no war with the angels, and a miracle of the sort she had never dared to dream of was happening. She, a vampire, carried a living, *human* child within her.

And the father of that little one, she reminded herself brokenly, had gone away.

Having delivered his message, Nemesis vanished in the blink of an eye, and Maeve was alone with her thoughts and the mysterious tapestry.

Dathan and Valerian must be told that the danger was past, that Nemesis and his Master had relented. Maeve would leave the spreading of this good news to them, however, for she had other things to do.

She stared into the tapestry for a long moment, her heart swelling with happiness and anticipation, then focused her thoughts on Valerian.

He was in a smoky saloon in the nineteenth-century American West, wearing rough-spun trousers, an old woolen shirt, six-guns, and one of the biggest hats Maeve had ever seen. A long, thin cigar protruded from one side of his mouth, and he was frowning at the hand of cards he held, as if the fate of the world depended on that very game of poker. A dance-hall girl hovered behind him, simpering and at the same time massaging Valerian's broad, powerful shoulders.

None of the mortals saw Maeve; she made sure of that. Valerian, however, looked up at her over his hand of cards. The merest shadow of a smile touched his mouth, and his eyes twinkled.

You and your games, Maeve told him.

He settled back in his chair, a gesture meant for the assortment of mortals sitting at the table and standing around it. *Eternity would be very dull without games,* he replied.

Maeve laughed. *I suppose you're right,* she said.

Nemesis came to me a little while ago—he and his Master have decided not to make war on us.

Valerian laid his cards out on the table in a flamboyant fan shape, and the mortals groaned in sporting despair and threw down their hands. *I am your creator, remember?* the great vampire finally said. *The instant you knew what had been decided, so did I.*

Maeve put her hands on her hips and tilted her head to one side. *Then you know about the child, too.*

Valerian gathered his winnings and tossed a chip to the dance-hall girl who was attending him so faithfully. *My dear,* he answered, *if you'd only troubled to look at the tapestry you were weaving, you would have seen the truth long ago. I've been aware of your delicate condition for days.*

Mild irritation moved in Maeve's spirit; sometimes Valerian's seeming omniscience really got on her nerves. *Well,* she retorted, *just tune out for a while, won't you please? There are things I want to settle with Calder, and I'd rather you weren't a witness to the whole encounter.*

He raised one shoulder in a shrug too elegant for the surroundings. *I have interests of my own,* he replied. *In fact, if you don't mind, I'd like to concentrate on my poker game.*

You'll tell Dathan and the others about the truce with Nemesis? Maeve pressed, eager to go but at the same time determined to accomplish her original purpose in coming to that rough, smoky place.

Certainly, Valerian answered, but he'd become absorbed in the new hand of cards he'd been dealt, and the dancing girl was perched on his knee. *The first time I see the warlock, I'll tell him. Then I'll tear his throat out.*

Maeve shook her head. *Have a care,* she warned. *Dathan is more powerful than you like to think.*

Valerian shifted his thin cigar to the other side of his mouth, clamping it between his white teeth. *I've been taking care of myself for centuries, Maeve,* he reminded her distractedly. *Believe me, I'm very good at survival. Now, get out of here and let me finish my game.*

She hesitated, then went to Valerian's side, bent, and kissed his cheek in gratitude, affection, and farewell.

Maeve found Calder in that same century, in a field hospital in northern Tennessee. He wore the uniform of a Confederate officer and carried a black leather bag packed with modern instruments and medicines.

When Maeve revealed herself to him, he was injecting a powerful painkiller into the arm of a boy who should have been at home, playing ball, doing chores, and going to school.

Calder raised his eyes to Maeve's face, and she saw his love for her in them, and his pain.

"Can they see you?" she asked.

Calder smiled sadly and withdrew the needle from the man-child's arm. "Yes," he answered softly. "They believe I'm a mortal, like them."

She looked down at the soldier. "Will he live?"

Calder nodded, then rounded the cot, took Maeve's elbow in one hand, and led her outside into the balmy southern night.

"That's quite a uniform," she said, noting his gray tunic and well-made trousers. "When did you switch sides and become a Confederate?"

"I haven't," he answered, studying her through narrowed, worried eyes. "I've always been on the side of life—I go back and forth between the two armies, helping where I can. Why are you here, Maeve?"

She hesitated, then said bravely, "Because I love you."

"And I love you," Calder answered, setting his bag down and laying his hands on Maeve's upper arms. "But I can't let you hold me prisoner, no matter what dangers you might be trying to protect me from. I need the freedom to be myself, Maeve—without that, I might as well not exist."

"I understand," she replied. "And I'm sorry for those times I held you captive. My intentions were good, but I realize now that I was wrong."

Calder raised one hand to touch her face. "Perhaps we could try again, you and I," he said gruffly. "You let me take my chances with the world, and I'll let you take yours."

Maeve felt unvampire-like tears burning in her eyes and clogging her throat. "We could always find each other," she said, "with just a thought."

He bent and kissed her lightly on the mouth, and she felt the old, savage passion stirring. "Always," he agreed.

She took his hand. "Would you come away with me, just for a little while?" she asked almost shyly. "There's something I want very much to show you."

"Of course," he replied, looking puzzled.

"I'll meet you in my studio," she said, feeling as though she could fly home on the wings of her joy, needing no other magic than that.

"To London," Calder said with a grand gesture of one arm, as though inviting Maeve to precede him.

She was standing in front of the tapestry when her mate appeared, and she watched his eyes widen as he took in the images and their meaning. Finally he turned to her in wonderment.

"A child?" His voice was low and gruff, and he sounded as though he were trying to restrain his rising hopes, to avoid disappointment.

Maeve caught both Calder's hands in her own and arranged them flat against her stomach. "Nemesis says the baby is mortal," she said.

Calder looked at once joyous and baffled. "But how can that be?" he whispered.

She put her arms around his neck. "I don't know," she said with a smile. "You're the doctor."

He ran his hands up and down her back, his eyes full of wonder. "It's a miracle," he marveled, and then he kissed her again.

Maeve was intoxicated when he finally drew back, and so weak that she clung to the front of Calder's tunic to keep herself upright. "How will we manage, Calder?" she asked. "How can vampires raise a mortal child?"

"The same way mortals do," Calder replied, smoothing her soft dress away from her shoulders to reveal her white, full breasts. "With a great deal of love and patience."

"But—"

Calder bent and took one of Maeve's nipples boldly into his mouth, effectively cutting off her words and swamping her doubts in a storm of physical and spiritual sensation.

Maeve threw back her head, abandoning herself to Calder's attentions, glorying in the wild appetites he had aroused in her. He smoothed the rest of her clothes away without leaving her breast, and then Maeve was clothed only in moonlight.

"Here's something else mortals do," he said gruffly when both Maeve's breasts were throbbing and wet from his tongue. He dropped to one knee before her, like a cavalier acknowledging his queen, parted the veil of silk that hid her most sensitive place from view, and kissed her there.

Maeve cried out, half in protest, half in glorious surrender. Calder's hands cupped her bare buttocks, and he pressed her hard against his mouth and suckled until she was trembling against him, whimpering softly in her need.

Calder lowered her to the bare wooden floor finally, and his own clothes were gone, quite literally, in a twinkling. He poised himself over her, and she parted her thighs for him willingly, even eagerly.

He entered her in one hard, desperate thrust and, as quickly as that, Calder's own control snapped. He and Maeve moved together in a graceful dance of passion, their sleek bodies rising and falling, twisting and turning, as each worshiped the other.

It ended with a simultaneous, white-hot melding, not only of their physical selves, but of their souls as well, and afterward they both lay stricken and exhausted on the hard floor.

Maeve was the first to move. She put her clothes back on, reached into the pocket of her gown, and took out the pendant the gypsy had given her, long, long ago. Crouching beside Calder, who was still splendidly naked and had managed to raise himself onto one elbow, she put the chain around his neck and then kissed him softly on each side of his face.

"This is my pledge to you," she said. "I will be your wife, now and throughout eternity, in heaven or in hell, in life or in death."

Calder sat up, took Maeve's face in his strong hands, and kissed her earnestly. "And this is my pledge to you," he replied then in a hoarse voice, drawing back only far enough to look deep into her eyes. "I will be your husband, faithful and brave and patient. I will love you beyond forever, and my soul will be a part of yours."

Maeve moved back into his arms. It was the closest they would ever have to a wedding, this exchange of vows they had just shared, but she and Calder had agreed to love each other for all eternity.

Forever sounded just right.